Take Time Out

Take Time Out

R. L. Johnson

YellowRoseBooks
a Division of
RENAISSANCE ALLIANCE PUBLISHING, INC.
Nederland, Texas

ISBN 1-930928-20-3

First Printing 2001

9 8 7 6 5 4 3 2 1

Cover design by LJ Maas

Published by:

Renaissance Alliance Publishing, Inc.
PMB 238, 8691 9th Avenue
Port Arthur, TX 77642

Find us on the World Wide Web at
http://www.rapbooks.com

Printed in the United States of America

Acknowledgements

There are many people that I would like to thank for helping me with this very rewarding writing experience. First of all, I would like to thank everyone who wrote me with such encouraging words along the way. I doubt I would have persevered if I hadn't gotten such nice feedback. Thanks to MaryD and Fanatic for hosting my story and giving me encouragement. I'd also like to thank my "official" beta readers, Alina, Kimly, MyWarrior, and Wendy, and my "unofficial" beta readers, Deb, Lisa, Fanatic's mom, and Kimiko. I've met some very special people who have written me with their feedback, and I hope our friendships last long into the future. And finally, I'd especially like to thank Marlys, who has graciously learned to share me with the Internet during this whole process, and who has given me unfailing support no matter how many times I asked her to read the same page over and over again.

For all the Capi's in the world.

Chapter
1

It was another rainy spring day in Comstock, and Robin Grant was slogging through the puddles on her way across campus. *Why aren't I wearing sensible shoes on a day like today?* Robin thought to herself.

A special meeting of the Athletic Advisory Committee had been called to introduce the new women's head basketball coach, and Robin was the faculty representative on the committee from the Economics Department. *I wonder why I think I have to dress up for a committee meeting, anyway?* Was it the hope that she would be named the new NCAA faculty representative when Frank Roberts finally retired that made her want to impress these people? She was sure that old Frank was delaying his retirement, and had even given up a few offers of better jobs elsewhere, just to retain that position. The annual trip to the national convention, free seats in the Athletic Director's sky box, and a few free trips to away games made the position very desirable for anyone who loved sports. And Robin *loved* sports, having been a two-sport athlete herself in college.

So here she was, sacrificing dry feet for fashion, making her way to the Athletic Director's office to meet the new basketball coach, Jessica Peters. Robin was pleased that they had hired a woman coach, but was more than a little annoyed by the complete disregard for affirmative action policies when it came to hiring practices by the Athletic Department. It would have taken the Economics Department at least six months to jump through the hoops to make a new hire, but the Athletic Department had managed to find a new coach only two weeks after the previous coach announced he was leaving, amid speculation of recruiting violations and an inappropriate relationship with a player. Yes, she understood it was recruiting season and the team would be at a huge disadvantage if it couldn't quickly name a new coach, but the double standard still irked her. It had not left her in a good mood to meet Jessica Peters, but she would try to keep her irritation with the Athletic Department separate from her assessment of the new coach. *After all, everyone deserves a friendly welcome, right? It's bad enough that half the faculty thinks athletics is a complete waste of time and money—I'll at least try to assure her that we don't all think that way.*

Jessica Peters was coming to Northern Oregon University from Idaho, after having been the head coach at Idaho State for the past five years. She had taken that team from a perennial cellar dweller to an appearance in the first round of the NCAA tournament last year, a feat that made her a hot commodity with a number of larger schools looking for coaches. Northern Oregon was just such a school, and had an inside track on the competition for Peters, given that she had been a star basketball player herself for NOU twelve years earlier, and "bled orange," as the alums liked to say.

"Hey, Robbie!"

Robin raised her eyes from under the dripping umbrella to see who was yelling at her from across the street.

"Hey, Flaxen, how you doin'?"

"You on your way to the gym? And why are you so dressed up?"

"No, I've got a committee meeting, and I'm *not* that dressed up. Jeez, you'd think I never wore anything but blue jeans and tennis shoes."

"You *don't* wear anything but blue jeans and tennis shoes, unless it's summer and you're wearing shorts and tennis shoes."

"So call me fashion-challenged—we can't all be as haute couture as you."

"Aw, you know I'm just teasing you. You'd look great in anything...or nothing, for that matter." Flaxen wiggled her eyebrows suggestively and added, "The women in the locker room will miss you today. Even the straight women have been doing double-takes."

Robin just groaned and said goodbye to her teasing friend.

It was true—Robin Grant was very easy on the eyes. Although only about 5'5", she kept her athletic body in great shape by lifting weights, running, and playing whichever team sport happened to be in season—basketball, volleyball, or softball. Add to that great body a sweet smile, sparkling green eyes, and blond hair carefully arranged to look completely windblown, and the result was simply stunning. Not that Robin really thought so, being a child of an overly critical mother who would have preferred a less athletic little girl, and who constantly criticized one thing or another about her. The adult consequence of this childhood was an interesting contrast of rebellion (blue jeans and tennis shoes) and conformation (dressing up for the big committee meeting). She had long since resigned herself to hearing her mother's voice in her head whenever she was trying to decide what to wear or how to behave in certain situations. She could only hope that her response to the voice was becoming less predictable over time.

The Athletic Director's office was large, but the dark paneling on the walls gave it a depressing feeling, and the gray day coming through the windows added to the effect. *Not exactly going to impress the new coach with these surroundings. I hope the basketball office at least has a little life to it.* There were six others around the large conference table, and Robin greeted them warmly, having served on this committee for a couple of years. Most of them were good old boys, representing the Booster Club or the Alumni Association, and mostly trying to stay on the good side of the Athletic Director in hopes of getting better seats, free parking, or maybe the chance to rub elbows with the athletes and reminisce about their own playing days. Robin could only hope that she would age more gracefully, and would have better things to do in her life than live vicariously through young athletes.

The sound of the door opening brought the casual conversation to a standstill, and all eyes were drawn to the incredibly good-looking woman trailing after the Athletic Director, Butch Dockman. She was a good head taller than he was, making him look rather comical as he craned his neck to talk to her. She smiled slightly at something he said, then turned to the table and flashed an even bigger smile, complemented by the most intense blue eyes that raked over everyone sitting there, obviously assessing each person in detail.

Not waiting for Butch to introduce her, she quickly strode over to the table and held her hand out to the nearest person, saying, "Hi, I'm Jess Peters."

An obviously impressed, if somewhat flustered, committee member replied, "How do you do? I'm Scott Reid, president of the Booster Club." She continued around the table, shaking each person's hand while looking them directly in the eye, and basically charming the pants off them before they even had a chance to think about it.

This is obviously someone who knows how to work a crowd—I guess it goes with the territory of being a public figure. I wonder what's behind the persona? Robin's skeptical thoughts were interrupted when the dazzling blue eyes locked onto her green ones, and the large, warm hand grasped hers firmly. "You must be Robin Grant. You played at Wisconsin a few years ago, right?" *Wow, she really did her homework. It wouldn't be hard to figure out I'm the only recent college athlete at the table, but she obviously looked into the committee members' backgrounds before the meeting—she's either really sharp or really paranoid.*

"Yes, yes I did," Robin managed to get out after staring dumbly for what seemed like minutes, but must have only been seconds. Recovering quickly, she added, "On behalf of the faculty, let me welcome you to Northern Oregon. We're really looking forward to the next season."

"Well, that's good to hear. I hope I don't disappoint you."

Somehow I don't think "disappointment" happens very much around you. How does somebody get looks, intelligence, charm, and athletic ability all wrapped up in one package? I'll bet NOU will be lucky to keep her a couple of years before she's off to even bigger and better things. Robin found herself wondering why that thought left her feeling so empty, but quickly forgot about it as Butch started going over Jessica Peter's resumé for the committee. Robin had read it all before in the newspaper and so spent the time looking more closely at the new coach, hoping she wouldn't get caught staring. Jessica Peters had long dark hair with bangs to just above the eyes. The hair at her temples was pulled back to the sides and clipped with a gold barrette at the back of her head, setting off the high cheekbones and dark eyebrows that periodically rose into the dark bangs at something Butch would say. She was dressed in a pair of tailored black slacks and a brilliant white shirt under a black vest with subtle orange trim. *My God, she can even make the school colors of orange and black look tasteful. That's reason enough to hire her.* Robin looked at her own chinos and cotton shirt and decided that "dressing up" was, indeed, relative. *I guess it's a good thing I decided to become a professor instead of a coach, because I could never pull off the wardrobe. It's one thing to have a bunch of half-asleep twenty year-olds looking at me in front of the class, but I'd never make it in front of 5,000 fans.*

Butch finished up the obligatory adulation for the new coach and asked if anyone had questions. Will Cox, president of the faculty senate, raised his hand.

"What is your philosophy regarding the academic careers of your athletes, and how will you ensure that academic standards are met?"

Robin rolled her eyes in her mind. The faculty senate saw itself as the watchdog for all things academic, and thought that athletics was an unconscionable waste of money that could be better spent on academics.

Jessica Peters didn't flinch. She gave a small smile and replied, "Well, I'm glad you asked that, Will, because I really believe in the term 'student-athlete.' Professional athletic careers for women are very rare, and while I would certainly encourage a gifted athlete to pursue such a career, I will also demand that all my athletes take advantage of this tremendous opportunity they are being given to earn a college degree."

Bingo! Right answer. Jessica went on to elaborate about mandatory study hall and other programs, but it really didn't matter—she had already won them all over. The faculty members and boosters alike were left wondering why this woman had been stuck at Idaho State, and why she was now sitting at Northern Oregon instead of UCLA or Georgia. Not that NOU didn't have a proud basketball tradition, but the small budget and small town atmosphere usually didn't attract the best of the best.

Maybe she's got some skeletons in her closet. Or maybe she just doesn't like the rat race that goes along with the big-time programs. Or maybe she's like me, and the quality of life offered by Oregon's natural resources more than offsets the lower pay and smaller markets. She doesn't really look like a mountain biker or fly fisher, though.

The meeting broke up and Jessica Peters took the opportunity to shake everyone's hand once again before they left, making sure to pin each of them with those incredible blue eyes in a way that would make her unforgettable. As Robin smiled and reached for her hand, she once again found herself at a loss for words. *How is it that I can speak regularly to hundreds of people, yet be such an idiot when it comes to talking to this woman?*

Jessica noted the slight blush in Robin's face and quickly filled in the silence. "I hope I'll be seeing you around campus, Robin. Do you get the chance to play ball anymore?"

"Well, I try to play at the recreation center a few times a week, and I play in the city league, but it's not as much as I'd like to." *Wow, I think that was a complete sentence. I'd better get out of here while I still sound mildly intelligent.* "It was nice to get a chance to meet you, and I hope you have a great season," Robin said quickly and dropped her eyes while heading for the door. She breathed a long sigh of relief as she walked back out into the rain, and headed straight for the gym where she hoped she could run the extra heat out of her body. If not, there was always the cold shower option.

Well, that went pretty well, Jess thought to herself. *They certainly didn't ask anything I wasn't expecting, and nobody even mentioned my early career. Maybe I can finally leave that part of my past behind me. I can hope, anyway.*

"Are you ready to meet your team, Coach?" Butch's question abruptly brought Jess back to the present.

"I'm looking forward to it."

In truth, this was the part of the day she was most worried about—meeting the group of women athletes that would ultimately determine her fate: success or failure as a coach. Because, regardless of what people said about "building character" or "producing high graduation rates," in big-time college athletics only one thing really mattered: winning. And a coach could only do so much to inspire her athletes to play beyond their abilities; at some point it came down to who had the most talented, self-motivated athletes. As a new coach, she had to take what was already at NOU, had to accept the previous coach's recruiting successes or failures. Oh, she might be able to pull in one or two junior college prospects at this late date in the recruiting season, but for all intents and purposes, she was about to meet the players that would make up the first team in the Jess Peters' era of NOU basketball.

And deciding what to say to these athletes is much more difficult than going through the motions with the athletic department staff, boosters, faculty, or any other adults, for that matter, Jess thought. *Most of these women are still teenagers, and most have been through a high school career where they walked on water. Follow that up with an intense period of recruiting, where coaches of major college programs are calling them more often than their boyfriends, and telling them repeatedly how great they are, and you have a recipe for a bunch of head cases for their college coach.* Not to mention their resentment over the abrupt departure of their previous coach, who had been popular with the players. *Maybe a little too popular with one,* Jess thought ruefully.

Jess followed Butch through the door to the team locker room and was visually assaulted by the orange and black décor. *I don't remember it being this awful when I played here,* Jess thought as she tried not to wince.

Twelve women sat around on the benches in front of the lockers, each of which had a fighting bobcat logo and a player's name prominently displayed. There were at least three pairs of high-top shoes in each locker, along with practice clothes and personal items. Most of the players were sitting back, looking skeptically at the imposing new coach, but a few were leaning forward with eager, welcoming looks on their faces. *Must be the walk-ons,* Jess thought, referring to the non-scholarship athletes who were hoping to make the team just to spend the next year working their butts off in practice and maybe getting a few mop-up minutes at the end of some blow-out games. *Everybody has a role to play—as long as they accept that role.* Jess knew that it wouldn't be the walk-ons that would complain about lack of playing time—it would be the scholarship player who had never sat on the bench before and now found herself behind someone bigger, faster, and better. It would be Jess's job to carefully massage their egos, kick their butts when necessary, and get them to accept their roles so that when they did go in to relieve the starters, they were ready to play and not pout on the court.

Jess looked around the room at the group of athletes, trying to make eye contact with each of them, striving for that look somewhere between intimidation (*I'm the new boss*) and camaraderie (*I'm not the enemy—we're all on the same team here*). Judging by the looks she got back, she thought she was successful. Butch then asked the women to introduce themselves, and Jess took that opportunity to scrutinize each of them in more detail. She already knew most of them, of course, having watched hours of film when deciding whether or not to take this job. Well, at least she knew their playing abilities; she knew little of what was going on behind each pair of eyes. And that would be her challenge in the next few months—to find out what made each player tick, how to get that last ounce of effort out of each one of them, and then get a little bit more.

"I'll turn it over to you now, Coach," Butch said. "I'll be back to pick you up in fifteen minutes for the meeting with the President." Jess nodded, and Butch left the locker room. Jess turned to see all the eyes looking at her expectantly again. She took the opportunity to walk slowly around the room, getting into each player's personal space while laying out her coaching philosophy for them.

"I want you to know that there's no history with me—each of you is starting with a clean slate. That also means that each of you has to earn your spot on this team. I don't care how many points per game you scored last year, or how many records you broke in high school. If you come into this gym every day and bust your butt in practice, you'll all have a chance to contribute to this team." Jess's look was definitely leaning toward intimidation at this point, and now she tried to soften it a little toward camaraderie.

"I expect you all to be motivated to give one hundred and ten percent all the time. I want you to play hard for yourselves— not for me, not for your school, not for some external reward. Those things aren't always going to be around to push you in life, and if you can learn to push yourself for your own pride and satisfaction, I guarantee you'll be successful in whatever you choose to do. I believe in respect and dignity for everyone on this team, players and coaches alike." Jess watched their expressions change from skepticism to something that looked like hope and anticipation. She knew that the previous coach had been something of a screamer, and she wanted to make sure they understood that wasn't her style. It would be hard, though, to take players that were used to being yelled at, who were used to having an adversarial relationship with their coach, and get them to internalize their motivation. Jess had been through it before, though, and was confident in her abilities.

"Any questions?"

There was a long pause, as each player waited for another to put a toe into these seemingly dangerous waters.

Finally, Natalia Schmidt, a 6-5 post player from Germany, who probably didn't have as many social phobias as the American players, asked in a thick German accent, "What offense will we run?"

"I like the 1-4 motion offense, but I need to see where our relative strengths are before deciding." Jess saw Natalia smile slightly, and knew that any good post would be pleased about running a post-oriented offense. "But I'd like to get as much offense as possible off our defense. Good defense will result in steals and fast breaks, and that means our post players are going to have to be in shape to run the floor." At that, the smile faded slightly, and Jess knew she had made her point. Natalia looked like she could lose a few pounds and still be quite effective in the low post.

Jess fielded a few more questions about the game and her expectations, and then Butch was back for their next meeting. She looked around at the players, trying to decide if it would work, and then told them to huddle up, putting her hand out in front for the others to join.

"Team, on three. One, two, three...TEAM!" Yeah, she knew it was corny, but she wanted them to know that she was now one of them—they were in this together.

"See you all in the weight room next week." Jess smiled warmly at them and then followed Butch out the door, feeling the admiring looks at her back.

Chapter
2

"Come on, Robbie! There's two RBI's out there for you!" Capi yelled from her spot in the coach's box along the third base line. "Just watch it all the way in—hit the middle of it!"

Robin stepped to the plate, glancing at the runners on second and third, and knowing that a base hit would score them both and end the game. She'd been in this position before, and had a very real fear of failure. *Damn my mother!* She thought angrily about her lack of self-confidence and decided it was time to change things. She narrowed her eyes and focused on the slow-pitch coming at her. *Middle of the ball, middle of the ball...*and proceeded to slap it right back over the pitcher's head and into center field, scoring both runs.

"Yeah, way to go, Robbie!" Capi yelled, while Robin gave her teammates high fives on the way back to the dugout. "I knew you could do it. You just have to believe in yourself."

"Thanks, Capi. I'll try to remember that in the future," Robin said with a big grin.

I'd be happy to remind you daily, Capi thought, as she looked longingly after her friend who was making her way through the line of handshakes with the other team.

Robin had known Capi for the three years she'd been at NOU, but it was only since joining her softball team last year that they'd become friends. Capi was the kind of person that always made you feel good about yourself, and she had a great sense of humor, too. Robin found herself spending more and more time with Capi, going for long walks and talking for hours. She thought that Capi might have a crush on her, and she was not averse to thinking about that possibility. But Robin definitely wasn't falling head over heels, and she was trying to figure out why not. Capi was tall and good-looking, intelligent, loved sports and the outdoors, and was basically everything that Robin thought she was looking for. But something seemed to be missing, and Robin was going to take her time before getting involved in anything that she wasn't sure about.

"Hey, Robin—nice game-winning hit." The low, smooth voice came from behind Robin, and she quickly turned around to see whom it belonged to. "Way to come through when the pressure's on. Maybe you could teach my players a little bit about mental toughness." Jess Peters was smiling broadly at Robin, and those blue eyes were sparkling with warmth. Robin thought she might melt on the spot. *THAT'S what's missing with Capi,* she thought, and it suddenly became crystal clear why Robin wasn't jumping into a relationship with her good friend. It had been a while since she'd been in a relationship that set her heart on fire, but she remembered what it was like and promised herself that she wouldn't settle for anything less.

"Thanks, but mental toughness is not one of my greatest assets. I think I just got lucky this time." Robin looked Jess over and saw that she was wearing a Tony's Pizza Parlor T-shirt, which meant that she was playing in the next game. "I didn't know you were playing in the league, Jess. How's your team doing?"

"Oh, I'm not much of a softball player, but some other coaches had a team and asked if I'd play. It's a good way to get to know people, not to mention a good excuse to get out for a few beers after the game." Robin smiled and nodded in agreement. "Well, I'd better go warm up. I'll see you next week—I think we play your team," Jess said with a big smile and just a hint of a wink.

"Hey, that will be fun. See you then," Robin said while giving a quick wave. Robin lingered around the field, gathering her equipment and changing out of her spikes. Of course, she was really stalling so that she could watch Jess warm up. *Will you look at those legs flying across the outfield. It would take me two*

strides for every one of hers. Not much of a softball player, huh?
She looks pretty damn good to me. And pretty good at softball,
too.

"Robbie, you want to go out for a beer?" Capi called out to
her from behind the backstop. "We're going to Tony's."

"Sure! I'll meet you there in a few minutes." Even though
they often went out to Tony's after the game, it now took on a
whole new significance. *I hope the Tony's team patronizes their*
sponsor after the game.

Robin's softball team had made their way to Tony's, com-
mandeered a few tables, and were now relaxed in front of strewn
pizza crusts and mostly empty pitchers of beer. Robin sat next to
Capi, reliving the game for the tenth time that night.

"I can't believe she gave me that flat pitch right down the
middle. She should have known that I can't hit anything high and
inside; she'd thrown me enough of those earlier in the game that
I popped up," Robin said with just the beginnings of a slight slur
to her speech.

"She was probably trying to make you look good, hoping
you'd ask her out after the game," Capi teased. "You should have
seen her looking at you when she was on third and you were
standing in front of her. Or should I say, leering at you?" They
both laughed and leaned their shoulders against each other for
support.

Robin's smile suddenly got wider as she saw the Tony's
team coming in the door, led by six feet of dark and beautiful.
Robin's team waved them over and brought a couple more tables
together to make room. After they'd placed their order at the
counter, Jess made her way over to the empty chair next to
Robin, noticing the slightly glassy-eyed look in Robin's eyes.

"Robin, I'd like you to meet my friend John," Jess said
while gesturing to a handsome, equally dark, man trailing behind
her. John gave Robin a dazzling smile while holding out his
hand. *Jeez, he looks like he's off the cover of GQ,* Robin thought.
In fact, the two of them look like they could be starring in some
sizzling Hollywood romance film. Suddenly Robin didn't feel so
good, but she smiled gamely and shook John's hand.

"This is my friend Capi Morgan. She's the Vice-Provost for
Student Affairs at NOU, so you'll probably be hearing from her

the next time one of your athletes ends up in trouble," Robin said teasingly. "Capi, this is Jess Peters, the new women's basketball coach."

"Nice to meet you," Capi said politely while giving Jess the once-over. She'd seen the look Robin had given Jess when they had first approached the table, and Capi sensed that her friend was more than a little interested in the new coach. *But what's with Mr. Macho there? Surely Robin wouldn't fall for a straight woman, would she? I guess I should hope she's straight if I want to have a chance with Robin.*

"So how'd the game go, Jess? You guys win?" Robin asked while pouring a beer for Jess and John.

"Yeah, the other team wasn't very strong, so we won pretty easily."

"You hit any over the fence? Throw anyone out at the plate?" Robin teased.

"Nah, our team has so many good players they wouldn't even miss me if I wasn't there," Jess said somewhat shyly.

"Oh, you're way too modest. What about that double you stretched to a triple, and the line drive you snagged on its way to the fence?" John was nudging Jess with his elbow to emphasize his points, and looking at her in a way that somehow reminded Robin of a puppy dog, although she usually didn't want to slap puppy dogs. Jess looked a little uncomfortable, and excused herself to go to the restroom.

"So John, what do you do for a living?" Capi asked, directing a sweet smile toward him, having seen the daggers Robin had sent earlier.

"I'm an assistant football coach. I coach the linebackers. I was a linebacker for Southern Cal, and I spent a few years in the NFL with Buffalo. I came to NOU to get some coaching experience so I can move up into the pro ranks after a few years."

Yuck! How many times can a person say "I" in ten seconds of conversation. Robin knew she wasn't being fair to John, but she wasn't exactly thinking clearly at the moment. In fact, she couldn't quite figure out why she was feeling so upset, and decided that maybe she had drunk more than she should have.

"So, you guys done talking about me?" Jess laughed as she slid back in between Robin and John.

"Oh, don't flatter yourself," Robin shot back with a grin. "John was just telling us about his football career. It sounds like a very exciting, interesting life." Jess and Capi caught the sarcasm, but John just beamed back at her. At that point, another of Jess's teammates caught John's attention, and Capi turned to talk to someone else, leaving Robin and Jess a moment to themselves.

They both spoke at once:

"So, how's your new team looking?"

"So, are you winding down your term?"

"Go ahead, you first." Jess smiled.

"Well, finals are next week, and I've got about fifty term papers to grade before then. This is the time of year when I hate being on the quarter system. We should be enjoying the beginning of summer instead of finishing the school year. And I definitely shouldn't be out drinking beer on a school night. They shouldn't be allowed to start the softball season before school is out," Robin said indignantly, drawing a warm smile from Jess. "So how are things going with your team?"

"Pretty well. We can only work in the weight room at this time of year, although the players can get together themselves for scrimmages. And of course, I can always find some reason to have to walk through the gym a few times during those scrimmages, and I've been pretty pleased with what I've seen. I think they're all working really hard. I'm also pretty busy with the recruiting end of things. That's going to take a lot of travel over the summer." Jess felt like she was running on about things that Robin probably wasn't really interested in, and couldn't help but notice how easy she found it to talk to such an attentive listener. She glanced up to see Robin's eyes looking intently at her, and gave her a shy smile in return.

"Hey, Jess. Isn't it true that I beat all the linebackers in the 40 this year? You were there—tell these guys that it's true." John was looking pleadingly at Jess, who politely confirmed his story for his admirers. When she turned back to Robin, she found Capi gripping her friend's elbow and looking with concern at Robin's face that had turned an unnatural shade of green.

"Hey, Robbie, how about I drive you home?" Capi asked gently.

"Is there anything I can do?" Jess asked, feeling like she had somehow missed an opportunity while responding to John, although she wasn't sure just what kind of opportunity it was.

"No thanks, Jess. I'll just take Robin home and she can pick up her car tomorrow." Both women got to their feet to help guide Robin to the door, and Jess gave Robin an encouraging smile before saying goodnight.

Water...I've got to have some water. Why am I so thirsty?
Robin tried to slowly open her eyes to see if, by some miracle, a
glass of water might be sitting on her nightstand. *No miracles
today.* That meant she had to somehow lift her head and get her
body to the bathroom. As she slowly rolled over in the bed, her
eyes flew open at the sight of another body curled up next to
hers. *Oh God, what did I do last night?* She recognized the dark
hair and innocent face of her friend Capi, and was relieved to see
that they were both relatively clothed. She gently slid out of the
bed and made her way to the bathroom, where she proceeded to
drink directly from the faucet. She fumbled around in the drawer
until she found the aspirin, and drank the equivalent of another
glass of water with three aspirin. She checked her watch and was
grateful to see that it was only four a.m. *If I can get back to
sleep, maybe the water and aspirin will have kicked in by six
when I have to get up.*

"Hey, how're you feeling?" Capi asked gently to Robin as
she returned to the bed. "Anything I can get for you?"

"Other than a new head? Preferably one with enough sense
to know when to quit drinking beer," Robin replied ruefully.
"Uh, we didn't...last night...you know..."

"Relax." Capi grinned at her. "I would never take advantage
of you when you're not in control of your faculties," she said
with mock seriousness. "At least not if I thought you would
remember in the morning."

Robin smiled back and reached over to give Capi a hug.
"What would I do without you? Thanks for taking care of me."
Capi pulled Robin in closer, rolling over to her back so that
Robin could nestle her head on Capi's shoulder. She placed a
tender kiss on the top of Robin's head, and soon they were both
back asleep.

❖ ❖ ❖ ❖ ❖ ❖ ❖ ❖

"Dr. Grant, could you give us the formula for price elasticity of demand again?"

Oh, why won't my head stop spinning? Robin thought to herself. She was using the last class period of the term for a review
session, and still suffering from the effects of the previous
night's indulgences. *Remind me again why I wanted to schedule
my class at eight a.m.*

"Sure, Gary, but I'd much rather that you understand the concept and not just memorize the formula. Think of it like this. Elasticity is like responsiveness," Robin said while pulling her hands apart in front of her like she had a big rubber band between them. "We want to know how responsive the change in demand is when price changes. Let's use an example that you can relate to. Suppose the price of beer went up by fifty percent." Robin's stomach lurched at the thought of beer, but she tried to keep her mind on the class. "Would you decrease your beer consumption by fifty percent?"

Gary thought about it for all of a half second and said, "No way."

"Well, how much less beer do you think you'd drink, in percentage terms?"

"I don't know, maybe ten percent less. I'd give up something else instead."

"Okay, so your demand response, ten percent, is less than the price increase, fifty percent, so your demand for beer is price inelastic. That means you think of beer as somewhat of a necessity instead of a luxury." A round of laughter came from Gary's classmates, even though most of them would probably agree.

"So Gary, if you're the local tavern owner, and you know that the demand for beer is price inelastic, do you raise or lower price to increase revenues?"

"Raise price," Gary said confidently.

"Great. Now do you still need that elasticity formula?"

Many heads nodded vigorously, and Robin sighed to herself. "Percentage change in quantity divided by percentage change in price."

Robin glanced at the clock and saw that time had run out. "See you all at the final next Tuesday at eight a.m." She had somehow made it through the fifty minute class without throwing up or passing out. She vowed never to let this happen to her again, and made her way back to her office.

Dropping unceremoniously into her chair, Robin doubleclicked on her mail icon and was chagrined to see thirty-two new messages waiting for her. *I wonder how much more time people spend on getting through their e-mail than they ever spent on snail mail.* She quickly deleted the messages that were announcing various seminars on campus, then her eye was drawn to a familiar name: Jessica.Peters@nou.edu. Robin quickly doubleclicked on the message.

Robin—
*I hope you're feeling better this morning. I just wanted to
check to make sure that you made it home OK last night,
although it looked like you were in good hands with Capi.*
See you at the game next week—
Jess

"Ughhh, how embarrassing," Robin groaned out loud. She
vaguely remembered being rather rude to Jess's boyfriend the
night before...*Boyfriend? Could that testosterone-laden airhead
have really been her boyfriend?* Robin concluded that she really
didn't want to think about that possibility, but decided she
should write Jess back to thank her for her concern.

Hey Jess—
*I'm doing much better this morning, thank you. I'm really
kind of embarrassed about the whole thing. I don't usually drink
that much, but I guess I just got carried away after the big victory. Sorry I couldn't stay longer to talk to you and John.*
*Hey, you know, I could really use some caffeine. If you've
got a few minutes this morning, I could meet you at the Java
Connection in the Union for a cup of coffee. I know you're probably busy, but if not this morning, how about tomorrow?*
Robbie

Robin felt a tightening in her stomach as she sent the message off and wondered why this woman made her so nervous.
She really wanted Jess to like her, and she was afraid that her
immature behavior of the night before wasn't going to help. *And
why do I want her to like me so badly? There were some pretty
good indications last night that she's straight...But I'm so
incredibly attracted to her. Would that happen if she really were
straight? I don't think I've ever fallen for a straight woman
before. My gaydar has always been better than that.*
Robin's attention was drawn to the box that flashed up on
her screen: "New mail has arrived. Would you like to read it
now?"
She clicked yes, and was delighted to see that it had come
from Jess.

Robbie—
It's a pretty slow morning over here, so I'd be happy to join
you for a cup of coffee. I'll meet you at the Java Connection in
ten minutes, unless I hear from you otherwise.
Jess

Robin quickly shot back an affirmative reply, then glanced
down at her attire that she couldn't even remember picking out
that morning. *Blue jeans and a cotton shirt—what did I expect? I*
wonder what basketball coaches get to wear to work?

Robin grabbed her wallet and headed for the Union. She
rarely went to the Java Connection for coffee, since Starbuck's
was much closer to her office, but the Java Connection was half
way between her and the athletic department. She found that the
fresh spring air and blooming rhododendrons helped to clear her
head, and she actually felt pretty good by the time she got to the
Union. She ordered a tall cup of coffee, put lots of cream in it,
and found a table by the windows. A few minutes later, her face
lit up as she saw Jess walk in the door, dressed in a very sleek,
black, warm-up jacket and pants. *I guess that answers that ques-*
tion. I wonder if there's anything that doesn't look good on her.
Robin was inordinately pleased at Jess's broad smile when she
spotted her sitting by the windows. The coach ordered her coffee
and joined Robin at the table.

"Hey, you look pretty good for someone who was nearly
green the last time I saw her," Jess said teasingly. "Still young
enough to recover quickly, I suppose."

Robin felt her face flush and wondered if her face looked
better in red or green. "Not quickly enough for my eight o'clock
class. I'm not sure how I managed to get through it. Did you and
John stay late at Tony's?" Robin asked, not really wanting to
know where they might have gone afterward.

"No, we left shortly after you did. John had a recruiting trip
this morning so I dropped him off at his place pretty early last
night." Robin felt a sense of relief that she knew was out of proportion with the situation.

"So how long have you known John?" *What am I, some kind*
of masochist? Why do I want to know about the two of them?

"Well, I met him shortly after I moved here, but we've only
been going out for a couple of weeks. We're both so busy with
work that we really don't get a chance to see each other very

much. I'm not sure I have the type of lifestyle that's conducive to a serious relationship, though. At least it's never worked out in the past." Jess looked away wistfully, and then turned back to Robin. "What about you? Are you seeing anyone?"

Oh boy, now what do I say? Robin was certainly not in the closet, but she didn't go around advertising that she was gay, either. She wasn't sure she was ready to come out to Jess, especially since it appeared that Jess was quite straight. *What if she's homophobic? Wouldn't that be just my luck?* Robin decided to play it safe.

"Oh, I go out every once in a while, but I'm not seeing anyone seriously." She felt a twinge of guilt when she thought about Capi, but decided she really hadn't lied. "Comstock isn't exactly the best place to live if you're looking for romance. Everyone says it's a great place to raise a family, but if you don't have a family, it can get kind of lonely. I sure have lots of great friends, though, so I can't complain."

"Yeah, your friend Capi seemed really nice. She must be a good friend to be willing to drive you home when there was a good chance you were going to be sick in her car," Jess teased with a wry grin on her face.

"Well, she's got leather interior so it cleans up easily," Robin shot back. They both laughed, and then Robin decided that the thought of vomiting might still be too real for her stomach to handle and she quickly changed the subject. "Speaking of small towns, Pocatello, Idaho can't be much different. Where did you live before you moved there?"

A dark look seemed to come over Jess's face, and she looked out the window while replying quietly, "I lived in a small town in western Montana for a few years." Turning back toward Robin, Jess forced a small smile onto her face and said, "I'm afraid I need to be getting back to my office. I'm expecting a phone call from a recruit. Thanks for inviting me for coffee," she said, already standing up to leave.

Wow, what did I say? Should I apologize? Robin was flustered as she quickly stood and said, "Sure, anytime, Jess. I'll see you next week at the game." Robin watched Jess's back as she left the coffee shop, then slowly sat back down, trying to figure out how the conversation got derailed so quickly.

Damn, I just panicked at the first mention of my past. It was a perfectly innocent question, and now I've just drawn attention to it. I hope Robin doesn't think I was brushing her off. I really like her—she's so easy to talk to. It's almost like we've been friends for years. Jess was making her way back to her office, and decided that an hour or so in the weight room might improve her mood a little. It was unlikely to be crowded at that time of day, and she would be able to get through her routine pretty quickly.

She warmed up for a few minutes on a stationary bike, then worked her way through the weights for a good fifty minutes. She found herself thinking about Robin and wondering how someone like her had ended up as an economics professor. *Do I know anything about economics? Supply and demand, right? Well, if she wants to talk about economics, I'm just going to have to admit to being a dumb jock.*

"Hi, Jess, I've been looking for you," Butch Dockman called out from the door to the weight room. "Do you have a few minutes?"

"Sure, what's up?" Jess asked as she dropped the weights she had been lifting back onto the rack.

"Well, if you're done here, maybe we could talk in your office," Butch said with a questioning look on his face.

"Okay, I was about to head back there soon anyway. I can catch a shower later." Jess tried not to show her worry on her face as she smiled at Butch and followed him out of the room. *Okay, don't be paranoid. I'm sure there's a perfectly innocent reason for him to want to talk to me in private.*

By the time they got to Jess's office, she was so nervous she had to put her hands in her pockets so Butch wouldn't see them trembling. She shut the door behind them and gestured Butch to a seat while she went around to sit behind the desk. Her office was spacious and decorated in the requisite orange and black, although in a subtle, tasteful way. A large TV and VCR dominated one corner of the office, where recruiting and scouting tapes could be watched. There were numerous glossy pictures of past NOU basketball players in action adorning the walls. There had been one of her in the office when she arrived, but she thought that was highly immodest and quickly had it moved out to one of the hallways.

Jess looked expectantly at Butch, who looked a little nervous himself.

"I had a phone call this morning from the mother of one of your recruits." He paused and shifted in his seat. "I guess it's best to just be direct, here. She asked me what I knew about your sexual preferences." He looked up to see what effect that had on Jess, but Jess only looked back steadily with a slight tightening to her jaw, so he quickly went on. "I assured her that that was absolutely none of my business, and I told her that I had complete confidence in your integrity and ethics."

Jess's expression softened slightly and she said, "Thank you, Butch. I appreciate that."

"Well, I could understand her concern as a mother, but it seems pretty unfair to assume that about you just because you're not married," Butch said indignantly, obviously never considering that a woman as beautiful and graceful as Jess could be gay.

Yeah, of course you can understand "her concern," Jess thought bitterly, *so why aren't you athletic directors ever "concerned" when you hire straight men to coach women athletes?* But she kept her sarcasm buried and asked, "Which recruit was it?"

"Angie Tomlinson, from Lake Oswego. Her mother said that the Southern Washington coach was hinting around that her daughter might be exposed to undesirable lifestyles if she came to NOU. Isn't that just what you'd expect from that...from Coach Runyon? If I were that mother, I'd be more concerned about exposing my daughter to that poison personality at Southern Washington."

At that, Jess had to laugh out loud, which helped relieve some of the tension. It was no secret that many coaches would try to influence the recruiting game by spreading rumors about opposing coaches. And one of the most effective rumors to use was that a female coach was gay. Even if the coach were married, some recruiters would suggest that the marriage was just for show. It never made sense to Jess that parents were completely secure in sending their daughters off to be coached by men, but would die before sending their daughter to be coached by a known lesbian. She knew of many examples of men coaches having inappropriate relationships with players, one right here at NOU, and more often than not, they were protected by the male athletic directors instead of being fired.

But regardless of the injustice toward lesbians, *in this case, it just isn't true,* Jess fumed. *Why does everyone think that all single women in athletics are gay?* Oh, she knew that a lot of them were, having had plenty of teammates through the years that were out, and even a few that had come on to her, but she had never had an attraction to a woman. She had nothing against gays, and considered herself very open-minded about the subject. But having had people assume that she was gay on numerous occasions in the past had made Jess somewhat defensive about the whole issue. So while she didn't want to say anything to Butch that would imply that she thought being gay was wrong, she also wanted to say something to let him know that she wasn't.

"Well, Butch, I can assure you that this won't be an issue in my program. I can't stop the lies that opposing coaches want to spread, but you won't have to worry about the integrity of my program. I will always maintain appropriate, respectful, relationships with my players."

"I wasn't doubting you, Jess. We heard only good things about your experience at Idaho State, and your athletes here are already showing how much they respect you. I just wanted to let you know what I had heard, so you didn't hear it from someone else." With that, Butch got up and smiled at Jess before leaving the office.

Oh God, not again. Maybe I should just get out of coaching. Or maybe I should just take the time to develop a real relationship that might actually last. If I were married, at least some of this would have to go away.

Jess thought about the guys she'd dated over the years, and wondered why they all seemed more like good friends, or brothers, instead of potential partners. *Well, maybe if you'd made any of them a priority in your life, instead of putting them after everything else, one of them would still be around.* But her teams and her career had always come first. It didn't take too many nights of watching film, or weekends of watching recruits, before her boyfriends had found someone else who appreciated them more. *Maybe I can do it right this time with John. I know he doesn't seem like a great match for me, but he's a nice guy and we really seem to have a good time together. God, I'm sounding desperate.*

Chapter
3

Ten o'clock, pause...two o'clock, pause...ten o'clock, pause...two o'clock, pause...wait for the loop to form...there! Now forward...Perfect. Mend the line...watch...watch...watch...

"YESSS! I got one! Capi! Bring the camera!"

Robin slowly tried to maneuver her way out of the current and back toward shore, all the while keeping the tension on her line. The rocks on the bottom of the river were covered with moss, and Robin was glad she was wearing her wading cleats as she slipped and skidded her way backward. Capi was making her way upstream, having reeled in her line after hearing Robin call to her. She was grinning broadly at Robin, who was obviously thoroughly enjoying her battle with the big fish. She loved to see Robin like this—looking like a kid at Christmas. The stress and fatigue of work was completely absent, and Capi thought her friend had never looked more appealing.

"We'll probably have every angler within ten miles here after that shriek of yours," Capi teased. "You'd think you'd never caught a fish before."

"I did not shriek," Robin said indignantly.

"Here, let me net it for you. Bring it in just a little closer...There, got it. Wow, that's a nice one, Robbie. Look at that red stripe down the side. I guess that's why they call these rainbows McKenzie River redsides, huh?"

Robin took the net from Capi and worked the fly free, knowing that Capi didn't particularly like touching the fish.

They had a running joke about whether Capi used fish repellant on her flies so that she wouldn't have to actually catch any fish.

"Okay, quick, get the picture so I can get it back in the water." Robin gave Capi her best full-toothed smile while holding the fish in front of her, and then gently set the fish back in the water, slowly moving it back and forth until it quickly swam away. "Wow, that was a great fish. Well, that's five to none in my favor, Capi. I guess some things never change. What do you say we break for lunch?"

"Yeah, I'm sure the fish will appreciate a break from your incomparable cunning and skill," Capi replied sarcastically. Robin threw her arm around Capi's shoulders with a laugh, and they made their way to the grassy bank and the daypacks they had left there.

"What a day, huh? We should do this more often on weekends," Robin said wistfully while leaning back and looking at the few, small clouds in an otherwise bright blue sky.

"That could be arranged," Capi said with a wry grin on her face. "You just have to decide that you don't need to work every weekend."

"Yeah, well you don't have to worry about getting tenure," Robin said with a worried look.

"As if you have to worry. You've only won the teacher of the year award in your college for the past two years, and I know you've got some impressive research projects going, too. I wish you thought as highly of yourself as everyone else does," Capi admonished.

"Yeah, I do too, but you didn't grow up with my mother," Robin said disdainfully. "I think I'm getting better though. Did you notice how I'm trying to just politely say 'thank you' when you give me compliments?" Robin grinned. "If I hang around you too long, you might start thinking I'm conceited."

"Yeah, right. I don't think we have to worry about that, no matter how long I hang around." Capi looked at Robin with a serious expression on her face, and Robin was afraid that the conversation was going to go in a direction that she wasn't ready for.

"Hey Capi, what did you think of that guy that was with Jess Peters at Tony's the other night?" Robin asked in an attempt to change the subject—and to change it to a subject she was particularly interested in.

"You mean John? He seemed like your typical macho jock, but a very good-looking macho jock." Capi looked intently at Robin. "You didn't seem to like him too much, judging by the way you were shooting daggers at him."

"I was not. At least I don't remember doing that," Robin replied sheepishly, realizing she might not remember everything that happened that night. "I guess I didn't think that he seemed very much like Jess's type."

"What you really mean, is that you were hoping Jess's type might come with different anatomy, right? And that maybe her tastes would run toward short, cute, blondes?" Capi grinned at the blush that was creeping up Robin's neck. "Oh, come on, Robbie, I saw how your face lit up when Jess walked into the room. But don't you think there's a real good chance that she's actually straight?"

"I hardly even know her," Robin protested. "So I don't know if I think she's straight, and I'm NOT scamming on her."

"Ah, what is that saying about 'protesting too much?'" Capi smiled gently at Robin and said, "It's okay if you have a crush on her, Robbie. God knows she's gorgeous enough. I'll bet she won't go fishing with you, though, and if she did, she wouldn't let you catch more fish than her."

"Oh right, like you *let* me catch more fish than you." Robin rolled her eyes. "It wouldn't matter anyway, Capi, you'll always be my best fishing buddy. It's good for my ego." At that, Capi lunged for Robin and they both went rolling over the grass in a half-hearted wrestling match. They ended up with their faces inches apart, looking intently into each other's eyes. Robin could see the silent request for something that she knew she couldn't give right now. So she turned her head slightly and gave her best friend a quick kiss on the cheek and a big hug, just for being Capi. Seeming to understand that the hug was some kind of consolation prize, Capi ruefully recognized that she was going to have to accept Robin's friendship for what it was—friendship only.

Robin felt profound regret at not being able to give Capi what she wanted. *I do love her, but it's a different kind of love than she wants from me. Why can't I feel more for her? She's so nice to me, and we have such a great time together; why can't I fall in love with someone who is so compatible with me?* Obviously love had not learned what the rules were, or had chosen to ignore them. Instead of taking the easy option and falling for Capi, she found herself increasingly thinking about a dark-haired basketball coach that was very likely straight, and didn't even seem that comfortable talking to her. Well, it wouldn't be the first time that Robin had chosen to do things the hard way, and it probably wouldn't be the last.

"Hey, I think I hear a fish calling my name," Robin said as she released Capi and stood up, offering her a hand. She didn't release Capi's hand as they walked back to the river, feeling very grateful that Capi seemed to be willing to accept their current relationship for what it was.

Chapter
4

Robin raced into her apartment from the carport when she heard the phone ringing. "Hello?" she said, breathing hard from her mad dash.

"Hi, Robbie. You sound like you just ran a marathon. Did I catch you at a bad time?"

"Oh, hi, Capi. No, I got tied up at work grading papers, and I was just getting home when I heard the phone ringing. What's up?"

"I wondered if you wanted me to pick you up for the softball game tonight. I was thinking that we'd probably go out afterwards, and I remember what happened last time when you had your own car."

"Thanks for reminding me, *friend*," Robin said sarcastically. "I'll be ready in about fifteen minutes, can you wait that long?"

"Sure, no problem. I'll see you then."

Robin hung up the phone and made her way into the bedroom to change. *I hope I remembered to wash my softball shirt after the last game. And where are my favorite black shorts? I hope I didn't leave them at school. God, look at my hair. I must have forgotten to comb it after the gym today.* Suddenly Robin stopped and looked at herself in the mirror. *Okay, why am I obsessing about how I look for a softball game? As if I don't know.* Robin knew that it made no sense to lie to herself about her feelings. She was already nervous about playing Jess's team that night. In fact, if she was honest, she'd been nervous about it

for the last two days. Not only was she worried about getting
beaten badly by a team that was much better than hers, but she
was also worried about how Jess had left so abruptly from their
last meeting at the Java Connection. *I hope I get a chance to talk
to her. Maybe she was just having a bad day or something, and
we can just pretend that it never happened.*

Robin found her shirt, which was clean and neatly folded,
and her favorite black shorts, which were in her gym bag, and
quickly changed for the game. She then raced into the kitchen to
wolf down a power bar and a soda before Capi arrived. She
grabbed her softball bag out of the trunk of her car and climbed
into Capi's SUV, throwing the bag in the back seat.

"Well, do you think we have a chance tonight?" Robin
asked. "They're kind of loaded with all those coaches playing
for them."

"Yeah, but we've got experience and wisdom on our side,"
Capi said grinning.

"You mean we're old and slow," Robin interpreted dryly.
"Speak for yourself."

"Well, you do tend to bring the average age of our team
down. It might be in the mid-thirties now. But unfortunately, you
can only play one position at a time, and they do make the rest of
us bat. So, to answer your original question—no, I don't think
we have much of a chance."

"Well, you're just going to have to believe in miracles, then,
because I think we're going to win," Robin declared triumphantly.

But when they got to the field and saw the other team warming up, Robin found her optimism waning. *Well, at least they
have a mercy rule, so maybe we'll only have to play five innings.*

Robin looked over at the other bench and saw Jess changing
her shoes. Just then, Jess looked up and their eyes met. Robin
immediately broke into a smile, and although Jess hesitated for
an instant, she smiled back and nodded. Robin's heart rate
seemed to pick up a few beats, and she had newfound energy as
she sprinted out to the field for the first inning.

The game went pretty much as expected. Robin's team usually went three and out, while Jess's team managed to score at
least one run in every inning. Robin did make some nice plays at
third base, including snaring a line drive of Jess's that would
have gone for a double. It was hit so hard that Robin really

didn't even have time to think about it, but just stuck her glove up and there it was. Jess had just grinned at Robin and yelled, "Happy birthday!"

The only thing that really detracted from the game was the constant, obnoxious hazing that was coming from one of the Tony's fans. Robin was appalled when she finally looked closer in the third inning and saw that the perpetrator was none other than John. *Oh God, what does Jess see in that guy? He's such a...a...man!* Robin knew that was completely unfair to half the population, but John just seemed to have what she thought of as all the negative male traits. *Obviously he can't be all bad, or Jess wouldn't be going out with him. Would she?*

Robin managed to tune John out for the remainder of the game, but couldn't help but gag a little when he greeted Jess after one inning with a big hug and a kiss on the cheek.

After the game, there were no hard feelings. The players on Jess's team were gracious winners, and Robin's team took the loss good-naturedly. They all agreed to meet at Tony's for a few beers, and made their way to the parking lot.

"Well, Robbie, you did all you could tonight," Capi said sympathetically as they climbed back into the SUV and headed for Tony's. "It's hard when you have to carry the rest of us."

"Oh, don't talk like that. Everyone did great. They're just stronger, faster, and better than us. It's just city league, anyway. It's not like it really matters whether we win or not."

"Yeah, right. Like you're not one of the most competitive people I know," Capi said teasingly. "I think you're going to need that competitiveness if you're going to try to sway one tall, dark, and beautiful away from one tall, dark, and handsome. They looked like quite the couple tonight."

Robin felt her gut tighten at the thought of Jess and John together, but tried to maintain a nonchalant face for Capi. "I'm not sure there's much chance of doing that, but you never know, Capi. Maybe Jess has just never really thought about being with a woman before, so she's just settling for some guy who happens to be available," Robin said hopefully.

Capi raised a disbelieving eyebrow at Robin. "How can anyone be in collegiate athletics and not have thought about the possibility of two women being together? She's gotta be in her thirties, so it's hard to believe that she wouldn't have found herself attracted to a woman by now if she's really gay. Unless, of course, she's homophobic and won't ever admit to being attracted to a woman."

"She doesn't seem like the type to be homophobic," Robin said defensively. "Maybe she's just never met the right woman."

"Right. And I suppose you know who the right woman is?" Capi challenged her with a grin.

"Alright, enough of this conversation. There's Jess now, so try to pretend like we weren't just talking about her," Robin admonished as they got out of the SUV in the Tony's parking lot.

"Hey, Jess, glad to see you could make it," Robin called out to her. The three of them made their way into the pizza parlor, and Robin was delighted to see that John didn't appear to be anywhere in sight. Leave it to Capi, of course, to bring the subject up.

"Where's John tonight? Did he wear himself out yelling at the umpire?" Capi asked with a smirk.

Jess looked embarrassed, and said, "He was a little loud tonight, wasn't he? I think he gets into the game and forgets that it's city league softball and not Pac-10 football. Anyway, he had to meet some other coaches to discuss a recruit, so it looks like it's girls' night out."

For some of us, every night is girls' night out, Capi thought wryly. "I'll order the pizza and beer, why don't you two go grab a few tables, okay?" Robin and Jess gave Capi some money for the order, and went to find some tables.

"You really played well tonight, Robin," Jess said. "Did you play softball at Wisconsin, too?"

"Yeah, but just for my junior and senior years. It was a new program, so we were kind of at a disadvantage in the Big 10. I got to play because they were just starting to recruit and had a lot of openings for walk-ons. I'm sure I'd never make the team now that they are fully funded and recruiting nationally," Robin said modestly.

"Oh, I wouldn't be so sure about that," Jess countered. "There's always room for good infielders, and you sure played a great third base tonight."

Robin felt herself blushing again, and cursed her fair coloring for making her discomfort so obvious. Remembering what she had told Capi earlier about handling compliments, she just smiled and quietly said, "Thanks." She really wanted to add *but I really just got lucky on a few of those,* but controlled her automatic urge to put herself down.

Capi and the rest of the players soon arrived with pitchers of beer, and the noise level rose considerably as everyone bantered back and forth about the game. Robin made sure to pace herself, not wanting a repeat of the week before. She was really enjoying the easy conversation around the table, especially the relaxing effect it seemed to have on Jess. There was no hint of the dark withdrawal that the coach had displayed at the Java Connection, and Robin decided that she must have just hit on some bad topic of conversation. *What were we talking about that day when she got up so abruptly and left? I think it was something about Montana, or Idaho. I wonder what happened there that she doesn't want to talk about.*

Robin was pulled out of her musings when Capi said, "Hey Robin, I've got an early morning meeting tomorrow, so I should probably get going. Are you about ready?"

Robin hesitated, because she was having a good time talking with Jess and didn't want to miss this opportunity, but then said, "Uh, sure Capi, I can leave now if you need to."

Jess picked up on Robin's reluctance, and quickly said, "Hey, I can give you a ride home if you'd like to stay a little longer, Robin."

Robin looked at Capi to see how disappointed she'd be if she didn't go with her, but Capi only looked reassuringly back at Robin and raised her eyebrows questioningly.

"Okay, that would be great, Jess, if you're sure you don't mind," Robin replied.

"Not at all. I don't have to be anywhere in the morning, so we can stay as late as you want."

Robin tried very hard not to think of all the possibilities that statement implied. She then got up to follow Capi to her car so that she could retrieve her bag.

"Well, it looks like this might be your big chance to see if your theories about the 'right woman' are correct," Capi teased. "Try not to do anything too drastic, just in case you're wrong. And if it does happen to work out, you can thank me later for giving you this opportunity."

Robin narrowed her look at Capi and asked suspiciously, "Do you even have a meeting in the morning?"

"You'll never know. See you later, hotshot." And with that, Capi was off and Robin made her way back into Tony's, wonder-

ing how Capi could possibly be so gracious in what had to be a
very difficult situation for her. It made her wonder again about
why she wasn't falling in love with Capi, but quickly forgot that
line of thought when she saw Jess waiting for her at the table.
Most of the other players had cleared out by then, and there were
just a few of them left talking in groups of two or three.

"Everything okay with Capi?" Jess asked as Robin sat back
down next to her. Robin nodded and Jess added, "She sure seems
like a good friend. How long have you known her?"

"About three years—ever since I got here, but we really
didn't start hanging out together until last year. She's my best
fishing buddy, and just a great friend to talk to. She has this way
of always making me feel better, no matter how bad things might
get," Robin said with a wistful look on her face. Jess wondered
why Robin seemed kind of sad about that, but decided not to pursue it.

"Well, everybody needs a best friend, so I'd say you're
pretty lucky to have found one here."

"How about you? Is John your best friend?" Robin said,
even though she couldn't imagine Jess confiding in John the way
she confided in Capi.

"I guess I don't really think of him as a best friend," Jess
said thoughtfully. "I don't really know him that well yet, but I'm
trying to give this relationship a chance without messing it up
like I have all the other relationships in my life."

"What do you mean, messing them up?" Robin asked. "How
do you know the other person didn't mess them up, or maybe
they were never meant to be?"

Jess noted the use of "other person" instead of "guy" or
"man," and wondered if Robin was making assumptions about
her sexuality just like everyone else. *Well, just to be sure...* "All
the other men were really nice guys—not like there were that
many of them—but I just always had something else in my life
that was more important than them. Usually basketball. I don't
blame them for looking for someone who would put them first in
their life."

"Well, if they really liked you, they would have found a way
to make what was important in your life, important in theirs,
too," Robin replied earnestly. *At least that's what I'd do*, she
added to herself.

"Well, thanks for the support, but I think it needs to go both ways. And I guess I haven't really been that interested in their lives." Jess then gave a laugh, and said, "Listen to me talk like I've had tons of boyfriends in my past. Really, we're only talking about a few casual, very short-term, relationships. In fact, the thought of really getting serious with John is pretty scary to me, but it seems like it's time to give it a chance. Maybe it won't work, but I don't want it to be for lack of trying."

Robin thought Jess's whole approach to the relationship with John sounded a little analytical, and predicted spectacular failure in the near future. Of course, she didn't share that thought with Jess, only smiled and nodded instead.

"But hey, enough about me. How can someone as smart, fun, and attractive as you still be single? Don't tell me you're bad at relationships, too?" Jess said with a smile toward Robin.

"Well, I've had a couple of relationships that have lasted for a few years, but then it seems like I move away and the other person doesn't want to come along with me. First it was moving from Wisconsin to Minnesota for grad school, and then it was moving out here for this job. I suppose I could have decided that the relationships were more important than the moves, but I think I was hoping that they would follow me after a year or two. At least that's what we talked about," Robin said with a far-away look in her eyes. "But it seemed that it didn't take long for them to forget about me once I had left, because they both went on to other relationships and I was left to start over." Robin had a wry smile on her face, and she added, "But I believe things happen for a reason, and I'm sure that I'm going to find someone else that is perfect for me, and I'll wonder what I ever saw in those other people." Robin looked up at Jess and raised her glass to toast her optimism.

Jess grinned back and said, "Here's to the future and perfection. May we both find it."

Oh, if only you were thinking about me when you said that, Robin wished.

They continued to talk for another hour, trading stories about playing basketball in college, going to grad school, and dealing with the psyches of college students. Before they knew it, they were the only ones left at the table, and midnight was fast approaching.

"Oh, look at how late it is." Jess gave Robin a worried look. "Do you have an eight o'clock class tomorrow?"

"No, it's finals week, and I gave my last final yesterday. So I just have to grade about two hundred exams before next Monday. But I don't need to be in the office at any particular time, so I can sleep in if I need to. What about you?"

"Things are really flexible for me right now, so getting in late isn't a problem. But we should probably be going before they kick us out of here," Jess suggested with a smile.

"Yeah, you're right. I really appreciate you giving me a ride home. I hope it's not too much out of your way," Robin said as they made their way out to the parking lot.

"Well, unless you live in another town, nothing in Comstock can be too much out of the way," Jess joked. "I think I can drive from one end of town to the other in about ten minutes."

Jess stopped at a late model Toyota Camry with dealer's plates on it and unlocked the door for Robin.

"I hope you don't mind riding in my 'family car.' It's not exactly what I would choose to drive, but all the coaches get complimentary cars from the local dealers, and we have to agree to drive them around town. I find it hard to believe that anyone is going to go buy a Toyota just because they see me driving this around," Jess laughed while shaking her head, "but I suppose the dealers get to write it off as an advertising expense, and they get lots of free tickets to all the athletic events for their donation."

"Well, at least they do it for both the men's and women's sports now. It sure didn't used to be that way," Robin replied.

"So where to?" Jess asked as she left the parking lot.

"Go right and head up to Elm Street. I live in those town-houses that are just up the hill from the shopping center."

"Hey, those look nice. They were all full when I moved here, so I ended up over on College Hill. It's a little too full of students for me, so I'm looking for something else. I think I might try to buy something small, but I want to wait until I learn the area a little more."

"Well, real estate is pretty expensive here, but I suppose a basketball coach makes a whole lot more than an assistant professor," Robin said with what she hoped wasn't too much sarcasm in her voice. "But I'm an economist, so I know how the laws of supply and demand work, and it's perfectly clear that basketball coaches are much more in demand than economics professors. And apparently football coaches are much more in demand than university presidents, since our football coach makes about three times what the president makes."

"Yeah, it does seem like we've lost some perspective when it comes to athletics, but as a coach, I have to play with the rules that are given to me. If we want to be successful at NOU, we have to be able to compete with the other programs."

Jess thought she was sounding a little defensive, and Robin was feeling bad for bringing the subject up. They both turned and looked at each other with apologetic expressions, and said "Sorry, I..." at the same time. Which caused them both to laugh and relax again.

"Maybe there are just some topics we should avoid, huh?" Jess offered.

"No, I agree completely with what you're saying, Jess. I think I was just feeling envious, or something. You know, I always wanted to be a coach when I was younger, but I thought it wasn't a 'proper' career. Of course, that was really my mother thinking for me, but I've always had some regrets that I didn't follow my heart. Not that I don't like what I'm doing, because I do, but I'm not sure that I could say with a straight face that I have a passion for economics." Robin laughed.

"I'll bet you're passionate when you teach, though, aren't you?" Jess asked with a knowing grin.

Robin blushed and said, "It's definitely the part of my job I like best."

"It's the part of my job that I like best, too," Jess replied. "Unfortunately, in collegiate athletics today, there's more emphasis on recruiting than teaching."

"Well, I'm sure you have an advantage in that department, too," Robin said with a smile. "You certainly do make a good first impression. I remember that day I first met you in Butch Dockman's office, you had the whole committee eating out of your hand."

Now it was Jess's turn to blush, and she noted with relief that they had arrived at Robin's apartment complex and she could change the subject by asking for directions to Robin's apartment.

Robin didn't want the evening with Jess to end, and debated with herself about inviting Jess in for another beer or some coffee, but decided that she shouldn't push her luck.

"Jess, thanks so much for the ride home," Robin said while turning toward her in the seat. "I was really glad that I could stay

R. L. Johnson

longer to talk to you tonight."

"Yeah, me too. I feel like we're already old friends," Jess said with a laugh.

"You know, if you're not doing anything at noon tomorrow, you should come by the recreation center," Robin offered. "We could show the boys a thing or two on the basketball court."

"Well, maybe you could show them a thing or two, but I've been spending a lot more time coaching than playing in recent years. I'd hate to embarrass myself. Besides, everyone loves to get the opportunity to 'beat the coach,' and that often leads to a bunch of wannabe basketball players trying to win at any cost, and I end up taking the brunt of it," Jess lamented.

"Yeah, I suppose that's true. I've never really thought about what it would be like to have everyone on campus know who you are," Robin said understandingly.

Jess laughed and said, "Well I sure wouldn't go that far. I'm sure there are plenty of people on campus that don't even know we have a women's basketball team, let alone who the coach is."

"Well, speaking from my personal experience, once they met you, they'd never forget you," Robin said sincerely. *God, I hope I didn't just go too far. I don't want to scare her away now.* But Jess just smiled, and their eyes met for a long time before Robin looked down and said, "Well, I guess I'd better get going. I don't want to keep you up any later. Thanks again for the ride." She reached out and gave Jess's hand a squeeze before climbing out of the car and shutting the door.

Jess sat there for a long moment, looking at her hand and wondering why such a casual gesture had felt so significant. *I guess it's been a while since I've had a good friend. Someone I can talk to and feel comfortable with. In fact, I can't remember the last time I let someone get that close. Closeness also means being vulnerable, though, and I'm not sure I'm ready for that.* Ironically, Jess had never had any of these thoughts about John, but that fact did not seem to register with her.

Chapter
5

Robin made it in to work by ten a.m. the next morning, having spent a leisurely morning drinking coffee and grading papers. Most of the students had already left campus for the summer, and things were very quiet around the department. As much as she loved teaching, it felt like such a relief when the students were gone. No more lines at Starbucks, plenty of parking spaces, and an uncrowded gym were just a few of the benefits.

Robin fired up her e-mail and found only five new messages waiting for her. *I guess even e-mail knows that summer break is here.* The first one was from Capi, and Robin opened it quickly, wondering what type of teasing she was going to have to endure from her good friend.

Hey Robbie—How did it go last night??? If you're reading this before noon, it's a bad sign. Does she still need help in figuring out who the "right woman" is? Want me to call her? I could give a great testimonial to your wit and charm. I could also tell her that there are plenty of women waiting in line if she doesn't have enough sense to know a good thing when she sees it.
Are you going to the gym later? Maybe I'll see you there.
Your not-so-secret-admirer, Capi.

Robin smiled and hit the "reply" icon.

Capi, you are so thoughtful—willing to act on my behalf in this matter. I hope you won't be offended if I respectfully decline your offer of assistance. I'm sure I'll be able to mess it up just fine on my own, without any help from you.

We did have a good time last night. We talked at Tony's until about midnight, and then she drove me home. I don't think she has a lot of close friends, but she seemed pretty comfortable talking to me. I'm certainly not going to push for anything more at this point. Besides, she made a few comments that made it pretty clear that she's straight. Or at least, she thinks she's straight! So I don't want to go scaring her away before we've gotten a chance to know each other better. I don't know how I'm going to handle the 'John' thing, though. She seems pretty intent on having a relationship with him. When I think about the two of them being intimate, it makes me want to throw up!

Well, I'll probably see you at the gym—I'm going over around noon.

Robbie

Jess was sitting in her office, looking at yet another tape sent in by a high school player looking for a scholarship. She had already started the tape twice, found herself daydreaming both times, and stopped to rewind it. *What is wrong with me this morning? Maybe I didn't get enough sleep last night.* What she really couldn't figure out, though, was why her mind kept transposing Robin into the basketball player on the tape. Yes, they were both small, blond, guard-types, but she'd never even seen Robin play. In her morning's fantasy, however, Robin was a dazzling point guard, flashing down the court and delivering no-look passes to a cutting power forward. Jess looked at her watch and saw that it was almost twelve-thirty. *Maybe I should just take a break and go see what the real thing looks like on the court.* Jess turned off the video unit and headed for the recreation center.

The gym at the rec center was on the lower level, but had large openings all around the main level so that spectators could look down on the courts. Jess ordered a smoothie from the food vendor on the main level, and headed over to one of the openings. Two of the three courts had games going on, and Jess quickly spotted Robin playing on the court nearer to her. She was the only woman playing, and definitely the smallest player on the court. She was being guarded by a much older man, probably in his fifties, and was clearly way too quick for him to keep up with. As a result, he often resorted to grabbing and holding Robin as she blew by him. Jess could tell that Robin was getting frustrated, as she threw her arm out to try and disengage herself from him. The next time down the court, Robin faked one way and quickly reversed directions for a back door pass. As she was about to leave her defender for a wide-open lay-up, he reached out desperately to grab her again. Robin took the ball and slammed it down on the court.

"Goddamn it, Glenn! If you grab my breast one more time, I'm gonna kick you in the balls so hard they come out your ears!" she screamed for the world to hear.

Everything went very quiet for a long moment, and then the other guys started snickering at Glenn's obvious discomfort.

"Well, that would make me stop," one of them said with a wry grin at his teammate.

"Hey, Glenn, why don't we switch—you take Bill and I'll take Robin," one of Glenn's teammates offered in an obvious attempt to smooth things over.

Robin let out a deep breath and looked up to the ceiling, obviously trying to calm herself down. It was then that she saw Jess up at the opening. *Oh my God, why today? It's not like Glenn hasn't been doing this for weeks now. Why did I have to choose today to lose my temper?* Robin put both her hands over her face and looked at Jess through her fingers. Jess was smiling broadly, not only at Robin's embarrassment at being "caught," but at the feistiness she had displayed with Glenn. She gave Robin a thumbs up sign, and went back to drinking her smoothie.

Robin continued with the game, now being guarded by a much more skilled, and therefore cleaner, player. The next time she looked up at the opening, Jess was gone. Robin realized that she had lost interest in playing anymore and decided to quit after the game was over, even though her team had won the right to stay on the court for the next game. She noticed that all of the guys made a point to come over and slap her hand, saying, "Nice game, Robin," and "He deserved it, Robin." Glenn apparently had enough sense to realize that his actions were completely unacceptable, even to the other guys, and had disappeared quickly after the game.

Robin slowly made her way towards the locker room, only to run into Jess coming out of the weight room.

"Hey, slugger, does Glenn still have all his private parts?" Jess asked with a big grin on her face.

Robin just groaned and asked, "Why do all the slimy guys have to guard me? Just because I'm 'the girl,' they think the oldest, slowest guy out there can guard me."

"Well, if it's any consolation, it was pretty clear that he *couldn't* guard you," Jess said sympathetically.

"Thanks. I just hope he never shows up again, although I suppose that's not likely," Robin replied. "Were you lifting weights?" she asked, nodding her head toward the weight room that Jess had come out of.

"No, I just saw a couple of my players in there and came down to talk to them. It's good to show up unexpectedly every once in a while so they think I'm keeping track of them," Jess said with a conspiratorial look. "Well, I should let you get to your shower, and I should get back to work."

"Hey, you know it's Friday, and it's the last day of finals week, how would you like to go out for a celebratory drink after work today?" Robin ventured. "Most of the students should be gone, so things won't be crowded."

Jess thought for a moment and then said, "Yeah, I think I can do that. Where do you want to go?"

"Well, Miguel's is just across the street from my office, and there's plenty of parking nearby."

"Robin, there's plenty of parking *everywhere* in Comstock," Jess replied with a smirk. "That would be great. See you there around five?"

"Sounds good; see you then." Robin waved a hand at Jess as she turned and made her way to the locker room. She had only gone a few paces when her friend Flaxen appeared at her side.

"Whoa, Robin, who is that gorgeous woman you were talking to?" Flaxen asked in a low voice while leaning into Robin.

Robin gave her a playful shove and said, "Back off, Flaxen. She's straight." But then she leaned close to Flaxen once again and whispered, "But I'm hoping to change that."

"Well, if anyone can, I'm sure you can. Is she new around here?"

"She's the new women's basketball coach. I can't believe

you haven't seen her before now."

"Well, I've read about her, but believe me, her picture in the paper didn't do her justice. I suppose it's hard to pack six feet of 'presence' into a newspaper mug shot. How do you know she's straight?" Flaxen asked.

"She's going out with this goon from the football coaching staff," Robin said while rolling her eyes. "Oh, I shouldn't be so harsh. He's actually a very good-looking guy, who just has a little too much macho in him for my taste. I suppose he's nice enough, though, and she seems to like him."

"Well, if my gaydar is in working order, I'd say he's in for a heartbreak," Flaxen replied.

"We can hope, can't we?" Robin answered with a smile, and they headed off to the showers together.

At four forty-five that afternoon, Robin was just starting to shut down her computer when there was a knock at her door.

"Come on in," she called.

Jess opened the door and stuck her head in. "Hi, I was walking over to Miguel's and thought I'd stop and pick you up, since it's on my way." She looked around the small office and said, "So this is how professors live."

"Well, it's how fairly new assistant professors live, anyway," Robin laughed. "There are actually some pretty nice offices in this old building, but you have to build up seniority before you get one of those."

Robin's office was long and narrow with a window at the end, making it difficult to arrange the desk, computer table, and filing cabinets in the room. Nevertheless, she had done a good job of making the office seem warm and comfortable. She had a number of posters with seascapes and mountain scenes from Oregon, as well as several posters of the men's and women's basketball teams from years past. Prominently displayed above the computer table was the poster of next year's team, which just happened to feature a big picture of Jess in the middle. Jess blushed when she noticed it, saying "Jeez, couldn't you find some better artwork for your office?"

Robin smiled back at her and said teasingly, "Ah, the price one must pay for being famous." She felt a little self-conscious about having the poster so prominently displayed over her computer where she spent most of her time, but hoped Jess didn't notice the significance of the location.

"Boy, the titles of these books are enough to make my head spin," Jess said while looking over Robin's bookshelves. "*Microeconomic Theory, Econometric Theory and Applications, Welfare Economics*...It's a far cry from John Wooden's *They Call Me Coach.*"

"Believe me, I'd much rather be reading John Wooden's book than those. Most of those are from my grad school days, but they cost so much that I can't bear to get rid of them. Occasionally, I actually even use one," Robin laughed. "Are you ready to head out? I'm getting hungry."

Having seen Robin polish off five pieces of pizza at one sitting, Jess figured that Robin didn't lack for appetite. She couldn't help but also notice that Robin's body didn't show any ill effects from her diet. *I guess she must work out enough to burn off all those calories. I just can't believe she doesn't have a long line of men waiting to go out with her—she's incredibly attractive, and a nice person, besides.* Jess felt something weird in her stomach in response to her thoughts, but her mind couldn't quite put a name to what she was feeling. She decided she'd have to think about it more later, and said, "Okay, let's go before you waste away from lack of food."

They quickly made their way across the street and found a table in the back room of Miguel's. Miguel's was a popular Mexican restaurant, and had a great selection of microbrews. After a few minutes, a server came over to take their order.

"Have you tried any of the brews from Deschutes Brewery?" Robin asked. "I really like their Bachelor Bitter, and they have some great seasonals, too."

"No, I haven't tried them, but if you recommend it, I'll have a Bachelor Bitter," Jess said with a smile toward Robin. After the server left, she added, "Why would someone name a beer after a grumpy, unmarried man?"

Robin laughed and said, "It's named after Mt. Bachelor, the ski resort. Didn't you ever go there when you were a student here?"

"No, I was really kind of a gym rat back in those days. My weekends were spent looking for pick-up games. Besides, our coach would have killed us if we'd injured ourselves skiing during the basketball season." The server returned with the beers, and after taking an appreciative swallow, Jess asked, "Do you ski?"

"I love skiing, but I probably do more cross-country than downhill. It's such a great workout, and you can really get into some spectacular backcountry in a couple of hours."

Jess was wondering just how much energy Robin had to burn in any given day. "How do you find time for all your hobbies, anyway? I feel lucky to find the time to take in a movie every once in a while."

"Well, I'd say you need to do something about that," Robin said with mock seriousness. "It's all a matter of priorities. I want to enjoy things like skiing and fishing and basketball while I'm still young and full of energy. Besides, who knows if I'll even make it to retirement age?" Robin finished off her beer and looked sternly at Jess. "I can see we're going to have to do something about your workaholic tendencies."

"I think it goes with the job. I don't think there's an hour of the day that you could go into the athletic offices and not find some coach watching films or working with athletes. There's just no nine-to-five about being a coach. I think that's why it's so hard to build good relationships and marriages. A lot of the men have wives and kids that they hardly see during the season. Somehow, I don't think husbands would be as understanding. At least boyfriends haven't been in the past," Jess said with chagrin.

Robin looked intently at Jess for a few moments, before asking, "Is being in a relationship something that's pretty important to you?"

Jess seemed startled by the question. "Well yeah, I guess so." She looked thoughtful for a moment. "Maybe I've just always assumed that I wanted to be in a relationship because it seems like everyone else is. The truth is that I've almost always been on my own, and it can get kind of lonely. Unfortunately, the few attempts I've made at relationships have never turned out to be the way I envisioned them in my head."

"How do you envision them in your head?" Robin asked gently, hoping that she wasn't pushing Jess too hard for personal details.

"I don't know." Jess stalled for time. "I guess I think of them as being equal partnerships, with lots of respect for each other, common interests, and, of course, a lot of passion." Jess smiled shyly at the last part, and Robin's heart nearly skipped a beat. Jess returned the question to Robin. "How do you envision the perfect relationship?"

"Well, I'm pretty sure I haven't experienced it yet," Robin laughed. "But I agree with all those things you said. I've never understood the couples that don't seem to have anything in common and basically only see each other in bed every night. They must be having some kind of great sex to make them stay together." Robin laughed.

"Yeah, well I wouldn't know about that either," Jess said, looking down at the table. "I've been unwilling to jump into bed with someone that I'm not really serious about, and I haven't ever gotten really serious about anyone yet. I know a lot of people appreciate good sex without any strings attached, but I've never been able to feel comfortable about that. I just don't see how sex can be that good if you don't have a close, trusting relationship with someone." Jess looked up at Robin and blushed. "I can't believe I'm sitting here talking to you about sex. I never talk to anyone about this stuff."

"Well, I think I probably brought it up," Robin said, smiling apologetically at Jess. "You can just tell me if I'm getting too personal. I know I have a tendency to just blurt out whatever's on my mind."

"Yeah, I kind of noticed that today at the gym," Jess teased.

"Oh God, that was so embarrassing," Robin said while the color rose in her cheeks. They both laughed lightly, and the somewhat uncomfortable moment before was quickly forgotten. "What's funny about it is that I hardly ever stick up for myself like that. I'm much more likely to just assume that somehow it's my fault and meekly let it go on. Yet another trait I attribute to my mother," Robin laughed. "Isn't it great to become an adult and be able to blame all your shortcomings on your mother? I wonder why fathers get off the hook so easily?"

"Well, I think they'd have to be around more in their kids' lives if they were going to have as much influence as mothers do. I can hardly remember my dad interacting with us as kids. He'd come home from work, eat, and disappear into his den for the evening. I always wondered what he had in that den that was so much more interesting than his family. I guess I'll never know," Jess said wistfully.

"Don't you see your dad anymore?" Robin asked, hoping again that she wasn't prying too much into Jess's personal life.

"Both my parents are dead. My mom died pretty young—I was just sixteen. Then my dad went into a major depression and basically drank himself to death ten years later. My brother and I tried everything to get him some help, but he just wouldn't accept it. I think maybe he felt bad about not being a better husband and father while my mom was alive, and the guilt just drove him to his death."

"I'm really sorry to hear that, Jess. It must get really lonely for you without your parents. Is your brother nearby?" Robin worried a little that she might be treading dangerously close to whatever topic had set Jess off at the Java Connection a week ago, but she didn't seem to be withdrawing.

"No, he lives on the east coast. He's six years older than me, so we were never very close. I probably talk to him twice a year, and I haven't seen him in about four years." Jess felt like everything she had to say was kind of depressing and was hoping to lighten the conversation a little. She looked up at Robin and asked, "What about you? I'd guess you were probably the youngest of three children, and you were so cute that you always got your way."

Robin laughed and said, "Not even close. I was in the middle of five kids, and I can't remember ever getting my way. My two older brothers got whatever they wanted because they were older and they were boys, and my two younger sisters were everything my mom wanted in little girls, and could do no wrong. I pretty much tried to remain invisible, since there was no way I could please my mom anyway. Being in the middle of a big family did make me appreciate food, though, because it seemed like I could never get enough. Which reminds me that I'm *really* hungry. How about if we order some nachos and get another round of drinks?"

Jess laughed at Robin's appetite and said, "Sure, sounds good. Do you want chicken, beef, or vegetarian?"

"I like veggie, but I'll eat anything, so why don't we get what you want?" Robin said while motioning the server over.

"Well, I probably would order beef, but I can live with veggie," Jess replied.

"I don't want you to just 'live with it,' I want you to enjoy it." Robin grinned back at Jess. She turned to the server and asked, "Can we get an order of beef nachos and another couple of beers?"

They continued to talk as they made their way through the food and drinks, and then Jess said that she should probably be going.

"Don't tell me you have to work tomorrow—it's Saturday," Robin said sternly.

"No, it's just that I told John that I'd be home tonight, so he'll probably be looking for me. I hope he wasn't planning on going somewhere for dinner or drinks, because I think I've had enough of both."

"Yeah, me too." Robin tried not to show her disappointment, but she was having a hard time accepting Jess's relationship with John, especially after having such a good time talking with her for the past two hours. "Well, I suppose you shouldn't keep him waiting. After all, you are trying to change your ways about relationships, right?" Robin hoped her smile didn't look as fake as it felt.

Jess thought Robin sounded a little sarcastic, but couldn't think of a reason for her to feel that way so she dismissed the thought. "Did you park near your office? I can walk you back that way since it's on the way to where I'm parked," Jess offered as they left the restaurant.

"I think I'll just go back to my office for a little while. I probably shouldn't drive right now anyway. I can spend some time surfing the Internet and sobering up. Are you sure you're okay to drive?"

"Yeah, I don't think three beers over two hours is enough to put me over the limit. I've probably got an extra forty pounds over you, too, so it doesn't affect me as much," Jess said with a chuckle.

"Well, I don't see any fat on that frame of yours, but you are a lot taller," Robin said, looking up more than a half foot into Jess's eyes. She got lost there for a few moments, then realized that she was staring when Jess gently took her arm and said, "Watch your step over this curb." Jess smiled when she saw Robin blush and look quickly away. *Maybe she's more drunk than I thought. She looks a little glassy-eyed. Maybe I shouldn't leave her alone.* Jess felt a little sense of elation at the thought of staying longer with Robin, but then remembered her commitment to John. Her mind clouded with irritation at that thought, and she wondered, *What is going on with me lately? I've got all these feelings I can't explain.* She decided that she needed to spend some time alone in the near future to try and sort out what was happening in her life.

They arrived at Robin's building, and Jess asked, "Are you sure you'll be okay? I could drive you home if you'd like."

"No, no, I'll be fine," Robin reassured. "I spend lots of evenings working in my office, and I feel perfectly safe there."

"And you call me a workaholic," Jess retorted.

"Yeah, well it takes one to know one," Robin replied with a grin. She reached for the door and said, "Thanks for joining me tonight. I really had a great time. Maybe we can make it a regular Friday event."

"I'd like that," Jess said sincerely. "I'll see you around, okay?"

"Okay, drive carefully tonight."

"I will. You too."

"I will. See you."

"Bye."

The lingering good-bye left both of them with a profound sense of regret, but only one of them knew why. Robin slowly made her way up to her third floor office and sank into the chair in front of her computer. Her eyes were immediately drawn to the poster with Jess's picture prominently featured in the center. *Why am I so attracted to you? Do I want you so badly because I know I can't have you? Is this just some kind of big, competitive challenge for me?* Robin didn't believe that was true, but she had never felt so obsessed about anyone before, especially anyone that she had known for such a short time. *Why don't I just quit torturing myself by doing things with her? She's made it perfectly clear that she wants to be with John. The more I hang around with her, the worse I'm going to get hurt.* But Robin knew she couldn't give up that easily, no matter how bad the heartbreak might be in the future. She sighed deeply and reached for the computer mouse. *There must be something on the Internet that can take my mind off of this.* She then gave a chuckle and thought, *It's a good thing that I don't dare access any lesbian erotica sites from my work computer—although I'm not sure that would really take my mind off of it. More like feed my fantasy.*

Chapter
6

Robin and Jess found themselves spending more and more time together over the summer—getting together for morning coffee, meeting for a late lunch after Robin's workout, or going out after softball games. Late in July, Robin was invited to join some of her softball teammates for a weekend camping trip in the Cascade Mountains. They were going to make a short hike in to a high mountain lake, and use that as a base camp for day hikes in the wilderness. Robin thought that it might be the perfect way to get Jess to unwind for a weekend, and to get familiar with some of the fantastic outdoor recreational opportunities in Oregon. So when Capi dropped by her office one day, Robin asked if it would be okay to invite Jess along on the camping trip.

"Oooh, two nights together in a small tent," Capi teased. "Maybe that will be enough to finally crack that cold exterior."

"Come on, Capi. She's not cold, just a little reserved. And I've already decided that I'm not making the first move. She has to decide that this is what she wants before I'm going to push her into anything." Robin had grown to appreciate her friendship with Jess, and didn't want to jeopardize it. Of course, she also couldn't deny her feelings for the coach, and sometimes the frustration level became almost unbearable. At those times, she tried to avoid Jess for a few days in order to get her emotions in check. Maybe two nights in a small tent wasn't such a good idea after all...

"Well, I, for one, would love to have her come along on the camping trip. It would give me a chance to get to know her a little better and see if she's really worthy of you," Capi said with a smile. "I'm quite good at probing for information, you know."

"Your skills are legendary, Capi," Robin said, rolling her eyes. "If I ever want to know something about someone, I can count on you to find it out. I think there's something about Jess's past that she doesn't want to talk about, though. I asked her once about where she was before Idaho and she practically got up and walked out on me. I've never brought it up again."

"Oh, that's like giving a scent to a bloodhound," Capi said while rubbing her hands together. "You just leave it up to me."

"Capi, I *don't* want you asking her about that. I want her to have a good time this weekend, not feel like she's being interrogated," Robin said sternly.

"You're no fun," Capi pouted. "What if I don't ask her directly, but just lead her in the general direction and see what happens?" she asked hopefully.

"Caaapiiii," Robin said threateningly.

"Okay, okay, I'll behave," Capi said, disappointed. "Hey, have you thought about the fact that everybody else on the trip is gay, and that's likely to be pretty obvious to anyone who pays attention? Does she even know that you're gay?"

Robin blushed and said, "Well, I've never told her, but I would think she might have a clue just from being around our softball team."

"Oh boy, this sounds bad," Capi said. "I can't believe you've spent this much time with her and the subject has never come up. What do you guys talk about anyway?"

"Well, we've talked about past relationships in general terms, but I've never gotten specific about who those relationships were with," Robin said guiltily. "It's hard to just tell someone that you're gay," she protested. "What do you say, 'Oh, by the way, did I mention that I'm a lesbian?'"

"Well, it's only going to get harder the more time you spend with her. Now it will seem like you've been hiding it from her, or that there's some reason you don't want her to know."

"There *is* a reason I don't want her to know," Robin whined. "I'm afraid she'll run away as fast as she can."

"Well, if that's true, then I don't think you should worry about it. Why would you want to be friends with someone that can't accept you for who you are?"

Robin's shoulders sagged and she looked down at her hands in her lap. "Oh Capi, I know you're right, but I guess I'm just scared. I know it's not rational."

Capi walked over to Robin's chair and knelt down beside her. She put her hands over Robin's and said softly, "I know there's nothing rational about being in love, Robbie. And I know it's even worse when the love isn't returned." Robin knew there was dual meaning to Capi's words, and felt profoundly grateful that Capi could be there for her even though it had to be hurting her at the same time.

Robin looked up into Capi's eyes and saw only acceptance and understanding there. "You're the best friend I could ever ask for," Robin said, giving Capi's hands a squeeze. "Someday you're going to be rewarded for being such a great person, and you're going to find the love of your life and you'll be glad you waited."

"Yeah, well she'd better hurry up and arrive or it's gonna to be too late to enjoy it." Capi laughed. "I'd better get back to work. I'll e-mail you with the details of the trip. I think we're going to leave around three on Friday. Can you get off that early?"

"No problem. I'm really looking forward to it," Robin replied.

"Me too. I'll see you later." Capi smiled and made her way out of the office.

Robin went to her computer and clicked on her mail program.

Jess—

How are things over in the glamorous world of athletics? Have you landed any great recruits today?

Some friends and I are going on a camping trip this weekend, and I thought maybe I could talk you into coming along. We're going to a great wilderness lake with a fantastic view of the mountains. You can hike, fish, or just relax for a full two days. What do you say?

(yes, yes, yes)--that was a subliminal message, in case you couldn't tell.

Robbie

Jess was sitting in her office talking to one of her assistant coaches when her computer chimed with the "new mail" message. Keeping one ear on what her assistant was saying, Jess double-clicked on the new message. She couldn't keep a small grin off her face as she read Robbie's note, and her assistant said, "I can come back later if you have something you need to do."

"No, no, sorry. It's just so hard to ignore that 'you have new mail' message when it comes through. I should find a way to turn off the audio reminder. What were you saying about the pre-season weight workout?"

Jess managed to give her assistant her undivided attention for the next five minutes, and then went back to her mail program when the door closed again.

Robbie—
I've always been able to resist television advertising, so I think I'm immune to subliminal messages, but the camping trip does sound like fun. Unfortunately, I don't have any camping gear, other than a sleeping bag, so I don't think I'd be prepared for the wilderness. Besides, shouldn't I have some survival training, or something?
Jess

Jess clicked the "send" icon and smiled at the thought of spending the weekend with Robin. *I wonder how much it would cost to get outfitted with the right gear.* Just then Jess's phone rang.

"NOU Women's Basketball, this is Jess Peters."

"Hey."

"Hey yourself."

"I have all the other gear you need. As long as you have a pair of hiking boots, that is."

"My, you're persuasive," Jess teased. "Do they teach advertising techniques in the economics program?"

"It comes up," Robin replied. "I told you that I never got my way when I was a kid, so I've worked hard to rectify that as an adult."

"Well, I'd say you've become very successful." Jess smiled. "As a matter of fact, I do have a pair of hiking boots, and I don't have anything particular planned for this weekend, so I'd love to go camping."

"Really?" Robin blurted. "I mean, that's great. We're going to leave around three on Friday, and we'll be back around dinnertime on Sunday. I can drive and I'll bring the tent, stove, food, and fishing gear. And I have an extra backpack that you can use." Robin realized that she was babbling and tried to slow down. "Have you ever been backpacking before?"

"No, I've done some car camping, but I've never spent the night in the wilderness before. Is there anything I should know ahead of time?"

"No, you'll be fine. We're only going to hike in a couple of miles, so we can take lots of things that we wouldn't be able to take on a longer trip. In fact I think I'm going to take my inflatable raft so we can fish the lake better," Robin said enthusiastically.

Jess chuckled at Robin's excitement. "Do you think you could make a list of things I should take?"

"Sure. And if you don't have something, let me know because I may have extra," Robin replied. "Hey, this is going to be fun. I'm really looking forward to it."

"Yeah, me too. So you'll pick me up at my apartment Friday afternoon?"

"Sounds good. I'll call you if anything changes."

"Okay, see you later."

"Bye."

Robin hung up the phone and pumped her fist. *Yes! Two days of having her out from under the influence of John. I can't wait.*

And it was true—she couldn't wait. Robin found it difficult to accomplish a single significant thing before Friday afternoon finally arrived.

Chapter
7

"Hey, looks like you didn't have any problem fitting everything in your pack," Robin said as Jess loaded her gear into Robin's car. Robin had dropped off a spare backpack earlier in the week, along with a list of things Jess should bring.

"Well it helps that you have the stove, food, and tent. We'll have to redistribute the load on the way back so I can carry my fair share. Of course, the food will be gone by then, so I'll still be getting the better end of the deal."

"Yeah, but I'm *sooo* much younger than you, I should carry more weight," Robin teased.

"And just how much younger would that be?" Jess asked with a raised eyebrow.

Robin put her chin in her hand as if deep in thought. "Well, I can't say I know exactly how old you are, but from your resumé that I studied carefully during that first meeting with the Athletic Advisory Committee, I would say you have to be at least thirty-three."

"Close. And that would make me exactly how much older than you?"

"Just close, huh? Then I would have to say about four years."

"You're telling me you're not even thirty yet?" Jess said incredulously. "What were you, some kind of child genius?"

"Hardly. I just didn't waste any time getting through school—two years for my masters and three for my Ph.D. If it makes you feel any better, I turn thirty in September."

Jess made a mental note to remember that. She'd have to ask
Capi for the actual date. "Well, I hope this *much older* woman
doesn't hold you up on the trail today. Maybe the fact that you
have to take two strides to every one of mine will be an equal-
izer."

"Oh fine, joke about my height now. Just because you're
used to being around basketball players all the time doesn't
mean that I'm not a completely average height for women,"
Robin said with mock indignation.

"I would never dream of joking about something as serious
as being vertically challenged," Jess teased back.

Robin just slapped Jess playfully on the arm and said, "Get
in the car, you Amazon."

The ride to the trailhead went by quickly, both women
relaxed and enjoying each other's company. When they arrived,
they found the rest of their group ready to hit the trail. Meghan,
Jennifer, and Sara joined Capi to make up the foursome. Meghan
and Jennifer owned a small restaurant in town, and had been
together for six years. Sara worked in the admissions office at
NOU, and had been a friend of Capi's for years. Sara had
recently split with her partner of two years, and seemed to
always have problems getting a relationship to last.

"Hey, come on you slowpokes," Capi called out with a
smile. "Daylight's a-wasting."

"We're all ready to go," Robin replied while putting on her
backpack. "We've got to get to the lake before the sun goes
down. I don't want to miss the hatch."

Capi rolled her eyes at Robin's obsession with fishing and
took the lead down the trail. The six women proceeded single
file, and the sounds of nature mixed with heavy breathing
quickly replaced the sounds of civilization. Shortly after leaving
the trailhead, they passed a sign marking the edge of the Jefferson Wilderness, and the trail headed uphill through a magnificent stand of old growth Douglas fir. A stream was running off to
their right, and the steeper the climb got, the louder the stream
became as it rushed over rocks and waterfalls. The fresh smell of
running water was mixed with the earthy smell of the moist,
dense forest, and the women breathed deeply, cleansing their
lungs with the fresh air. After about a mile, the trail leveled out
and the forest got thinner, allowing for glimpses of the distinc-
tive peaks of Three Fingered Jack and Mt. Jefferson in the dis-

tance. The group stopped to catch their breath and take a drink of water.

"How are you doing?" Robin asked Jess. "No blisters or anything?"

"Nope, I'm doing great. I can't believe how beautiful it is up here."

Robin couldn't help but agree as she found herself staring at Jess's sweat-glistened face. She managed to tear her eyes away before Jess caught her, and asked, "Is that backpack adjusted okay? Let me see how it's fitting on your hips and shoulders." Robin walked over and placed her hands under Jess's hip belt to see if it was riding on her hips properly. She then pulled on the shoulder straps to see how much weight was resting on Jess's shoulders. "You know, you can connect this strap in front that pulls the two shoulder straps together if that makes it more comfortable," Robin said while grabbing each end of the strap and buckling it over the upper part of Jess's chest. Suddenly Robin realized where her hands were and abruptly dropped the strap and, blushing, looked down, afraid to meet Jess's gaze.

"Yeah, that is better," Jess replied. She had felt an inexplicable tenseness as Robin was adjusting her pack, but decided it must have been from feeling like a little kid getting dressed by her mother. She dismissed the thought and smiled her thanks at Robin, wondering why the younger woman was blushing again.

"Everybody ready?" Capi asked. They all nodded and set off single file once again. It was only another half hour before the trail rounded a corner and opened up to a spectacular view of a high mountain lake. The clear sky gave the water a magnificent deep blue color, and the still waters carried a perfect reflection of Mt. Jefferson that loomed over the horizon.

My God, it's just like the pictures at the travel agencies, Jess thought. While she'd lived in the Pacific Northwest for many years, she had never experienced the beauty of the mountains from this close before. *I can't believe this is within an hour of a highway. Why aren't there fifty other people here?* As if on cue, a pair of hikers appeared on the far side of the lake, but headed away from them, deeper into the wilderness.

"Which side of the lake do you want to camp on?" Capi asked. "You have your choice of views—sunset over Mt. Jefferson from this side, or sunrise over Three Fingered Jack from over there," she said pointing across the way.

"I vote for sunrise," Robin said. "That way I won't have to be squinting into the sun when I'm fishing the evening hatch."

Everyone groaned at Robin's single-mindedness, but happily made their way to the other side of the lake. A well-worn campsite, complete with fire pit and logs arranged for sitting, gave testament to the popularity of the easily accessible lake. The women quickly shed their packs and started setting up tents. Robin chose an area well away from the fire pit and asked Jess if she wanted to help her.

"Sure. What do you want me to do?"

"Well, why don't you start by finding the flattest spot you can, clear any rocks and sticks from it, and put down the ground cloth."

While Jess was doing that, Robin snapped the tent poles into place and then they both worked at getting the tent set up. Robin retrieved both of their sleeping pads and bags, and spread them out in the tent. *Boy, it's going to be cozy in here,* she thought as she looked around the small tent. There would barely be room for a few extra clothes in the tent with them, and their packs would have to stay out under the rain fly. *I can only hope I don't snore all night, or roll over on her,* Robin thought. *Then again, rolling over on her might not be so bad...*

The group reconvened by the fire pit and organized the preparation of the night's dinner.

"Hey Robin, why don't I cover dinner tonight, and you can do breakfast in the morning," Jess offered. "I don't want to keep you from those fish."

"You sure you don't mind?" Robin questioned. "Evenings are the best time for dry fly fishing. Maybe tomorrow we can both offer to do clean-up, and then we can fish the evening hatch and clean up after dark."

"Sure, that would be great. But you know, I've hardly ever used a fly rod before, and I'm much more likely to be catching those trees than any fish."

Robin laughed and said, "Then I'll inflate the raft tomorrow and we can use that in the evening to fish. That should give you plenty of room for flailing around."

"Well, the trees would be safe then, but I'd say you'd be in great danger in a small raft with me handling a fly rod."

"I'll remember to wear safety glasses," Robin replied dryly. "And I'll be sure to give you flies with barbless hooks, just in case you find any other body parts to snag."

Jess just smiled good-naturedly and went to see how she could help with food preparation. Robin made her way down to the water's edge with her fly rod and surveyed the area for the best place to stand. The lake was ringed with trees, which made it difficult to find a place with some room for a backcast. She looked down the shore and saw a fallen log extending about twenty-five feet into the lake. Carefully making her way out on the log, she felt her heartbeat pick up as she saw fish rising to flies all around her. She quickly tied an elk hair caddis to her leader and made a short cast to her right. The fly had barely hit the water before she saw the strike. Unfortunately, the fish missed and Robin found herself setting the hook on thin air. Robin nearly lost her balance on the slippery log and admonished herself to be more careful. On her next cast, she hooked a small brook trout, about ten inches long, and carefully disgorged the hook and set it back in the water. *This is almost too easy. But I know the hatch is only going to last for a few minutes, so I'd better take advantage of it.* Robin looked around at the serene lake, the virgin forest, and the rugged slopes of Three Fingered Jack bathed in the red light of sunset and thought, *It can't possibly get any better than this, can it? And I'm not even wishing I had someone here to share it with, because the one person I'd like to share it with is here.* Robin took a deep breath and smiled as she resumed casting.

Jess sat on one of the logs near the fire pit, chopping some onions and mushrooms that would go into the spaghetti sauce. One of the advantages of taking such a short backpacking trip was that they could actually eat fresh vegetables on the first night out. Capi mixed some salad dressing to go over a bag of fresh lettuce, while Jennifer and Meghan worked on setting up the two backpack stoves. Jess felt her eyes start to water from the onions, and looked away to give her eyes a break. As she looked out over the lake, she saw Robin silhouetted against the light reflecting off the water. The rhythmic motion of the fly rod sent the line snaking behind Robin in a perfect loop, only to shoot forward and settle perfectly onto the still lake. Jess found herself mesmerized. *That is so beautiful.*

Capi looked over at Jess and saw the look of open admiration on her face. She followed Jess's gaze over the water to see Robin's silhouette. *She's so beautiful,* Capi thought wistfully.

She looked again at Jess, who was still caught in the trance. *Well, Robin, it looks like you may have caught the biggest fish after all.*

"Hey Jess! Do you have those onions and mushrooms chopped?" Meghan called out, breaking Jess out of her reverie.

"Uh, almost. I'll have them done in a few seconds." Jess shook her head to clear her thoughts, and wondered once again about why she had been so spacey lately. It seemed like she was always daydreaming about Robin, and she couldn't figure out why she was so intrigued by the young woman. *Maybe I've been spending so much time around people in athletics the past few years that it's just refreshing to talk to someone different.* Satisfied with that explanation, Jess finished her chopping and added the ingredients to the pot. Soon the aroma of Italian spices filled the air and the campsite grew dark outside the circle of the fire. Jess looked toward the lake repeatedly, thinking that Robin couldn't still be fishing in the dark, and wondering if she should go check on her. Just then, Robin emerged from the darkness with a big grin on her face.

"That was some of the best fishing I've had in years. I must have caught twenty fish in a half hour. You should have been there, Jess. Tomorrow, huh?"

"I wouldn't miss it." Jess smiled at Robin's enthusiasm. "But now you'd better join us for some dinner before it gets cold. Meghan's been slaving over a hot stove for the last hour creating this masterpiece."

"Yeah, right," Meghan snickered. "More like I opened a couple of jars and turned the stove on high."

"Well, it smells great," Robin said as she dug into a huge helping of spaghetti.

"Uh-oh. Hurry everyone. If you want any dinner, you'd better get it quick before it's gone," Capi teased, watching Robin devour her meal.

"Oh, very funny, Capi," Robin said sarcastically. "Just because you wouldn't know what it's like to work up an appetite by catching twenty fish..."

Capi laughed and replied in an equally sarcastic tone, "Yeah, that right arm of yours must have really gotten a workout."

"You just watch what this right arm is going to do to you," Robin said menacingly while putting her plate down and advancing on Capi with a mock snarl on her face.

"Oh no. Robin, I'm eating," Capi pleaded while almost fall-ing backward off the log she was sitting on. She barely got her plate set down on the ground before Robin pounced on her and tickled her mercilessly. They both rolled over the log together and ended up laughing so hard they could barely catch their breath. They slowly untangled their limbs and helped each other up, laughing and brushing off the pine needles they'd accumu-lated on their clothes.

Jess watched the interaction between Robin and Capi and felt a twinge of jealousy. *They have so much fun together. It must be great to have such a close friend. The way Capi's looking at Robin makes me think she'd like to be more than close friends, though.* That thought caused Jess's eyes to pop wide open with the sudden realization that Robin might be gay. She thought back on all the time she'd spent around Robin, looking for anything that might have given her a clue to Robin's sexuality. Other than the fact that some of her softball teammates were quite open about being gay, Jess couldn't think of anything that would have indicated that Robin was. *Listen to me. I hate it when other peo-ple speculate about whether I'm gay, and here I am doing the same thing.*

"Hey Jess, are you going to finish that spaghetti?" Robin asked while looking hungrily at Jess's half-eaten dinner.

Jess was startled by the interruption to her thoughts and looked down at her plate. "Oh...well...I guess I'm not very hun-gry." She smiled up at Robin. "I take it the bottomless pit wants more?"

"Well, only if you weren't going to eat it. I'd hate to see it go to waste, you know."

Jess laughed and handed her plate over to Robin, who eagerly polished off the remaining spaghetti. Jess took the opportunity to look around at the others in the group of campers. She knew that Meghan and Jennifer were together, because they often engaged in public displays of affection, or PDA's as an old friend of hers used to call them. She didn't know Sara very well, and she had never really thought about Capi's sexuality, but she realized that there was no reason to think they weren't all gay. But then, there was no reason to think they weren't straight either. *Maybe I can try to bring it up somehow with Robin, hope-fully without offending her.* Jess started to think about the various conversations she could have that might reveal the information she sought. Her musings were interrupted again by Capi asking if she'd like to take a walk around the lake while the others cleaned up.

"Sure, that sounds great. Do you have a flashlight?"

"It's a full moon, so I don't think we'll need one," Capi replied. "The trail is really well-worn, so I'm pretty sure we'll be able to pick it out."

Capi and Jess got to their feet and headed down to the lake. As Capi predicted, the moonlight shining down and reflecting off the lake provided plenty of light to see the trail. They ambled off at a leisurely pace with Capi in front.

"So Jess, did you spend much time in the mountains when you lived in Idaho?"

"No, I spent most of my summers working basketball camps. We had our own camp at Idaho State for two weeks, and then I'd travel around and work other camps. And, of course, once the preseason conditioning started, I was pretty tied to campus."

"Sounds like a busy life. Did you grow up in the Pacific Northwest?"

"No, but close. I grew up in Montana."

"Really? I spent some time in Montana after grad school. Whereabouts in Montana did you live?"

Jess paused for a moment before answering quietly, "Oh it was just a little town near Missoula. I'm sure you've never heard of it."

Remembering her promise to Robin not to probe too much for information about Jess's past, Capi decided that she should change the subject. "So how do you like NOU and Comstock? Have you met very many people?"

"Mostly just people at work—I haven't had time for much of a social life yet."

"It can be kind of frustrating to be single in Comstock, and let me tell you I speak from experience."

Jess thought she might have found her opening to get the information she sought. "Have you been single the whole time you've been here? I'm not sure I even know how long you've been here," she added.

"I've been at NOU for seven years, but I'm relieved to say that I haven't been single that whole time," Capi said with a laugh. "I had a partner for three years after I first moved here, but she got a great job offer on the east coast, and I guess she decided that our relationship wasn't worth turning down the job offer. I suppose you could say that I didn't think our relationship was worth following her, either, so I guess we were both at fault."

Well, that answers my question about Capi, Jess thought. "So nobody else has come along since then?"

"Well, to tell you the truth, I've had a huge crush on Robin ever since she got here, but she's made it pretty clear that she just wants to be friends. And we have a really great friendship, so I don't want to give that up or jeopardize it by pushing for something more."

Well, that doesn't exactly tell me whether Robin is gay or not, but I'd say it's a distinct possibility, Jess thought. She felt a powerful sense of jealousy at Capi's admission of a crush on Robin, and wondered how she could feel so possessive of Robin's friendship.

"You two sure seem to get along great. Why do you think Robin's not interested? Is she interested in someone else?"

Whoa, I thought I was supposed to be the queen of interrogation, Capi thought. *I think I've met my match.* "I'm not really sure, Jess. I don't think she's seeing anyone else, but maybe she's got her heart set on someone who just hasn't realized what a catch she is." *Well that will either confuse her or hit her over the head with a two-by-four.*

"Yeah, I told her the other day that I couldn't believe she didn't have guys lining up at her door, asking her out," Jess replied.

Looks like we're gonna need a four-by-four, or maybe a railroad tie, Capi thought ruefully. "Oh, I'm sure Robin has plenty of offers. I think she's holding out for someone special, though."

The women walked in silence for a short while, each lost in their own thoughts, and then the light from the campfire became visible around the next bend in the trail. They walked back into the campsite to find their companions roasting marshmallows and sharing stories of previous backpacking trips.

"You should have seen the size of the grizzly bear we saw in Alaska," Sara said. "Luckily it was downwind of us, and it never even knew we were there."

"We had a black bear come into our camp down on the Rogue River, and we spent half the night throwing rocks at it to get it to leave our cooler alone," Meghan added. "I don't think I slept more than an hour the whole night."

"And did you read that story in the paper about the guy who got attacked by a grizzly on the trail, and all they found was his backpack and a few scattered bones?" Robin asked.

"Whoa. What are you guys trying to do—keep us from getting any sleep tonight?" Capi protested. "Can't you think of something more pleasant to talk about?"

"Oh, relax Capi," Robin replied. "You know there aren't any grizzlies in Oregon. And besides, I'm much sweeter than you, so they should come after me first," she teased.

"Well, you know what they say: you don't have to be faster than the bear, you just have to be faster than me, and there's no question that I'd be the last one in line," Capi said with a laugh.

"Well, on that happy note, I think I'm going to go hang the food bag and then turn in," Meghan said. "You coming, Jen?"

"Someone has to protect you from the bears," Jen said with a grin while putting her arm around Meghan's shoulders and heading off.

"Yeah, I think I'm about ready, too," Robin said. "I'll take the far side of the tent, Jess, so you won't have to crawl over me when you come to bed."

"Okay, I'll be there in a little while. I'm just going to watch the fire for a few more minutes." Jess found herself alone with her thoughts as everyone else made their way to their tents.

What do I really feel for Robin? I get jealous, and nervous when she touches me...Not exactly what I'd expect if I just thought of her as a friend. But I've never been attracted to a woman in my life. I'm sure I'm not gay. I can't *be gay. I know things are going to work out with John. I just have to give it a chance. And when that happens, these other feelings will just go away. I'm sure of it.*

With a renewed sense of purpose, Jess doused the fire and headed off to bed. Her resolve was sorely tested however, when she crawled into the tent and found herself within inches of a sleeping Robin. The younger woman was sleeping on her side, facing Jess, and had a peaceful, open look on her face that made her more attractive than ever. Jess sighed deeply and turned her back to Robin, hoping sleep would come quickly.

Chapter
8

"Robin! Robin, wake up," Jess was whispering harshly in Robin's ear. "There's something outside the tent."

"Huh...what? Something what?" Robin blinked her eyes open, trying to make sense of where she was and what Jess was saying.

"There's something *big* outside the tent. Don't you hear it?"

Robin was fully awake and sitting up now, straining to hear what Jess was talking about. Jess crept back away from the tent door, practically sitting in Robin's lap.

"Craaack!" A branch snapped somewhere very close to the tent, and they could hear the sound of dry leaves being stepped on.

"What do you think it is? Are there bears around here?" Jess asked worriedly.

"I think you listened to too much bear talk around the campfire," Robin replied, "but yes, there could be bears around here. Only black bears, though, so they'd be interested in our food, not us." Robin put her hand on Jess's back and rubbed in small circles reassuringly. She felt Jess relax slightly and breath a little slower. "I'm pretty sure it's not a bear, though, because it doesn't sound that big. I'm going to unzip the door and take a look around, okay?" Robin didn't want to belittle Jess's feelings, but she was pretty amused at how scared the self-confident woman seemed to be. She moved around from behind Jess and crawled over to the tent door. She quietly unzipped the door and moved her hands and head outside the tent. About ten feet away, a big mule deer was chomping on the leaves of a bush. Robin smiled to herself and made her way back inside the tent. "I think we're safe," she said with a sly grin. "At least I've never heard of Bambi attacking campers before." Jess visibly relaxed her shoulders and felt a blush creeping up her neck. She was thankful that it was dark in the tent. Robin crawled back over to her and put a reassuring hand on her thigh giving her an understanding smile. "Hey, you should have seen how scared I was on my first backpacking trip. I was convinced that every chipmunk outside the tent was either a grizzly or a mass murderer."

Jess gave a small laugh and said, "Thanks, but I feel pretty foolish."

"Hey, no reason for that. Come on, let's try to get back to sleep." Jess lay down with her back to Robin again, and Robin faced her and put a hand lightly on Jess's back in a reassuring gesture.

"Thanks," Jess said softly, and soon she could hear Robin's breathing indicate that she had fallen asleep again. Jess found sleep harder to come by, and she lay awake listening to the sounds around the tent and thinking about how nice Robin's hand felt on her back.

Daylight came way too early for Jess, and she groggily stumbled out of the tent to find the others drinking their morning coffee around the now cold fire ring. Robin gave Jess a little teasing smile, but didn't say anything about the previous night's excitement. Jess responded with a raised eyebrow that seemed to warn Robin to keep it just between the two of them.

"Ready for a cup of coffee, Jess?" Jennifer asked. "It's not exactly Starbucks, but it's hot and has caffeine."

"Sounds great," Jess said gratefully. "Don't we have breakfast duty, Robin?"

"Actually, Capi offered to make her famous poppy seed pancakes, so I guess we'll do clean-up instead."

"Mmmm, famous pancakes, huh? I won't argue with that," Jess replied. She took a long sip from her coffee and closed her eyes in appreciation. Capi was mixing her pancake batter, and the others were gathering up plates, silverware, and syrup.

"So what does everybody want to do today?" Sara asked.

"Jennifer and I were thinking we might just hang around the lake, maybe do a little swimming, and just generally relax," Meghan replied.

"Sara and I talked about taking a short hike to another lake that's about two miles further down the trail," Capi said. "There are supposed to be some great wildflower meadows along the way."

"Well, I was thinking it might be fun to try to get part way up Three Fingered Jack," Robin said while looking hopefully at Jess. "I've heard that it gets kind of dicey near the top, but I don't think you need any technical rock climbing skills for the lower slopes."

"That's gotta be a good eight miles, round trip, not to mention a 2,000 foot increase in elevation" Capi said. "I think that's more than I'm up for."

"Yeah, me too," Sara said. "I think I'll stick to the wildflower hike."

Robin looked over at Jess and raised her eyebrows questioningly. Jess found she couldn't resist that look, even though eight miles and 2,000 feet did not really sound like fun to her. "Well, I don't think you should go by yourself, so I guess I'm game," Jess said resignedly, but with a smile toward Robin. "Better make extra pancakes, Capi."

After breakfast and clean-up, Jess and Robin filled a daypack with lunch, water, and basic first-aid supplies and headed off toward Three Fingered Jack. The trail was an easy grade for the first three miles, and the two women covered the distance in a little under an hour. But then the trail steepened, and soon the women were trudging up a series of switchbacks. After another half-hour, the trees disappeared and the trail was barely visible through a field of loose rocks. The footing got continually worse, and the hikers found themselves sliding a half step back for every step they took forward. They finally came to a small plateau about halfway up the peak, and Robin suggested they take a break.

"How are you doing, Jess?"

"I'm okay. A little tired, and I'm sure I'm going to be sore tomorrow, but nothing I can't live with," Jess replied good-naturedly. "How about you?"

"So far, so good. I'd like to see if we could get up to that notch between the first two 'fingers.' Do you think you can make that?"

"Hey, where you go, I go," Jess joked. "I can't let you think I'm too old to keep up."

"Not too competitive now, are we?" Robin teased. "Come on, we can have lunch up there. I'll bet the view is fantastic."

"Oh, lunch. Now that ought to be incentive for you. You'll probably set a new land speed record," Jess said sarcastically as she trailed after Robin who had already set off.

The trail narrowed as it wound around the side of the mountain, in some places barely wide enough to put one foot in front of another, with a steep slope on both the uphill and downhill side of the trail. Jess kept taking deep breaths and tried not to look down, concentrating instead on Robin's strong calf muscles just in front of her feet. After another half-hour of nerve-wracking, thigh-burning climbing, the pair made it to the notch. Jess breathed a deep sigh of relief and collapsed on the nearest rock. After catching her breath, she sat up and looked around.

"Oh my God. Look at that view." Jess stood up and slowly turned three hundred and sixty degrees, seeing Mt. Jefferson, Mt. Hood, Mt. St. Helens, and Mt. Adams to the north, and Mt. Washington, the Three Sisters, and Mt. Thielson to the south. In between were endless acres of forest interspersed with a cookie-cutter pattern of clearcuts and the occasional high mountain lake.

Robin smiled as she watched Jess's expression of awe. "Hey, we'd better get a picture so they believe we actually made it up here." Robin dug the camera out of the pack and adjusted it on a rock so that she could use the timer on the shutter. She focused Jess in the viewfinder, pressed the shutter, and quickly ran over next to her. She leaned in close and put her arm around Jess's waist while they both grinned for the camera. She felt Jess's arm go around her shoulders just as she heard the shutter click. She looked up into Jess's blue eyes and gave her a big smile and a congratulatory hug. "You did great, Jess. You'll be bagging the rest of these peaks in no time."

"Is that the lingo—bagging peaks?" Jess asked with a smile. She didn't take her arm from Robin's shoulders as she looked down the slope. "I think I'll be happy just to make it back down this one."

Robin leaned her head against Jess's shoulder and the two

women stood there admiring the view and enjoying the undeniable pleasure of their contact. Robin's stomach chose that moment to growl loudly, and both women laughed.

"Well, I guess that means it's lunch time," Jess said. She reluctantly broke away from Robin and grabbed the lunch out of the pack. They sat next to each other and shared crackers, cheese, and dried fruit. Robin did her best not to take more than her share, but Jess insisted that she didn't want any more, and Robin quickly devoured what was left.

Jess looked at Robin out of the corner of her eye with a wry smile and asked, "How much would it be worth if I offered you a bag of M&M's right now?"

"You're kidding," Robin said disbelievingly, while making a grab for Jess's pockets.

Jess smiled and leaned back, batting Robin's hands away. "How much?" she repeated.

I don't suppose a kiss is what she has in mind, Robin thought ruefully, but then seized on another idea. "How about a complete leg and back massage when we get back to camp tonight?" Robin offered.

"Ooooh, that is tempting," Jess said while experimentally flexing her tired leg muscles. "Throw in a flycasting lesson and you've got a deal."

"Yesss!" Robin yelled while lunging again for Jess's pockets. Jess just laughed and held her arms out while Robin rummaged through the five different pockets in her shorts, finding the chocolate treasure in the side cargo pocket. She happily tore open the package and even offered to share with Jess, who politely refused. Jess didn't want to renege on the deal, which she was now looking forward to.

The two women gathered up their things for the return trip. Jess was a little worried about the top part of the trail, which was very narrow with poor footing. *All we can do is go slow, I guess. Hopefully Robin knows what she's doing.*

Robin led the way down the treacherous trail, picking her way slowly and looking for solid footing for each step. She could hear Jess right behind her, and panicked slightly every time she heard one of Jess's feet slip on the rocks, but each time, Jess managed to stop herself before sliding into Robin. They were nearly back to the plateau when the rocks under Robin's right foot went sliding out from under her. Robin grabbed at thin air while her body slowly fell outward over the steep cliff. A scream escaped her lips as she looked desperately at Jess who reached for her while trying to maintain her own balance. Jess couldn't reach her in time, and she screamed, "Robiiiin!" while watching her friend tumble down over the rocks.

Robin went head over heels for about fifty feet before coming to an abrupt halt on the plateau. She lay there, crumpled and unmoving, while Jess stood in shock up above.

Chapter
9

Move, damn it! Move! Jess was vaguely aware of a voice in the back of her head telling her to do something, but her consciousness wasn't registering it. With a glazed look in her eyes, she moved down the trail, blindly putting one foot in front of the other. She was oblivious to the treacherous footing, which turned out to be advantageous since she wasn't trying to brake on the slippery rocks. Within minutes she had reached the plateau and her head was clearing. When asked later, Jess would have no memory of how she made it down the trail to the plateau.

She quickly looked around for the best path back to the place where Robin had fallen and set off at a dead run. When Robin's body came into sight, there was still no movement. *Oh God, please be okay!* Jess knelt down next to Robin and saw a pool of blood spreading out from the back of her head. She could see no other obvious injuries, such as compound fractures, and put her face next to Robin's to see if she was breathing. Just then, Robin groaned, and Jess felt a wave of relief rush over her.

Jess had enough first-aid training from her coaching career to know that Robin shouldn't be moved until she was sure there wasn't a spinal cord injury. However, she also knew she had to stem the bleeding from whatever cut Robin had on her head. Robin groaned again and rolled slightly to her side. Jess noted with relief that Robin's hands and feet had both moved.

Jess decided that her priority had to be the head wound. She pulled her bandana out of her back pocket, folded it into her palm, and very carefully slid her hand behind Robin's head. Unfortunately, the first-aid kit was in the pack on the prone woman's back, and Jess was not yet prepared to turn her over. *Oh jeez, what am I gonna do? We're a good three miles from our camp, and another two miles from the cars. I can't leave her here to go for help, but the chances of someone else coming by are slim to none. Oh God, Robin, please wake up!* Jess settled herself behind Robin, holding her head in her hand, trying to think of anything else she could do. Just then, Robin groaned again and her eyes slowly blinked open.

"Robin! Can you hear me? Try not to move," Jess said worriedly while scooting around so that Robin could see her better.

"Ughhhhh... Jess? What happened?" Robin whispered while squinting her eyes at the light. "My head hurts. Everything hurts."

"You fell a long ways, and you have a cut on your head. But I don't want to move you until I'm sure that you haven't hurt your back. Can you feel your hands and feet?"

Robin closed her eyes and wiggled her toes and fingers. She felt an excruciating pain in her right ankle and gasped loudly.

"What? What's wrong?" Jess asked, leaning closer to Robin and trying to figure out what was causing her pain. She wanted so badly to be able to help the injured woman, to ease her pain, and she had never felt so frustrated in her life. She put her palm on Robin's cheek and gently stroked her thumb over lips that were pursed in pain. "Tell me what hurts, Robbie," she pleaded.

"My ankle," Robin gasped. "It feels like it's broken."

Jess looked down at Robin's foot, which was still securely held in her hiking boot, and didn't see any obvious sign of dislocation. She decided that the compression offered by the boot would be the best thing for Robin's ankle until they could get some ice on it. She returned her attention to the head wound, which seemed to be most in need of immediate attention. "Robin, do you think you could sit up? I need to get the first-aid kit so I can take care of the cut on your head."

Robin nodded weakly and struggled to sit up. Jess got her arm around Robin's shoulders and helped her to a sitting position, keeping the pressure on the back of Robin's head with her other hand. Robin swayed a little, and her head hung down, but she remained conscious. Jess wedged her body behind Robin's for support and dug the first-aid kit out of the pack. The pack was torn in a number of places, and Jess realized that it had probably provided some padding for Robin during her fall. With her free hand, Jess opened the first aid kit and found some gauze pads. She then grabbed a water bottle and drenched one of the pads. Taking the bandana from the back of Robin's head, Jess started gently wiping the blood away from the hair, trying to determine the extent of the wound. She found about a one-inch gash, and it appeared that the flow of blood had already slowed. She took another gauze pad, soaked it in cold water and pressed it against the wound.

"How are you doing?" Jess asked when she realized that Robin hadn't made a sound for the last two minutes. She leaned her head around to look in Robin's eyes and found them glazed over. *God, she must have a concussion on top of everything else. This only gets better and better.*

"Robin! Talk to me. How does your head feel?"

Robin groaned again and blinked her eyes, seeming to bring things into focus again. "My head hurts," she repeated.

"I know, but you're gonna be okay. I found the cut on your head, and the bleeding is slowing down. You've just got to stay awake and try to keep talking to me, okay?"

"Okay," she mumbled in reply. "How did I fall? I don't remember falling."

"You slipped on a rock and lost your balance. I tried to catch you, but I couldn't." Jess looked crestfallen. "I'm so sorry, Robin," she whispered. "But we're going to get through this. You just stay with me, okay?"

Jess's soothing voice was having a calming effect on Robin, and she was starting to think more coherently. Unfortunately, that meant that she was also becoming aware of all the places on her body that hurt, and the tally was getting longer and longer. Most of them were just bumps and bruises, overshadowed by the pain in her head and ankle.

"Do you have a bandana? I need something to tie around your head to keep this bandage in place."

"I think it's in my back pocket," Robin replied.

Jess wiggled her hand into Robin's back pocket and found the bandana. "Do you think you can hold the bandage in place while I tie this on? Here, just put your hand right here," Jess said while guiding Robin's hand to the bandage. She finished tying off the bandana, which freed her to look more closely for other injuries. She moved around to face Robin and looked closely at her face. She wasn't bleeding from her nose or ears, but her pupils were definitely dilated and she had a slightly blank stare on her face. Jess grabbed the water bottle and helped Robin to take a drink. Once again, Robin's eyes seemed to focus, and she grimaced in pain. Jess carefully looked at Robin's arms and legs, and didn't see anything other than a few scrapes. She couldn't see whether Robin's ankle was swelling inside her boot.

"We're going to have to figure out how to get you out of here. Do you think you can stand up?"

"I can try, but I'm pretty sure I can't walk on my ankle."

Jess looked around for something to use as a splint, but there was nothing but rocks for about another quarter mile down the slope. She was reluctant to leave Robin alone to go get something, and decided that she could try to carry her that far. *She's so small—how much can she weigh?*

"Robin, I'm going to pick you up and carry you down to the tree line so we can find something to use for a splint and a crutch. Put your arms around my neck and hang on, okay?" Robin did as she was told, and Jess very carefully lifted her up, trying not to jostle her ankle. Nevertheless, Robin grimaced in pain at the movement and clutched even harder at Jess's neck. Tears streamed down her cheeks, and Jess felt heartbroken that she couldn't do more to help her companion. She moved down the trail as quickly as she could, but the steep, rocky terrain made the going slow. By the time they hit the first trees, Jess's arms and legs screamed with fatigue, and she unceremoniously dropped to the ground with Robin in her lap.

"How are you doing?" Jess asked between gasps for air. She looked into Robin's eyes and thought they looked better and more alert than before, despite the tears that were coming from them.

"I'm okay. I can't believe you could carry me all that way. I'm not exactly a lightweight."

"It was all downhill, and it wasn't that far," Jess replied modestly. "I'm sure you would have done the same for me."

Robin looked skeptical at that, but decided not to respond. She was just grateful that Jess was holding everything together, and it looked like they might actually find a way to get back to their campsite.

Jess carefully moved Robin off her lap and got up to find

some sticks that could be used as a splint and a crutch. Within a few minutes she was tying a splint to the injured ankle with a cord that she had stripped from the top of the pack. Even though she was as gentle as possible, Robin gasped in pain a number of times during the ordeal.

"Let me take another look at your head before we start back," Jess said. She carefully removed the bandage and saw that the wound was barely seeping. She got a fresh gauze pad out of the first-aid kit and replaced the bandage. Satisfied that she had done all she could with the supplies they had, Jess was anxious to get started back to the campsite. She had found a tall, sturdy stick that could be used as a crutch, and helped Robin to her feet. It took the groggy woman a moment to gain her equilibrium, but she gave Jess a determined look and said, "I'm ready—let's go."

The trail had much better footing in the trees, but still had a fairly steep grade. Jess went in front of Robin, and stayed close enough to catch her if she should stumble. They had only gone about a hundred feet when Robin said she needed to stop. It was obvious that her ankle was killing her, but her eyes seemed much better. Jess found a log and helped Robin down onto it, holding her steady with an arm around her shoulders.

"Hey, you're doing great, Robbie," Jess said encouragingly. "We've got plenty of time, so there's no need to rush." Secretly, Jess was a little worried about how long it would take them to get back at this pace, but there was obviously no alternative. "Do you want to try some ibuprofen for your ankle?"

"Yeah, anything that might help, I'm willing to try," Robin replied. Jess retrieved the water bottle and gave her three tablets. After a few minutes, Robin said she was ready to go again, and they started off down the trail. This time they got to the bottom of the switchbacks before Robin needed to stop again. After that, the trail leveled out and they slowly made their way toward the lake, Jess watching Robin carefully for any signs that she might be getting worse. The trip was going excruciatingly slowly, and Jess was worried about whether Robin was going to last. Just when Robin was dragging to a halt for another break, Jess heard some voices up ahead.

"Robin. Did you hear that?" she asked excitedly. "I think someone's coming."

Around the bend in the trail appeared Capi and Sara, laughing and talking until they saw Robin and Jess. Capi's expression changed to one of shock as she sprinted over to Robin.

"Robbie! Are you okay? What happened?" Capi asked with

concern while grabbing Robin's arm and helping her to sit down.

"It's okay, Capi. It's not as bad as it looks. Just a cut on the head and a sprained ankle," Robin replied, while trying to catch her breath. Capi glanced over to Jess for confirmation of Robin's account and saw a raised eyebrow and a look of skepticism.

"We were just coming out to give you guys some company for the walk back to the lake. I'm so glad we found you," Capi said while looking over Robin's injuries and rubbing her back reassuringly. "How far have you had to hobble on that crutch?"

"She fell about halfway up Three Fingered Jack, so we've probably gone about a mile so far. I was beginning to wonder if we'd have enough energy left to make it the rest of the way, so I'm *really* happy to see you guys, "Jess said gratefully. Capi was busy tending to Robin and wasn't listening, and Jess found herself feeling a little left out.

"Capi, between the two of us we can make a 'chair' and carry Robin the rest of the way. The sooner we get back to the lake, the sooner we can do something about that ankle," Sara said with concern. She and Capi helped Robin to her feet once again, and Robin put one arm around each of their shoulders. They then each supported Robin under her thighs and made off for the lake. Jess trailed behind, watching Robin's two friends take over. Now that she was no longer solely responsible for taking care of the injured woman, she felt the stress of the day come crashing over her. *She could have been killed. What if she'd never regained consciousness? What would I have done? And why didn't I catch her before she fell? All I had to do was reach out and catch her...*Jess could feel the tears stinging the back of her eyes and blinked furiously, willing herself not to cry. She slowed down to distance herself from the other three, not wanting them to see her emotions. *What do I have to be crying about? I'm not the one who got hurt. What the hell's the matter with me?*

It took the group another hour and a half to go the remaining two miles, having to stop frequently to rest and reposition Robin. Jess offered to take a turn carrying Robin, but Capi wouldn't let her, saying she had already done her part and should take it easy. When they finally made it back to the camp, Jess quietly stood to the side while the other four women hovered over Robin, discussing what their next step should be.

"I think we need to get her to a hospital and make sure her head's all right, and get her ankle x-rayed," Capi stated firmly.

"What do you think is the best way to get her back to the

car?" Jennifer asked.

"We could make a stretcher," Sara offered. "There are plenty of long sticks around here, and we could use one of the ground cloths."

"Good idea," Capi replied. "Sara, why don't you and Jennifer work on that while the rest of us pack up camp? Jess, can you pack up Robin's things? We can tie her pack onto the stretcher and take turns carrying it."

Jess just nodded and turned away from the group, walking over to where she and Robin had pitched their tent. Jess felt like she was running on autopilot as she quickly dismantled the tent and stuffed everything into their packs, not bothering to fold or organize anything. She returned to the others to find Robin sitting alone, leaning against a tree, while the others were busy breaking camp.

"Hey, c'mere," Robin called out when she saw Jess lugging both of their packs. Jess set the packs down and walked over, dropping to the ground beside Robin. "Are you okay?" Robin asked with concern when she noticed that Jess was looking a little depressed.

Jess looked down with a chagrined look on her face. "Yeah, I'm fine. I just wish I could have done something to keep you from falling."

"Jess, I don't remember falling, but I'm sure you did everything you could. And I'd really have been in trouble if you hadn't done such a good job of taking care of me afterward. I'm just sorry that you had to be put in that situation."

Before Jess could reply, Capi interrupted to tell them that they were ready to go. "Jess, where's Robin's pack? We need to tie it onto the stretcher."

Jess took the pack over to Sara, who strapped it onto the head of the stretcher. Capi and Sara then helped Robin onto the stretcher, and the rest of the women donned their packs. Capi and Sara took the first shift, carrying Robin for about a half mile. Once again, Jess was left out, the other women pairing up to take their turn.

The sun was just going down when they arrived at the parking lot. Capi insisted on driving Robin's car and taking her to the nearest hospital in Salem. All the other women wanted to make sure Robin was all right, and they followed along in their own cars. Jess rode with Sara, but couldn't find the energy to engage

in conversation. Sara seemed to sense that Jess wanted to be left
alone, and they made the hour and a half drive in silence.

Chapter
10

Capi was allowed to accompany Robin into the emergency room, while the others sat in the waiting area. After about half an hour, she came out to inform them that Robin had a slight concussion and strained ligaments in her ankle, and had needed ten stitches in her head. Amazingly, she had no broken bones.

"She's just about done in there, and the doctor said it was okay for her to go home tonight. He wants someone to wake her up about every two hours, so I'll stay with her. Why don't the rest of you head back and get some rest? It's been a really long day."

You *think it's been a long day,* Jess thought sarcastically. She was getting a little annoyed at the way Capi had just taken over responsibility for Robin's welfare. But then she remembered that Capi was Robin's best friend, and was probably who Robin wanted looking after her. With a profound sense of regret, Jess followed the others out the door to the parking lot.

Jess tossed and turned all night, worrying about Robin, and wishing she had been the one to stay with her instead of Capi. Around five a.m., she finally gave up trying to sleep and got up and put on her running shoes. She headed north from her apartment, and before she knew it she was within a block of Robin's apartment. She couldn't help herself; she detoured into the parking lot and ran past Robin's apartment. Her Outback was parked in its space, and the shades were drawn in the front window. Jess slowly jogged past, her stomach tightening at the thought of Capi and Robin in bed together. *I'm just worried about her—it's a perfectly natural reaction to yesterday,* Jess tried to convince herself. Still, she felt unusually depressed as she ran back to her apartment.

Robin awoke for the fourth time that night, Capi shaking her gently and calling her name.

"Hmmm....yeah, I'm awake," Robin said groggily.

"Let me see your eyes," Capi said gently, putting her hand on the side of Robin's face and turning it towards her. Robin blinked sleepily and squinted into the light, her pupils contracting properly. "Hey, you seem much better," Capi said with a half grin at Robin. "Do you have a headache?"

"My head hurts, but I think it's mostly from the swelling around the cut. Do we have any ibuprofen handy?"

"Yeah, I've got it right here on the nightstand," Capi said, retrieving three ibuprofen tablets and a glass of water.

Robin downed the tablets and sank back into her pillow. She sighed deeply and closed her eyes. "Capi, do you think Jess is okay? It had to be awful for her yesterday, and I didn't get to talk to her at all after we left the lake."

Capi reclined on her elbow next to Robin. She hadn't even thought about Robin's feelings for Jess during the hectic events of yesterday. *I guess I just kind of took over, didn't I? And I didn't even tell Jess how grateful I was that she rescued Robin. I wonder if anyone did? We were all so concerned about Robin that we just kind of forgot about the heroic effort that Jess made. I definitely owe her an apology.*

"Well, she seemed okay when she left the hospital last night, but I actually don't remember her saying much of anything after we found you guys on the trail," Capi said. "Now that I think about it, she was probably suffering from a little bit of shock herself. It must have been really scary for her to be all alone when she found you. She really did a great job of first-aid, though, didn't she?"

"I'm sure she saved my life," Robin said solemnly. "I wish I could have told her that last night."

"You'll get another chance," Capi said gently. "Why don't you try to get some more sleep now? I'll wake you up again in a couple of hours, and by then it will be time for breakfast."

"Breakfast?" Robin perked up. "I didn't even get dinner last night."

Capi laughed and put her hand on Robin's belly. "Well, you're nothing if not predictable. Try not to keep us awake with your growling stomach." She rubbed her hand in small, soothing circles on Robin's stomach, and soon she could hear Robin's breathing slow down into the steady rhythm of sleep.

Jess heard the phone ringing from the deck of her apartment. *It's probably John. I just don't feel like talking to him right now.* She had been moping around in a funk all morning and didn't seem to want to do much of anything. She thought about calling Robin at least ten times, but didn't want to disturb her in case she didn't feel well. *I'm sure Capi is taking good care of her,* Jess thought sarcastically.

After five rings, Jess relented and got up to answer the phone.

"Hello?"

"Hey, how are you doing?"

"Robin? I should be asking you that question Are you okay?" Jess asked, relief flooding her voice.

"Yeah, I'm fine, thanks to you. I didn't even get a chance to say thanks for saving my life yesterday," Robin said with a smile in her voice.

"Oh, I certainly didn't do anything as dramatic as that," Jess protested. "I just did basic first-aid—what anyone else would have done in that situation."

"Yeah, well it wasn't anyone else, it was you, and if you hadn't been there and kept your wits about you, I would have been in serious trouble. Anyway, I just felt bad that I didn't get a chance to tell you that last night."

"I was sorry I didn't get to talk to you last night, too," Jess replied softly. "I was really worried about how you were doing, but Capi seemed to have everything under control."

"She was a little overprotective, wasn't she?" Robin replied with a small laugh. "I know she was just worried about me and was trying to do what she thought was best."

"I know that, too. And I'm sure it was comforting for you to have your best friend there with you."

Robin thought that she could sense some resentment in Jess's voice, and wondered if Jess might be jealous of Capi. *Now that would be interesting, wouldn't it?*

"You know, I'm really feeling a lot better today. I'm supposed to take it easy, but I could cook us some dinner tonight if you'd like to come over," Robin said hopefully.

Jess thought about that for a moment and decided she really wanted to see Robin and make sure she was doing all right. "I'll tell you what, I'll come over for dinner if I can do the cooking and you promise to relax."

"Ohhh, that sounds like an offer I can't refuse! How about six o'clock?"

"Sounds great. Is there anything you don't eat?"

"Are you kidding? I like everything."

"Of course, what was I thinking?" Jess laughed. "Okay, I'll see you at six."

Both women hung up the phone with a smile on their face, looking forward to the evening.

Jess arrived promptly at six, arms laden with groceries. Cooking was not her forte, but she was pretty sure that she could make a decent stir-fry, and fresh vegetables from the local farmer's market would enhance her chances of success.

She and Robin sat at the counter that separated Robin's kitchen from her dining room and chopped vegetables while Robin recounted her experiences at the hospital. "The doctor said I was very lucky to have such minor injuries after falling fifty feet." Robin paused in her chopping and looked up at Jess, catching her attention with a smile. "And, he said you did an excellent job of splinting my ankle and treating the cut on my head." She reached out and covered one of Jess's hands with hers and said seriously, "I'm really glad that you were there with me, Jess. I would have been in real trouble without you."

Jess felt her throat constrict with emotion and said, "Hey, c'mere," reaching over and drawing Robin's head into her shoulder. "I'm just sorry that I didn't catch you before you fell." Her voice cracked as she said, "I was so scared, Robin. You weren't moving, and there was all that blood around your head..."

"Shhhhh..." Robin stroked Jess's back soothingly and said, "Jess, you did everything you could. You did everything right. If you were scared, you sure didn't show it to me. You made me feel like everything was going to be all right, and it was."

Jess held on to Robin until she felt her emotions come back under control. She cleared her throat and pulled away, saying, "Well, let's just not do it again anytime soon, okay?"

Robin accepted Jess's attempt at humor as a way to ease the tension, and gave her a big smile in return. "It's a deal. The next time I invite you on a camping trip, I promise the most excitement will be when you catch a twenty inch rainbow on a dry fly."

Jess laughed and got up to begin her stir-fry. The next hour was spent in easy conversation while enjoying Jess's cooking. Afterward, they moved into Robin's living room and turned on the TV, although neither of them was very interested in watching it.

"Are you sure you shouldn't be getting to bed early? What did the doctor say you should be doing for your head?" Jess asked.

"He basically said that if I got through twenty-four hours without any problems, I could resume my normal activities...within reason of course. I'm probably not supposed to play tackle football for a while, but with my ankle, I don't think I'm going to be playing much of anything for a long time," Robin said sadly.

"That's going to be hard for you, isn't it?" Jess said with a sympathetic smile. "How do you feel about swimming?"

"Ughhh. You mean other than to reach the shore from a sinking boat? I hate putting on a swimsuit, and I hate jumping into cold water, but other than that, swimming's fine," Robin joked.

"Well, it's probably going to be the best thing you can do to keep in shape for a while. And look at the bright side, you won't have any run-ins with Glenn in the pool."

"Yeah, well there are probably lots of other lecherous old men that go to the pool just to leer at women in swimming suits," Robin retorted.

Jess just laughed in response. "Speaking of your sprained ankle, aren't you supposed to be icing it and keeping it elevated?"

"Yeah, I was pretty good about icing it during the day, but I should probably do it again before I go to bed."

"You lie down there on the couch, put your foot up, and I'll go get you some ice," Jess offered. Before Robin could protest, Jess was off to the kitchen for a bag of ice. She returned to the couch, putting Robin's foot in her lap and placing the bag of ice on the injured ankle. Just then the phone rang, and Robin reached over to the end table to answer it.

"Hello?"

"Hey, babe, how's it going? You sound pretty good."

"Hey, Capi. Everything's fine. Jess is here and she just coerced me into icing my ankle again," Robin said while smiling at Jess.

"Well, Jess is a very smart woman and you should do whatever she says," Capi said with mock seriousness.

"Oh great. All I need is for you two to gang up on me, like I can't take care of myself," Robin retorted.

"Well, I think you pretty much proved that yesterday," Capi teased. "Do you want me to come and stay with you again tonight? I don't mind, if you're worried about your concussion."

"Thanks, Capi, but I think I'm going to be fine tonight. I haven't had any dizziness, and my headache has really gotten better."

"Ah, but I'll bet the real reason you're going to be fine tonight has something to do with six feet of dark and beautiful, right?"

Robin could feel the blood rush to her face, and it made her head pound. She looked away from Jess, hoping that she wouldn't notice her discomfort, and replied, "Yeah, it was nice talking to you, too, Capi. I'll see you tomorrow. Bye."

Before Capi got a chance to reply, she reached around and hung up the phone, hoping that she didn't look as flustered as she felt.

"Is Capi worried about you?" Jess asked, while rearranging the ice bag on Robin's ankle. It was too cold to rest her hands on the ice bag, and Jess had found herself wondering where to put them while Robin was talking on the phone. She had hesitantly placed one on Robin's shin and the other on her foot, and now she was unconsciously lightly rubbing Robin's leg and toes.

"Mmmm, that feels good, thanks," Robin said while closing her eyes. "Yeah, she was offering to stay here again tonight, but

I think I'll be fine."

Jess was startled by Robin's response and almost jerked her hands away, but recovered quickly and put more thought into her impromptu massage. She carefully avoided the swollen ankle, but gently worked the tight calf muscle while adding some warmth to the cold toes.

"I distinctly remember that I promised *you* a massage, not the other way around," Robin said, smiling contentedly with her eyes still closed.

"Yeah, well that was before your whole world turned upside down, and now I'm sure that you need it more than me. Why don't you just sit back and relax for a while?" Jess offered.

"Hmmm, twist my arm," Robin replied, snuggling down into the couch. She let her mind wander while Jess's movements took her attention away from the cold ice on her ankle. Within minutes, she was softly snoring.

Oh great. What am I gonna do now? Jess thought to herself. She carefully removed the ice bag from Robin's ankle and checked to make sure that it wasn't leaking before placing it on the floor. *I hate to disturb her because I know she needs her rest. She'll probably wake up pretty soon,* Jess thought as she leaned her head on the back of the couch and shut her eyes.

Jess awoke with a sharp pain in her neck. She slowly lifted her head from the back of the couch, neck and shoulder muscles complaining about the awkward position they'd been left in for hours. *Damn that hurts. I can't believe I fell asleep like that.* She looked over to see Robin sleeping soundly. Jess's stomach contracted with a feeling of intense longing, and alone with her thoughts, she allowed herself to consider what it would be like to physically be with a woman. *Do I want to kiss her? And what would come after kissing?* Jess started to feel distinctly uncomfortable at the thought. *No, that's not what I want. When I think about physical attraction, I think about men, not women.* But she could not deny the intense emotional attraction she had for Robin. She thought about her all the time and loved being with her. *Maybe I've just never had such a close friend before and that's why this seems so different to me.*

Jess felt a sense of great relief that she had ruled out a physical attraction to Robin. That train of thought, however, had reminded her of her relationship with John. She found herself with an intense curiosity about whether she had a physical attraction to him. *I enjoy kissing him, although it's not like fire-works go off or anything. And we've certainly had a couple of times where things have heated up to the point where I know he wanted more. Maybe I just need to let it happen—to see what I've been missing all these years. And maybe it would put to rest these doubts I'm having about an attraction to Robin.* Convinced by this line of reasoning, Jess decided that she would invite John over for dinner in the very near future, and would encourage things to go farther than they had in the past. *If it doesn't happen, so be it. But I'm pretty sure that John will be more than happy to accommodate me.*

Right now, however, Jess had to decide what to do about her present sleeping arrangements. She decided not to disturb Robin, but she thought she should stay for the remainder of the night just to make sure that Robin was all right. She carefully lifted Robin's feet and slid out from under them. Grabbing the blanket on the back of the couch, she gently spread it over Robin's sleeping form. She took one last look at Robin's peaceful face, turned out the light, and made her way to Robin's bedroom. She shucked her jeans and socks and crawled between the covers, sleep claiming her quickly.

Robin was slowly returning to wakefulness, thinking about strong hands on her legs and feet. As she awoke that thought was quickly replaced by a throbbing in her ankle and a distinct sense of emptiness as she realized she was alone on the couch. The early morning light streamed in through the front window, and she squinted at her watch to see that it was six a.m. *I can't believe that I slept on the couch all night. And when did Jess leave? I never even heard her. Some hostess I am—I fall asleep in the middle of our conversation and don't even thank her for dinner.*

Robin groggily got to her feet, grabbed her crutches, and made her way into the bedroom to access the attached bathroom. She abruptly stopped in the doorway when she saw Jess's long frame stretched out on her bed. She had shed the covers during the night, and long, bare legs were sprawled across the mattress. Robin's eyes made their way up the legs, somewhat disappointed to see that the rest of Jess remained clothed. Her lips were parted slightly, and she appeared to still be deep in sleep. *God she's beautiful. Even if she were gay, there's no way I'd have a chance with someone like her,* Robin thought dejectedly. She knew that was really her mother talking in her head again, but she had never even dreamed of falling in love with someone like Jess. *Wait a minute...falling in love? Come on, Robin, let's not go overboard here. Yeah, you're attracted to her, but you can't set yourself up for a major heartbreak. Get a grip.* She gave a quiet sigh and turned away from the bed.

Robin quietly went over to the bathroom and shut the door behind her. After brushing her teeth and taking a quick shower, she returned to her bedroom. The running water must have awakened Jess, because she was sitting on the edge of the bed, fully clothed once again.

Robin gave her a big smile and said, "Hey, sorry I fell asleep on you last night. Believe me, it was no reflection on your company—I just must have been more tired than I thought."

Jess laughed lightly. "No problem. I hope you don't mind my crashing in your bedroom. I didn't feel comfortable leaving you alone last night, so soon after the accident."

"That was thoughtful of you, Jess, but I'm sure I would have been fine. However, now that you're here, the least I can do is make you some breakfast. How about a cheese omelet?"

"Sounds great, but you don't have to go to any trouble. I can always just stop at Starbucks on my way home."

"It's no trouble at all, and it will only take me a minute. Do you have to go to work today?"

"Yeah, but I don't have to be there too early. I have a meeting with my assistant coaches at eleven, but nothing before that."

"Great. I'll go get breakfast started. You're welcome to take a shower, and I'd offer you some clean clothes, but I don't think they'd fit," Robin said with a wry grin.

"That's okay, I'll just wait until I get home." Jess followed Robin out to the kitchen and helped her get the coffee started. Jess retrieved the ingredients for the omelet, and then the two of them sat at the counter grating cheese and beating the eggs. *What a nice thing to wake up to. I'm usually so cranky in the morning, but today I really feel good. It's so pleasant here,* Jess thought peacefully as she looked around at the soothing earth tones of Robin's kitchen, and the contagious cheerfulness of the woman herself.

Robin interrupted her thoughts with an offer of coffee. "Do you need cream or sugar?"

"No, black is fine. I think it gets into the bloodstream faster that way," she quipped.

Robin laughed and replied, "Well, I always thought that a little cream might help protect my stomach lining, but I'm sure I'm kidding myself."

Robin returned to the stove, and in no time she put two plates with steaming omelets on the counter and moved around to join Jess. They ate in a relaxed silence, each thinking about how nice it was to spend the morning with the other. When they were finished, Robin insisted that she could clean up on her own, and that Jess could head back home. Jess drove herself across town, thinking about how different it felt to start the day in a good mood.

Chapter
11

Jess looked up at the knock on her office door and saw John's head poking around the edge.

"Hey, baby, I missed you this weekend. How was your camping trip?" John walked over to Jess's desk and gave her a quick hug and a kiss on the cheek, before sitting on the edge of the desk.

Jess leaned back in her chair and gave him a big smile in return. "Well, it was actually quite eventful. Robin and I were on a hike when she fell off a fifty foot cliff, and I ended up having to practice my first-aid skills."

"You're kidding. Is she all right?"

"Surprisingly, she only had a gash on her head, a slight concussion, and strained ligaments in her ankle. The hard part was getting her back to the campsite."

"Wow, it sounds like more excitement than you wanted, huh? It's amazing she wasn't hurt worse than that. Fifty feet is a long way to fall."

Jess felt queasy thinking about that, and the great mood that had been with her all day threatened to flee. She took a deep breath and decided to change the subject. "So what did you do all weekend?"

"Other than mope around because you weren't there?" John asked with a pouting look. "A couple of other coaches and I went to a Mariner's game up in Seattle, and decided to stay and taste the nightlife in the big city."

"Oh yeah, it sounds like you were really moping around missing me," Jess said sarcastically. "And how was the night-life?"

"It was great. We must have hit three or four different clubs before closing time. Luckily they were all within walking distance of our hotel, because we certainly weren't in any shape to be driving."

Men are so proud of their drunken exploits. I wonder if they think it's charming. Before her mood changed, Jess remembered her resolve to make things work with John, and turned another smile on him. "Hey what are you doing for dinner tomorrow? I was thinking maybe you could come over, and I'd cook something for a change. And if you want, you could bring a video to watch after dinner."

John seemed startled by the offer, but quickly accepted. "That sounds great. Anything in particular you want to see?"

"No, you can surprise me. But how about if you get something romantic instead of those blood and guts movies you like?" Jess suggested with a seductive smile.

Whoa, what's gotten into her? I should encourage her to go away for the weekend more often, John thought, his mind running away with the possibilities for tomorrow night. "Okay, I'll pick out something good. What time should I come by?"

"How about six?"

"Great. See you then—I can't wait." John leaned over and gave Jess another quick kiss, then got up and left the office with a distinct spring in his step.

Jess just sat in her chair and shook her head. *Men are so predictable.* Her smile faded though as she thought about what tomorrow night might bring. *Is this really what I want? Or am I just trying to convince myself that I'm not attracted to Robin? I guess it doesn't matter. I've waited too long to find out if what's been missing in my past relationships has been a physical connection. If nothing else, at least I'll get this milestone in my life over with.* Jess felt a little regret at having that attitude toward losing her virginity, but she had gone enough years waiting for that magical someone that would make her glad she had saved it. She no longer believed it happened like that—Mr. Right, falling in love at first sight and knowing that "this is the one." Now she believed that you had to work to fall in love in with someone, and part of that meant being willing to give of yourself physically. At least it was worth a try—nothing else had worked in her past.

Robin went into her office on Tuesday after having spent Monday continuing her recuperation. Her headaches had mostly disappeared, and she was getting along pretty well on her crutches. She needed to get over to the library to pick up some journal articles that were related to one of her research projects. *I'll be glad when the whole world is on-line and I won't have any need to ever go to the library again*, she thought as she made her way across campus on her crutches. She decided to detour past the Java Connection and grab a cup of coffee on her way. As she walked in the door, she was surprised to see Jess and John sitting at one of the tables drinking coffee. Jess looked up and saw her and gave a big smile and a wave.

"Hey Robin, come on over and join us."

As happy as Robin was to see Jess, she felt almost nauseous at the sight of Jess and John together. Nevertheless, she mustered up a smile and said, "Sure, I'll be right over," and headed off to the counter to place her order. She was just trying to figure out how she was going to carry her coffee and use her crutches at the same time, when Jess appeared at her elbow.

"Here, let me get that," she said smiling, taking the coffee from Robin.

Robin looked up into the warm blue eyes and felt her heart melt all over again. *Oh, jeez, I've got it bad.* She quickly looked down before the blush could start, and said, "Thanks," while following Jess over to the table.

"Hey, Robin, I heard you took quite a tumble," John remarked. "You don't look bad for someone who fell fifty feet."

"Thanks, John...I think," Robin replied with a smirk. "I was just lucky Jess was with me and she knew a thing or two about first aid," Robin said with a shy smile toward Jess.

Jess smiled back, but didn't reply. She felt a little uncomfortable having both Robin and John at the table with her, and found herself comparing her feelings towards the two of them. She was more than a little surprised when she realized she was hoping John would leave so that she could talk to Robin alone. *Maybe I just want him to leave so that he won't say something to make a fool of himself in front of her,* she thought wryly.

"Well, I should be getting back," John said. "I have to meet some athletes in the weight room in about ten minutes. You coming, Jess?"

"You go ahead, John. I still have half a cup of coffee."

"Okay, I'll see you tonight then?" John said with a wink and a big grin on his face.

Jess felt herself blushing and quickly said, "Yeah, around six. See you then."

John walked out of the coffee shop, and Robin noticed Jess's blush. "So, you've got a big date tonight?" she asked, trying to keep the disappointment out of her voice.

Jess looked up shyly and replied, "Yeah. Remember when we were talking that night at Miguel's, and I said that I didn't think I tried hard enough in the past to make relationships work?" Robin nodded but didn't say anything, not liking where this conversation was heading. "Well, I decided that I need to try harder with John. I think I need to find out if what I've been missing is the physical part of a relationship, and that's why I've never been successful in the past. So I invited him over for dinner tonight, and if events end up heading toward the bedroom, I'm not going to stop it this time."

Robin felt like someone just punched her in the stomach. She swallowed hard, and clenched her jaw, trying not to let her reaction show. Somehow, she managed to mumble out an appropriate reply before getting up out of her chair and saying that she really had to get to the library.

Jess was startled by Robin's abrupt reaction, and asked if she needed any help carrying things.

"No, thanks, I've got my backpack," Robin replied while gathering up her crutches. As she turned to leave, she said, "Have a good time tonight. I hope everything works out the way you want." And then she was out the door, heading for the nearest restroom she could find. She barely made it there before the tears started falling from her eyes, and she locked herself into a stall, sobbing uncontrollably.

Robin made it through the rest of her day in a state of severe depression. When Capi called her at the end of the day and asked if she wanted to join her for dinner, she quickly accepted, knowing she didn't want to be alone with her thoughts.

Robin met Capi at Mazzi's, a local Italian restaurant. Capi could immediately see that something was wrong, but waited until they were seated with a glass of wine before gently asking Robin what had happened.

"Who says anything happened?" Robin said defensively.

"Oh come on, Robin, you've got heartbreak written all over your face. Now spill it. What happened between you and Jess?"

"Oh, Capi, nothing happened between us. It's what's happening between her and John that's the problem."

"Uh-oh, this sounds bad. Do you mean to tell me she's actually getting serious about him? As much as I teased you before, I didn't really think she was that interested in him."

"That's the really awful part. I don't think she *is* that interested in him. She's got this crazy idea in her head that the reason her relationships with men don't work is because she won't go to bed with them."

"You're kidding. Isn't that supposed to be the guy's line?"

"Capi, it's not funny," Robin protested. "She feels like she's been holding back, and now she wants to see if having sex with the guy will make a difference. Why couldn't she have experimented with her last boyfriend, before I even knew her," Robin lamented.

"Hey, come on, Robbie," Capi said gently. "Maybe she'll come to her senses before it's too late."

"I don't think so. She's invited him over for some romantic dinner tonight, hoping that he'll ask to spend the night."

"Oh God, what a way to ruin my appetite," Capi said with disgust. They both sat there in silence for a few minutes, not wanting to think about what Jess and John would be doing tonight, but unable to think about anything else.

"You know, I'm not really hungry either. Would it be okay if we just finished our drinks and went home?" Robin asked hopefully.

"Sure, Robbie. Do you want me to come over and keep you company for a while?"

"No thanks, I think I'm just going to try to go to bed early. The sooner I fall asleep, the less time I have to think about it."

The two women finished their drinks and walked back out to the parking lot. Capi took Robin in her arms and felt Robin give her a ferocious hug in return. She could tell that Robin was crying, and she just held her tight, oblivious to the other patrons walking to and from their cars. After a few minutes, Robin broke away and wiped at her tears with the back of her hand. Capi gave her a reassuring smile and said, "You'll make it through this. If you and Jess were meant to be, this will all work out, you'll see. Have faith, Robbie."

"Thanks Capi, and thanks for putting up with me. I'm sorry you always have to listen to my troubles."

"Hey, I love you, Robbie, and I'll always be here for you."

Robin smiled up at Capi through her tears and said, "I love you, too, Capi. You're the best friend I could ever ask for."

They both knew that "I love you" meant different things for each of them, but they were also both comfortable with that. Capi helped Robin into her car and gave her a wave good-bye. With a deep sigh, she headed for her own car and her empty house. *I want Robin, Robin wants Jess, and Jess wants John...or at least thinks she wants John. Why does love have to be so complicated?*

The unconsciousness of sleep that Robin hoped would claim her never came that night. She tossed and turned in her bed, trying not to think about Jess and John, but failing miserably. Finally, at the first light of dawn, Robin gave up and crawled out of bed. *I know I shouldn't do this, but I have to know. I can't go another minute without finding out for sure.* She threw on some sweats, grabbed her crutches and her car keys, and headed out to her carport. No one else was on the road as she made her way toward Jess's apartment. She slowly drove past, hoping beyond hope that she wouldn't see John's truck parked next to Jess's car.

Chapter
12

The huge Dodge Ram parked next to Jess's Camry could not be missed. Robin sucked in a breath and momentarily closed her eyes in pain. As she let the breath out, she felt empty. Not sick, not like crying...just empty. She wanted to be angry, to feel betrayed, but she knew that wasn't rational. *Jess has no emotional commitment to me. There's no reason for her to think that sleeping with John would affect me at all. Oh God, why didn't I tell her how I feel? Maybe she wouldn't have run away. Maybe she would have felt the same way. Maybe this wouldn't be happening, and my heart wouldn't be breaking. It's my own damn fault for being so insecure and afraid of rejection.*

Robin made a U-turn and headed back to her apartment, but changed her mind on the way and drove to the trailhead at McHenry's Peak, just outside of town. There was a short, well-maintained trail to the top of the peak that afforded a 360-degree view of the valley and surrounding mountains. She noticed the "handicapped accessible" sign on the trail, looked down at her crutches, and thought, *I guess now I can appreciate these trails.* Twenty minutes later, out of breath and with a throbbing ankle, she was cresting the top of the small peak and watching the sunrise over the Cascade Mountains. The punishment of the walk up the hill, combined with the exhilaration of reaching the top and seeing the sunrise, seemed to cleanse Robin's senses. It was like she had exorcised her demons and was now ready to take the next step. She knew that she wasn't going to be able to see Jess for a while, and they would probably never be able to regain the close friendship they'd developed. *But I'm going to accept Jess's choice and not let it ruin my life.* Unfortunately, the feelings she had for Jess were not just going to go away because she wanted them to. *But if I can just avoid her for a while, keep my distance, maybe time will heal things.* She could hope.

Jess awoke feeling distinctly uncomfortable. Something was crowding her, pinning her right arm to the bed. She slowly opened her eyes to see John's semi-clad body sprawled across the bed, his right arm on top of hers. Momentarily shocked at the sight, she quickly recovered, remembering the previous night's events. *Poor John, I really didn't mean to lead him on like that and then tell him "no."* Jess had every intention of making love with him last night, but when they got to her bedroom, what had previously been only a thought in her head became a reality, and she knew immediately that it wasn't right. They had talked and kissed, but when John started to unbutton Jess's shirt, she stopped him. She said she thought she was ready, but she wasn't, and hoped he'd understand. To his credit, he immediately backed off and told her that he would wait until she was ready—he didn't want to pressure her into doing anything she didn't want to do. Jess was profoundly relieved, and asked him to just stay with her for the night, which he did.

Now in the light of day, Jess looked at John and realized what a big mistake she'd almost made. She didn't love him, and making love with him wasn't going to change that. Maybe she would come to love him in time, but they needed to get to know each other better. If she'd had sex with him, she would have regretted it, and the relationship would have gone no further. *Thank God I came to my senses in time. What was I thinking, anyway?* Reflecting back, Jess realized that part of her motivation was to prove that she was physically attracted to men, not women. *Oh come on, be honest, you wanted to convince yourself you didn't want Robin...Well, I'm pretty sure that if it had been Robin in my bed last night, the result would have been the same.* She still couldn't get her mind around the thought of having sex with a woman. *And besides that, I just...can't...be...gay. All the pain and suffering that poor girl, her family, and I had to go* *through ten years ago...*No, the irony would be too cruel if it turned out that Jess really was gay.

Jess extricated herself from beneath John's arm and slid out of bed without waking him. After a quick trip to the bathroom, she made her way to the kitchen to make some coffee. As she was pouring herself a cup, John appeared in the doorway.

"Hey, how'd you sleep? I've got some coffee here if you'd like some."

"Mmmm, sounds good," John replied sleepily. "Why are you up so early? It's barely light out."

"A little cranky in the morning, are we?" Jess teased. "It's not that early—it's nearly seven. And I've got to get to work early this morning because I'm meeting with the strength coach to plan our preseason workouts." Jess opened the refrigerator door and poked around for some breakfast. "I've got some bagels and cream cheese if you're interested."

"Sure, sounds good," John said while making his way over to the kitchen table with his coffee.

"You want poppy seed or cinnamon raisin?"

"Cinnamon. And lots of cream cheese. Toasted," John said as he picked up the newspaper on the table and began reading.

A "please" would be nice, Jess thought. Suddenly she had a flash forward to what life would be like with John, and it wasn't a particularly pleasant thought. She couldn't help but compare this scenario to the enjoyable morning she had spent at Robin's two days ago. It had been so comfortable, and so easy to engage in conversation with the cheerful woman.

Jess finished preparing two bagels and gave one to John, who barely looked up from his paper to take it.

"I'm going to take a quick shower and get ready to go. Take your time—you can stay as long as you want."

John mumbled an okay, and Jess headed off to her room, munching on her bagel and anxious to get out of the apartment.

Robin managed to avoid Jess for the rest of the week, letting voice-mail answer her phone and not returning e-mail messages. She knew she couldn't avoid her forever—they were sure to see each other eventually at a softball game, since all the women's teams played on the same night. This week, her game didn't

overlap with Jess's, and she declined Capi's offer to go to Tony's
afterward. The weekend arrived, and Robin was feeling progressively more depressed. *I thought it was supposed to get better
with time. There's not an hour that goes by that I don't think
about her.*

Robin decided that she had to get out of town, and called
Capi to see if she wanted to go to the beach.

"Do you just want to go for the day, or are we talking overnight trip here?" Capi asked.

"Let's take overnight stuff so we can play it by ear. If the
weather's nice, we could make a fire and camp on the beach."

"Sounds great. When do you want to pick me up?"

"Can you be ready in a half hour? We can stop and get coffee on the way out of town."

"Oh, so now you're bribing me with coffee...Well, that usually works. I'll see you in a half hour."

Robin drove up to Capi's house, gave a quick honk on the
horn, and saw Capi wave through the front window. Two minutes
later, Capi was loading her things into the Outback and they
were off to Starbucks.

"Did you find somebody to take care of your cats?" Robin
inquired.

"No, I figured they could just stay inside. It won't kill them
if they don't get to go hunting for one night. Besides, I won't
have to come back to half-eaten carcasses this way, just a full lit-
ter box."

"Ah, life is full of trade-offs, isn't it?" Robin quipped.

They arrived at Starbucks and found the line ten people
deep, as usual on a weekend morning.

"Why didn't I buy stock in Starbucks when they were first
getting started?" Robin lamented.

"Probably the same reason we didn't buy Microsoft, or
Pfizer," Capi replied. "Who knew that so many men were impo-
tent?"

Robin laughed and found herself feeling better than she had
all week. They retrieved their lattes and Robin put her arm
around Capi's waist as they headed back to the car. "You know, I
love how you can make me laugh. I think that's the best quality a
friend can have—the ability to make you laugh."

Capi smiled back at Robin and returned the hug with her
free arm. "Glad to be of service, friend."

Jess was feeling restless as the weekend arrived. Things had gone better than she'd hoped with John. He seemed content for things to slow down for a while, and he had some traveling to do at the end of the week that would keep him away until Monday. Work had been fine—her team would be back on campus soon, and she should be excited and looking forward to the preseason. But something had been missing all week, and she knew that something was Robin. *Why wouldn't she answer my e-mails or return my phone calls? It just doesn't make sense.*

Jess thought back to the last time she'd talked to Robin. *We had a good time when I stayed there last Sunday, and everything seemed fine when I left in the morning. Maybe something happened to her. But I talked to one of her teammates at Tony's on Thursday night, and she said Robin was fine. I don't get it.*

Frustrated, Jess grabbed some money from her wallet and left her apartment. *It's such a nice day, I think I'll just walk to Starbucks.* She headed off for downtown and made the easy walk in about fifteen minutes. When she was a block away, she saw Robin and Capi leaving the coffee shop, arms around each other and laughing. Jess froze as the sight of the two women made her stomach clench painfully. *Could that be why Robin's avoiding me? Did she and Capi finally get together, and she doesn't know how to tell me?*

Jealousy rose up in Jess like it never had before in her life. *Capi's not right for her. If she didn't want to be with her for the last three years, why would she change her mind now? She's just settling for something that's easy and available.* Her alter ego could not remain quiet at that thought. *Kind of like you, huh? So desperate to be with a guy, to prove that you're not gay, you just settled for what was easy and available.* Jess felt disgusted with herself, but it didn't stop her from being angry with Robin. The alter ego spoke again. *Angry? How can you be angry with her? She has every right to be with Capi if she wants to. Do you wish she were with you instead?* Even in her thoughts, Jess refused to answer that question.

Well, she could have at least told me she was gay. I thought we were friends. That's not exactly something you would hide from your friend, is it?

No longer interested in coffee, Jess turned around and

headed back to her apartment. She retrieved her car keys and headed to her office, determined to punish herself by working all weekend.

"What an incredible sunset. Makes me glad I live on the west coast instead of the east," Robin said, watching the wispy clouds on the horizon turn a brilliant shade of red as the sun sank below the Pacific Ocean. As usual along the Oregon coast in summer, it was twenty degrees colder than it had been in the valley, and the loss of sunshine added to the chill. Robin shivered and put her arms around herself, trying to keep her body heat in.

"Let's get that fire started before we freeze to death," Capi said when she saw Robin's discomfort. They found a spot among the dunes that was protected from the wind and gathered up driftwood. Within minutes, they had a roaring fire going, and they huddled together under a blanket they had brought along.

"So Robin, the subject of Jess has been noticeably absent from your conversation lately. Have you talked to her since her big date with John?"

"Oh jeez, did you have to bring that up? I was having such a good time," Robin said sarcastically. "No, I've been studiously avoiding her because I don't have any idea what to say to her. 'So Jess, was he a good lay?' I think I'd throw up if she said yes. Heck, I'd probably throw up if she said no, because either way I'd have to think about the two of them doing it," Robin said with distaste dripping from her words.

"Yeah, that's a visual I'd just as soon avoid myself," Capi replied. "But if you don't talk to her, how are you going to know what she decided about her relationship with John? Maybe she hated it, and she's come to her senses."

"It doesn't matter," Robin said dejectedly. "I've already decided that I need to move on. Anybody that's that hung up on being with a guy—any guy, apparently—isn't going to be thinking about women any time soon. The longer I keep kidding myself, the worse it will hurt in the end."

Capi put her arm around Robin and softly rubbed her back. "Things will get better. Just give it time."

"That's what I thought, but it only seems to be getting worse. How do I stop wanting someone who has consumed my thoughts for the last two months? I felt like we had something between us. But it seemed like the closer we got, the more obsessed she got about making her relationship work with John."

Capi seized on that thought. "Well maybe that's it. Maybe she couldn't handle getting that close to a woman, and she freaked out."

"Like that's supposed to make me feel better?" Robin did her best Jess impersonation: "Gee Robin, the thought of being with you gives me the creeps, so I'm gonna hop in the sack with the first guy I can find." Robin shook her head. "I don't think I've ever had that effect on a woman before."

"Oh come on, Robbie, you know what I mean. Maybe she just needs a little more time to think about it—to get used to the idea," Capi said persuasively.

"Well, I can't sit around waiting for something that might never happen. I just have to figure out how to get over her."

"Well, I can tell you that you don't just get over it because you want to. I don't know what it takes...maybe somebody else to come along...but don't be surprised if you feel this way for a while."

Robin looked sympathetically at Capi. "Some pair we are, huh? A couple of hard-luck love stories." She leaned her head on Capi's shoulder and the two women stared into the fire, thinking about what could have been.

Chapter
13

The rest of the summer slipped by without Jess and Robin talking to each other. They would see each other occasionally, at softball games and on campus, but since neither one was interested in starting a conversation, a quick hello or a nod was as much as they shared. It probably didn't help that Robin was usually with Capi when Jess saw her. Similarly, Jess was usually with John when Robin ran into her. Jess and John had mutually agreed that they made much better friends than lovers, and actually were enjoying spending more time together. Of course, Robin didn't know this, and the sight of the two of them together always sent Robin into another bout of depression.

I wonder why Jess stopped calling and e-mailing me after that first week? It sure didn't take her long to get over me, did it? But then I guess she's got someone else to occupy her thoughts now, Robin thought sarcastically. *Listen to me. I'm the one who wouldn't talk to her, and now I'm mad because she's not calling? Get a grip, Robin,* she admonished herself.

Robin found herself wondering if she should just acknowledge that Jess wanted John instead of her, and try to reestablish their friendship in spite of that. *I couldn't be any more miserable than I am now, could I? But would I really be able to accept her and John together? I guess I wouldn't have a choice,* Robin thought while trying to imagine how she could initiate a conversation with Jess.

How would I explain my refusal to talk to her before? I can't just tell her that I was jealous of John. Robin was frustrated as she tried to think of some way out of her current depression.

Jess was equally frustrated with her inability to figure out what went wrong between her and Robin. *I know why I got mad at her, but why is she avoiding me? Does she really think I can't handle knowing that she and Capi are together? Maybe she's just embarrassed because she never told me she was gay.*

Jess sighed deeply. *I guess I could get some answers to these questions if I'd just swallow my pride and call her.* But Jess couldn't quite figure out how to start such a conversation, and procrastination prevailed.

The end of September brought the beginning of another school year. Robin was busy preparing for classes and trying to finish up a research project before the hectic term began. She was sitting at her computer, staring blankly at the women's basketball team poster above her monitor, when Capi appeared in her doorway.

"Still thinking about her, huh?"

"Wha...Capi, you scared the shit out of me."

"Uh-uh-uh," Capi said while shaking her index finger at Robin. "None of that kind of language now that the students are back on campus. You don't want the head of Student Affairs after you now, do you?"

"I thought I already had the head of Student Affairs after me," Robin quipped. "Not that I'm complaining, of course," she quickly added.

"Yeah, well a lot of good it's done me. I wonder if I'd have more luck if I got promoted to Provost. That way I'd be the one to decide on your tenure," Capi said mischievously.

"And give up all those days you get to spend with the juvenile delinquents on campus?" Robin teased.

"Well, believe it or not, I do have more responsibilities than dealing with bad fraternities, students that cheat, and athletes that get arrested," Capi replied. "Those are just the fun aspects of my job," she joked.

Robin laughed and said, "So what brings you down here? Some economics student gone bad?"

"No, I just wanted to talk to you about the Fall reception for the Faculty Women's Group this Friday. You're on the steering committee, right?"

Robin looked chagrined. One of the other members of the committee had decided that this would be a great opportunity to introduce the women faculty to the new women's basketball coaches. The reception was going to be at the Alumni Center, and Robin was desperately trying to think of a way to get out of going. "I might be on the committee, but nobody asked me if I thought this reception was a good idea," she grumbled. "I think I might be sick that day. I feel a fever coming on," Robin said as she dramatically put the back of her hand to her forehead.

"Come on, Robin, you can't avoid her forever. Maybe this will be a good opportunity for you to break the ice," Capi said while looking sympathetically at Robin. "I hate to see you so unhappy."

"What if she doesn't want to talk to me? It's not like she's been breaking my door down."

"Well what do you expect? You gave her the deep freeze for a whole week. How persistent do you expect someone to be?"

"I know," Robin said resignedly. "And I have been trying to think of a way to approach her, but I don't know if I'm ready yet."

"It may never seem like the right time, Robin, but the sooner you try, the sooner you'll know whether there's any chance that you can become friends again."

"Okay, I'll go to the reception, but I can't promise I'll get up the nerve to talk to her."

"Great. If it'll help, I'll go with you, and I promise to disappear at the first subtle hint you give me."

"Thanks, Capi, but I doubt there'll be any need for that."

"I'll swing by and pick you up at four on Friday, okay?"

"Okay. Thanks for stopping by."

"No problem." Capi gave Robin a big smile and said, "Chin up!" on her way out the door.

The Alumni Center was on the south end of campus, perched on a small rise that afforded a great view of the surrounding hills. Capi and Robin walked over at four p.m. on Friday, arriving well before the four-thirty start time for the reception. At Robin's suggestion, the event was being catered by

Meghan and Jennifer's restaurant. Robin and Capi arrived in time to see the finishing touches being placed on an exquisite spread of appetizers.

"Hey, Meghan," Robin called to her friend. "You've out-done yourself. This looks great."

Meghan smiled broadly in return. "Thanks, but you know Jennifer's the culinary expert—I just try to make everything look pretty on the table."

"Well, I'd say you're exceptionally qualified for your job, then," Capi replied, admiring the layout.

The two made their way over to a group of women standing out of the way of the last minute preparations.

"Hi, Robin," one of the women called out to her. "We were just talking about how to introduce the coaches. We were think-ing that we'd wait until about five, so everyone would have a chance to get here and get some food first."

"Sure, that sounds good," Robin replied.

"Since you're on the Athletic Advisory Committee, we thought maybe you'd like to introduce them. Aren't you friends with the head coach?"

Robin paled noticeably. "I think it would be more appropri-ate for someone else to do the introductions," she said quickly. "Maybe someone who represents the administration?"

All heads in the group turned to look at Capi.

"Whoa, wait a minute," Capi said while putting her hands up in front of her. "I'm not even on your committee."

"That doesn't matter. You'd be perfect, Capi," one of the women said.

Capi turned to look at Robin and saw an Academy Award-winning imitation of puppy dog eyes. "Oh, all right," she sighed. "Do you at least have some resumés I can work from?"

One of the women quickly handed her some papers, and Capi went off to prepare.

The basketball coaches arrived promptly at four-thirty. Jess was accompanied by two of her three assistant coaches. Pam Campbell was her first assistant, and had followed Jess to NOU from Idaho State. She was in her late twenties and had been a standout guard for Washington before playing professionally in Japan for two years. Her second assistant, LaTeisha Bolton, played for USC and then served as a graduate assistant coach for Long Beach State for three years. She was Jess's primary recruiter, especially of African-American players in talent-laden southern California. The third assistant coach, Jeff Walters, worked mostly with the post players, and he asked to miss this event so that he could catch up on some paperwork. Jess knew that the real reason had more to do with him being in a room full of nothing but women faculty members, and graciously let him off the hook.

The Steering Committee members were stationed near the doorway, greeting everyone as they arrived and directing them to the food and drinks. Jess was startled to see Robin in the receiving line. She knew that it would be possible that Robin would be a member of the Faculty Women's Group, but given Robin's avoidance of her, she didn't expect to see her at this event. Jess recovered quickly, however, and returned her focus to the first woman in the line.

"Hi, I'm Jess Peters, and these are my assistant coaches, Pam Campbell and LaTeisha Bolton," Jess said while extending her hand and giving the woman a dazzling smile.

"Oh, we're so glad that you could make it, Coach Peters," the woman gushed. "These are the members of the Steering Committee—I'll let them introduce themselves," she said as she turned to fawn over the two assistant coaches.

Jess made her way down the line with characteristic grace and charm, making eye contact with each woman, and asking her what her role was in the University. Robin waited nervously at the end of the line, wishing she were anywhere else, yet desperately wanting to be right there waiting for Jess. As Jess finally got to the end, blue eyes turned toward Robin, who was looking up hesitantly. Jess's eyes seemed to be asking a question as she extended her hand and simply said, "Robin."

"Jess," Robin replied while taking the hand and reflecting an equally questioning look back at Jess.

The moment became awkward as they stood with their hands clasped, neither one knowing what to say. Capi, standing nearby for just this reason, quickly stepped forward and said, "Hey, Jess, it's good to see you again," while reaching out her hand toward Jess.

Their eyes broke away from each other as Jess turned to talk to Capi. Robin felt a dull ache at the loss of contact with Jess, but quickly realized that she needed to pull herself together to meet the other coaches. She turned back to find a *very* attractive woman smiling at her with what appeared to be a mischievous look in her eye. *Oh my, what have we here?* Robin thought while smiling back cautiously.

"Hi there, I'm Pam Campbell, and you look way too young to be a faculty member." Pam's dark eyes sparkled as she reached out to take Robin's hand.

"I'm Robin Grant, and believe me, I won't look this young by the end of the year. I still have that summer vacation glow." She smiled back at Pam, her gaydar pinging loudly.

"Let me guess...I'll bet you're an exercise physiology professor," Pam said while looking appreciatively at Robin's toned body.

"Not even close." Robin smiled. "I teach economics."

"Hey Pam, move along—you're holding up the line," LaTeisha said jokingly, giving Pam a little nudge.

Pam gave Robin's hand one last squeeze and said, "I hope we get a chance to talk more later."

"Yes, me too," Robin replied politely. She then turned to LaTeisha and introduced herself, looking up a good eight inches to meet her eyes. *Wow, where does Jess find these assistants? Between the three of them, they could just as easily be models as basketball coaches. It's going to make it hard for the fans to keep their eyes on the game instead of the bench. Well, at least some fans...*

After completing her reception line duties, Robin made her way over to the food table. She watched as Capi got everyone's attention and displayed her usual wit while introducing the coaches, giving a short bio for each one. The coaches stood with Capi, trying not to look self-conscious as she highlighted their previous accomplishments. Robin couldn't help but take advantage of the opportunity to study Jess without reservation, since everyone else was looking at her, too. Jess let her eyes roam around the room, but when they made contact with Robin, she quickly looked away. Mercifully, Capi's introductions were short, and soon everyone was mingling once again.

Robin made her way through the crowd, catching up on the summer activities of many of her colleagues. Eventually, she took refuge by the food table again, and looked around discreetly to locate Jess. She was surprised to find her still talking to Capi, and quickly turned away before she got caught looking. *I sure hope Capi isn't taking it upon herself to try to smooth things over between Jess and me.* Her thoughts were interrupted by a touch on her elbow.

"Hey, Robin."

"Oh, hi, Pam. Did you get to meet everybody?"

"Well, probably not everybody, but you seem by far the most interesting economics professor here, and I figured you'd be the perfect person to explain Greenspan's latest tweaking of the interest rates," Pam said with a shyly seductive smile on her face.

Robin saw deep brown eyes appraising her, and couldn't help blushing slightly. "Well, I'm the only economics professor here, and just about anything is more interesting than the Federal Reserve," she said dryly. She was starting to feel a little flustered by the blatant come-on from Pam. "Say, have you tried the food? It's really outstanding. A couple of friends of mine have a restaurant in town and they catered this. Have you had much chance to get around Comstock and try out the restaurants? *Jeez, Robin, slow down. What are you so nervous about? You'd think no one had ever flirted with you before.* She realized that part of her discomfort came from the fact that Jess was nearby, and she didn't want Jess to think that she was reciprocating Pam's attention. *On the other hand, maybe it would be good for her to see that at least someone thinks I'm attractive.* It was also true that after going for months without making any headway with Jess, Robin's ego needed a little boost.

Pam laughed lightly at Robin's flurry of words, and said, "Well, I've been here for almost five months, so I think I know my way around town pretty well. How long have you been at NOU?"

"Three years now. I guess that makes me an old-timer compared to you."

"Yeah, I guess so." Pam reached behind Robin to grab a piece of celery off the food table, brushing her breasts against Robin's arm as she did so. She placed the celery stalk halfway in her mouth and twirled her tongue around it. "So how many classes do you teach?"

"I have a couple of the intro classes, and a grad class in labor economics."

"Well, I have to say that none of the economics professors where I went to school looked anything like you. Most of them were men over fifty with thick glasses and pocket protectors."

Robin smiled and felt herself blushing again. "Yeah, I had a few econ professors like that, too. We're not all geeks, though."

"I should say not," Pam replied while giving an approving look up and down Robin's body.

"Uh, if you'll excuse me for a minute, I need to check on the caterer. It looks like we're getting low on punch." Robin nearly ran from the room, taking refuge in the nearby kitchen.

Jess had been watching the interaction between Robin and Pam, getting progressively irked at her assistant coach for the way she was leering at Robin. *Usually I can count on Pam to be discreet, but she sure is being obvious tonight. I guess it's a good thing she's flirting with Robin, who I know is gay, and not some straight faculty member.* Before she could think twice about being glad that someone was flirting with Robin, Capi was introducing her to yet another professor. Jess once again smiled charmingly at the woman, offered some appropriate small talk that made the woman feel like the most important person on campus, and then politely excused herself to talk to Capi again.

As she turned back, she noticed Capi watching the interaction between Pam and Robin with a concerned look on her face.

Nodding in Pam and Robin's direction, Jess leaned over and said, "I suppose that could make one jealous, watching people flirt with Robin all the time. She's a very attractive woman—it must happen to you a lot."

Capi's attention snapped back to Jess. "What did you say?"

Jess shrugged. "I was talking about Pam flirting with Robin. You must feel very secure about your relationship not to get jealous."

It took Capi a moment to make sense of what Jess had said. "You think Robin and I are...? I thought I told you on our camping trip that Robin's not interested in a relationship with me. If that's changed, no one's told me yet." Capi looked questioningly at Jess. "What gave you the idea that Robin and I were together?"

"Well, I saw you..." Jess stopped and thought about what she had really seen that day outside Starbuck's. *Maybe it was nothing more than friends sharing a hug.* "Uh...I don't know, Capi. It just seemed like I always saw you two together. I'm sorry," she stammered. "I guess I jumped to conclusions."

"That's okay," Capi replied. "I suppose a lot of people might assume that Robin and I are together just because we do so many things with each other. But believe me, we are just friends...unfortunately, for my sake," she added.

Jess needed some time to think, and excused herself to go to the restroom. She splashed some water on her face and looked at her reflection in the mirror. *If Robin and Capi aren't together, then why did Robin stop talking to me? And does this mean that maybe Robin's not gay after all?* Sighing in frustration at never getting any answers from the voice in her head, she decided it was time to quit acting like a teenager and go talk to Robin.

As Jess walked back into the room, she saw that most people had left the reception. She didn't see Robin anywhere, and decided that she must still be in the kitchen where Jess had seen her disappear to earlier. She walked through the door and saw Robin sitting on a counter talking to Meghan. She hesitated, not wanting to interrupt, but Meghan waved hello to her and quickly said she had to start retrieving dishes from the other room. Jess watched her leave, then turned back to Robin. She slowly walked over to where Robin was sitting, the questioning look back in her eyes.

"Hey, can we talk?"

Robin looked up hopefully and said, "Sure...I'd like that."

Jess stood in front of Robin and tilted her head to look into the younger woman's eyes. "I'm not exactly sure what happened between us..." Jess paused, taking a breath. "But I know I'd like to figure it out, because I really miss having you as a friend."

Robin waited for Jess to say more, but nothing else was offered. *That's it? Now it's up to me? What am I supposed to say?* Robin looked down at her hands resting in her lap, stalling for time. *Well, apologizing usually works,* she thought wryly.

"I'm sorry if I've been avoiding you, Jess. I just thought that since you wanted to work on your relationship with John that I shouldn't be monopolizing your time." *Well, that was pretty close to the truth.*

Jess's eyebrows furrowed in confusion. She gently placed her fingers under Robin's chin, silently requesting Robin to meet her eyes. "John and I aren't even dating anymore. But even if we were, that doesn't mean that I can't have other friends."

Robin tried to hide her surprise at Jess's revelation, and she could feel her heartbeat pick up. "But you talked about how you

wanted to do it right this time, to give the relationship the attention it deserved. I just didn't want to get in the way."

"Oh, Robin, you couldn't have gotten in the way. If John
was the right guy for me, it would have worked out, but I realize
now that 'trying harder' is not all it takes to make a relationship
work. There has to be some chemistry there in the first place."
This time Jess looked down at her hands. "I don't know why I
was so bent on having that relationship. Sometimes I wonder
why I bother with romance at all, when friendship is so much
easier, and from my experiences anyway, so much more rewarding." At that, she looked up again at Robin with a tentative half-
smile on her face.

Robin smiled back, relieved beyond words that things might
actually be working out between them. Well, not working out
exactly in the way she'd like, but right now, having Jess's friendship seemed like more than enough.

"Hey, don't give up on romance. When you find the right
person, it will all be worth it."

"Are you speaking from experience? Last time I looked, you
were single," Jess teased.

"Yeah, well you know that saying about 'those that can't do,
teach'? I think there's a corollary there somewhere," Robin said
laughingly.

The two women smiled at each other for a long moment,
happy that some semblance of their previous relationship had
returned, and with it, the easy banter between them.

There were still a lot of unanswered questions in Jess's
mind about how things had gone so awry between them, but she
didn't want to dwell on those right now.

"You know, if you didn't eat too many appetizers, I'd be
happy to buy you dinner," Jess offered tentatively. "That is, if
you're not busy."

"No...no I'm not busy," Robin quickly replied. "I'd love to
get some dinner. Let me just find Capi and tell her I'm leaving."
Robin gave Jess a big smile as she jumped down from the
counter. She hesitated for a second, and then stepped over and
gave Jess a hug. She intended it to be just a quick hug, but once
she felt Jess's arms go around her, she clasped the taller woman
tightly, burying her head in her shoulder. Some unspoken understanding passed between them, and then Robin released Jess and
went in search of her friend.

Jess stood there in temporary shock for a moment, wondering how things could have changed so drastically in such a short time. She shook her head and decided that she felt better than she had in weeks, and she wasn't going to waste time wondering why.

Robin spotted Capi at the food table, helping Meghan stack dirty dishes. Capi couldn't help but notice the big grin on Robin's face as she approached.

"Is it safe to assume that you and one basketball coach worked out your differences?" she queried while smiling warmly at Robin. "Maybe I'd better clarify that, since more than one basketball coach seemed to have their eye on you tonight," she teased.

"Oh please...what was that all about, anyway? Do I have some big sign on me that says 'available and easy,' or what?"

"You don't need a sign. You're just plain irresistible." Capi laughed. "But seriously, I think the head coach was getting a little perturbed at her assistant and the attention she was giving you. Now I know she's not supposed to be interested in women, but it looked a lot like jealousy to me."

"She was probably just worried about the reputation of her program. Can't have people thinking there are lesbians in the coaching ranks, you know." Robin said the word "lesbian" like it was some dreaded disease.

"Say what you like, I say she was green with envy," Capi said emphatically. "You want to know what was really strange? She told me *I* should be jealous—she thought you and I were together."

"You're kidding. What gave her that idea?"

"I guess she just saw us together a bunch of times and assumed you'd finally given up trying to resist me," she joked. "Anyway, I think it kind of rattled her when I said we were just friends. She made a beeline out of here, and the next thing I know, you're coming out of the kitchen with a cat-that's-got-the-canary grin on your face. So what gives?"

Robin couldn't help smiling again. "I'm not sure we know exactly what happened between us yet, but we both agreed that we wanted to go back to being friends again. She offered to buy me dinner, so I wanted to see if it would be all right if I abandoned you for the rest of the evening."

Capi put on her best pout and sighed deeply. She then grabbed Robin around the shoulders in a one-armed hug and said, "Of course I don't mind being left alone...again. Have a great time, and I hope everything works out. You deserve it."

"Thanks, Capi. I'll make it up to you, I promise."

"Yeah, sure you will. G'wan, get outta here," she said with a smile.

Chapter
14

Robin and Jess walked over to retrieve the coach's car from the Athletic Department lot, since it was closer than Robin's car. They headed for the *Green Dragon*, a local Thai restaurant, and soon Robin was happily digging into her paht thai with abandon.

"I see you haven't lost your appetite over these past few weeks," Jess said while watching Robin with amusement.

Robin looked up and smiled back at Jess, a noodle still clinging to her lower lip.

"Actually, I've just started to be able to run on my ankle again, and it feels so good to get off that stationary bike that I've probably been overdoing it a little. It does make for a healthy appetite, though."

"What's the prognosis for your ankle?" Jess asked with concern. "Will you be able to get back to basketball soon?"

"Everything looks good, according to the doctor. It's just a matter of slowly building up strength again before putting too much stress on it from jumping or cutting sharply."

"That's great. I'm sure the boys at the rec center all miss you."

"Oh, I stop by all the time and shoot a few baskets, just so they know I'm still around. I think they're happy they don't have to deal with the 'shirts and skins' thing, though. It was always a hassle when I was supposed to be on the skins...the other team would pass me the ball by accident, and my team would never pass it to me. There were times when I just wanted to strip my shirt off and be done with it."

Jess laughed, but didn't share how much that thought intrigued her. She certainly didn't want to give Robin the wrong impression.

"So how is your team looking, Jess? When do you get to start practicing?"

"We don't start until the middle of October when we have our Midnight Madness event with the men's team. But the players have been working real hard on conditioning. I don't think anybody wants to be embarrassed at the first practice by sucking wind in front of the new coach," she said with a satisfied grin on her face.

"I guess there are some advantages to being new, huh?"

"A few, but they don't last for long. The honeymoon is pretty short. I'll have plenty of players cursing me behind my back after a few tough practices, and we all know how many losses it takes before the fans turn on you."

"Well, I, for one, promise to be loyal to the bitter end," Robin said confidently. "At least until they fire you, then I'll say 'I told you she was a terrible coach,'" Robin said with a mock scowl on her face.

Jess laughed and said, "With friends like you..."

"Hey, I'm just kidding. I think you're going to do great. I predict an appearance in the sweet sixteen," Robin said, referring to the round of sixteen in the NCAA playoffs.

"Well, I'm glad you have such confidence in me, but really Robin, you don't know anything about whether I'm a good coach or not. I still have a lot to prove."

"That's not true. There are lots of things I know about you that tell me you would be a great coach."

"Oh yeah? Like what?" Jess challenged, half afraid at how embarrassed she was going to be with what Robin would say.

Robin started ticking off the points on her fingers. "One, you have great presence—you command respect, which all coaches need. Two, you're very intelligent, and you obviously know the game inside and out. Three, you have great rapport with the alums and other fans, so you'll get lots of support from them. Four, you're honest—there are no hidden agendas and you won't be playing mind games with your players. Five..."

"Okay, okay, that's enough," Jess interrupted, laughing and blushing slightly. "I sure hope I can live up to the reputation you've just given me." Privately, Jess cringed at Robin's last point. *Well I've always prided myself on being honest, and I still am with others, but I'm starting to worry about whether I'm being honest with myself about some things.*

Robin enjoyed seeing the self-confident woman struggle with her modesty. *She's such an interesting mix of contradictions. So competent and in complete control, yet obviously sensitive, and almost shy sometimes. It's incredibly appealing.* Robin decided she needed to change the subject quickly before her infatuation was seen on her face.

"Did you get enough to eat? We could order some dessert," she added hopefully, not quite ready to have the evening end.

Jess wasn't anxious to leave Robin either, and she seized upon an idea. "Hey, you know I've got some great Haagen Daaz ice cream at home. We could let our dinner settle and go over to my place for dessert instead."

"Let me guess, chocolate chocolate chip, right?" Robin asked with a mischievous smile.

Jess looked startled for an instant, but quickly recovered. "Well, I've got mocha almond fudge, too," she said defensively. Then she cocked her head and held her chin as if thinking hard. "I'd guess you're a cookie dough kind of person."

Robin laughed, not wanting to think too hard about what kind of person that was. "Well, cookie dough is probably on the list of my top five, but number one has to be rocky road."

"Then we'll stop at the store on the way home and get some rocky road," Jess stated emphatically.

Jess grabbed the bill and insisted on paying for dinner as promised, and soon they were on their way to dessert.

"You know, I've never been in your apartment before Jess. It's really nice." Robin sank into an overstuffed black leather couch and sighed with delight. "Oh, I could get used to this."

Jess headed for the kitchen and came back with two bowls of ice cream. Robin's was piled high above the rim, while Jess had a small single scoop.

"What are you trying to do, fatten me up?" Robin joked, even as she eagerly grabbed the bowl and dug into the generous serving.

Jess sank down into the other end of the sofa and stretched her feet out toward Robin. They ate their dessert in silence for a few minutes, Robin finishing hers before Jess was halfway done.

Robin looked at Jess's long legs stretched out beside her and said, "Hey, if I remember correctly, I owe you a leg massage."

Jess stroked her chin in thought. "Well, it's true that there was a deal made fair and square for a bag of M&M's, as I recall."

Robin smiled and scooted over on the couch, lifting up Jess's legs and resting them across her thighs. Jess was wearing a pair of light chinos, and Robin could easily feel the strong muscles underneath as she kneaded Jess's calves.

"Mmmmm, I didn't know those were so sore," Jess said while leaning back contentedly and slowly licking the ice cream off her spoon.

Robin saw the sensuous way that Jess was making love to her double chocolate chip, and could barely keep her mind on her task. *If that's the way she handles her ice cream, I'd love to see how she'd handle...Stop it. Stop it.* Robin shook her head and took a deep breath, trying to will away the blood that was rushing to her face, among other places.

After spending a good ten minutes on Jess's calves, Robin slowly made her way up to the thighs, stopping to gently probe around the knee on the way. She knew she was getting into dangerous territory here, and kept her hands well away from the sensitive inner thighs.

Jess had long ago closed her eyes and rested her head on the arm of the couch. She had a small smile on her lips, and every once in awhile would moan softly with pleasure.

"I can tell you don't have this done nearly enough," Robin said with a soft laugh.

Jess raised her eyelids slightly and replied, "I can't remember the last time. It always seems so self-indulgent. I guess I don't feel like I've done anything to deserve such treatment."

"You don't need to *do* anything to deserve it Jess. Everybody deserves to be pampered once in awhile for no reason at all."

"Hmmm, if you say so." Jess closed her eyes again and wondered when she became such a hedonist.

Robin continued working the strong leg muscles until she noticed that Jess hadn't made a sound for a few minutes. Worried that she had fallen asleep, Robin whispered, "Jess?"

Jess blinked open her eyes and looked questioningly back at Robin. "Are you getting tired? I can take you home if you'd like."

"No, I'm fine, but I think you're the one who's tired," Robin replied with an understanding smile.

"Well, I have to admit that the combination of the massage and this couch was making me a little sleepy," Jess said sheepishly. "But I'm awake now. Do you want to watch a video?"

"Are you sure you're not too tired? I don't want to keep you up."

"No, I'm fine, really. But why don't we get more comfortable on the floor, and then if I do fall asleep, at least I won't wake up with a kink in my neck."

"That sounds good. Do you have a blanket and some pillows?"

"I've got better than that. Let's get the mattress off the hide-a-bed in the den and be really comfortable."

"Oh, now you're asking to fall asleep," Robin teased.

The two women dragged the mattress out to the living room, and then Jess retrieved some extra blankets and pillows.

"I'm going to change into something more comfortable. Do you want to borrow some sweats or something?" Jess asked tentatively.

"Well, a T-shirt and some shorts would be nice," Robin replied. "Hey, if we're going to watch a movie, aren't we supposed to have popcorn and soda and candy and..."

Jess groaned loudly. "You've got to be kidding. How can you even think about more food right now?"

Robin faked a look of disappointment before relenting and saying, "Yeah, I am kidding. That ice cream ought to hold me for at least a couple of hours."

Jess smiled and headed into her bedroom. She came back with an NOU Women's Basketball T-shirt that had TEAM written in eight inch block letters on the back, and a pair of plaid flannel boxer shorts that looked only slightly too large for the smaller woman. Robin excused herself to use the bathroom and change.

Robin pulled the T-shirt over her head and smiled at the thought of wearing a shirt that was obviously made for Jess's team. *If I'd had a coach like her in college, I might have killed myself from working too hard to please her.* Which was saying a lot, since Robin had worked harder than anybody else on her team anyway.

She emerged from the bathroom, boxers slung low on her hips, and found Jess throwing a blanket over the mattress. Jess had changed into an Idaho State T-shirt and a pair of athletic department-issue gray shorts. Noticing Robin looking at her T-shirt, she said, "Now that I'm at NOU, I can only wear these at home where no one will see me and think that I have split loyalties."

"Well, I won't tell anyone." Robin smiled.

"What do you want to watch? I don't have a huge selection, but there should be something we can agree on."

"Oh, I'm easy." *Did I really just say that?* Robin mentally slapped herself. "Whatever you want is fine," she quickly added.

"Do you like Sigourney Weaver? I've got *Copycat.*"

"That's the one with Holly Hunter, isn't it? That would be great. I haven't seen it."

"Okay, *Copycat* it is," Jess said and popped the tape into the VCR. Robin had already settled back onto her pillows, drawing the blanket up to her waist. Jess lifted the blanket and slid onto her side of the mattress. She started the video and soon both women were engrossed in the thriller.

After about a half hour, Jess looked over to see Robin's eyes closed and her lips parted slightly. *Uh-oh, looks like we lost one. I wonder if she would want me to wake her up and take her home.* Jess thought about how wonderful the evening had been up to now, and really didn't want it to end. *But I should at least give her the choice. I wouldn't want her to wake up later and be mad at me for letting her fall asleep.* Jess reached over and gave Robin a gentle nudge while softly saying her name.

Robin's eyes slowly opened and a look of confusion crossed her face. *Where am I...Who...*Then she saw Jess gently touching her arm, and instantly became wide-awake. "Oh geez, I fell asleep didn't I? I'm really sorry."

"Hey, don't worry about it. It's fine if you want to fall asleep here, but I thought I should at least offer to take you home in case you want to sleep in your own bed," Jess said with a small half-smile on her face.

Whoa boy, what am I going to do with that offer? Robin thought worriedly. *Is she going to sleep here with me, or go into her own room? If she stays here, can I trust myself to keep my hands off her all night? We just got back together. I sure don't want to send her running off again.* Robin looked up and realized that Jess was waiting expectantly for her reply.

Chapter
15

What am I waiting for? Of course I want to stay here. "Well, if you're sure you don't mind, I am pretty darn comfortable here," Robin said, smiling back at Jess.

"Great. Do you need anything else? Do you want to borrow a toothbrush?"

"Well, that probably depends on whether the toothbrush that I'm borrowing is used or not," Robin laughed.

The laughter relieved the tension that both women could feel, and Jess finally relaxed a little, reclining back on the pillows.

"Well, I happen to have a *new* toothbrush in the bathroom that you could break in."

Robin got up and headed toward the bathroom, calling back over her shoulder, "As long as you promise not to offer it to someone else later."

Jess watched the young woman disappear into the bathroom, her gaze lingering on Robin's flannel-covered derriere much too long for a woman who thought she was straight. She blinked hard a few times and brought herself back to reality. "Hey, I think the toothbrush is in the right-hand drawer in there," Jess called out.

"Thanks," came the muffled reply from behind the door.

Minutes later, Robin returned, shut off the light, and settled underneath the blanket. Jess rolled onto her back and double-checked to make sure she was on her own side of the bed. *God, why is this making me so nervous? Or is it excitement, not ner-*

vousness? Oh geez, that would be worse, wouldn't it?

The two women laid there in silence for a few minutes before Robin turned on her side facing Jess. She propped herself up on her elbow, her head resting on her hand. "Hey Jess?" she asked softly.

"Yeah?"

"Tonight was the best time I've had in weeks, and I just wanted to thank you for taking the initiative this afternoon." Robin took a deep breath and willed herself to continue. "I'm really sorry that I jeopardized our friendship by not coming to talk to you sooner."

Jess turned on her side and mirrored Robin's position. "Hey, you don't have to apologize any more than I do. You don't know how many times I wanted to just call you, or stop by your office to talk to you, to figure out what went wrong, but I never did." She tried to see Robin's eyes in the dim moonlit room, but could only see shadows.

"Why didn't you?"

Jess swallowed hard. *I can't tell her it was because I was jealous of her and Capi. And I can't tell her it was because I was mad at her for not telling me she was gay, which I'm not even sure she is anymore. Well, I'd better say something.* "Well, you know I did try to contact you for about a week, but you never returned my calls or messages. I guess I just figured that you didn't want to talk to me, and I didn't want to push it." *Oh right, like you can take the high ground in this.*

"You're right, and I should have returned your calls and not just assumed that I was getting in the way with you and John. I'm really sorry, Jess."

Jess felt extremely guilty that she'd prompted Robin to apologize again, when in reality she knew she was as much to blame. "Don't be. I shouldn't have given up so easily. I don't know what I was thinking. I'm just glad that we figured out it was all a misunderstanding." Jess's eyes had adjusted to the darkness, and she saw a relieved smile on Robin's face.

"Yeah, me too." Robin reached over and put her hand on top of Jess's. "I promise I'll make a better effort to communicate in the future, and I won't just make assumptions about what you're feeling, okay?"

"Okay, me too," Jess replied while turning her hand over and gently clasping Robin's.

They stayed that way for a moment, smiling at each other in the dim light, until Robin started to worry about how Jess would react to prolonged physical contact between them. She gave Jess's hand a squeeze before releasing it and turning over onto her back. Jess remained on her side, looking at Robin.

"Thanks," Jess said softly.

"What for?"

Jess paused. "Just thanks."

Robin wasn't exactly sure what Jess meant, but knew it wasn't something she should question.

"You're welcome."

Jess smiled and turned onto her back and stared at the ceiling for a while, thinking about the events of the last six hours. *I am so glad we worked that out. I've missed her so much.* She thought about whether she'd ever had a friend like Robin before, one that meant so much to her. *I can never remember being so close to anyone like this. Where it meant so much to see them happy. Where I spend so much time thinking about them, and thinking about when I'll get to see them again. And I know I've never felt this way about any of the guys I've dated. Is it possible that people are actually closer to their friends than their lovers? Or am I just kidding myself about what I really feel for Robin? Maybe this is what real love feels like, and I've just never experienced it before.* At the thought of real love, Jess's mind couldn't help but go to the next logical step. She looked over at the attractive woman lying beside her and felt nervous again. *I just don't feel comfortable with the thought of having sex with a woman. I mean, we can share hugs, hold hands, and that kind of thing feels great, but lots of women friends do those things.* Jess sighed deeply and closed her eyes. *But it's never felt like this with any other women friends I've had. Maybe I need to just stop analyzing everything and let whatever happens, happen.* Satisfied with that strategy for the time being, Jess turned onto her side and allowed the happiness of the evening to wash over her and lull her into sleep.

Robin awoke feeling uncomfortably warm. She had already thrown off the covers, and when she blinked her eyes open she saw that it was still dark. Not too dark to see the long body that she had somehow snuggled up against during the night, however. The same body that was now acting as a furnace. Robin slowly extricated herself from Jess's side, relieved to see that the taller woman was still asleep. She took the opportunity to study Jess's face for a moment, seeing the peacefulness of sleep etched in her features. Her stomach clenched painfully with the longing she had for this woman. *Am I just torturing myself with this friendship?* Robin shook her head, denying that thought. *I just can't give up on the hope that her feelings will change for me. I mean, there are already signs of affection. I just can't tell if it's the affection between friends, or something more. Maybe she doesn't even know herself.* Robin admonished herself to be patient, turned back over and closed her eyes. In moments, she was back asleep, already inching her way unconsciously back toward Jess.

Robin awoke the next morning feeling rested and content, despite the fact that she was alone in the bed. She could smell the aroma of coffee coming from the kitchen, and she stretched her arms above her head, inhaling the welcome scent. Looking at her watch, she saw that it was already ten a.m., and wondered how long Jess had been up. After standing up and working the kinks out of her body, Robin made her way into the kitchen.

"Hey sleepyhead. I thought maybe you were going to stay in bed till noon," Jess teased.

Robin rubbed her eyes and replied, "I probably would have if I hadn't been enticed by the smell of coffee." She walked over to where Jess sat drinking her coffee and reading the paper. She leaned slightly against Jess's chair while putting her hand on her shoulder. "Anything happen in the world yesterday that I need to know about?"

"Well if it did, it wouldn't make the Comstock Gazette until tomorrow anyway," she joked. She looked up at Robin. "Let me get you a cup of coffee to open those eyelids a little more." She rose out of her chair, the nearness to Robin causing her to have a strong desire to lean down and give the smaller woman a soft kiss on the top of her head. She resisted the temptation, thinking, *Sure, friends always feel like that, don't they?*

Robin dropped into a chair next to Jess's, and looked around at the kitchen. It was clean and functional, but didn't give the impression that it got a lot of use. Robin supposed that coaches spent a lot of evenings away from home, and that Jess had probably gotten in the habit of eating out.

"Just cream, right?" Jess called out from over at the counter.

"Right, lots of it, please."

"Here you go, one cream with a little coffee," Jess said, handing the mug to Robin. "How about some breakfast? I probably can't make omelets as well as you, but I think I could handle some French toast."

"Mmmm, that would be great. But let me help. You don't have to wait on me like I'm some guest, you know," Robin said, getting up out of her chair.

"But you are a guest," Jess pointed out with a little smile, even knowing what Robin meant.

Robin gave her a little push in the back and said, "You know what I mean. Now get going and start heating up the pan, while I get the eggs and milk. I'm hungry."

"Hmmm, why doesn't that surprise me?" Jess asked sarcastically.

The two women happily worked together to prepare the French toast, occasionally running into each other in the small space, and smiling apologetically when it happened. Jess was once again struck by the contrast of this morning with Robin and her ill-fated morning with John. In fact, she couldn't ever remember feeling so comfortable and happy in the morning.

As they sat down at the table to eat, Robin asked, "So what do you have on the calendar for today?"

"Nothing really. I usually spend some time in the office on Saturdays, but there's nothing urgent that needs to get done. I do need to get to the gym sometime, though, especially after this big breakfast," she said while looking at her stack of three pieces of French toast. "What do you have planned?"

"Pretty much the same thing. If you want, I could meet you at the rec center later this afternoon," Robin said hopefully.

Jess thought for a moment before replying, "Sure, that sounds great. Usually I work out over at the arena, but the rec center shouldn't be too crowded on a Saturday afternoon."

"Great. How about if we meet there at three? That should give us enough time to digest this."

"Sounds good to me," Jess replied, as she finished off her breakfast and took her dishes to the sink.

The two women cleaned up the breakfast dishes, and put the mattress, blankets, and pillows away.

"Do you want to use the shower?" Jess asked.

"No, I'll just wait till I get home. That is, if you don't mind my keeping your clothes for a day or two till I get a chance to wash them."

"Keep them for as long as you'd like. It's not like I don't have drawers full of T-shirts and shorts."

Robin chuckled and replied, "Sounds a lot like my wardrobe."

She gathered up her things and Jess drove her back to her apartment. She spent the rest of the morning feeling decidedly happy, looking forward to seeing Jess again that afternoon.

Jess arrived at the rec center in her workout clothes, and was already warming up on a stationary bike when Robin showed up. After changing in the locker room, Robin jumped on a Stairmaster next to Jess and started climbing.

"I should have asked you to meet me at two instead of three," Robin said, as she started to breathe a little heavier. "I've been starving for the last hour, but I knew if I ate anything, I'd never be able to exercise without throwing up."

"Well, in that case, I'm really glad you waited," Jess replied dryly. "Tell your stomach it will only be another hour before you make it happy again."

"I hope you don't expect me to stay on this Stairmaster for an hour."

"No," Jess laughed. "I thought we could lift some weights for about twenty minutes or so when we're finished here."

"Whew. You had me worried there for a minute," Robin said with a big smile.

The two women increased their level of intensity on the exercise machines, and soon they were too short of breath to continue conversation. Thirty minutes later, they were both drenched in sweat and leaving the exercise room.

"Hey, what do you say we shoot a few baskets? There shouldn't be anybody in the gym at this time of day," Robin said hopefully. "I'll take you on in a game of H.O.R.S.E.," she challenged.

Jess grinned and said, "You'll be sorry. Want to bet dinner on it?"

"Oh, pretty confident, are we?" Robin taunted. "I'll bet dinner *and* a movie on it."

"You're on. I'll even let you go first."

They checked out a basketball and found the gym empty, as predicted. Robin dribbled over to the nearest basket and made an easy lay-up.

"Is that the best you can do for your first shot?" Jess taunted.

"That was just a warm-up shot, smart aleck," Robin retorted. "Here, you can have one, too," she said as she passed the ball crisply to Jess.

Jess dribbled the length of the court, made a left-handed lay-up, then dribbled back and made a reverse lay-up.

"Show-off. That was two warm-up shots," Robin said with a grin.

Jess passed the ball back to Robin and said, "Go ahead, take your best shot."

Robin decided she would start slow and get her range before trying anything too difficult. She walked over to the free-throw line, took three dribbles, and swished a high arcing shot.

Jess retrieved the ball, walked over to the free-throw line, and calmly repeated Robin's feat, raising her eyebrow and smirking at Robin.

Robin gave her a mock glare in return, and sank a twelve footer from the baseline. Jess smiled and did the same.

Robin then backed up and drained a three-point shot from the top of the key. Jess calmly walked over and effortlessly sank hers.

Oh geez, I should have known she'd have ice-water in her veins, Robin thought ruefully. *Why didn't I think about the fact that this woman spends her life on a basketball court?*

Robin decided it was time to get fancy. She started at the top of the key, took one dribble, wound the ball around her waist once on her way to the hoop, and laid it softly off the glass.

Jess scowled at her. "I don't let my players do that kind of trash on the court."

"Oh come on. This is a game of H.O.R.S.E., not the NCAA championships," Robin admonished her with a smile.

Jess reluctantly took the ball and repeated the maneuver to

perfection.

"Oh, like you've never done that before," Robin said indignantly.

"I never said *I'd* never done it, I just said I don't let my players do it."

"Okay, fine. Let's see how good you are with your left hand."

Robin started from the left side of the basket, drove underneath it and attempted the reverse lay-up with her left hand. Unfortunately, she missed.

Jess smiled with the look of a predator about to enjoy its dinner. "You want to see how good I am with my left hand?"

Oh, Robin, don't even go there, she admonished herself as her mind took off with Jess's question.

Jess took the ball near the basket on the right side, took one dribble across the key, and neatly made a left-handed hook shot.

"Of course you'd use a post move," Robin said as though Jess was cheating.

"Oh, and what about your three pointer?" Jess shot back playfully. "I didn't have a lot of occasion to shoot those in my playing days."

Robin just grumbled and picked up the ball, flailing badly on her attempt to make a left-handed hook shot.

"That would be H," Jess said triumphantly. She proceeded to run out O, R, S, and E without too much more difficulty, once she had figured out Robin's weaknesses.

"Double or nothing on a game of one-on-one to eleven," Robin challenged quickly.

"Don't know when to quit, do you?" Jess replied with a big grin. "Okay, you're on."

She tossed Robin the ball at the top of the key, and jumped in close enough to keep her from getting a shot off. Before she had barely come to a stop in front of Robin, the smaller woman was by her on the left and in for an easy lay-up.

"A little slow in your old age?" Robin said over her shoulder, walking back to the top of the key. She tossed the ball to Jess who immediately backed her down to the low post. Robin did her best to use her body to keep Jess from getting position in front of the basket, but she couldn't stop her from doing an easy drop step for a lay-up.

The play continued in this fashion, Jess leaving more room

to try to stop Robin's drives, and Robin getting increasingly more physical to try to stop Jess's post-up moves, but neither being very successful. In reality, both women were enjoying the physical nature of the play, taking every opportunity to push, shove, grab, and hold each other. Had there been a referee present, both would have fouled out before they got to seven points.

In the end, as is often the case in basketball, size won out and Robin graciously accepted defeat.

"What do you say we skip the weight room and go directly to dinner?" Robin asked hopefully.

Jess just laughed and said, "You're so predictable, but I love it."

"How about if I go take a shower and then I'll pick you up at your place for dinner?" Robin offered.

"Give me about a half-hour and I should be ready."

Robin put the ball under her left arm and put her right around Jess's waist as they left the gym. She leaned in close to Jess's ear. "You know, I only let you win because I didn't want you to feel bad." Before Jess could react, Robin bolted for the locker room, throwing a big smile back over her shoulder. Jess just shook her head and headed for her car.

Chapter
16

Jess sat in her office, daydreaming about how great her weekend had been. She and Robin had gone to dinner and a movie Saturday night, and Jess had talked Robin into coming back to her apartment afterward for a drink. As it got late, Jess again asked Robin if she wanted to stay, and this time, Robin didn't even try to think of reasons not to. They got up Sunday and spent a leisurely morning together before Robin returned to her own apartment. All in all, Jess couldn't think of a weekend she had enjoyed more. Her pleasant reminiscing was interrupted when LaTeisha knocked on her door.

"Hey, what's up?" Jess asked as her assistant coach came into the office.

"Well, we may have a little problem with Bennie." Benita Gonzales was a sophomore point guard who had more than her share of attitude. While she and Jess hadn't had any run-ins yet, she clearly had a chip on her shoulder and wasn't about to give the new coach an ounce of respect that she didn't earn.

Jess just raised her eyebrow, encouraging LaTeisha to continue.

"I've heard from some of the other players that she's skipping a lot of her classes. It's early enough in the term yet to not be that much of a problem, but she's got to realize that our league season doesn't start 'til January, and she has to pass all her classes this term to stay eligible. Now I know she's a lot smarter than she lets on, but she's going to have a hard time doing that unless she goes to class."

Jess thought for a moment. "Do you have a copy of her class schedule?"

"Sure, I already pulled it out," LaTeisha said, handing the piece of paper to Jess.

Jess studied the schedule for a few seconds, and then a small smile crossed her lips. "I think I just might have to pay a visit to one of her classes and see for myself."

Later that afternoon, Jess wandered through the halls of the Social Science Building, looking for the main auditorium. When she found it, she slipped in one of the back doors and took a seat on the edge of the last row where she could see everyone in front of her, as well as anyone coming in. She was five minutes early for the start of class, and the auditorium was about a quarter full. Bennie was nowhere in sight.

About two minutes later, the door in the front of the auditorium opened, and the young economics professor strode quickly over to the podium, arms laden with books and notes. Robin wore a pair of blue jeans and a neatly pressed short-sleeved shirt. The bright auditorium lights were focused on the front of the room, and they highlighted the sun-lightened streaks in Robin's hair. Jess thought she looked fantastic.

Robin started the class right on the hour, and Bennie still had not arrived. Jess decided she'd stay for a few more minutes in case the student was running late. In no time, she was mesmerized by Robin's engaging voice and enthusiastic approach to her class. She almost missed Bennie when she wandered in ten minutes late. She looked up as the young woman passed her seat and Bennie looked back at her. The athlete's eyes widened in shock, and she quickly moved ahead a few rows to take a seat. She grabbed her notebook and began to furiously take notes. Jess couldn't help but smile a little.

"So Dr. Grant, are you saying that economics assumes that all people are greedy?" one of the students toward the front of the class asked.

"No, I'm saying that all people are motivated by utility maximization. While some people may maximize utility by consuming as many material goods as possible, others may maximize utility by actually giving money away, to charities, for example. All I'm saying is that we assume people act rationally, and they make choices that they believe are in their best interests."

"That seems ridiculous to assume that people act rationally all the time," the student retorted.

"That may be true." Robin smiled easily, not taking offense at the tone of the student's statement. "But it depends on what your definition of 'rational' is. Suppose I give you ten dollars and tell you that you can share part of it with the person sitting next to you, but if you don't share any of it, you have to give it back. How much money would you offer to your neighbor?" The neighbor turned with renewed interest to her classmate, wondering how generous he would be. The student thought for a moment and said, "I'd probably give her a couple of bucks."

"Now some people would say that isn't very rational," Robin replied. "After all, you could give her one cent and you could keep the other $9.99. What made you decide to give her two bucks?"

"I don't know, it just seemed like I should share a little, and I still get to keep a lot more than I'm giving her."

"So what you're saying is that you would receive some utility from sharing, and that utility outweighed the utility you would have gotten from keeping the extra $1.99, right?"

"Yeah, I guess so."

"So you did act rationally, even though you didn't act greedily."

"Hey, he could have given me five," the neighbor complained.

Robin laughed. "Okay, so maybe he was a little greedy. But this demonstrates that economic theory is compatible with people doing things for altruistic reasons, or religious reasons, or even for love. We just have to put it into the framework of utility maximization."

Jess sat in the back of the room, appreciating Robin's rapport with the students and her uncanny ability to explain things in a way they would understand. *I'm going to have to think a little bit more about this idea of love being related to utility maximization, though.*

When the class ended, Bennie fiddled around with her notebook, clearly not wanting to have to get up and face the head

coach. Jess just waited patiently until Bennie could no longer
hold out. She slowly got up and walked back toward the door,
keeping her head down.

"Hey, Bennie," Jess said softly as she approached her seat.
Bennie looked up reluctantly. "Have a seat here for a minute."
Jess motioned to the seat in front of her and Bennie sat down,
turning halfway towards Jess. "That was a pretty good lecture,
didn't you think?"

Bennie shrugged her shoulders and mumbled, "Yeah, she's
cool," without looking at Jess.

"Don't you think it shows a little disrespect to show up late
for class?"

"I don't know. Lot's of people come late," Bennie replied
defensively.

"Yeah, but you're not lots of people. You're a scholarship
athlete who's getting an all-expenses paid college education."
Bennie still wouldn't look at Jess. "And besides that, you're an
athlete on *my* team, and *my* athletes are going to go to class,
because I think it's just as important that you get an education as
it is for you to excel on the basketball court." Bennie looked at
Jess as if she was trying to figure out whether the coach was
really serious about that. After all, athletes hear that kind of talk
all the time, but when it really came down to it, a lot of coaches
let the academics slip if it means keeping an athlete happy and
productive. Jess looked intently back at Bennie, not blinking an
eye, letting her know she was completely serious.

"The next time you skip a class, Bennie, you're going to pay
for it with a week of six a.m. workouts with me, okay?" Bennie
nodded reluctantly. "Oh, and one more thing. That professor happens to be a friend of mine, so I'd appreciate it if you'd show her
the respect of showing up on time."

Bennie looked startled, like she couldn't imagine the coach
actually having a friend, but quickly nodded.

"In fact, I want you to show up to all of your classes on
time."

Jess got up to leave and put a hand on Bennie's shoulder.
She gave her a smile and said, "Maybe you'll find out you even
like economics. Stranger things have happened." And with that,
she left the young athlete to ponder her future actions.

Chapter
17

"Student Affairs, this is Capi Morgan." It was a busy day in the Office of Student Affairs, and Capi was answering her phone for the tenth time since lunch.

"Hi Capi, this is Jess Peters."

"Oh, hi Jess. How are things going over in athletics?"

"Fine. Don't worry, I'm not calling you because one of my athletes has been arrested."

Capi laughed. "So what can I do for you?"

"Well, remember when I asked you when Robin's birthday was?"

"Yeah, it's coming up this weekend."

"Well, I wanted to do something nice for her, and I was thinking about taking her on a fishing trip. The problem is, I don't know too much about the fishing opportunities around here."

"Oh, I think we can fix that problem," Capi said conspiratorially. The two women spent the next half hour scheming about the weekend trip.

"When am I going to get to find out where we're going?" Robin asked from the front seat of Jess's car. Jess had told her to pack for two and a half days, all casual clothes for fall weather, and had picked her up from her office on Friday afternoon. Capi had taken Jess over to Robin's apartment earlier in the day, using the extra key that Robin had given her good friend months ago, and packed up the fishing gear that Robin would need. Jess had borrowed Capi's gear for herself, promising that she wouldn't use anything without Robin's instruction before hand.

"You'll find out when we get there. It's supposed to be a surprise," Jess admonished. "Now just sit back and relax for a couple of hours, and try not to ask me if we're there yet every ten minutes."

"Couple of hours, huh? And we're heading east, so that narrows it down to somewhere in the mountains. Do you have camping gear in the trunk?"

Jess sighed with exasperation. "You're not going to give up are you? Aren't you supposed to be more gracious when somebody is doing something nice for you for your birthday?"

"Well, when you put it like that," Robin said with a little pout, resigning herself to being more patient. "You know, you really didn't have to go out of your way for my birthday. I know this is a busy time of year for you."

"I know I didn't have to, but I wanted to. Practices will start in a couple of weeks, and then I'll never get a chance to go away for a weekend. Believe me, this is going to be as much fun for me as it is for you," Jess said while giving Robin a warm smile.

Jess turned south on I-5, then headed west again out of Salem towards the Santiam Pass. When they continued beyond the pass, Robin really got curious about their final destination. Jess could see her squirming in her seat, dying to ask about it, and had to smile at the younger woman's distress. About twenty minutes later, Jess slowed down and turned north off the highway. Robin's eyes immediately lit up.

"Are we going to the Metolius River?" she asked excitedly. The Metolius was not only an excellent fly-fishing river, it was also one of the most beautiful rivers in Oregon. The water was a unique aquamarine color, and the river flowed swiftly through magnificent Ponderosa pine stands. Although it was used heavily in the summer months, the last weekend of September would give the two women a good chance of finding some solitude along the river.

Jess turned onto a dirt road, and wound around to a cabin perched within a couple hundred feet of the river. She pulled to a stop and the two women jumped out of the car and walked toward the river in the twilight.

"Well, how do you like it?" Jess asked with a big smile.

"Are you kidding? I love it." Robin looked at Jess and couldn't stop herself from throwing her arms around the taller woman in a big hug. Jess just laughed and hugged her back, glad she could do something to make Robin so happy.

"I can't believe you got a cabin right on the river," Robin said. "These are all private—how did you manage to rent one?"

"My secretary knows someone who owns one, and when she heard that I was looking for a place to go fishing for a weekend, she called them up and arranged it."

"This is so wonderful," Robin sighed, looking around. "Let's get unpacked so we're ready to go fishing first thing in the morning."

The two women quickly unpacked the car and got settled in the cabin, which was rustic but very charming. The fact that the place only had one bedroom was just an additional bonus as far as Robin was concerned. *I can't believe I have her all to myself for a whole weekend. And it was her idea.*

Indeed, things had been very good between them over the last couple of weeks, and they had grown closer and closer. Robin was trying not to get her hopes up too high, but as their relationship grew, they spent more evenings together, found themselves touching each other more often—a quick hug, a clasp of the hand, a back rub or leg massage—and Jess seemed to be fine with all of it. Robin couldn't be happier.

The two women decided to turn in early after the long day, and were up and ready to go by seven the next morning. Robin helped Jess get her equipment sorted out, and they found that Capi's waders were a perfect fit. They donned their fishing vests over a couple of layers of clothes, knowing that the temperature would heat up as the day wore on.

They walked down to the river by the cabin and took a look at the water.

"It doesn't look like there's much happening in the way of a hatch right now," Robin said while looking up and down the banks. "But there will be plenty of fish feeding on nymphs. In fact, look. Right over there behind that boulder," she said pointing upstream and across the river, "there are three or four fish hanging out."

Jess strained her eyes to see what Robin was pointing at, but saw only rocks under the water. Just then, one of the rocks moved about a foot, and Jess's eyes widened. "Yeah, I see them," she said excitedly.

"I can't tell if they're rainbows or whitefish, but either way, they'll give us some good action," Robin said, referring to the healthy population of mountain whitefish in the river. While no self-respecting fly angler would admit to fishing for whitefish, since they were in the river with the rainbows you were bound to catch a few of them. And most anglers couldn't tell the difference between playing a rainbow or a whitefish. Once the fish was identified, however, the angler would scowl and mutter some oath about "damn whitefish." Robin, on the other hand, accepted the whitefish as a good opportunity to practice her technique.

"Okay, let's get your rod set up for nymphing," she said as she took Jess's fly rod from her.

"Set up for *what*?" Jess asked skeptically.

"Nymphing. And no, it's not related to nymphomania. Get your mind out of the gutter—we're fishing," Robin said with mock seriousness.

Robin held the fly line out in front of her. "We're going to use what they call a dropper system." Jess watched as Robin tied an additional piece of tippet onto the end of the leader, leaving a little tag of about five inches coming off the old leader. She tied a small hare's ear nymph to the tag, and a large, weighted stone fly nymph to the end of the tippet. She held the finished product out away from her and looked it over. "Casting this won't be pretty, but it's the results that count, right?"

"Whatever you say, maestro," Jess replied while watching Robin intently.

Once both rods were set, Robin stepped off the bank and into the current, turning around to offer Jess a hand.

"Why don't you just hang onto my arm until you feel comfortable in this current," Robin offered, while making her way out into the stream.

Jess had a death grip on Robin's forearm until she figured out not to fight the current. Eventually she found her balance and released Robin's arm. They walked to within about ten feet of the fish they had seen earlier.

"Aren't we going to scare them away?" Jess asked.

"Not unless you fall in the river and thrash around," Robin

joked. "We're downstream of them, so they shouldn't notice us. Even if we do spook them, if we stand here long enough, they'll be back."

Robin positioned herself just behind Jess on the upstream side and told her to let a little line out. "Just let it float downstream with the current until you get about fifteen feet out."

Jess complied with Robin's instructions, and then Robin put her right arm around Jess and gripped the rod over Jess's hand. "Do you mind?" she asked, not wanting Jess to feel uncomfortable about such a close position.

"No, of course not," Jess replied while smiling back over her shoulder at Robin.

"Okay, now we're going to lift the tip of the rod as high as we can, and then sling the line directly upstream, like this." The two flies went soaring overhead and slapped the water upstream from them. "Now keep your rod tip up and gather in the slack line as the flies float back down to us. You want to be able to feel a hit, but still have the drift look natural." The weighted fly bounced along the bottom of the river, the lighter fly floating above it in the water. Jess and Robin were watching the line intently when the downstream motion stopped and Robin jerked their hands back, almost sending Jess into the water.

"Sorry about that," Robin said, grinning at Jess who looked accusingly back at her. "It was only a rock. But you never know, so anytime the line stops, you have to set the hook."

"I just can't believe we're going to catch any fish this close to our feet," Jess said.

"You'd be surprised," Robin replied. "But as you get better at casting—if you can call slinging this line 'casting'—you'll be able to fish farther away from you. There's really no need to, though. The water is fast enough that you can stand pretty close to the fish without a problem."

Robin helped Jess with a couple more casts, and then stood back to let Jess try it herself. The tall woman had no problem getting the rod high enough to make the short cast easily. As the line came back downstream, Robin saw it stop and yelled, "NOW!" Jess jumped at Robin's exclamation and set the hook way too late. She turned and scowled at Robin for scaring her.

"Here, give me your line and I'll put a strike indicator on it," Robin said, digging a bright orange piece of foam out of her vest. She attached the adhesive-backed foam about six feet up

Jess's line and told her to try it again. This time Jess could easily see when the line stopped moving in the current and quickly set the hook. Her line took off across the river and Jess's face lit up.

"You've got one!" Robin yelled. "Way to go, Jess! Keep the tension on the line and just let it run for a few minutes."

The fish was about twelve inches, and Jess was able to bring it in quickly. Robin netted it for her and efficiently got the hook out while keeping the fish in the water.

"Do you want me to take your picture with it?" Robin asked.

"No, that thing's just a baby," Jess protested.

Robin laughed and released the lively fish back into the current. She looked up and saw Jess's blue eyes smiling back at her. She gave Jess a big smile in return, and said, "I think you're a natural. That's more fish than Capi catches in a month. And now she won't be able to say it's her equipment that's the problem."

"Yeah, well maybe I was an expert in a past life," Jess said with a wry grin.

"I suppose we can't rule out that possibility, can we?" Robin replied. She looked around for other good places to fish, and said, "Think you can handle it here by yourself for awhile? I'm going to head upstream a ways."

"Sure, just don't go too far in case I catch that lunker and need my picture taken," Jess joked.

"I'm sure I'll hear the scream," Robin replied as she waded up through the current.

The two women leapfrogged their way upstream for a couple of hours, then took a break before fishing their way back down to the cabin for lunch. They each caught a number of whitefish and a few rainbows, all around ten to fourteen inches.

After a leisurely lunch eaten along the bank of the river, Jess asked Robin if she'd like to go into the town of Sisters to look around. There were some nice shops along with the usual tourist traps, and Robin readily agreed. In truth, Jess needed to stop at the bakery and pick up a birthday cake she had ordered. She was able to get away from Robin for a few minutes, under the guise of needing to go look for a bathroom, and hid the cake in the trunk of the car. When they got back to the cabin, Robin suggested they fish for a little while before making a late dinner.

"Maybe there will be an evening hatch and we can try some dry fly fishing," she said hopefully.

"That sounds good, but you know, I'm a little tired from this morning. Why don't you go fish, and I'll just hang out on the deck and relax for a while. I can start dinner in about an hour and then everything will be ready when you get back."

"Are you sure you don't mind? I can help with dinner..."

"No, no, you go fish. It's your birthday, remember?" Jess said, smiling at Robin.

"Well, actually my birthday is tomorrow, but since you insist..."

"Think of it as your birthday weekend and you get to celebrate both days," Jess insisted.

Robin donned her fishing gear and headed down to the river, while Jess grabbed a book and headed for the recliner on the deck. The book was ignored for a good half hour, as Jess couldn't take her eyes off Robin fishing just downstream. Robin effortlessly cast across the river, the line snaking out behind her, then shooting forward to land feather-light on the water. The sight was mesmerizing and Jess could feel a distinct pull at the center of her being toward the young woman standing in the fading sunlight.

Jess finally shook herself out of her reverie, and went back into the cabin to start dinner.

Chapter 18

"Wow, it smells great in here," Robin exclaimed as she returned to the cabin from fishing. "What are you making?" she asked as she wandered over to the stove and poked her head around Jess's shoulder to see what she was stirring. Her eyes widened in surprise and she looked at Jess incredulously. "Are those the glazed onions that go with marinated pork tenderloin? How did you find out about that?"

Jess smiled at Robin's reaction. "An informant told me you had a fondness for one of the dinners in there," she said, nodding at the cookbook sitting next to the stove. "Said you'd first had it while at a fishing lodge on the Umpqua River, and the lodge had a cookbook, so since this is a fishing weekend, I thought it was only appropriate."

Robin's mouth still hung open in surprise, and Jess reached over and gave her a one-armed hug. "This is just the first of many birthday surprises I have for you," she said mischievously.

Robin returned the hug with both arms and buried her face in Jess's shoulder. "You're incredible, you know that?"

Jess laughed and said, "Hey, watch it," as Robin got between her and the stove. "You're going to end up with glazed onions on you if you're not careful."

Robin looked up at Jess. "I thought you said you couldn't cook."

"Well anybody can follow a recipe, can't they? I hope so, anyway, but maybe you should hold your praise till we taste it."

Robin finally released Jess so she could return her attention to the stove. "How about if I set the table and open a bottle of wine?"

"I'm afraid I already beat you to the wine," Jess said with a guilty look on her face. "You didn't expect me to cook without something to relieve the stress, did you? Besides, the recipe calls for a little wine, so I had to open it anyway."

"Hey, quit rationalizing it and pour me a glass," Robin said with mock indignation.

"Coming right up."

The two women finished the preparations and sat down to an elegant spread of marinated pork tenderloin over glazed onions, three-pepper stir-fry, salad, and bread. Robin dove in like she hadn't eaten in weeks, and Jess just looked on in amusement. *I can't believe how making her happy makes me so happy. I've never been so focused on someone else's feelings before.*

The women finished their dinner over casual conversation, and Jess cleared away the dinner dishes. "I hope you left room for dessert," she said.

"You're kidding. How could you have had time to make dessert?"

"Oh, I have my ways," Jess replied as she opened a cupboard. "Close your eyes for a minute." She looked over her shoulder to make sure Robin complied, and then brought the cake out onto the counter. She had already put the candles in, and she lit them quickly.

"Happy birthday to you, happy birthday to you...." Robin opened her eyes as Jess walked over with the cake, singing with perfect pitch in a rich alto voice. Robin couldn't decide whether to stare at the cake or the stunningly beautiful woman carrying it. Her eyes chose the latter, and she found herself drowning in pools of blue. Robin felt her emotions rise to the surface, and thought Jess could see into her soul if she only looked hard enough. The thought made her blink her eyes self-consciously and look back at the cake.

She took a deep breath to steady her emotions. "Well, at least you didn't try to put thirty candles on it. We wouldn't want to set off the smoke alarm," she joked in an effort to relieve her inner tension.

"Well, you'd better make a wish before they burn out," Jess warned.

Robin closed her eyes. *Oh God, do I dare wish for what I'm afraid I can't have? Why not—isn't that why they're called wishes?* She opened her eyes, took a deep breath, and blew out the candles.

Jess looked at her with a warm smile. "I hope it comes true," she said sincerely.

"Me too." *You don't know how much.*

Robin proceeded to cut a couple of pieces off the cake, and the two women took their dessert into the living room and settled onto the couch.

"How about if I make a fire?" Jess offered. "It's going to get a little cold tonight."

"That would be great. I'll go get some wood off the porch if you want to get it started."

Jess found some old newspapers and some kindling, and soon had a good start to the fire going. Robin came in with an armload of wood, and added a couple of smaller logs to the fire. In no time, they had a roaring blaze going in the fireplace, and they sat back on the couch, watching the flames.

"Hey, how about a nice shoulder massage to round out your birthday presents for today?" Jess offered.

"You're going to spoil me, you know that, right?"

"That's the whole point. Come on, sit down on the floor in front of me here and I'll see if I can't put you to sleep."

"Mmmmm, you don't have to ask twice," Robin said gratefully. She slid off the couch to the floor and scooted over between Jess's legs. Jess leaned forward and started kneaded the muscles between Robin's shoulder blades. As she worked her way over the tops of her shoulders, Robin sucked in a breath.

"Is that too hard?" Jess asked worriedly.

"No, it's good, I think I'm just sore there from all that casting today."

Jess focused her effort on Robin's right shoulder and arm for a few minutes, eliciting a long string of groans from the sore woman. As she worked her way back to the center of Robin's upper back, she found the straps from Robin's sports bra getting in the way. "You know, I could do this a little better if you'd take this off," she said, pulling on one of the shoulder straps under the T-shirt.

Robin quickly turned her head to see if Jess was serious, and just got a smile and raised eyebrow in return. She turned back around, and quickly pulled her T-shirt and bra over her head. As she started to put the T-shirt back on, Jess put her hand on Robin's arm and said, "Leave it off—it will be easier this way."

Robin slowly lowered the shirt back down, her arms still partially through the armholes, and brought the T-shirt to her chest, leaving her back and shoulders exposed. *Oh God, give me strength!* Robin thought, as Jess's hands touched her bare skin. Jess moved her hands across Robin's back in a soft caress, slowly increasing the pressure with each pass. She worked her way over the tops of the shoulders, her fingers dipping down into the hollow below the collarbone. Robin's head tilted back, eyes closed, and she leaned against Jess's legs, still holding the T-shirt across her breasts. Jess massaged the front of Robin's shoulders and arms that were exposed, watching the blissful expression on the young woman's face. Jess's fingers gently made their way up the sides of Robin's neck, into the hairline behind her ears, and forward to her temples. She made small circling motions around Robin's temples and across her forehead, watching the facial muscles relax under her fingers. She traced two fingers gently between her eyebrows, then across the strong cheekbones and down to the jaw line.

Jess found her own eyelids half closed as she looked at Robin's full lips that were slightly parted. *What would they feel like? Are they as soft as they look?* She resisted the temptation to run her fingers over them, and instead moved her hands back into Robin's tousled hair. She took a deep breath and continued the soft head massage until she noticed that Robin's breathing had changed and the young woman was fast asleep. *Mission accomplished.* Jess lightened her touch and ran her fingers softly through Robin's hair, enjoying the chance to just sit and appreciate how attractive the young woman was. *Oh Jess, what are you going to do? There's no denying what you're feeling anymore. There's only trying to figure out what to do about it.*

Chapter
19

Robin awoke to the feeling of something being draped over her upper body. She blinked open her eyes to see Jess wrapping the blanket from the back of the couch around her shoulders. She was still sitting on the floor, nestled between Jess's legs, and her head was resting against a thigh.

"Sorry...I didn't mean to wake you up, but I thought you'd want to be covered, and I knew I'd wake you if I tried to put your shirt back on," Jess said apologetically. Robin looked down at herself and saw that her hands had dropped to her lap, taking the T-shirt with them, and leaving her torso completely bare. She immediately felt the blood rush to her face, not because she was modest, but because the thought of being that close to Jess while naked from the waist up sent a rush of heat through her body. She gathered the blanket close in front of her and tried not to let Jess notice her discomfort.

"I can't believe I fell asleep on you again. I seem to be making a habit of that, aren't I?"

"Hey, it's not a problem," Jess said reassuringly. "It's a compliment to my massage technique."

"Believe me, your technique is flawless," Robin replied while rolling her head around and noticing how much better her neck and shoulder muscles felt. "If you ever lose your job as a coach, you can start a new career as a massage therapist."

"Oh, I'm not willing to put my hands on just anybody."

"Oh really?" Robin replied inquisitively. "Then I count

myself as very lucky that I get to be one of the chosen few."

"Well, it would be more correct to say the chosen one," Jess said with a lopsided grin. "I'm really not a very touchy person. I don't know what it is about you that brings it out in me."

"Probably the fact that I *am* a touchy person," Robin laughed. "I don't really give you much of a choice."

"Yeah, I guess that's true," Jess acknowledged.

Robin yawned, and blinked her eyes sleepily.

"Hey, what do you say we get you up off the floor and in to bed before you fall asleep again?" Jess said as she stood up and held her hand out to help the younger woman up.

Robin gripped the blanket in front of her with one hand and let Jess pull her up with her other one. To Robin's surprise, Jess didn't let go of her hand, but just turned toward the bedroom and pulled Robin along behind her. The two women quickly prepared for bed and crawled between the cold sheets, each gravitating toward the middle to try to share some of the other's body heat.

"Jess?"

"Hmmm?"

"This has been the best birthday I've had since I was eight and got to go to Disneyland."

"Wow, as good as Disneyland?" she teased. "But you know, it's not over yet, so maybe it will end up being better than Disneyland."

"I can't imagine what you can do to top this day," Robin replied sincerely. To herself, she thought, *except take me in your arms right now and make mad, passionate love to me. Oh, Robin, don't even go there.*

"We'll just have to see what tomorrow brings, won't we?" Jess said mischievously.

Robin rolled over on her side facing Jess. "And just what is that supposed to mean? Do you have some surprises planned?"

"I'll never tell."

"Oh yeah? I have ways of making you talk," Robin threatened as she pounced on Jess, straddling her waist and grabbing her wrists. Jess put up a token struggle, letting Robin pin her wrists to the bed next to her head, grinning back at her. As she felt Robin relax slightly, she quickly freed her wrists and arched her back, sending Robin flying off of her. Before Robin could react, their positions were reversed and the taller woman had Robin immobilized underneath her. She tickled Robin's ribs, causing the younger woman to convulse with laughter so hard that tears sprang to her eyes. Robin's arms flailed at Jess, trying to stop the torture, and Jess grabbed each of Robin's hands and forced them over her head. The action brought Jess's face mere inches above Robin's, and the two women looked deeply into each other's eyes, breathing hard from the playful exertion. Just when Robin thought sure that Jess was going to kiss her, the older woman closed her eyes with a sigh, and rolled off to the side.

I can't do this yet. I'm not ready for it. She put her forearm over her eyes and breathed deeply, trying to calm her racing heart.

Robin raised herself onto one elbow and gently put a hand on Jess's arm. "Hey, are you okay? What happened?" she asked softly.

"I'm fine. I just got a little out of breath there," Jess said lamely. *Please don't push it, Robin. I won't know what to say.*

"Do you want me to get you some water?" Robin asked worriedly.

"Yeah, that would be great," Jess said, relieved to have a minute to compose herself. By the time Robin came back from the kitchen with a glass of water, Jess was sitting up in the bed with a relaxed smile on her face. She took a long drink from the glass and said, "Thanks. I feel much better now." She lay back down on her pillow and closed her eyes. "Come on, we'd better get some sleep or we'll never get up in the morning."

"And that's a problem...why?" Robin quipped. Jess laughed and Robin settled back down into the bed, facing the taller woman who was lying on her back.

Jess reached over and put her hand on top of Robin's. "Goodnight. Sleep well."

"You too," Robin said as she took the hand and brought it closer to her body. Jess didn't pull away, and Robin smiled contentedly, quickly drifting off to sleep.

Jess let Robin sleep in the next morning, finally bringing her a cup of coffee in bed around nine. She sat down on the edge of the bed and watched as Robin slowly blinked her eyes open and focused on her surroundings.

"Happy birthday, sleepy head," Jess said with a smile, holding out the cup of coffee for Robin. The smaller woman sat up and leaned against the headboard, taking a long swallow of the coffee.

"Mmmmm, thanks. Can I wake up like this every day?"

Jess laughed and replied, "Not unless you win the lottery and pay me a lot of money to deliver your coffee in bed."

"Remind me to buy a megabucks ticket on the way home."

"Hey, that reminds me..." Jess reached into her pocket and took out an envelope and handed it to Robin. The young woman took it with a questioning look on her face.

"What's this?"

"Open it and you'll find out," Jess said, grinning.

The envelope said "Happy Birthday, Robin" on the outside, and the young woman put her finger under the flap to open it. Inside were two tickets between a folded piece of paper. She opened the paper and read, "I hope you'll invite me to go along—J." She looked closer at the two tickets and a big smile lit up her face.

"Two tickets to the Wisconsin women's game versus Washington in Seattle! Jess...how did you...you can go with me? You won't have a game?"

"It's still preseason, so everybody's schedule is different. And this will give me a chance to scout Washington anyway," she said, pleased at the happy reaction from Robin.

"This will be great. I haven't gotten to see my Alma mater play for over five years. I heard they were coming out here for a holiday tournament, but I hadn't gotten any of the details yet." She looked at the tickets again, then up at Jess, who smiled at her. She set her coffee down on the nightstand and crawled over to Jess. She put her arms around the taller woman's neck and hugged her tight.

"Thank you," she whispered into the ear next to her face. "Thank you for the tickets, thank you for dinner last night, thank you for this whole weekend. It's been the best birthday ever."

Jess shivered at the breath in her ear, and hugged Robin back, feeling the emotion of the woman in her arms. "You're welcome. I'm glad I could make you so happy," she said sincerely.

Tears ran down Robin's cheeks, and she pulled back, wiping them away with her sleeve. "Sorry, I didn't mean to get you wet," she said while smiling sheepishly.

"No problem. You can cry on me any time you want, as long as it's because you're happy," Jess said.

Robin sniffed, regaining her composure. "Guess what?"

"You're hungry."

Robin laughed and swatted Jess on the arm. "Am I that pre-dictable?"

"Yup. Come on, I've got breakfast all ready to go," she said, holding her hand out to Robin as she got up. They walked into the kitchen hand-in-hand, both women thinking about how close they had become, and how wonderful it felt.

Jess and Robin packed up to leave in the early afternoon, after spending a couple more hours fishing. As they stood at the car, they took one last look at the cabin and the river.

"It's going to be hard to go back to work tomorrow," Robin said wistfully.

"Yeah, I know what you mean. The inside of the weight room is going to feel pretty stifling after this."

Robin put her hand on Jess's shoulder and smiled up at her. "So when did you say your birthday was?"

"I don't recall saying." Jess grinned back. "But if you're going to bring me someplace like this, I might be willing to tell you."

"Hmmm, I think I'd rather surprise you," Robin replied mis-chievously. "Come on, let's get going so we get back in time for dinner."

"There you go again, thinking about food."

The two women had a quiet ride back home, each lost in their own thoughts about the weekend.

It feels like something fundamental has changed about our relationship, Robin thought, *but I still don't get the feeling she wants things to go to the next level. And I'm just not willing to make the first move that way. It's pretty clear that she's never been with a woman before, and I don't want to scare her away by pushing things too fast. But what about the hugs? And holding hands? And that near kiss? Maybe she's just too scared to take the next step and she's waiting for me. Oh God, why is this so hard?*

Across the car a similar scenario was playing out in the mind of the basketball coach.

Okay, so I admit that I'm attracted to her as more than a friend, Jess thought. *So how do I know for sure that she really feels the same way about me? Do I just ask her? What if I'm wrong—how embarrassing would that be? But how could I be wrong? I can feel something when she touches me—I can see something in her eyes when she looks at me. So what's stopping me? Am I afraid of rejection, or am I afraid of learning something about myself that I don't really want to know?*

Chapter
20

The next couple of weeks flew by, with Jess getting ready for practice to start and Robin getting into the thick of the term. In mid-October, Robin attended Midnight Madness, where they introduced the men's and women's teams, and had the first practice allowed by NCAA rules. It was mostly a fun night, with contests for the fans and scrimmages by the teams. Robin sat in the upper stands with Capi, watching Jess direct her players and have some fun with the men's coaches. She seemed relaxed and confident, and Robin could tell that Jess was in her element—she belonged on a basketball court, guiding and encouraging these young athletes.

Capi looked over at Robin and saw the proud smile on her face. "See something you like down there?"

Robin blushed. "You could say that. I don't get to see enough of it, though," she said ruefully.

"Ahh, college coaches have a busy life, I suppose," Capi said sympathetically. "Are things going well otherwise?"

"I guess so. We manage to see each other pretty often, for coffee or dinner or something like that, but I really miss the intimacy we had that weekend on the Metolius."

Capi raised her eyebrows. "Intimacy? I don't think you told me about that part," she admonished.

"No, not like *that*. I just mean that we spent every minute together, and we could hug, or hold hands, and it just felt right."

"Whoa. What do you mean, 'hug and hold hands?' I thought

you said things hadn't progressed to a physical level."

"They haven't...Not really. It's more like when good friends hug or hold hands, but yet I feel like there's more behind it than just good friends." She looked down at her hands in her lap. "But neither one of us has said anything, or done anything to really cross the line and see how the other one reacts. So we just keep going along in this state of limbo, and it's driving me crazy."

"So why don't you do something about it?" Capi asked gently. "Have some confidence in yourself—you would know if she didn't return your feelings. Just believe in it and go with what you feel."

Robin thought about what Capi said, and decided that she couldn't live with the regret if she lost this chance for love without ever even trying. Feeling like a weight had been lifted off her shoulders, she took a deep breath and said, "You're right, Capi. I will."

"Okay, two on one, full court," Jess called out. The players split into two groups, half at each baseline. "Bennie, start out on defense on that end. Chris and Heather, you ready? Go!" The two players sprinted down the court, passing the ball back and forth between them. As they neared the other basket, Bennie faked a move toward Chris, prompting her to pass the ball, and then quickly stepped in front of Heather and intercepted the pass.

"Nice job, Bennie," Jess yelled. "Chris, don't give up the ball until you're sure the defender has committed to you. Go again with Julie. Natalia, play defense on that end," she called out. Chris and Julie took off toward the other end of the court, and this time Chris kept the ball until Natalia was within a foot of her before passing it off to Julie.

"That's the way, Chris. Nice pass," Jess congratulated her. The drill continued, Bennie staying in the defensive position for a few rounds, and repeatedly getting steals. *God she's quick,* Jess thought. *If I can just get her to play up to her potential.*

Jess blew her whistle. "I want three on two now, half court, two groups, point guards in the middle." The players split into two groups, this time at mid-court. Two from each group positioned themselves in the key to play defense, and the others formed three lines at mid-court. On one end of the court, Bennie had the ball in the middle and dribbled toward the top of the key, while her wing players sprinted ahead on either side. The top defender picked her up at the free throw line and she took a step to the right, looking at her right wing player. The bottom defender went for the fake and Bennie threaded a no-look pass to the wing on the left for an easy lay-up.

"Great pass, Bennie. Just make sure you don't get too deep in the key before you pass it. If you get too close together, one defender can guard both of you." Bennie didn't acknowledge Jess's comments, just ran back to get in line for the next round. *She's just going to have to learn to take a little constructive criticism,* Jess sighed to herself.

After another ten minutes, Jess blew her whistle. "Take a break and get some water." As she walked over to the bench to check her notes, she noticed someone watching practice from the upper stands. She did a double take, and saw Robin give her a little wave and a smile. Her spirits immediately soared, and she gave Robin a big smile in return. *Amazing what she can do for my mood,* Jess thought.

"Okay, let's get back out there. I want to run some half-court offense against a player-to-player defense. Bennie, Chris, Natalia, Heather, and Julie on offense, the rest of you rotate yourselves in and out on defense." Bennie took the ball near mid-court and dribbled up court, her defender shadowing her. When she got to the top of the key, she made a quick behind the back dribble, lost her defender, and drove down the lane for a lay-up.

"Nice move, Bennie. But where's the help on defense, people? Everyone is responsible for more than just her own player. You have to see the ball and your player, and if the person with the ball is heading for the basket unguarded, there better be somebody stepping up, okay?" Heads nodded and the players set up to run it again. The next two times, Bennie again easily beat her defender, but someone else stepped in to pick her up. Using her quickness and excellent vision on the court, Bennie dropped the ball off to the player whose defender had come to help, and another easy lay-up resulted. *This isn't exactly giving us any practice in running our offense,* Jess thought. *And pretty soon, Bennie's head is going to be so big there won't be any room in the gym for the rest of us.*

Jess blew her whistle again. "Pam, step in there and guard

Bennie." The player who had been trying to guard Bennie hung her head and walked to the sidelines. Jess walked over to her and said softly, "Just keep working hard, Tara. You're doing fine. Bennie is a tough assignment." She gave the player a soft pat on the back, and walked back to mid-court. Pam, the assistant coach, took up the defensive position opposite Bennie. Pam was not only equal in quickness to Bennie, she had a few more years experience. Bennie, of course, took this as a personal challenge and dribbled towards the key, doing her best to lose Pam, but completely ignoring her other teammates. Pam anticipated Bennie's spin move, and deftly stole the ball from her.

After a repeat of this the next time through, Jess blew her whistle again. "Bennie, the last time I looked, our offense included four other players. If you have an open shot, or an open lane to the basket, I want you to take it. But if you don't, I want to see you run the offense, okay?"

Bennie just looked down at her shoes, her hands on her hips.

"I didn't hear you, Bennie," Jess said with a warning tone to her voice.

"Okay," Bennie mumbled without looking at Jess.

Why does she think it's her against the world? Jess asked herself. *And how am I going to make her a part of this team...no, the* leader *of this team?* Jess sighed and returned her attention to the court, watching the offense run smoothly. Bennie was distributing the ball to her teammates, all the while trying to maintain a bored look on her face. *Well, I'm not sure I'd call that coachable, but at least she can follow directions,* Jess thought resignedly.

The team practiced for another half hour, ending with a relay race that injected a little fun into what otherwise would have been wind sprints. The players then gathered at mid-court with the coaches for a team cheer. As they walked away, Jess saw Robin had come down from the bleachers and walked towards her. Just as their eyes met, Robin's attention was diverted.

"Robin. Nice to see you again," Pam said, flashing a bright smile at the economics professor and reaching out to shake her hand. "Did you come by to watch practice?"

Robin had to pull her hand away from Pam, who seemed reluctant to let go. "Yeah, I wanted to see how the team was coming along," she said with a polite smile back at Pam. Jess walked up next to Robin, and took a possessive stance close to Robin's shoulder. "That was some pretty amazing defense you displayed out there," Robin complimented the assistant coach.

Pam beamed back at Robin, not noticing the scowl on the head coach's face. "Well, these youngsters have to be convinced that they can still learn a thing or two from us, right, Coach?" Pam said, glancing over at Jess.

Jess immediately tried to hide her irritation and muster up a smile while agreeing with Pam.

Pam seemed oblivious to Jess's demeanor, and returned her attention to Robin. "Say, any chance you'd be interested in dinner? I'd really like to try out that restaurant you said your friends run."

Robin gave Pam an apologetic look and said, "I'd really like that, Pam, but I'm afraid I've got other plans tonight. Maybe we can do it another time?"

Pam looked disappointed but said, "Sure. I'll call you sometime." She gave her another big smile and walked off to talk to some players.

"Geez, why do you encourage her?" Jess asked with annoyance.

"What do you mean, encourage her?" Robin asked with a look of disbelief on her face. "I was just being polite." Robin looked closer at Jess, trying to read her facial expressions. *Could she be jealous?* Robin softened her look and tried to get the coach to relax a little.

"The truth is, I don't have any plans yet tonight, but I was hoping I could have dinner with you."

Jess looked guiltily away and took a deep breath. She looked back at Robin and said, "I'm sorry, I didn't mean to snap at you. And I would love to have dinner with you tonight." She gave Robin a warm smile and her eyes asked for forgiveness.

Robin smiled back, being the type who was always quick to forgive. "Where do you want to go for dinner?"

"Well, if you don't mind, how about if we pick up some Thai food and take it back to my place? I need to watch a scouting video of our first opponent so I can plan part of tomorrow's practice."

"You have practice on Saturday?"

"Hey, it's preseason. We have practice of some kind every day."

"Oh," Robin replied, thinking again what life with a coach would be like. "Well, why don't I go get the food while you finish up here, and then I'll meet you at your place in a half hour?"

"Sounds great. See you there," Jess said with a lingering look at Robin before turning away.

"Hey, isn't that Dr. Grant, the economics professor?" Chris whispered to Heather, nodding her head toward where Robin and Jess were talking.

"Yeah, it is. What do you think she's doing here?" Heather whispered back.

"Maybe somebody's flunking her class," Chris speculated.

"I don't know...they don't look like they're talking about someone flunking class. Have you ever seen Coach smile like that before?"

"No, I can't say I have. You don't think..." Chris looked disbelieving at Heather.

"Well, if it is, all I can say is she has great taste," Heather said with a cocky grin.

Chapter
21

Robin arrived at Jess's just five minutes after the coach got home. They quickly got out some plates and dug into the cartons of Thai food.

"Do you mind if we watch this video while we're eating?" Jess asked. "It will only take about a half hour."

"No, it will be interesting to see what kinds of things you scout," Robin replied.

Jess plugged in the video and the two women settled in on the couch, Jess balancing a clipboard on her knee. The top sheet had a number of diagrams of a basketball key area, and some spaces to write the defense, offense, starting line-up, and other key pieces of information.

"Hey, if you'd like to help, you could fill out this shot chart for me," Jess said, handing another sheet of paper to Robin. "Just write the number of the player shooting in the location she's shooting from, and circle it if she makes it."

"Okay," Robin replied, impressed at the amount of detail that was involved in game preparation. Jess used her sheet to diagram in-bounds plays and variations of the offense. The two women ate in silence, diligently recording the opponent's strategies between bites.

Jess turned the VCR off when they were finished and said, "Well, it looks like my predecessor managed to schedule somebody we could beat in the preseason. Let's just hope we play up to our potential."

They cleared the dinner dishes, returned to the living room, and settled once again on the couch.

"It was nice of you to come by practice today," Jess said.

"Hey I owed you one since you sat through an entire economics lecture."

Jess looked startled. "I didn't think you saw me there."

Robin smiled. "You think I don't know exactly what's going on in my classroom?" she teased. "I have to admit it made me a little nervous."

"Well, you could have fooled me. I thought you were great. I was ready to sign up for credit."

Robin blushed and said, "Thanks. You know, I don't know how you can do your job in front of all those fans. I've always thought about what it would be like if everyone had to do their job like that. Like there would be somebody yelling at me from the back of the lecture hall, 'Hey Grant, that's the stupidest example for elasticity I've ever seen!' And the next morning some newspaper reporter would be calling for my resignation, saying too many of my students got D's on the last test."

Jess laughed. "It's not really that bad. You just learn to tune all that stuff out. And if you're good at your job, you get to hear a lot more good things than bad. That's probably something you don't get to enjoy, either."

"Well, that's true. Nobody much cares if I manage to explain production theory so well that every student understands it," she said with a chuckle.

"Hey, I'm sure those students care," Jess said seriously. "I think you're a great teacher."

"Thanks. That means a lot to me," Robin said sincerely. She felt a little embarrassed and decided to change the subject.

"I thought your team looked really good today. That Bennie is a great point guard."

"Yeah, she is, but she's got a chip on her shoulder the size of Manhattan. I just have to figure out a way to bring her into the team concept."

"Well, I thought that having Pam guard her was a good move. A little reality check for her."

Jess's expression clouded at the mention of her assistant coach's name. "Yeah, well Pam could use a little reality check herself. I think she's used to getting her way with people most of the time."

"Well, she is a very attractive woman," Robin noted.

"Do you think so? She's a little too perfect for my taste."

"How can someone be too perfect? Isn't that an oxymoron?"

"You know what I mean. I like someone who's a little more real. They might have a few flaws, maybe a couple of insecurities, something that makes them human."

"Well, I'm sure that Pam has plenty of flaws, just like the rest of us. But I have to admit, I don't find her particularly appealing either. She comes on just a little too strong for my taste."

"So what do you find appealing?" Jess ventured, looking up shyly into Robin's eyes. "What are you looking for that you can't seem to find?"

"Who says I can't seem to find it?" Robin asked mischievously.

"Well, unless you've been hiding someone, you appear to be quite single," Jess replied with a smile.

Robin smiled back and reclined on the couch, laying her head next to Jess's thigh with her feet up on the armrest. "What am I looking for?" she repeated, staring at the ceiling deep in thought. "I'm looking for someone who sets my heart on fire. Who makes my mouth go dry. Who consumes my every waking thought. Who makes me laugh, and feel more alive than I've ever felt before."

Jess smiled down at Robin and gently ran her fingers through her hair. "You don't ask for too much, do you?"

Robin laughed softly, closing her eyes at Jess's gentle touch. "But I don't care if the person is short or tall, blond or brunette, black, white, or purple...I'm not that concerned about what they look like, or what they do for a living—I'm concerned with how they make me *feel*. So no, I don't think I do ask for too much," she said with a self-satisfied smile.

"Have you ever found someone who made you feel that way?" Jess asked softly.

Robin was silent for a moment. "I'm not sure," she finally replied. She sat up next to Jess, drawing her feet underneath her and facing the taller woman. "Look at me," she said gently, drawing Jess's eyes into her own. She reached over and took Jess's hands into hers. *I really hope I'm not making a mistake here.* "The only person who has ever made me feel even close to all those things...is you."

Jess felt like the room was closing in on her. Her mind was switching back and forth between feelings of elation and panic faster than she could keep track of them. She couldn't hold Robin's gaze, and looked down at their hands, still unable to respond.

"Hey, I'm sorry if I made you feel uncomfortable," Robin said quickly, looking away and feeling like she was going to die right then and there. "I shouldn't have assumed..."

"No! No, don't be sorry," Jess interrupted, finally getting a grip on her emotions and looking up. She gently put her fingers under Robin's chin, and turned her head to look at her. "I...I want you to feel that way. I feel that way about you, too. I'm just scared...I've never felt like this before."

"What are you afraid of, Jess?" Robin asked gently. "Are you afraid to be with a woman?"

"No...yes..." Jess closed her eyes and took a deep breath. "I don't know what I'm so afraid of. But I know that I can't deny what I feel for you anymore. And I don't want to." She opened her eyes and looked into Robin's. They were mere inches apart, and Robin's eyes closed as she leaned closer to Jess.

It was like a magnet, more powerful than anything Jess had ever experienced, and she found her own eyes closing as she turned her head and parted her lips. The touch of Robin's lips was soft and electrifying at the same time. The sensation quickly spread throughout her body, as if her lips held the switch to every nerve ending.

Robin drew away a bit and looked at Jess with hooded eyes. When she saw desire mirrored back from the pools of blue, she leaned forward again and drew Jess's bottom lip softly between her own, the tip of her tongue lightly reaching out.

Jess moaned softly at the contact, and parted her lips further, seeking out Robin's tongue. Robin shifted on the couch, never breaking contact with Jess's mouth, and settled herself in Jess's lap while wrapping her arms around her neck. Her fingers wound their way into Jess's hair, pulling the taller woman more forcefully to her. Jess's hands were everywhere on Robin's back, reaching underneath her shirt and caressing warm, soft skin. Robin groaned at the contact and deepened the kiss, pressing herself so close to Jess that they were almost one. Desperately needing air, Robin slowly withdrew her mouth from Jess's, leaving small kisses on her upper and lower lip as she pulled away.

The two women looked at each other in silence, both breathing heavily.

"Are you sure this is what you want?" Robin asked softly.

"Do you need to ask?" Jess replied, leaning forward and giving Robin another small kiss.

Robin chuckled and returned the kiss, drawing away after a moment. "I know this is hard for you, and I don't want to push you to do anything you're not ready for," she said sincerely.

"Why don't you let me worry about that," Jess said, smiling gently. "Right now I don't feel like worrying about anything. I just feel like kissing you." She put her hand behind Robin's head and drew her closer, kissing her forehead, then her temple, then drawing a breath next to Robin's ear and gently taking the soft lobe between her lips. Robin shuddered at the sensation and leaned her head back, exposing her neck. Jess didn't miss the invitation, and placed gentle kisses up and down the soft skin. Robin's audible response was arousing a passion in Jess that she had never experienced before, and with a soft moan of her own, she unbuttoned Robin's shirt, kissing the soft skin as each inch was uncovered. Her lips traced the breast above the laced top edge of Robin's bra, her fingers softly touching the delicate material. *God, how can anything be this sensual?* Jess thought. She laid her cheek against Robin's chest and breathed deeply, inhaling the intoxicating scent of the younger woman.

Robin was breathing hard, trying desperately to keep her emotions under control and let Jess set the pace. She was more than a little surprised by Jess's assertiveness, and was barely able to keep herself from responding with total abandon. She put her hand over Jess's cheek and held her head tight against her chest, hoping that Jess could hear her heart pounding in response.

Jess pulled back from Robin and without a moment's hesitation, rose up off the couch, lifting the smaller woman in her arms. Robin looked startled, but then put her arms around Jess and planted soft, wet kisses on her neck and ear while they moved quickly toward the bedroom. Jess laid the smaller woman gently on the bed, following her down and laying softly on top of her. Her lips found Robin's again, and she could feel the young woman's hips moving up toward hers as their passion increased.

Jess broke away and looked at Robin in the dim light coming from the hallway. "I want you so much, but I don't know if I know how..."

"Shhhh," Robin hushed her, placing her fingers over Jess's lips. "You couldn't possibly disappoint me." But knowing that Jess was probably anxious about being with a woman for the first time, Robin gently pushed on her chest and turned her over, reversing their positions. "All we have to do is communicate," Robin said softly, and placed a kiss on Jess's cheek. "Tell me if I do anything you don't like." She took her finger and ran it lightly down Jess's neck and around a breast, eliciting a soft moan. She smiled and said, "I think I'll be able to tell if I do something you like." She tugged on Jess's shirt, and the taller woman lifted her shoulders so Robin could strip off the shirt and the sports bra underneath. Robin sat back, her gaze lingering over Jess's full breasts. "You are so beautiful," she whispered.

Jess pulled Robin back down into a searing kiss, her bare breasts touching Robin's lace covered ones. She pulled Robin's unbuttoned shirt off her shoulders, and reached around to unclasp her bra. Pulling the lace garment out from between them, Robin gasped as skin touched skin for the first time.

Robin slowly kissed her way down Jess's neck, her body sliding down so that her thigh was between the taller woman's legs. She could feel Jess's hips move, and Robin could no longer hold back. She slid her hand up to the side of a breast and covered it with her mouth. Jess drew in a breath sharply and arched her back in response, her hips picking up their rhythm against Robin's thigh. Robin lavished attention on Jess's breasts, delighting in the moans and ragged breathing from the woman beneath her. She shifted slightly to the side and moved her hand over Jess's bare stomach, gently raking her fingernails over the soft skin. She dipped her fingers under the waistband of Jess's pants, feeling the muscles clench in response. She lifted herself off the taller woman, rose up to her knees, and put both hands on the top of Jess's pants, pausing to look in her eyes before giving them a gentle tug.

"You too," Jess replied while sitting up and reaching for Robin's belt.

"I thought you'd never ask." Robin smiled back.

Jess rose up to her knees, mirroring Robin's position, and slowly tilted her head to meet the shorter woman's lips. Her hands moved to release Robin's belt and she gently lowered the zipper. She put the palms of her hands on Robin's stomach and slowly moved them under the top band of the exposed underwear. She hooked her thumbs over the top of the pants as she moved her hands lower, and slid them over Robin's hips, taking the underwear along with them. Her hands kept contact with Robin's skin as they moved down to her knees, causing a shiver to run down the younger woman's legs.

God, I can't believe she's never done this before. She's driving me crazy. Robin lifted one knee, and then the other, as Jess slid the pants the rest of the way off. Robin quickly reciprocated the act with Jess's pants, then put her arms around the taller woman's neck and drew their bodies together, feeling the heat radiating from Jess's skin. She kissed the full lips that were now parted with desire, and pushed Jess back onto the bed, entwining her legs with the longer ones beneath her.

Robin murmured sweet, reassuring words to Jess as she kissed her way back down to her full breasts. Her hand caressed Jess's stomach, occasionally making a foray down her hip to her thigh. She pushed gently on the inside of Jess's thigh, making room for her own hips as she continued to kiss her way lower on the tall woman's body. As her lips found the soft inside of a well-muscled thigh, Jess moaned loudly.

Jess grasped the blanket under her hands, trying to control her breathing. *Oh my God, if she kisses me there I'm gonna die.* Jess could feel Robin's warm breath against her wetness, and was about to hyperventilate from anticipation. *But if she doesn't kiss me there soon, I'm gonna die anyway.* Robin didn't disappoint her, and Jess gasped as she felt Robin's tongue caress her intimately.

Jess's hips bucked in response, and Robin realized that Jess wasn't going to last very long. She reached up and took one of Jess's hands while the taller woman quickly spiraled out of control. Robin held on as Jess's hips jerked beneath her, and she could feel the muscles clench as Jess cried out loudly. Robin stilled her motion, and squeezed Jess's hand tightly. She slowly released her pressure, kissing Jess softly as the aftershocks shook her body. Robin turned her head and kissed the inside of Jess's thighs, not wanting to leave this most intimate of places.

"You're so beautiful," Robin murmured between kisses.

Jess finally opened her eyes as she felt her breathing return to normal and her heart rate slow down. She reached down for Robin, saying, "C'mere. I want to see you...I need to see you."

Robin gave one last kiss to the inside of Jess's leg and slid back up her body. She looked into the desire-darkened eyes and lowered her lips to Jess's. When she pulled back, Jess had a look of wonder on her face.

"I can't believe what you just did to me. That was incredible."

Robin smiled shyly. "I think you were more than ready."

"Yeah, I guess so. Thirty-four years is a long time to wait."

Robin was struck by the significance of what they had just done, and tears sprang to her eyes.

"Hey, what's wrong? Why are you crying?" Jess asked worriedly.

"I just can't believe I'm the one who gets to experience this with you for the first time. You don't know how much that means to me," Robin said sincerely.

"No, you don't know how much it means to me," Jess said softly. She hugged Robin to her tightly. "I'm so glad I waited for you. It would never have felt this wonderful with anyone else."

They laid together like that for a while, Jess rubbing Robin's back soothingly while the smaller woman was draped over her. Robin started kissed the bare skin that was next to her lips, and Jess felt desire stir in her again. Robin's hips started moving in a slow rhythm, and Jess raised her knee slightly, bringing her strong thigh between Robin's legs. She could feel the wetness on her skin, and it inflamed her senses. She took Robin's head in her hands and brought their mouths together. Robin breathed hard as she kissed Jess passionately. She grabbed one of Jess's hands and said, "Please, Jess. I want you now." She guided the hand between their bodies, lifting slightly to allow room. Jess didn't need to be told twice. She quickly matched Robin's rhythm, their perspiration-slicked bodies sliding together easily. Jess watched as Robin threw her head back, eyes closed, crying out in ecstasy, and thought she had never seen anything more beautiful in her life.

Robin collapsed on top of Jess, and kissed the shoulder where her head was. Jess continued to rub Robin's back, listening as the smaller woman's breathing returned to normal. She felt Robin shiver as the cool air moved over her sweat-covered body, and Jess pulled the blanket over the two of them. She sighed contentedly and closed her eyes, not ready to think about how much her life had just changed. Their exhausted bodies adjusted to a more comfortable position, and sleep quickly claimed them.

Chapter
22

Jess awoke early the next morning, the unfamiliar sensation of bare skin touching bare skin alerting her senses that something was different. She looked over at the small woman sleeping peacefully beside her, blond hair tousled and an incredibly peaceful look on her face. Jess couldn't help but smile, even while her mind raced with the implications of what they had done last night.

Feeling nervous and self-conscious, Jess quietly slipped out of bed and headed for the bathroom, picking up her clothes that were discarded around the floor on the way. She stepped into a hot shower and looked down at her body—the same body she'd looked at every day that had now experienced something she'd never known before. *It was incredible. I had no idea what it would feel like to make love with someone I care about...I never would have believed that making love with a* woman *could be like that. A woman...*Jess swallowed hard. Did this mean she was gay? *No, of course not. I've never been attracted to other women. It's just Robin. Maybe I'm bisexual.* Jess sighed deeply, wondering why she had to be *anything. Because I know other people are going to label me. Oh God, what if someone else finds out about this?* Panicky feelings overtook Jess, and she switched the temperature to cold before turning the shower off and stepping out.

She quickly dried off, put on clean clothes, and headed for the kitchen. As she finished getting the coffee started, she heard

Robin in the bathroom. Nervousness set in again, Jess wondering how things would be different between them this morning.

Robin shuffled into the kitchen sleepily, her eyes barely open. "What are you doing up so early?" she asked while trying to stifle a yawn.

Jess's heart rate picked up at the sight of the adorable woman, and she couldn't help the smile that crossed her lips. "I see you found a T-shirt to wear," Jess noted, nodding at the extra large shirt that hung mid-way down her thighs.

"Yeah, I hope you don't mind," Robin said apologetically, walking over to Jess. She put her arm around Jess's waist and leaned her head into her shoulder. "Mmmmm, you smell good," she said while closing her eyes and inhaling deeply.

Jess stiffened for a moment at the contact, but then her arms found their way around Robin's shoulders without thought, and she rested her cheek on the top of Robin's head. She took a deep breath and tried to think clearly. *Am I supposed to say something about last night? Do we have to talk about it?* Jess's emotions kept circling from ecstatic, to scared, to confused, and she felt an urgent need to be alone to sort things out.

She pulled back from Robin and said, "Why don't you go back to sleep for awhile. I have to go into the office early today anyway, so I'll just grab something to eat on the way. You can stay here as long as you want," she said with a small smile.

Robin looked questioningly at Jess, wondering if the coach was having second thoughts about what had happened. Seeing the small smile, she decided not to press the issue, and instead agreed that more sleep was exactly what she needed.

"What time is your practice today?"

"From eleven to one," Jess replied.

Robin desperately wanted to ask if they could see each other later, but decided that she had to leave it up to Jess.

"Okay. I'll probably go into work today for awhile, too, so maybe I'll see you around campus."

Jess sighed with relief as she turned around to grab a travel mug for her coffee. She filled the mug and turned back around to find Robin looking at her with a questioning look on her face.

"Would it be too much to ask for a kiss goodbye?" Robin asked hopefully.

Jess felt her heart flip, and couldn't deny the powerful urge to feel Robin's lips again. The kiss was sweet and chaste, but the feelings it invoked in the coach made her weak in the knees. She pulled back, looked one more time into the green depths of Robin's eyes, and quickly made her way out of the apartment.

Robin stood there, leaning against the counter, trying to make sense of what was happening. *No "thanks for the great evening." No "last night was wonderful." No "I can't wait to see you again."* Robin sighed deeply and made her way back to the bed, feeling a strange mix of hope and desperation. She hugged Jess's pillow to her face, inhaling the scent that lingered there. Eventually, she fell back into a fitful sleep, afraid that she would wake up and find that last night had just been a dream.

Robin made her way into work around ten, and spent some time preparing her lectures for the next week. Around twelve-thirty, she wandered over to the arena, hoping to catch the end of Jess's practice. She quietly took a seat in the upper stands, and watched as the team worked on defending some of the play sets they had seen on tape last night. Her eyes were repeatedly drawn back to the tall coach, and she couldn't help but think about what they had shared last night, and how different things had felt that morning.

I've just got to give her some time to get used to it. Of course she's going to feel a little uncomfortable the next day. My God, she's thirty-four years old and she's just discovering that something as basic as her sexuality has changed. I've just got to be patient with her and give her all the time she needs to adjust to this. After all, what's my hurry? It's not like I'm going anywhere.

Jess was watching Heather race down court after stealing the ball on an inbounds play, when her eye was drawn to the upper stands. She saw Robin sitting there, and quickly looked away. The blood rose to her cheeks and she hoped no one was watching her. She felt like her body was betraying her and sending some kind of broadcast signal to the world that she had, in fact, slept with the woman in the stands last night.

I can't believe she came to watch practice again today—on a Saturday. *Somebody's going to notice. And what are the players going to think?*

Jess managed to compose herself and get through the rest of

practice. As the team huddle broke up, she saw Robin making her way across the gym. She felt the heat rise to her cheeks again, and willed herself to retain control over her emotions. She gave Robin a weak smile as the young woman neared.

"Hey," Robin said softly, trying to read the different emotions flickering across the coach's eyes.

"Hey yourself," Jess replied. "I didn't expect to see you here. Did you finish your work?"

"Oh, there's nothing that I really had to get done today. I was just trying to get ahead a little bit. How was practice?"

"Pretty good. It's hard to get them going on a Saturday morning, but once they woke up, it went fine." Jess looked over Robin's shoulder toward the water station and saw Chris and Heather with their heads together, whispering and smiling while casting glances at her and Robin. Jess immediately backed farther away from Robin. "Hey, I really need to meet with my coaches for a few minutes before they get away. Maybe I'll see you a little later, okay?"

Robin tried to hide her disappointment as she said, "Sure, no problem. See you around." She quickly turned and walked out of the gym, feeling the weight of depression settle over her.

Jess put her head down and walked toward her office, afraid to meet her players' eyes for fear that her secrets would be revealed.

Robin waited in vain on Saturday for Jess to call, finally going to bed early in the hopes of losing consciousness and not having to think about how miserable she was. *I know she felt something last night. There's no way I was imagining that. Did I do something to scare her away? Did I push too hard?* She thought about the previous night and knew that Jess was not only a willing partner, she was often the aggressor. *She can't deny what she's feeling, can she? What is she so afraid of that she would give up something like this?* Robin tossed in her bed, no nearer to sleep. *Maybe I'm just being paranoid. Just because she didn't call today doesn't mean she never wants to see me again, right?* But Robin couldn't shake the depression that had blanketed her, and she found herself awake late into the night.

The next morning, Robin decided that she would rather

know that Jess didn't want to see her than to spend another day wondering if something was wrong. After waiting until a respectable hour, Robin called Jess at home.

"Hello?"

"Hey Jess, it's Robin," she said in the most cheerful voice she could muster.

"Oh hi, how are you doing?" Jess replied somewhat hesitantly.

"Good...well, actually that's a lie. I've been better. I was wondering if we could get together for dinner tonight."

Jess paused, not knowing what to say. *I want to see her, but I'm not ready to commit to this relationship and I don't want to lead her on and then have to tell her no.*

"Jess?"

"Yeah...yeah, that would be fine. Do you want to go out somewhere?" *I can't invite her over here again. I'd just be thinking about last night.*

"Why don't you come over here and I'll cook something?" Robin offered.

That should be safe. At least I can leave if I need to. "Okay, is six o'clock alright?"

"That would be...good. See you then." Robin hung up the phone, trying to figure out what Jess was feeling. In spite of her apprehension, Robin's spirits were lifted, and she quickly made a list of what she would need for dinner, and then headed out to the grocery store.

Jess hung up and immediately started worrying about the upcoming evening.

When Jess arrived, Robin gave her a quick hug and a kiss on the cheek, but didn't push for anything more intimate. They fell into relaxed conversation as Jess helped with last minute preparations.

From the moment Jess had walked in the door, she couldn't resist the strong attraction she felt for Robin. The young woman made her laugh and relax, and was undeniably attractive as her green eyes sparkled with emotion.

Dinner was fabulous, and Robin was starting to think that maybe she had conjured up problems that weren't even there.

Afterwards, they went into the living room and sat close together on the couch.

Jess put her arm around Robin and pulled her close, kissing the smaller woman's temple while breathing the scent of her hair. Robin felt a tidal wave of relief wash over her. She wrapped both arms around Jess's neck and pulled the taller woman to her for a searing kiss. Remembering her promise to let Jess set the pace, Robin pulled back and caught her breath. They sat together for a while, content to hold each other and silently communicate their feelings.

Eventually, Jess cleared her throat and said, "I really can't stay too late tonight. I have a budget meeting with the Athletic Director first thing in the morning, and I still have to go over a few more numbers tonight."

"That's okay," Robin replied quickly, not wanting to pressure Jess into staying longer than she wanted to. "I'm just glad we got to spend a little time together. I missed you over the last twenty-four hours," she said with a shy smile.

Jess smiled back at her and leaned down for a soft kiss. Before she lost herself again in the young woman's lips, Jess pulled herself away and stood up, holding her hand out to help Robin up.

"Dinner was really great tonight. Thanks for inviting me," Jess said as she walked toward the door, still holding Robin's hand.

A little formal tonight, aren't we? Robin thought. *You'd think it was our first date. But then again, I guess in some ways it is.*

"You're always welcome here, Jess. I mean that," Robin said sincerely. She reached up on her toes to give Jess a kiss goodnight, and could feel her heart race again at the contact. *Oh, if you only knew what you did to me.*

Little did Robin know that she had the same effect on the taller woman, and Jess left Robin's feeling more confused than ever.

Jess arrived early to work the next morning, and found LaTeisha already in the office.

"Hey, you're here early," Jess remarked.

"Yeah, I wanted to get those travel budgets done so you'd have them for your meeting with Butch."

"Thanks, that'll be really helpful."

"Hey did you hear about the Northern New Mexico coach?"

"No, what happened?" Jess asked.

"They found out she was gay and then the rumors started flying that she had an affair with one of her players. They canned her ass. Can you believe that?"

Jess blanched noticeably and looked away from LaTeisha, hoping the assistant coach wouldn't notice her reaction.

"Man, I can't believe how hard the world of athletics is on gays," LaTeisha said sympathetically. "But if she was messing with one of her players, she was asking for trouble."

Jess mumbled some reply and walked blindly into her office. *What am I gonna do? That could be me. Oh God, am I jeopardizing my whole career by this?* She sat stunned at her desk until LaTeisha knocked much later, bringing her the travel budgets.

"Hey, you okay? You look a little pale?" LaTeisha said with concern.

"Yeah, yeah I'm fine. Just a little tired, I think," Jess replied. "Well, I'd better get over to Butch's office before I'm late." She shook her head to try to regain her composure, and walked out of the office.

Jess called Robin later that morning and asked to meet her for lunch at the Union. They found an out-of-the-way table, and Robin knew that something was wrong by the look on Jess's face and the fact that she wouldn't meet her eyes. Soon after they sat down, Jess looked up and stated bluntly, "I can't do this, Robin."

"What...what do you mean?" Robin asked lamely, desperately hoping that Jess was referring to her ability to eat fast food for lunch, and not what she knew Jess was really talking about.

"You and I...I can't be with you. Not like that. Not in a relationship." Jess paused and took a deep breath. "I'm saying this badly...I'm sorry. What I mean is that I want us to be friends, like we were, but we can't be...lovers." Her voice lowered so she was barely whispering the last word. She looked up and saw the anguished look on Robin's face and felt her own heart breaking, but she had to go through with this. "It just isn't who I am...who I want to be."

"You mean you don't want to be gay," Robin clarified for her.

"No. I mean, right. Don't you see, I can't be gay and have my career, too," Jess pleaded.

"Why do you have to be anything? Why can't you just choose who you want to love, and forget about the labels?"

"Because it's not up to me. Somebody else is going to find out about this and it's not going to matter what I call it because every opposing coach and athletic director is going to say that I'm gay," Jess hissed.

"I can't believe you're the only coach in America that has slept with a woman and still has a job," Robin said sarcastically.

Jess looked up at the ceiling in exasperation. "I have no idea how other people do this—I just know that I can't."

Robin looked pleadingly at Jess. "So you would just give up everything that we feel for each other? Give up what we had two nights ago? Jess, that was the most incredible night of my life!" Robin felt like she was begging now, but she didn't know what else to do.

"Life is always about choices," Jess said coldly. "There are lots of times when things we care about conflict, and we have to choose between them. I've lived without love for thirty-four years, and I'm not willing to jeopardize my career now because I suddenly can't live without it."

Robin was stunned at Jess's cold analysis of what they had shared. "So being a basketball coach is more important to you than being true to your heart."

"Being a basketball coach is what I am," Jess said emphatically. "I wouldn't be true to myself if I tried to be something else. I'd be miserable if I had to give it up, so what good would it do to be happy with my love life if I'm miserable with the rest of my life?" Jess paused but Robin just looked at her in disbelief so she continued. "If I have to give something up, it's going to be this thing that's brand new in my life...that I don't even understand yet...that might not even work out...not the thing that is at the core of who I am."

"But why can't you have both, Jess? We can be discreet...no one has to know what you do in your bedroom."

"*I* would know," Jess replied, looking Robin in the eye. "I'd always be worried about someone finding out. I'd always be looking over my shoulder. That's no way to live." Her look softened and she added, "And that certainly wouldn't be fair to you. You deserve to be with someone who would cherish their relationship with you, not be ashamed of it."

Robin felt her world crumbling around her. *I will* not *cry. I will get through these next few minutes and I will find a way to walk out of here.* Robin looked down at her hands on the table. "I don't know what else I can say. You know how I feel about you, and I'd do almost anything to make you change your mind. But if this is the way you truly feel, then I guess I just have to accept it. I can't force you to feel something you don't." She paused and looked up into Jess's eyes, her own eyes glistening with unshed tears. "But I could have sworn you felt something for me two nights ago."

Now it was Jess who couldn't maintain eye contact. "That's not it. You know I felt something—I felt *more* than something. It was incredible, I told you that and I meant it. But it doesn't change the fact that I have to make a choice." She sighed and looked up at Robin. "Something happened to me many years ago, something that showed me first-hand the consequences of being gay in the world of athletics. Those consequences ruined a young person's life. And I can't take the chance of having that happen again."

Jess's words were said with such finality that Robin knew there was no point in arguing any more. At least not today. *I need to get out of here before this escalates into something we both regret later.*

She looked directly into Jess's blue eyes and said, "I'm sorry you feel that way Jess. Sorrier than you'll ever know." And with that, Robin got up and left the table.

Jess put her face in her hands and closed her eyes. She couldn't watch the young woman walk away. After she was sure Robin was gone, she got up and headed back to her office.

Chapter
23

Robin sat in her office, staring at her computer screen without really seeing, when she heard a knock on her door. "Come in," she said dully, without turning her head from the computer.

"Professor Grant?"

Robin swiveled slowly around in her chair and looked up at her visitor.

"Heather?" She was surprised to see the basketball player in her office. Although Heather was in her introductory economics class, she always sat to the back of the room and never asked questions. "What can I do for you?"

Heather looked nervously down at her feet, which were shuffling back and forth on the floor. "Well...um...I'm worried about the test on Thursday. I, like, didn't do too well on my last homework, and I don't think I really understand those indifference curves, you know?"

Robin smiled sympathetically at the young woman and told her to sit down. "What exactly don't you understand?"

"Well, like, I don't get how you know where to draw them on the graph, when they represent those 'utils,' you know, which are just some made-up idea, and not, like, real."

Robin chuckled and got out a piece of graph paper and slowly worked through a few examples for Heather. Finally, it looked like the light went on, and Heather's eyes widened a little.

"So, you mean, like if I prefer oranges a lot more than

apples, then my indifference curve would be steep, like this?" she said as she drew the example on the paper.

"Exactly," Robin said emphatically, while giving Heather a congratulatory smile.

"Cool, I think I get it," Heather replied, looking relieved. "Can I keep this?" she asked while picking up the piece of paper with the examples on it.

"Sure. And don't be afraid to come back, or send me an e-mail, if you have questions later, okay?"

"Okay, thanks," Heather said as she got up and started toward the door. She stopped midway and turned back around. "Professor Grant?"

"Yeah?" Robin looked up.

"I think it's really cool that you come by to watch us practice. Will you go to the games, too?"

Robin felt her heart clutch as she thought about watching Jess at practice, but she quickly recovered and replied, "I'd like to. Do you think you're going to have a good season?"

Heather's face took on a look of excitement as she replied, "Oh yeah, I think we're gonna kick butt this year. Coach Peters is really working us hard, but we're learning a lot of new stuff, too. I've never seen everybody so excited about practice before."

Robin paled a little as she tried not to think about what had happened just hours earlier. "That's great, Heather," she said weakly. "Now if I can just get you that excited about your economics homework..."

Heather looked a little guilty, but Robin smiled at her and wished her luck in the coming season, and the player cheerfully walked out of the office.

Robin couldn't help feeling left out—she had so looked forward to sharing the experience of the upcoming season with Jess, and now she would be on the outside looking in...if she could even bring herself to do that.

Robin somehow went through the motions of the next few days, teaching her classes and grading homework, but could do little else. Her e-mail and voice-mail went unanswered and her fitness was suffering as well. Finally on Thursday she managed to drag herself to the gym at noon for a workout. Stopping at the

Union to pick up lunch on her way back to her office, she ran into Capi.

"Hi stranger. Where have you been? Didn't you get my messages?" Capi asked with a smile.

"Hey. Sorry about that. I guess I haven't been keeping up with my messages. Things just seem to be so busy lately..." Robin did her best to smile and act like everything was okay, but Capi was much too wise to let it slip by.

"Say, do you have time to join me for lunch?" the administrator asked.

"I was just going to get something to go. I'm pretty busy at work..." Robin started to make an excuse to avoid having to tell Capi about her and Jess.

"Come on, just a quick bite to eat? I haven't talked to you in ages," Capi pleaded.

Robin couldn't resist her good friend's request and gave Capi a weak smile and an affirmative nod.

Capi smiled broadly in return, trying to lift Robin's spirits. "Great. What do you want to have—pizza, Chinese, or burgers?"

"Chinese, but you can get whatever you want and I'll meet you back at a table over by the window." Robin pointed to an area well away from the table where Jess had broken her heart three days earlier.

"Chinese is fine with me," Capi replied while the two women got in the Panda Express line.

Once at the table, Capi looked gently into Robin's eyes and said, "So tell me what's wrong."

"Who says anything's wrong?" Robin said defensively.

"Is it personal or professional?"

Robin gave Capi an exasperated look. "Why can't I hide anything from you?"

"Because I'm your best friend and I love you," Capi said seriously. "So give. What are you so upset about that you can't even return your best friend's messages?"

Robin sighed heavily. "I feel like I'm always running to you when things go bad, and it doesn't seem fair that you always have to listen to my problems."

"Hey, that's what friends are for. You'd do the same thing for me, right?"

"Of course, but you never ask me to," Robin protested. "It just seems so one-sided."

"Well, when I fall for someone besides you, I'll be sure to bring all my problems your way, okay?" Capi said with a wry grin on her face. Robin blushed and smiled back. "So let's hear it. I'm assuming it's not professional, so tell me what's gone wrong between you and one basketball coach."

Robin couldn't help it—the tears immediately sprang to her eyes and she looked down at her lap.

"Hey," Capi said gently, putting her hand on Robin's arm. "It can't be that bad, can it?"

"It's worse," Robin replied dismally. She proceeded to tell Capi the details of the past week, going from elation to depression.

"I've never felt as wonderful as I did last Friday, and I've never felt as horrible as I have since Monday. How can one woman make me feel both of those in such a short time?"

"Well, it's obvious that she has many skills," Capi said sarcastically. "Unfortunately, it doesn't seem that honesty and integrity are two of her better traits."

As bad as Robin felt about what Jess had done to her, she couldn't keep herself from defending the coach. "That's not fair, Capi. She was perfectly honest with me. She just changed her mind...or maybe she had to experience being with a woman to know that it wasn't right for her."

"Oh bullshit. Being with a woman is exactly what's right for her, she's just too chicken, or too stupid to admit it. I've seen the way she looks at you—there's no question she feels more for you than just friendship."

"But she's not denying how she feels," Robin protested. "She's just saying that her career is more important than her feelings...than me." The tears fell from her eyes as she looked down at her lap.

Capi could feel Robin's pain in her own heart. "Awww, Robin, please don't cry. She's not worth it—not if she can't see how lucky she is to have someone like you that cares about her. Just give it some time. You'll get over this, you'll see."

"I don't want to get over it," Robin said vehemently. "I want her to come back to me."

"But how can you take the risk of having this just happen again in the future? She might come back when she realizes how she really feels about you, but then at the first sign of trouble with her career, she'll be gone again. You don't deserve to be jerked around like that."

"But what am I supposed to do, give up?" Robin pleaded. "Lose this chance to be with her? Isn't it worth staying and fighting for? I really believe that I can get through to her if I can just spend more time with her." Robin looked away wistfully. "If you could have felt what I did that night we were together, you'd know that she feels something for me, and that's not going to go away just because she wants it to."

Capi looked earnestly at Robin, gauging the depth of the young woman's feelings. "Well, maybe it would be a good thing to put a little distance between you for awhile. Give you a chance to get yourself together, and give her a chance to see how much she's lost."

"You're probably right," Robin sighed. "But I don't know how long I can do that. I can barely get through my day now, and it's only been three days since I've seen her."

"Hey, you just give me a call whenever you're having a bad time, okay? Anytime, day or night. I'm there for you," Capi said sincerely.

"Thanks—I really mean that. And even though I owe you for all the times you've listened to my problems, I really hope that I never have to return the favor," Robin said with a little smile.

"Me too," Capi replied, reaching over and patting Robin's hand.

Chapter
24

It had been two weeks since Robin left Jess sitting in the Union, and it wasn't getting any easier for the young economics professor. Robin told Capi that she wasn't even sure she wanted to go to the women's basketball games in the upcoming season.

"But Robin, you love basketball. You always get season's tickets," Capi admonished her. "If you stay away just because of your feelings for Jess, you'll only be punishing yourself."

"I know that, Capi, but I'm just not sure I can stand watching her for that long. Maybe if we get tickets behind the visitor's bench I won't really have to look at her while I'm watching the game."

"Oh great, then we have to watch people like the Southern Washington and USC coach throw temper tantrums instead. You're asking a lot."

"Well, let's just go to the first preseason game and see how it goes. Then we can buy season's tickets after that if we want to."

"I guess that would be okay," Capi acquiesced. "It's not like the games sell out or anything. I'm sure there will still be plenty of good seats available."

"Thanks Capi. And if I end up not going anymore, I'm sure there are lots of other women on campus that would love to go to the games with you."

"Yeah right. Name two."

"Debbie and Laura," Robin immediately replied.

Capi laughed. Debbie and Laura were the two people that seemed to be perpetually single and available in Comstock, and whenever anyone complained about the lack of women in such a small town, their names always came up.

"Well, for my sake, let's just hope that you decide to keep going," Capi said with a grin. "When is the first preseason game, anyway?"

"Next Monday. I think they're playing some traveling team from Australia. I don't know how those international teams do it. They're on the road for a month straight, getting beat up by all these Division I schools. I can't believe they get that big of a paycheck out of it."

"Well, at least the Australians will be able to understand the referees. I always love it when the Lithuanian National Team comes and the coaches are yelling at the refs in their language and the refs are yelling back in English, and nobody knows what the other one is saying," Capi laughed.

"The Australians might be able to understand the refs, but I'm not sure the refs will be able to understand the Australians," Robin joked. "Anyway, it should be a good game. I've heard that the Australians have some pretty good teams."

"I just hope we're as good as we were last year," Capi replied. "We kind of lost a recruiting year with the untimely departure of our previous coach. I guess it will be a good test of Jess's coaching abilities."

Regardless of the rift that had developed between them, Robin wanted to see Jess succeed. She still had strong feelings for the coach, and it would hurt her to see anything bad happen to Jess. *I just wish I could be sharing the ups and downs of the season with her...be there to support her, and celebrate with her. Oh damn, why am I thinking about this again?*

"How about if I pick up the tickets for the first game?" Capi offered. "You can buy the beer afterward."

"Sounds like a deal. I'll call you on Monday to arrange a time to meet."

Jess was becoming increasingly frustrated with each day that she went without seeing Robin. Little things started to annoy her, and her temper was on a very short fuse. It seemed like her team was getting worse instead of better, and practices had become tense for everyone involved.

"Deny! Deny! Meg, you've got to deny that pass!" Jess yelled at her wing player. "If you're too lazy to do it, I'll get someone else in there who will. Now set it up and run it again." The team hung their heads and slowly shuffled into their positions to start the defensive drill again. After receiving the ball on the wing, Heather threaded a neat pass into the post player for an easy turn-around.

"Natalia! You've gotta beat her to that spot! If you let her get that kind of position on you in the key, she's gonna kick your ass. Go again, and I want to see some defense this time or you'll all be running suicides."

Jess dropped her forehead into her hand and took a deep breath. *What is the matter with me? I sound just like all those coaches I hate.* She looked up and blew her whistle. "Take five and then shoot twenty-five free throws. Meet at the bench when you're done."

Jess took the time to settle herself, and to think about how she'd been acting for the past couple of weeks. *I just haven't been having any fun. Life hasn't been fun. How can one person— or should I say the absence of one person—make such a difference?* Jess shook her head and made her way over to the bench to talk to her team.

Looking around at the sweaty and tired faces, Jess saw a mixture of indifference and resentment—not what she was used to seeing from one of her teams. "Look, I know I've been pretty hard on you for the last few weeks. Probably too hard," she acknowledged. "I just want to let you know that I appreciate how hard you've been working, getting in shape, and learning a new system. And I'm making a promise to you right now, that it's going to get better, for all of us." Jess saw a few of the players look up hopefully at her words. "Next Monday we're going to get a chance to beat up on somebody besides ourselves...a team that won't know all our plays...that won't be cheating on defense because they know exactly what we're going to do. I know it's hard to practice against ourselves every day, but you're all doing a great job of challenging each other. And it's going to pay off in the long run, believe me." Jess paused and walked up and down in front of the bench, looking at each player, some whom refused to meet her eyes.

"So let's make this the beginning of a new season for us, okay? From now on, we think positively, we work hard, we help each other, and we get better. As a team, okay?" The players' expressions had become filled with positive anticipation, and heads were nodding. Jess smiled broadly at them, and said, "Okay, one more time through the match-up zone defense. Let's go!"

The players ran onto the court with renewed energy and the sound level in the gym increased dramatically. The players were talking on defense, calling out the cutters, and encouraging each other. Jess smiled and felt immeasurably better about herself. She realized that smiling wasn't something that she had been doing very much of lately and vowed to change that.

After practice, Jess went back to her office and reflected on the past couple of weeks and her estrangement from Robin. *God, I miss her so much. All the good times we had together. How happy I was just to see her smile. How easy it was to talk to her. I want to call her so badly, but I feel like I need to wait until she's ready to see me again—as a friend. If she* ever *wants to see me again.* Jess sat in her office staring dejectedly at the wall until she could muster up the energy to go home. She hated to go home now...home to the place where she had experienced the most incredible night of her life, only to throw it all away two days later. She had taken to sleeping on the couch in the den, unable to bear spending the night in her bed—the bed she had shared with Robin that one glorious time.

"Starting for the Australian National Team, at forward, number 22, Jane Lattimore. At center, number 43...."

"Wow, they've got some size," Robin noted while looking over the game program. "I wonder how we'll match up."

"Well, as long as Natalia stays out of foul trouble, we should be okay," Capi replied.

The two women were sitting four rows behind the visitor's bench, among a group of rowdy Australian fans.

"I think every Australian in Oregon must be here tonight," Robin mused.

"Yeah, and I think they've all been to the bar ahead of time," Capi laughed, looking at a group of young men who had the Australian flag painted across their bare chests.

"...and the head coach for the NOU Bobcats, in her first season, let's welcome Jess Peters!" The crowd got to its feet and gave Jess a rousing welcome, which the coach acknowledged with a smile and a short wave. Robin watched and felt her heart ache at the sight of the tall, good-looking woman. Capi, knowing how hard this was for Robin, reached over and patted her on the leg, giving her a little smile for encouragement.

The Australians came out ready to play, and quickly got an eight point lead on NOU. Jess's players were clearly nervous and tight, missing easy shots and making turnovers. Jess called a thirty second time-out with only five minutes gone in the game. The players sprinted over to the sidelines and huddled around the coach, panting heavily, many with dazed looks on their faces.

"Okay, everybody take a few deep breaths and relax," Jess told them calmly. She waited a moment until she could see a few of the expressions change. "Now we're not trying to do anything out there tonight that we haven't done a hundred times in practice. We've seen the defense they're playing; we've practiced against their offense. I want you to forget about the crowd, forget about the fact that this is our first game, and think about how hard you've worked in practice over the last month, and how successful you've been. Those same things that worked in practice are going to work now, you just have to concentrate on executing." She could see a renewed sense of purpose in the players' eyes as she looked around the group. "Okay, let's get out there and play with confidence." She raised her hand up in front of her and the players around her joined their hands to hers. "Team," Jess said, and the players repeated it loudly, broke the huddle, and sprinted back on the court with a new energy.

On the next possession, Bennie beat her player at the top of the key and drove into the lane. As the post player came to help on defense, she flipped a pass around her to an awaiting Natalia for an easy lay-up.

As the Australians brought the ball back up court, Heather anticipated a long pass down the sideline and intercepted it in front of the bench. Jess jumped to her feet, yelling encouragement as Heather raced back the other way for the lay-up.

On the next Australian possession, NOU played good defense for twenty-eight seconds, forcing a long shot to try to beat the thirty second shot clock. The shot missed badly and

Natalia rebounded it and made the quick outlet pass to Bennie. As they ran the controlled fast break up the court, Bennie stopped at the free throw line, not seeing either of the wings free on the side. Just as she was about to throw the ball back out to set up the offense, Natalia yelled "trailer!" as she sprinted past Bennie on the right, Natalia's defender a good five feet behind her. Bennie lobbed the pass into Natalia as she neared the basket, and NOU had quickly gotten within two points.

Jess was going crazy on the sidelines, cheering her team on, and especially encouraging Natalia for hustling on the fast break. The tall German couldn't help but give a little smile toward the bench, knowing that she never would have been in on a fast break in previous years.

"Wow, I wonder what she said to them during that last time-out," Capi said in awe.

"I have the feeling that motivating her players is something Jess is very good at," Robin replied, thinking about the powerful presence of the tall coach. Robin was secretly delighting in seeing the enthusiasm that Jess displayed on the bench. *She can seem so reserved and in control—I'm sure the players love it when they see her like this. And the fans kind of like it, too*, she thought wistfully.

NOU continued to play solid basketball for the remainder of the half, and left the court up by six at the break. A couple of the Australian players had gotten into foul trouble, obviously not being used to the tighter foul calls of the American referees. Midway through the second half, the Australian's big, talented post player had fouled out on what their coach thought was obviously a bad call.

"You were so far away, that call was long distance!" the coach yelled at the ref. "Get your bloody ass into position before you make a call like that!" Which, of course, drew the coach a technical foul and two more free throws for NOU. Jess's team finished the game ahead by fifteen, and all the players got to see some playing time. Smiling faces were in abundance as the Bobcat players and coaches shook the opponents' hands and gathered in the center of the court for a final cheer and wave of thanks to the crowd before heading to the locker room.

Jess went over to the press table and put on some headphones for a post-game interview with the local radio station. As she was adjusting her microphone, she looked up and saw Robin looking back at her from behind the visitor's bench. Her throat tightened and she managed a weak smile before diverting her eyes and trying to concentrate on what the play-by-play man was asking her. Robin also offered a little smile, knowing that whatever else happened between them, she would always be happy for Jess and her team's success. *Maybe that's a sign of true love*, Robin thought wistfully, *that I care more about her happiness than my own.*

Robin and Capi slowly made their way out through the crowd, and headed for the parking lot.

"Do you want to go get a drink?" Capi asked.

"You know, I'm kind of tired," Robin replied. "Would you mind if I took a rain check on it?"

"Of course not. As long as you promise you aren't going to go home and mope around," Capi admonished.

Robin smiled back at her good friend. "You know, I really don't feel as bad as I thought I would. I loved watching the team, and I was really happy for Jess—to see all of her hard work pay off. I can't just change my feelings for her, but I think I realized that there's a real, solid friendship that we had between us, too. Maybe there is a way we could get that back, even if we can't be more than that."

Capi looked skeptically over at Robin. "I don't know. I don't want you setting yourself up to get hurt again. Do you really think you could be happy with just being friends?"

Robin sighed. "I guess I don't know either. All I know is that I'm miserable with the way things are now, and I feel like I have to try something."

"Well, just be careful, okay? Don't go giving your heart away to somebody who's going to break it."

Robin reached over and gave Capi a hug. "Always looking out for me, aren't you?"

"Oh, I don't know...I suppose some would say I'm just looking out for *me*," Capi laughed, returning the hug.

Chapter
25

Jess unlocked her apartment door and stepped into the empty, quiet space. She went to the kitchen, got a beer out of the refrigerator, and returned to the living room to watch the game tape. After a few minutes of staring at the TV screen and not writing a single thing on her notepad, she realized her mind wasn't on the tape. Instead she was thinking about seeing Robin for the first time in over two weeks, how good she looked, and how good it made Jess feel when the young woman smiled at her.

I just had my first win at NOU, my first real test at this level, and all I can think about is that I wish she was here to share it with me. When did my happiness get so tied up with someone else? I've never let anyone interfere with my career before, and now it seems like success in my career isn't enough. Jess closed her eyes and sighed, thinking about the irony of it all.

Across town, Robin was pacing back and forth in her living room, gripping her own bottle of Sierra Nevada pale ale. *Just call her. You know you want to—what's stopping you? I mean, what's the worst thing that could happen?* Inspired by that age-old argument, Robin went over and picked up the phone.

"Hello?"

"Hey, it's me," Robin said softly. "Great game tonight."

"Hey," Jess replied with surprise in her voice. "Thanks." She paused awkwardly. "It was good to see you there—thanks for coming to watch."

"Sure...I enjoyed it."

When Jess didn't immediately reply, Robin felt an urgent need to fill in the silence. "I like how up-tempo you played. I've never seen Natalia run that much in the three years she's been here."

Jess laughed. "Yeah, well we had a little talk when I first got here about what I expected out of a post player, and she's done a really good job of getting herself in shape."

"I thought they all looked like they were in good shape," Robin complimented. "You've really done a nice job with them, Jess."

"Thanks," the coach replied softly. "That means a lot to me."

Another awkward silence ensued and Robin plunged ahead with the conversation. "And Bennie looked great tonight. It looks like you've gotten her to play within the offense."

"Yeah, she's really improving in that area. And she's done everything I've asked of her, even if it is a little reluctantly sometimes," Jess chuckled.

There was another long pause as both women thought about what subjects they could safely discuss.

"You know, Bennie's been coming to class regularly, too," Robin offered.

"On time?" Jess queried.

"Well, for the most part," the young professor said with a laugh. "And she's doing well on her homework and exams. It's obvious that she's a lot smarter than she likes anyone to know."

"That's pretty clear on the basketball court, too. I've never had a point guard that adjusted so quickly to changes in the opponent's defense. It's like having another coach out there on the court. Of course, I'll never tell her that because her ego is already out of control," Jess chuckled.

Robin laughed, too, and both women started to relax a little.

"So why aren't you out with Capi tonight?" Jess asked, having noticed them at the game together.

"Well, it is a school night," Robin noted, "and I just didn't feel much like going out and being social." She cleared her throat. "But...umm... the truth is, I wanted to come home and call you...I...I've missed talking to you, Jess," she finished softly.

Jess drew in a deep breath that could clearly be heard over

the phone line. "I've missed you, too. But I didn't know if you still wanted to be friends, after...well, everything."

"I wasn't sure myself," Robin sighed in return. "But tonight I realized that I was missing your friendship more than anything else. So I guess I'm willing to try just being friends...that is, if you still want that."

"Yes! Yes, I still want that," Jess said, trying not to sound too desperate.

A comfortable silence ensued, while both women felt the tension and frustration of the past few weeks drain out of them.

"Jess?" Robin said softly.

"Hmmm?"

"Can I come over there for a little while? Just to talk," she added quickly.

"Sure," the coach replied with surprise. "But don't you have to get up early tomorrow for class?"

"I'll only stay for a few minutes, I promise."

"Hey, it's okay with me, I just don't want you to be tired in the morning," Jess said with concern.

"I'll be right there," Robin said, the excitement evident in her voice.

Jess hung up the phone, feeling better than she had in weeks. She quickly picked up her papers, which were strewn across the coffee table, and went to the kitchen to put two days worth of dishes in the dishwasher. She was just wiping down the counters when she heard the doorbell ring. Taking a deep breath to calm herself, she walked to the door and opened it up to the woman she had been missing. She had an overwhelming desire to wrap the smaller woman up in her arms, but she resisted, not knowing how it would be received.

Robin stood there, smiling a little uncertainly, until Jess finally stepped aside, saying, "Sorry, come on in." She turned and Robin followed her into the living room, both women taking opposite ends of the couch. Jess jumped up and offered Robin a beer, which she graciously accepted, and then they sat there for a moment, sipping their drinks and trying to get comfortable with being in each other's presence again.

"So how does it feel..."

"So what did you think..."

They both started at the same time, and then laughed as they each waited politely for the other one to continue.

"You first," Robin said with a smile.

"I was just wondering what you thought about the other team tonight," Jess replied. "They had a real nice inside game, and their point guard could really light it up from the 3-point line."

"Yeah, but they didn't adjust very well to how the officials were calling the game," Robin noted. "I think you could learn a thing or two from their coach about how to bait the refs, though."

"I really can't see myself saying 'Get your head out of your bum' to a referee anytime soon," Jess laughed.

"No, I suppose that's not your style, is it?" Robin smiled over at Jess, grateful beyond words that they could sit there and talk like friends again.

Jess looked back for a few moments, and finally said, "What?"

"I was just thinking about how much I missed this."

"Me, too." Jess looked down at her hands, and decided that they really needed to clear up some things if they were going to make this work. "You know, I'm really sorry that I can't be what you wanted."

Robin felt the tears immediately spring to her eyes and she looked away quickly.

"But I don't want to lose you as a friend," Jess continued. "I don't think I could stand it. I've been miserable these past few weeks."

Robin looked back at Jess, the tears rimming her eyes, and said, "I have been, too. I'd rather be just friends than not have you in my life. I can't promise that my feelings for you will ever change, but they don't have to get in the way of us being friends."

Jess looked guiltily at Robin's tear-streaked face, and wanted to try to make her understand why she couldn't be the lover Robin wanted.

"I know you don't understand why I feel the way I do," Jess began. "But I had something happen to me in Montana that changed my life...forever, so it seems. I didn't want anyone here to know about it, but I think I need to tell you so you can maybe understand why I would give up what we could have had."

"Jess you don't owe me any explanations..."

"Yes I do," Jess interrupted. "I want to tell you

this...please," she said softer.

Robin realized that this was something very important to Jess, and she simply nodded her head in encouragement.

"My first job after college was coaching basketball at a high school in Kalispell. I was barely older than the players, and we got along great. Looking back, I see now that I should have kept more distance between me and them, but at the time, I think I was just flattered that they liked me." Jess paused and took a sip from her beer. "There was one girl, Julie, that was the classic coach's pet. She was always the first one to practice and the last to leave. She'd help me close up the gym, and sometimes I'd give her a ride home after practice. I knew she kind of had a crush on me, but I thought it was just one of those harmless things that all kids go through."

Jess was facing Robin, but looking at the back of the couch as she told her story, a faraway look in her eyes. "Well, towards the end of my first season, Julie's mom comes to see me in my office. She accuses me of being a pervert and seducing her daughter. I was shocked. I told her that simply wasn't true, and asked her what Julie had told her. She said that Julie told her she was in love with me. Her mother said that Julie wouldn't feel that way if I hadn't seduced her. I was incredulous—all I could think about was that it wasn't true, and that my very first job was going to end in some sordid scandal that I wasn't even responsible for."

Jess pushed her hair away from her face in a gesture of frustration. Robin waited patiently for her to go on.

"Well, I knew we had to clear this up, so I told her to bring Julie into the office the next day and we could figure out what the truth was." Jess shook her head resignedly. "I didn't even think about how hard that would be for Julie. All I could think about was my own innocence. Well, they came in the next day, and I asked Julie if I had ever done anything to make her think that I was attracted to her. The poor kid was so scared she could hardly speak, but she shook her head no. I told her I wasn't gay, and that she was risking my reputation by saying things that would make people think I was gay." Jess sighed. "I was so worried about people thinking I was gay, I made it seem like the plague or something.

"Well, the mom was embarrassed, and she took it out on Julie, too. I was so relieved to have the truth out that I didn't even think to defend her. I mean, all she had done was tell her mother how she felt. She never lied about me; it was just her mother that had jumped to conclusions."

Jess shifted on the couch, her eyes finally coming into focus on Robin's. "Julie didn't come back to practice," she said sadly.

Robin couldn't help it—she reached over and took Jess's hands, rubbing her thumbs over the back of them soothingly. "Jess, you were young then. You were just protecting yourself. No one can blame you for that." She looked sympathetically at the coach. "We all had crushes on our teachers in high school. I'm sure Julie got over it."

"Julie's dead. She committed suicide the day after I met with her and her mother."

Robin's mouth dropped open as she stared at Jess. She recovered from her shock after a few seconds, and realized how devastated Jess must have felt—must still feel.

"Oh, Jess, I'm so sorry," Robin said sincerely. "But you've got to know that it wasn't your fault."

"I believed that at the time. I had no reason back then to think I *was* gay. I could honestly say that there was no reason for this girl to be attracted to me. But now...don't you see...now if it turns out that I am gay, maybe was gay, I might have been giving her some mixed signals that I didn't even know about."

And I thought she didn't want to be with me because she was worried about losing her job, Robin thought ruefully. She was starting to understand Jess's fear of her own sexuality, and she was overwhelmed by a feeling of fierce protectiveness for the coach.

"Jess, listen to me. It doesn't matter if you are, or were gay. What matters is that you never acted inappropriately toward her. It's no different than having a man coach a girl's team. Some of the players are going to fall in love with the guy, but that doesn't make him responsible for their feelings." She softened her tone and said, "It's awful that someone wasn't there to support Julie. That our society is so sick that it would condemn a young girl for her feelings. But you can't blame yourself for not being the one to support her. She needed someone to validate her feelings, and her sexuality, and you were in no position to do that. You were young and struggling with your own issues."

"But my actions made it seem like I was condemning that lifestyle—that I was telling her there was something wrong with her. I was as much to blame as the rest of society for making her feel worthless. Here I was the object of her affection, and I became her adversary," Jess said hopelessly.

Robin moved over on the couch and gently wrapped her arms around Jess, cradling her head in her shoulder. She could feel the older woman crying, and she rubbed her back soothingly, whispering words of sympathy and compassion. When Jess's breathing finally returned to normal, Robin pulled away, but didn't move back to the other end of the couch.

"Thank you for telling me," Robin said while looking into Jess's eyes. "Maybe you needed to talk about it. Maybe this will give you a chance to see another perspective, and to see that you don't have to be so hard on yourself after all these years. Have you ever talked to anyone else about it?"

"The Athletic Director at the high school talked to me about it, and we both agreed that it would be better if I just left after the season, and no one else would have to know what happened. He wrote me a nice letter of recommendation, and I went off to be an assistant college coach. I've never talked to anyone else about it, because I just wanted to put it all behind me."

"Well, I'm no psychologist, but it doesn't seem like something that you just 'get over' without a little help," Robin said gently. "Maybe you've been letting something that happened over ten years ago keep you from finding happiness in your personal life."

"I don't know...I'm not sure I could talk to anyone else about it," Jess said uncertainly.

"Yeah, I know how hard that can be," Robin replied sympathetically. "But you can talk to me about it anytime you want, okay? I'm no professional, but I can listen and maybe I can help you find a way to forgive yourself."

Jess looked up at Robin and saw nothing but compassion and acceptance in her green eyes. She had been afraid that if she told Robin about what had happened, that the young woman would be ashamed of the way Jess had acted, just like the coach had been ashamed of herself. But that's not what had happened, and now Jess could see just a glimmer of hope that maybe she, too, could learn to accept her actions of so long ago. Not justify them, or make excuses, but just accept that it was the best she could do at the time.

They sat together on the couch in companionable silence for

a long time, shoulders leaning against each other and just thinking about all they had talked about. Robin was reluctant to push
Jess to talk anymore that night, knowing that the experience had
already taken a lot out of the coach.

*She should be celebrating her first big win tonight, and
instead she's reliving a nightmare from the past,* Robin thought
sadly. *But maybe this can be the start of a healing process for
her. I just hope that I can be what she needs to help her through
this.*

Jess shifted on the couch and looked over at Robin. "I'm
sorry to keep you up so late," she said with a faint smile. "I
really didn't intend to spill out my life story to you tonight."

"Hey, I'm fine," Robin responded with a reassuring look.
"How about you? Think you'll be able to sleep tonight?"

"I haven't been sleeping very well lately anyway, so I'm
sure it won't be any worse."

"I could stay with you if you want—just as a friend, I promise," Robin offered.

Jess laughed lightly. "It's not like I think you're going to
force yourself on me, you know." She added more seriously, "I
miss the closeness we had, and I don't think we have to lose that
if we're just friends. At least I hope not."

"Me, too," Robin said, although she couldn't help but be
worried about how much closeness she could stand and not go
crazy with desire. "Come on, I'll give you a nice backrub and see
if I can't put you to sleep," Robin offered while standing and
holding her hand out to help Jess up. The coach didn't hesitate,
and the two women made their way to the bedroom.

After finding a T-shirt and shorts for Robin to wear, the two
women slipped into the bed that had not been slept in for weeks.
Suddenly it seemed like a very welcoming place to Jess, and she
quickly relaxed under the gentle massage of Robin's fingers. In
no time, she was fast asleep. Robin gazed at Jess's face for a few
moments before snuggling up close to the tall woman's side and
drifting off herself. It was the best night's sleep either of them
had in a long time.

Chapter 26

Jess awoke the next morning with a feeling that something good had happened to her, but not yet conscious enough to remember what it was. As she blinked her eyes open, she saw Robin's tousled blond head poking out from under the covers and it brought a smile to her face. *God, I hope we can find a way to work this out. I'm miserable without her yet after one evening together, I feel like I'm alive again.*

Jess crawled out of bed, showered, dressed, and made coffee before deciding that she needed to wake Robin so that the professor wouldn't be late for her first class. Jess couldn't help but laugh at Robin's groggy appearance in her kitchen as she stumbled in for her first cup of coffee.

"I thought you said you were going to be fine without much sleep last night," Jess teased while leaning against the counter, sipping her own coffee.

"I lied," Robin growled, casting an evil glance at the grinning coach.

Jess raised her eyebrow with a smirk. "A little cranky when you don't get enough sleep, hmm?"

"You haven't seen the beginning of cranky yet," Robin warned. "Wait till it gets to be three p.m. and some student is telling me he didn't get his homework done. There will be no sympathy from me today."

"Well, I'll make sure I'm nowhere near you at the end of the day. Unless you manage to take a nap sometime beforehand."

"I think that would be a wise strategy on your part," Robin replied.

"But if you think you'll still be civil at lunch time, we could meet after your workout and grab a bite to eat," Jess said hopefully.

"Sure, that sounds great. I could meet you at the rec center at one. Right now, I'd better get my butt in gear and get ready for work. Can I wear these clothes home and get them back to you later?"

"No problem." Jess smiled.

Robin gulped down the rest of her coffee, gathered up her other clothes, and set off for home, relieved that they seemed to have been able to pick up their friendship where they had left off. Well, sort of where they had left off, if you didn't count that one night they spent together...

Jess and Robin fell into a comfortable routine—meeting for coffee, having lunch occasionally, and spending many evenings together. They avoided talking about their one night together and their different aspirations for their relationship, preferring to focus on less emotional topics that allowed them to reestablish their friendship. They both had more things they wanted to say, but neither could seem to find the right time or place to bring them up.

Jess's team won its first three games against relatively easy preseason opponents, but the schedule was about to get tougher. And then the conference season would start in January, and things would be anything but easy then.

In mid-November, the weekend of the Wisconsin-Washington game arrived, and Robin looked forward to cashing in on her birthday present from Jess. Since the coach had a limited amount of time available, they decided to drive up to Seattle after Saturday morning's practice, stay overnight, and return in time for Sunday afternoon's practice. It would be a quick trip, but it would also be the most uninterrupted time Robin would have with Jess since basketball practice had started.

Robin arrived at the NOU arena about a half hour before Saturday practice was over and took her usual seat in the upper stands. While the team worked on a shooting drill, Jess was on the sidelines talking to a Hispanic woman holding a notepad who was considerably shorter than the coach. She laughed at something Jess said, revealing a dazzling smile that was set off by her dark curly hair and dark eyes. Robin couldn't help but feel just a little twinge of jealousy as she watched Jess smile back at the attractive woman. The woman wrote a few things on her notepad, and then headed out of the arena.

Robin's eyes were drawn back to the court, where Jess was setting up a rebounding drill for the team. As one of the assistant coaches shot the ball, the defensive team worked on boxing out, while the offensive team worked on their moves to get around the defenders. As often happens with these types of drills, the play got very physical as everyone scrambled to grab the rebound. Some of the players found this fun, laughing with their opponent as they grabbed and held each other, but others lost their temper at what they considered cheating by the other player. The thing about these types of drills, though, is that there is no such thing as cheating—however the players can get the job done, they do it. Of course, the players wouldn't always get away with this in a game, but Jess thought it was good practice to have a few drills where no fouls would be called. There were plenty of times in a game where someone blatantly grabbed a player's jersey or held a player's arm down without getting a foul called, and Jess wanted her players to be able to handle those situations without always looking to the officials to make a call. In practice, however, she had to make sure that things didn't get out of control, resulting in a fight or, worse, an injury.

After a few rounds of the drill, Jess blew her whistle.

"Bennie, Tara has gotten around you the last three times," the coach called out. "Just because you're a point guard away from the basket, doesn't mean you don't have to box out. I want to see your butt in her stomach for at least five seconds after this next shot," Jess challenged. The other players were smiling and trying not to laugh at the coach's choice of words, knowing that they could easily be next to get singled out.

As the next shot went up, Bennie turned toward the basket and stuck her rear into Tara's midsection so hard that the smaller player went sliding five feet backwards on her butt. Bennie looked over at Jess with a big grin on her face and the coach couldn't help but smile back, saying under her breath, "Well, I guess that works, too." Louder, she said, "Try to be just a little more subtle next time, okay?"

The team finished up practice with some sprints and free throws, as Robin made her way down to the sidelines. Jess gave her a big smile as she walked over and the professor couldn't help but grin back.

"They're looking better all the time," Robin commented.

"Do you think so? I see them every day, so sometimes it's hard to notice the improvements," Jess replied.

"Oh yeah, I can see a lot of improvement from that first game, and it shows in the confidence they seem to have on the court."

"Well, they're going to need it next weekend in the Thanksgiving tournament. Washington and Colorado State are going to be a far cry from what we've seen so far."

"At least you'll get a chance to scout Washington tonight—that should help," Robin said encouragingly.

"Yeah, I hope you don't mind that I'll be taking notes during the game instead of cheering on your beloved Badgers."

"Hey, I'll be enough of a fan for the both of us," Robin replied as she held open her jacket to reveal a red sweatshirt with white "WISCONSIN" emblazoned across the chest.

Jess grimaced. "Well, just don't wear that around here, because it really clashes with the orange."

"Oh, I have another complete wardrobe of NOU clothes," Robin warned, "although they lean more toward the black than the orange."

Just then, the small, dark woman that Jess had been talking to earlier appeared at her elbow, saying, "Sorry to interrupt Coach, but I need the probable starters for the next game to give to the newspaper."

Jess turned a charming smile on the woman, eliciting another twinge of jealousy in Robin, and replied, "LaTeisha's got that information for you—she probably just forgot to give it to you earlier today."

"Okay, no problem," the woman said, as she turned and sped off toward the assistant coach. Jess watched the small bundle of energy, and shook her head with a smile.

Robin couldn't stand it any longer—she had to ask. "Who is she?"

Jess turned back to Robin with an open look on her face. "Her? That's Carmen Ricardo, our sports information director, and let me tell you, she's *very* good at her job."

Robin didn't like the way "*very* good at her job" rolled off Jess's tongue. "She does seem to have lots of energy," Robin replied dryly.

Jess just looked at Robin questioningly, wondering what the tone in Robin's voice meant, but then shook it off and changed the subject.

"Well, we'd better get moving if we're going to get there in time for the game. Let me run and get my bag from the office, then I'll meet you back here."

"Okay," Robin replied, while Jess headed off the court. Robin went to sit on a chair along the sideline, watching a few players getting in some extra shooting practice. After a few minutes, Heather approached the economics professor.

"Hi, Dr. Grant."

"Oh, hi, Heather. How's it going? You looked great in practice today."

"Thanks," she replied shyly. "Things are going really well."

"You did a really nice job on that rebounding drill—you were about the only one who was consistently boxing out your opponent."

Heather looked a little surprised that Robin would notice something so subtle, and asked, "Do you play basketball?"

"Well, I try to play a few times a week, but I don't get to play as much as I'd like."

"Did you play in college?"

"Yeah, I played at Wisconsin, but that was a long time ago."

"Really?" Heather asked, obviously impressed. "When was it?"

"Trying to embarrass me, huh?" Robin asked, chagrined. "I graduated eight years ago."

"That's not that long ago," Heather admonished. "Wisconsin usually has a really good team."

"Well, I hope they have a good team this year, because we're going up to Washington to watch them play the Huskies tonight, and I'd sure like to see those dawgs get beat."

Heather looked surprised. "You and Coach Peters are going?"

"Yeah, she got me tickets for my birthday. I'll bet you didn't know she could be so nice, did you?" Robin said teasingly.

"I think I'd better not answer that," Heather replied, blushing a little. "Well, I should get going. See you in class next week."

Jess had entered the gym again and looked over to see Heather and Robin talking and smiling. She came to a stop, her first reaction one of fear that somehow her player was going to think that she and Robin were together. But she quickly shook those feelings off as paranoid, and found herself glad that one of her players seemed to like Robin. She saw Heather wave good-bye to Robin and come running off the floor in her direction. As she neared, Heather grinned and said, "Have a good time at the Washington game, Coach," and quickly ran off to join her teammate Chris before Jess could reply.

Jess looked bewildered and watched as Chris and Heather put their heads together, talking excitedly and giggling. She shook her head as she turned back toward Robin, thinking *I'll never understand nineteen-year olds.*

Chapter
27

"Come on, Red! Play some defense! Front her! Yeah—way to come from the weak side to help!" Robin stuffed another handful of popcorn in her mouth. "That's an illegal pick!" she yelled, slightly muffled by the mouthful of popcorn. "Come on, ref, quit sucking on that thing and blow it!"

Jess leaned back in her seat and looked on with amusement at Robin's display of enthusiasm. The young professor had been yelling all night, one of the very few Wisconsin supporters in a sea of purple and gold. Since the Badgers were winning by about ten points late in the game, the Husky faithful were none too happy with Robin's vocal support of her team. This, of course, just made Robin yell all the louder. Jess was just hoping that they'd get out of there without a confrontation and was relieved when the horn finally sounded, the Badgers still up by eight. Robin stood up and yelled "Go Badgers!" a few times while turning around to the opposing fans.

Jess smiled and got up, taking Robin by the elbow and saying, "Come on, Bucky, let's get out of here before someone takes their frustration out on you."

"Hey, how did you know the Badger mascot's name was Bucky?" Robin asked with an incredulous look at the coach.

"Lucky guess," Jess replied, grinning. "Come on, let's go."

They gathered up their things and walked out to the parking lot. Traffic was slow getting away from the arena, but eventually the two women made their way to a restaurant for dinner and were seated in a quiet table by the window. They were both tired from the long day and glad to just sit and relax for a while. Jess ordered a bottle of pinot noir and they sipped their wine with a view of the lights reflecting off Lake Washington.

Jess leaned over the table and tilted her glass toward Robin. "Here's to the end of a very successful, and very drawn out birthday present," she offered. Robin brought her glass up to meet Jess's and looked into the coach's smiling eyes. She took a sip of the wine, raised her glass again and said, "And here's to friendship...our friendship." Jess smiled in return and they found themselves staring into each other's eyes for a long moment.

"Are you two ready to order?" the server interrupted them.

Jess quickly returned her eyes to the menu. "Uh, yeah...let's see...I think I'm going to have the alder smoked salmon."

"Baked, whipped, au gratin, or French fried potatoes?"

"Au gratin."

"Salad or clam chowder?"

"Salad."

"French, Italian, bleu cheese, thousand island..."

"Bleu cheese," Jess interrupted before the server could get any further into her rote response.

"And for you?" the server turned toward Robin.

"That all sounds pretty good. I'll have the same thing, except for Italian dressing instead of bleu cheese." The server looked relieved at not having to recite the same litany of choices again, and took their menus and went off to place the order.

Both women grabbed their wine glasses and took a drink, thinking about the moment before the interruption, and not wanting things to be awkward.

I have to behave myself tonight, Robin admonished herself. *I can't sit here and stare into her eyes with a lovesick expression on my face. Just lighten up and everything will be fine.*

Across the table, Jess was also having a little talk with herself. *Come on, I can't say I want to be just friends and then look at her like I want to undress her right here. She's been so good about not pressuring me, so I can't start sending her mixed signals now.* Jess looked up at Robin again, grateful to find the young woman looking out the window. She couldn't help but stare again. *She is so beautiful...how am I going to do this?*

Robin turned back from the window and Jess looked away before she got caught staring.

"So, how do you think you'll match up with Washington next week?" Robin asked in an attempt to steer the conversation to lighter topics.

"Well, I think we'll be okay inside, but I'm a little worried about our perimeter defense and our ability to handle their press. Sometimes Bennie thinks she can just do everything herself, and we end up using too much of the shot clock just to bring the ball up the court. But we'll work on those things in practice this week, and I think we'll have a real good chance against them."

"That would be a big win for you, wouldn't it?"

"Yeah, it sure would," Jess said wistfully. "I'm a little nervous about it because it's our first real test, and it's on their home court. If we don't at least make it competitive, it could really have an effect on the players' confidence."

"From what I've seen, you've done an incredible job with their confidence in the short while you've been here," Robin complimented. "I don't think one loss will make too much of a dent in that."

"Thanks, I hope you're right. We sure work on that aspect of the game a lot, because I really believe that the mental aspect is at least as important as the physical skills that they have."

"Well, according to Heather, you're very good at preparing them mentally."

Jess blushed a little and replied modestly, "She probably just knows you're a friend of mine and she wanted to be sure to say the right thing. I have to admit that there were a couple of weeks there when I was a complete failure at building their confidence." She looked up sincerely at Robin. "I couldn't believe what an effect our separation had on my professional life. I was a total bitch, ask any of the players." Jess looked guilty at the admission. "Luckily I finally snapped out of it, and realized not only that I needed to change my attitude, but that I needed to somehow find a way to make our friendship work again. I can't tell you how happy I was that night when you finally called me."

Now it was Robin's turn to blush. "I'm just sorry I waited so long, because I was pretty miserable, too. I think I just needed a little time to be sure that I could adjust to being friends again, without pushing you for something you can't give me." She looked up with a worried expression on her face, afraid that she was going to make Jess feel guilty by her last statement, but was relieved to find only understanding in the coach's eyes.

"I know it must have been really hard for you, and I'm so sorry that I put you through all of this," Jess said sympathetically. "I should have known myself well enough before I ever let our relationship go that far. That was so unfair to you."

"I would *never* regret that night we spent together, Jess, no matter how things turned out," Robin said with complete sincerity. "Please don't think of that as a bad thing that happened between us."

"I don't," Jess said emphatically. "I just thought that it made things more difficult for you and I felt badly about that."

"I suppose that if I'd never gotten to experience it, I wouldn't be able to miss it, but that seems like a bad argument to use for depriving yourself of all the pleasures in life," Robin said with a half smile.

Jess smiled back, thinking it amazing that Robin could always make her feel better, even when she had done something to hurt the young woman.

Their food arrived and they used the opportunity to take a break from the serious discussion and enjoy their meal. When the server returned later with a dessert tray, Jess put her hand over her stomach and said, "Not for me—I'm stuffed."

Robin's eyes lit up at the array of tempting dishes on the tray. She pointed at a tall glass cup of chocolate mousse covered with whipped cream and said, "I'll have one of those, please."

"Any coffee for either of you?" the server asked.

"Decaf, please," Robin replied.

"Me, too," added Jess.

Minutes later the server came back with the coffee and dessert, and Robin eagerly plunged into the chocolate mousse. A look of pure bliss crossed her face as she closed her eyes and savored the mouthful of chocolate and whipped cream. Jess couldn't help but smile at the sight. She reached over with one finger and wiped off a bit of whipped cream that was lingering on Robin's lower lip. Robin opened her eyes in time to see Jess licking the whipped cream off of her finger, and she felt her heart beat pick up. She took another spoonful of the dessert and moved it toward Jess's mouth, her eyes silently asking if the coach wanted to share. Jess's eyes were locked on Robin's as she opened her mouth to accept the spoon. As Robin slowly withdrew the spoon, she saw Jess's eyes mirror her own earlier look of bliss. Robin smiled and said, "Can you think of anything more decadent?"

"Mmmm, maybe one thing," Jess replied sensually.

Robin blushed and looked away. *What is she trying to do to me?* She took a deep breath and felt her cheeks return to their normal color. *I can do this...keep it casual,* she admonished herself.

"More coffee?" the server interrupted, then refilled both their cups.

This woman's timing is impeccable, thought Robin, grateful for the distraction. She finished the rest of her dessert, Jess declining any further offerings, and the server brought the bill. Robin reached for it, but Jess clamped her hand over Robin's wrist, saying, "Oh no you don't. This is part of your birthday present, remember?"

"The *tickets* were the birthday present, if I recall, and it seems only fair that I should pay for dinner."

"The tickets are just part of the whole package, and there's no way I'm letting you pay for part of your own birthday present," Jess said firmly.

Robin didn't want to argue, so she acquiesced with a smile and a sweet thank you. "I hope you realize you're setting a pretty high standard for when your birthday comes around," she warned.

"Well, I don't believe in standards or expectations for presents," Jess replied. "The only thing that matters is that someone *wants* to get you something, no matter how big or small it is. And besides, doing something for you on your birthday made you so happy that I feel like *I* got the present just to be able to watch you."

Robin smiled back at Jess. "You're way too nice to me. Come on, let's get out of here before you make me cry."

Jess laughed and the two women gathered their coats and left the restaurant. It was raining, making the underground parking at the hotel a welcome relief. They checked in and took the elevator to the 15th floor, where they found a spectacular view of the Space Needle from the window of their room. Jess closed the door behind her but didn't turn the lights on right away, and instead moved over to the window where Robin was looking out at the lights from the city.

"It's beautiful, isn't it?" Robin asked, looking over her shoulder at Jess.

"It sure is," the tall coach replied, never taking her eyes off of Robin.

Robin turned back to the view and leaned into the taller woman behind her. Jess put her hands on Robin's shoulders and softly kneaded the muscles there, eliciting a soft moan from the younger woman. Jess found the scent of Robin's hair and the feel of her body intoxicating, but her mind was sending a warning signal. *Careful how far you take this. You can't afford to lose control again, and you definitely don't want to hurt Robin again.*

Jess decided to be safe, and asked, "Is this okay?" giving a little squeeze of her fingers to let Robin know what she was talking about.

Robin turned slightly to look at Jess. "It feels wonderful, and I promise that I won't get any false expectations from it. I'm not going to push you, Jess—I promise."

"I know, and I appreciate that, I really do," Jess replied sincerely.

Robin turned back to the window and put her hands over Jess's on her shoulders. They stayed like that for a few minutes, before Robin gave a big yawn, prompting Jess to release her and suggest they get ready for bed.

The room had two queen size beds, and Jess pulled the covers back on the one facing the TV and sat down to wait for Robin to finish in the bathroom. When Robin came out, Jess grabbed her bag and took her turn in the bathroom. She reentered the room to find Robin in the other bed watching the TV she had left on. A wave of disappointment rolled over the taller woman as she slipped back into her bed. She turned off the light and asked Robin if she wanted the remote control for the TV.

"No, you can turn it off. I'm really tired, anyway."

Jess clicked off the TV, sending the room into darkness, lit only by the glow from the city lights. She turned on her side facing the other bed, but could only make out Robin's silhouette.

"Goodnight," Jess said softly.

"Sweet dreams," Robin replied.

But Jess's eyes didn't close for a long time. She looked over at Robin and tried to sort out her feelings, which were becoming more confused with every day she spent in the young woman's company. *Am I just kidding myself that we can be friends? Is it okay for friends to hug like we do? Is it okay for friends to sleep together? Friends kiss each other sometimes, but I know if I felt those soft lips on mine again, it wouldn't feel like I was kissing just a friend. How am I going to draw the line here?* Jess thought with frustration. *And why am I so intent on drawing that line in the first place? I thought I knew exactly what I wanted three weeks ago, and now I'm not so sure anymore.*

Jess sighed loudly and turned over to her other side. She continued to wrestle with her thoughts, and her body took its cue from her mind and refused to settle down. After tossing and turning for an hour, Jess got up to get a glass of water from the bathroom and then felt her way back to the bed in the dark.

"Hey," Robin said softly. "Can't sleep?"

"Oh, sorry. I didn't mean to wake you."

"You didn't. I couldn't sleep either. I've been listening to you turn somersaults over there for the last hour."

"Sorry," Jess repeated. "I should have tried to be more quiet." She had worked her way around the bed and was standing next to Robin. She could just barely make out the green eyes in the dim light.

Robin extended her hand toward Jess. "Join me? Maybe I can help you get to sleep."

Jess worried for all of a second that she was getting close to that line she didn't want to cross again, and then took Robin's hand and slid in between the sheets as the smaller woman moved over to make room for her. Jess settled onto her back and Robin snuggled in close to her side. Robin's hand was gently caressing Jess's arm, shoulder and neck, but instead of putting her to sleep, it rapidly aroused her senses. She self-consciously turned over, her back to Robin, and took a few deep breaths to try to slow her heart rate down. Robin continued to stroke Jess's back, kneading the tight muscles she found there, and eventually the taller woman relaxed. Soon she was breathing deeply in sleep, and Robin joined her moments later, her hand still resting on the coach's back.

Sometime in the night, Jess returned to her back and she awoke in the morning with Robin snuggled up against her side, sleeping soundly. A sense of peace came over her as she looked at the smaller woman, feeling like everything was as it should be.

Chapter 28

The following weekend was Thanksgiving, Robin had four days off and Jess's team was playing in a preseason tournament in Seattle. Robin talked Capi into going to watch, and on Friday, the two women embarked on a road trip. They stopped at Starbuck's for coffee and cinnamon rolls before heading up I-5.

"So it seems like things are going pretty well for you and Jess," Capi remarked.

Robin couldn't stop the smile that crossed her lips at the mention of the coach. "Yeah, it's been great."

"Has it been hard to just be friends when you'd really like to be more than that?"

"Sometimes, I guess. There are times when she smiles at me, or looks at me a certain way, that my heart nearly does flips in my chest, but I do my best not to look completely lovesick."

"Well, you show remarkable restraint, if you ask me. Do you still think there's a chance that she'll come around and realize what a mistake she's made?"

"I can't help but believe that," Robin said emphatically. "I know the feelings are there, it's just a matter of her working through a few issues that she's got. One of which is the fear of losing her job. I just don't know how to convince her that it's possible to be a gay woman and be a successful basketball coach. Hell, I'll bet more than half the woman basketball coaches are gay."

"Do you think she knows that? It seems hard to believe she

wouldn't know it," Capi said thoughtfully.

"I think she's made it a point to keep a certain distance from other coaches, so I'm not sure she really knows much about their personal lives. And she's definitely not the type to speculate, given that she doesn't want people speculating about her."

"Hmmm, I suppose that's true. It's too bad you don't know any of those coaches—maybe you could talk to them about how they handle it."

Robin's eyes lit up. "Hey, I do know one. Sara Graebel was an assistant my first year here and was going out with my roommate, Ellen, at the time. Since my roommate was a little flaky, Sara and I spent many long nights talking about how she could get Ellen to be more serious about her. I think Sara and I ended up being closer than Sara and Ellen," Robin laughed.

"So where is she coaching now?" Capi asked.

"She's at Cal State Monterey as the head coach. It's not Division I, but I'm sure the same issues about recruiting and job security would be there. I'm going to give her a call." She turned and gave Capi a big grin and a high five. "Way to go, partner. This just might help."

"Whoa, hang on a second," Capi warned. "If you're going to tell Sara about Jess, are you sure you can trust her not to tell anyone else?"

Robin thought about that for a minute, because the last thing she wanted to do was violate Jess's trust. "You're right, but I know I can trust Sara. Not only would she respect my confidence because of our history, but she's also a professional with a lot of integrity. There's no way she'd go spreading rumors about another coach."

"Okay, I just didn't want you making a mistake you'd regret later," Capi replied.

Robin smiled and said, "Always looking out for me, aren't you?"

"I try, but it's a pretty hard job sometimes."

Robin got out her cell phone and address book, and dialed the coach's number in California. She was somewhat surprised to actually reach Sara, thinking that she would have either Thanksgiving weekend plans, or coaching responsibilities over the holiday.

"No, I gave the team two days off to see their families," Sara explained. "Most of my kids are from around here, so they can drive home and still be back for Saturday practice. How are things going with you? It's been awhile since I've talked to you."

"Things are great," Robin replied. "My classes are going well, and I'm still finding time to play basketball, so I can't complain. How is your team doing?"

"Oh, we're rebuilding a little bit this year. I lost my two senior post players, so we have to adjust to a different style of play. But I think we'll do okay, and I've got a couple of new recruits that are coming along faster than I thought they would. So we might surprise a few people."

"Well, I'm sure you'll find a way to make them play above their potential—you were always really good at finding ways to motivate your players."

Sara laughed modestly. "Thanks. I guess that degree in sports psychology has paid some dividends. So are you still living by yourself or have you found that perfect woman you've been waiting for?"

"I'm still single, thank you very much, and there's nothing wrong with being picky," Robin said indignantly.

"Well, it's not like there's lots of opportunities in Comstock, so you can't be too picky," Sara laughed.

"Actually there is a new opportunity, as you put it, that I'm interested in, but it's not going as well as I'd like. In fact, that's why I'm calling you—I need a little advice."

"What kind of advice would you need from me? You've seen how successful my relationships have been. I'm not exactly a role model, you know."

"Yeah, but this is a coach, so I thought you might be able to relate."

"Oh really," Sara said with interest. "What kind of coach?"

"This has to be completely confidential Sara, okay?" Robin asked seriously.

"Hey, you know me better than that. You don't even have to ask—my lips are sealed."

"Well, I've been spending a lot of time with the head basketball coach..."

"Whoa," Sara interrupted. "Jess Peters is gay? You've got to be kidding me—the way she keeps her distance from everybody I didn't think she even had feelings."

"Oh, come on. She's really nice," Robin protested.

"Not around other coaches she's not," Sara replied. "It's not like she's mean or anything, she just ignores everybody else—never socializes."

"Well, she seems to have some issues about whether it's possible to be gay and be a successful coach, and that's what I wanted to talk to you about. How do you handle the whole recruiting thing if people know you're gay?"

"I don't think that many people do know I'm gay. It's not like I advertise it, you know. It just hasn't been an issue to my knowledge."

"But you always hear about how opposing coaches will use it against you in recruiting. Doesn't that happen?"

"Yeah, I've heard that, but I've never actually seen it happen. I suppose there are a few severely homophobic parents out there that would respond to that kind of thing, but most athletes want to play for the best team they can get on, and are going to look at the coach's credentials, not some rumor about their sexuality."

"Well, what do you do if someone comes right out and asks you?"

"It depends on who it is," Sara replied thoughtfully. "I won't lie about it, but if it were a parent of a recruit, I would probably say that my private life was private, and that I hoped they would help their daughter make a decision based on the integrity and quality of the program. If that made somebody choose not to go to my school, then I wouldn't want them in my program anyway. But if my athletic director asked me, I would tell him the truth, because I really believe he'd support me. But the reality is, it just doesn't come up, Robin. As long as a coach is discreet and doesn't get involved with her players, it's just a non-issue."

Robin sighed heavily. "I wish you could tell Jess that," she said ruefully. "How am I ever going to convince her?"

"I'd say that Jess Peters is crazy if she's turning down a chance to be with you because she's worried about her job," Sara said emphatically. "Doesn't she know that every lesbian in Comstock would have given their right arm to go out with you?"

Robin laughed. "You mean all three of them? Come on, it's not like they were lining up at my door."

"You're way too modest. I would have asked you out in a heartbeat, but your roommate would have killed me."

"Ah, so it's Ellen's fault that I'm still single. I didn't realize that she was acting as the gatekeeper all that time."

"Well, there's no excuse now, so I think you'd better turn those considerable charms of yours on that basketball coach and see if you can't get her to lighten up a little."

"Okay, I'll see what I can do. You've given me a few things that I can talk to her about, so maybe things will get better."

"I'm sure they will. Keep me informed, okay?"

"Okay, I promise. It was great talking to you. Keep in touch."

The two women hung up, both deep in thought about what they'd learned.

Capi, who had been patiently listening to one side of the long conversation while driving, couldn't remain quiet any longer. "Come on, I'm dying here. What did she say?"

Robin was startled out of her thoughts, and smiled at Capi's frustration.

"She said Jess is a fool not to marry me tomorrow," Robin teased.

"Well, you could have saved a long distance cell phone charge—I could have told you that." More seriously, she asked, "What did she say about the coaching issues?"

Robin proceeded to relate the other side of the conversation.

"Well, that sounds pretty positive, don't you think?" Capi replied.

"Yeah, but now I have to convince Jess," Robin said somewhat despondently. "And then there's another related issue that I haven't even told you about yet."

"What's that?"

"Well, I can't give you the details, but basically Jess had one of her high school players fall in love with her many years ago and it didn't turn out well. She feels responsible for what happened, and she associates all that guilt with being a gay coach. I think she knows in her head that what happened had nothing to do with whether she was gay or not, but she hasn't learned to get over her negative gut reaction to the thought of being gay." Robin put her head in her hands. "God, this is complicated."

"No kidding," Capi replied sympathetically. "But it sounds like maybe you're making some progress if she's talking to you about these things. That's a sign that she's at least willing to deal with the issues, rather than just shut you out."

"Yeah, that's true," Robin said hopefully. "I know it's probably going to take a while, but I swear she feels the same way about me that I do about her. You should see the way she looks at me sometimes—it's everything I can do not to throw myself at her on the spot."

Capi laughed. "Well, if talking doesn't work, maybe you should try that next."

Robin smiled back at her good friend, wondering again why she couldn't have fallen in love with some less complicated—someone like Capi.

Chapter
29

The two friends arrived at the arena a good hour before game time. Jess's team was scheduled to play Colorado State in the tournament opener, and then Washington would play Montana State in the prime seven o'clock spot. The tournament organizers expected Colorado State and Washington to advance to the championship game the following night, which would be a good draw for the fans. Jess's team had other ideas, though.

The arena was practically empty, most fans not arriving until a half hour or less before game time, and most Husky fans not arriving until the second game. Jess's team was shooting around, getting used to the lights and the court, while the coach was standing off to the side talking to Carmen Ricardo.

"Who's that with Jess?" Capi asked as they found their seats behind the visitors' bench.

Robin's face clouded as she replied, "That's the sports information director, Carmen something or other, and every time I see her she's making eyes at Jess."

Capi looked over at Robin with surprise. "She's hardly making eyes at her; they're just looking at a piece of paper." Capi looked over at the two women again. "And besides, she's really cute. She can make eyes at me any time she wants."

"You think so?" Robin asked skeptically. "She's a little short for my tastes."

"Well, I happen to like them short. I guess I don't have to tell you that. Let's walk down there, maybe we'll get introduced."

Robin rolled her eyes, but got up and headed over toward Jess. In truth, she was dying to talk to the coach, and if Capi could divert the SID's attention for a few minutes, all the better.

Jess saw them coming and gave Robin a big smile, which immediately warmed the smaller woman's heart and made her forget all about Carmen what's-her-name.

"Hi Capi, did you guys have a good ride up here?" Jess asked.

"Yeah, Robin entertained me with stories of all the hearts she's broken, so the time went fast."

Robin blushed and swatted Capi on the arm. "Do you think you could tell the truth just once in your life?" she admonished her friend.

Jess noticed Carmen smiling at the banter between the two good friends and realized that her manners were lacking.

"Carmen, this is Robin Grant, an economics professor at NOU, and this is Capi Morgan, the Vice Provost for Student Affairs." She turned back to Carmen. "And this is Carmen Ricardo, our new Sports Information Director."

The women shook hands, and Robin noticed Capi holding on just a little longer than necessary while smiling engagingly at Carmen.

"Ah, you're someone I'll probably be dealing with in the future," Carmen said, smiling back at Capi. "There's always some athlete getting into trouble and ending up in your office, and some coach wanting me to control what gets said in the local papers. In fact, I'm surprised I haven't met you before now."

"Well, the football season did seem a little too quiet this fall. Are you sure you guys haven't been hiding some things over there in Athletics that I should know about?" Capi replied teasingly.

"I'll never tell," Carmen said with a wink.

"Hey, I've gotta get back to the locker room for last minute preparations," Jess interrupted. She turned to Robin with a hopeful look on her face. "Are you staying for the next game? I have to scout both teams for tomorrow night, and I could use some help if you're going to be around."

"I'd love to," Robin replied immediately, and then remembered that she was there with Capi and quickly turned to her friend to see if it would be all right with her.

"Yeah, sure, we'll stay," Capi replied easily.

"Great. See you after the game," Jess said as she headed off to the locker room.

"Good luck," Robin called after her, which earned her another smile over Jess's shoulder.

"Well, I've got to go make sure things are all set up at the press table," Carmen said. "It was very nice to meet you both, and I hope we get another chance to talk soon." This last part was definitely directed at Capi, who had a silly grin on her face as she watched the small woman walk away.

"God, you're easy," Robin said with mock disgust as she grabbed Capi by the arm and dragged her back to their seats.

"Whaaat? I was just being polite," Capi protested.

"Sure you were."

Thirty minutes later, both teams took the floor for their pre-game warm-ups. Jess strode onto the floor behind her team, looking stunning in a black suit with a white silk shirt underneath. Her shoes had a slight heel, making her stand out above most of her players. Robin found herself mesmerized by the sight, until Capi elbowed her and said, "Hey, snap out of it. It's not like you don't see her every day."

"Not like that, I don't," Robin said reverently. "God, Capi, what would she want with me? Look at her—she could have anybody she wanted, male or female."

"Stop that right now. How am I ever going to convince you that you are just as attractive as her or anyone else? And besides, she doesn't want anybody else, she wants you."

Robin sighed. "I want to believe that, really I do, but it's just so hard for me."

"Well, I'm going to keep telling you that until you do believe it, so you'd better get used to it."

Robin smiled gratefully at Capi. "OK, I'll do my best."

The game started at a furious pace, both teams pushing the ball up the court after a steal or a rebound, and by the first official timeout at the sixteen minute mark, the players were sucking wind as they ran over to the bench.

"Okay, listen up," Jess shouted over the noise of the band. "The defense looks great and we're getting some good shots off the break, but we've got to cut down on the turnovers. I want to see a ball fake before you try to pass it in to the post. The posts are working hard to maintain their position, so they can't always move to your pass. Make sure you give it to them where they're calling for it, okay?" Heads nodded as Jess looked around the huddle. She then proceeded to diagram a defensive adjustment to counteract a screen that was being set on the baseline, and the time-out was over.

Robin looked up from the huddle that she had been watching to see Capi looking across the court. She followed her gaze to the press table and saw Carmen smiling back at the administrator. *Jeez, what is this—love at first sight?* Robin felt that irrational sense of jealousy one gets when something is being lost, even though that something wasn't really wanted in the first place. But she quickly scolded herself for wanting anything but happiness for her friend who had always been there for her.

She leaned over and whispered in Capi's ear, "You know, you're right—she is pretty cute." Capi blushed furiously and returned her attention to the action on the court.

The NOU team cut down on their number of turnovers and continued to play relentless defense, resulting in a six point half-time lead. After the break, the Bobcats came out even more determined to prove the odds makers wrong, and ended up cruising to an eleven point victory. The players from the bench ran onto the court to congratulate their teammates, as their coach walked down to shake hands with the opposing coaches. Jess was able to maintain her professional decorum until that formality was taken care of, and then she sprinted onto the court with her players and joined in the celebration.

Robin grinned from ear to ear while she watched Jess let down her guard as she congratulated her players, giving them big hugs and high fives. This was Jess's first big win against a top-ranked opponent, and Robin couldn't be happier for her. She and Capi made their way down to the floor and stood by the corner where the teams would leave the floor. The two teams for the next game were waiting patiently for the celebration to end before taking the court for warm-ups. Finally, Jess's team came running off the court, still shouting and laughing as they headed for the locker room. The coaches trailed behind, and when Jess saw Robin standing there, her smile got even bigger.

Robin couldn't stop herself—she reached up and gave Jess a big hug, and to her surprise, the coach returned it without pulling immediately away. Robin took the opportunity to whisper in Jess's ear, "You guys were great. I'm so proud of you."

"Thanks," Jess whispered back into the ear that was dangerously close to her mouth. "And thanks for being here to share it with me."

Robin released her hold and smiled back at the coach. "Always," she said aloud.

Chapter
30

Jess emerged from the locker room twenty minutes later and saw Robin and Capi in their seats. She motioned for them to join her, and they walked back down to the edge of the court.

"There are some seats at the press table for coaches, so why don't you two join me?" Jess offered.

"Are you sure that's okay?" Robin questioned.

"As long as you help me scout, it shouldn't be a problem."

"Well, you'll have to tell me what to do, because I've never scouted a team before," Capi replied.

"No problem, we'll put you to good use," Jess said with a smile as she led the two women over to the press table. There were four empty seats at the end of the table, and they took the last three. Jess handed out scouting sheets and told Capi to just help Robin with the shot chart.

"Aren't your assistants going to need to sit here?" Robin asked.

"No, they're taking the team to get dinner, then I'll meet them back at the hotel later. I was hoping I could catch a ride back with you, but if you've got other plans, I can just call one of them to come back and pick me up."

"Sure, we can give you a ride, right Capi?" Robin looked questioningly at her friend.

"No problem," Capi replied easily. "I think that women's bar we wanted to go to is pretty close to the hotel, so we could drop you off on our way."

Jess's expression changed noticeably as she took in that information. *Are they going to a gay bar?* The little voice in her head answered with impunity. *Of course they're going to a gay bar. What did you expect? You wanted to be "just friends," remember? Did you expect her to never look for another girlfriend, just because you weren't willing to fill that role?*

Jess looked crestfallen as she returned her attention to the court, shaking her head and trying to get her attention back on the game. She recorded the starting line-ups as they were being announced, when Carmen slipped a piece of paper in front of her.

"Here are the final stats, Coach. I faxed them back home to the newspaper and talked to the reporter after he finished your post-game interview. I think they have everything they need. If you're still around after the end of this game, the local TV sports reporter would like to talk to you about tomorrow's opponent."

"Thanks, Carmen," Jess said distractedly. "We'll see how this game goes. I probably won't need to stay 'til the end of it, but I will if it's close."

Carmen moved around to the empty chair that was left next to Capi and sat down to watch the next game.

"Hello again," Carmen said with a smile as Capi looked up from her scouting sheet.

"Hey, do you have to work this game, too?" Capi replied, returning the smile.

"Not really. Somebody else will provide all the statistics, but I wanted to check out the opposition for tomorrow. And I have to phone the results back to our local paper when it's over so they can say a few things about tomorrow's match-up in the morning story."

"Sounds like a job with a lot of late nights," Capi remarked.

"Yeah, it can be. The hours aren't regular, that's for sure. But I like traveling with the different teams and getting to spend time around the students. You must get to spend a lot of time with students in your job, too, don't you?"

"Probably more than I want to," Capi said with a short laugh. "Actually, I love the time I get to spend with the good ones—those that are trying to make a difference and help their fellow students. It's the ones that make trouble that I could stand to see less of."

Carmen gave an understanding smile as she laid her hand on Capi's forearm. "Well, I'll bet even the bad ones are glad that they have someone like you who cares about them."

Capi blushed slightly and was about to make a modest reply when Robin interrupted.

"Hey, who took that last shot? I couldn't see her number."

"Uh-oh. Sorry, I didn't see it either," Capi replied sheepishly.

Robin gave the administrator a mock glare and said, "Try paying attention to the *game*, okay?"

Capi leaned over to Carmen and surreptitiously whispered, "I think I'm in trouble. We'll have to continue this conversation later."

Carmen grinned back. "Okay. Maybe at halftime the boss will give you a break."

Washington got off to a quick start against Montana State, dominating inside and pressuring their smaller guards into numerous turnovers. Jess tried to concentrate on ways to defend the Husky post players, but her mind kept returning to the thought of Robin going to a gay bar later that night. *Capi called it a women's bar—I wonder what that's like? I've never been to a gay bar. Are they different than any other bar? Will women be hitting on Robin all night? Do they just talk and play pool, or is there dancing?* At the thought of Robin dancing with another woman, Jess blanched noticeably. *Oh God, how am I going to handle this? I've never felt so jealous in my life, and nothing's even happened yet.*

The horn sounded at the end of the first half, jolting the coach out of her distressing thoughts. Robin looked over at Jess's pale face and asked, "Hey, are you all right? You don't look like you're feeling very well."

"Oh...no, no, I'm fine. Probably just a little hungry since I haven't eaten since lunch," she offered lamely.

"Do you want me to get you something from the concession stand?" Robin offered.

The thought of food actually made Jess blanch even further, but after giving Robin the excuse about not eating, she couldn't say she wasn't hungry. "No thanks. I really don't like to eat that junk food. I'll be able to pick something up when I get back to the hotel."

"You sure? How about a soda just to settle your stomach?"

"Okay, that'd be great, thanks," she replied and managed a small half smile towards Robin.

Robin smiled back with a concerned look on her face, and got up to go to the concession stand. When she returned with a soda for Jess and a big bag of popcorn for herself, she saw the tall coach sitting with her forehead in her hand, looking at the table in front of her. As she approached, she noticed that nothing was on the table in front of Jess, and her eyes were actually closed. Robin walked over and casually put her hand on Jess's back. She leaned over and asked gently, "Are you sure you're okay? We could take you back to the hotel if you want."

Jess slowly raised her head and managed a weak smile. "No, really, I'm fine. Just tired, I guess. *And where did this headache come from?* she wondered as she felt her pulse pounding behind her eyes. *Stress, that's where it comes from. And nothing has ever stressed me out like the woman sitting next to me, and my own damned inability to figure out what I really want. Oh hell, who am I trying to kid? I know exactly what I want—I want her, in every way imaginable. But I also want my job, and my reputation, and I don't want to feel guilty about my past...*She stole a glance over at the attractive professor, who had sat back down and was talking with Capi. Robin laughed at something Capi said, putting her arm around the administrator's shoulders as they shared a private joke. Jess felt her chest tightening, as if someone was squeezing her heart. *I don't think I could stand it if she was with someone else. I'd have to find another job—move to the east coast or something. Or maybe I could catch on with that Australian team,* Jess thought ruefully.

The teams had come back on the court for the second half, and Jess tried to return her attention to the scouting sheets. She had already gathered most of the information she needed, and now she was mostly waiting to see if Washington would continue their dominance at the start of the second half. If Montana State didn't make a run early, the game was as good as over.

"Hey, babe, feeling any better?" Robin asked softly.

Jess was startled by the term of endearment, but unmistakably heartened by it. She gave Robin a crooked smile and said, "Yeah, a little bit, thanks."

"I talked to Capi and we agreed that we can leave anytime you want. So just say the word, and we'll get you back to the hotel so you can get something to eat and get some rest. You really look like you could use it," Robin said sympathetically. She was dying to touch the taller woman, to stroke her hair, rub her shoulders, and try to make her feel better, but she knew that it would be a risk to display even the most casual signs of affection, so she kept her hands to herself.

"I just want to see the first five minutes or so," Jess replied, "then we can go. Are you sure you don't mind missing the end of the game?"

"Nah, we'll see Washington tomorrow night, and I've been in this gym long enough for one day." She turned to Capi to find out if she'd be ready to go soon, but found the administrator deep in conversation with Carmen once again. Robin rolled her eyes as the two women leaned together laughing about something. She nudged Capi, who turned around to see what Robin wanted.

"Think you can tear yourself away from *the game* in a few minutes?" she asked with sarcasm dripping from her voice. "Jess said she'd like to leave soon."

"Oh...um...actually, I was going to ask for a favor," Capi said with a pleading, puppy dog look on her face.

Robin sighed. "You want me to come back and get you later because you're so fascinated by the game you can't tear yourself away, right?"

Capi's face lit up. "Right. How did you know?" She smiled gratefully at Robin and added quietly, "How would you feel about Carmen going out with us later?"

"It's okay with me," Robin replied easily, "but are you sure she wants to go out to a women's bar?"

"Well, I guess I'm not positive, but come on. Look at her. What do your instincts tell you?"

Robin discreetly looked over at the SID who had returned her attention to the game. She had a compact, athletic body and was wearing tailored black pants with a crisply pressed white shirt and black Italian loafers. Her black, curly hair was cut just above the ears and collar, and helped to set off a strong jaw and high cheekbones. She was unadorned by jewelry, other than a functional watch and diamond stud earrings. *Pretty androgynous, but with a definite sense of style,* Robin thought to herself. She couldn't help but compare the small woman with herself, thinking that the only thing they seemed to have in common was that they were both short. *I guess it's egotistical to think that Capi is going to go looking for a clone of me.*

"Okay, I suppose you're right," Robin finally replied.

"Well, I'll leave it up to you to make the big move and ask her out," she teased. "Do you remember any good pick-up lines?"

"I don't think I'm going to need any. She's not exactly shy. I'll bet you tomorrow's dinner that she asks me before I even get a chance."

"Mmmm, pretty sure of yourself, aren't you? Okay, you're on," Robin agreed with a smile. "I'll expect a full report when I get back."

"Deal. How about if I call you on your cell when Carmen's done with her post-game duties? Can you keep yourself occupied 'til then?"

"Sure. If Jess doesn't want to stay up, I'll wait for your call in the hotel bar."

"Great...and Robbie?"

"Yeah?"

"Thanks."

"Any time, my friend. I'm very happy for you," Robin said sincerely as she briefly laid her hand over Capi's before turning back toward Jess.

Jess looked up from her work and said, "You about ready? I could leave anytime."

"Yeah, let's get out of here," Robin said, gathering her papers and standing up.

The two women were headed for the exit when Jess stopped to ask why Capi wasn't accompanying them.

"She has a sudden fascination with learning more about the world of sports information," Robin replied dryly.

Jess looked confused for a moment, but then her expression cleared as she realized what Robin meant. "Oh, I see. Well, she couldn't have asked for a more attentive teacher," Jess replied with a smile.

It was raining hard as they left the arena, and Robin insisted on going to get the car so that Jess wouldn't get her good clothes wet. She pulled up at the curb a few minutes later, and the tall woman folded herself into the front seat. Jess found herself immediately relaxing now that the two of them were alone in the car, and her headache was reduced to a dull throbbing.

"Have you eaten dinner yet?" she asked the younger woman.

"No, I had some popcorn at the game, but that hardly counts. You know me, I'm always ready to eat."

"There's a pretty good restaurant at the hotel if you'd like to get something," Jess suggested hopefully.

"Well, I've probably only got about forty-five minutes before I have to be back at the arena, so I don't think I have time for that. But I wouldn't mind grabbing something quicker. Do you think you could stomach some Taco Bell or McDonald's?"

"I think there are a couple of items at Taco Bell that won't kill me," Jess chuckled.

Robin pulled into the drive-through lane, and they got their order and went to park in a corner of the parking lot. They finished their dinner in silence before Robin spoke up. "Does a little food help? Are you feeling any better?"

"I'm feeling much better, thanks. I can't seem to shake this headache, though."

"Here...give me your drink and put your seat back," she suggested as she took Jess's cup and put it in the holder. She put her own seat back as well so that both of them were reclined at the same level. Robin turned on her side and reached her left hand over to brush Jess's bangs off her forehead. "Close your eyes and relax, okay?"

"Mm-hmm," Jess replied as the smaller woman massaged her forehead and temples. "Oh God, that feels good," Jess groaned.

Robin watched the muscles in Jess's face slowly relax as the tension drained out of the coach. She worked her fingers back farther into the thick, dark hair, and eventually made her way down to the neck and shoulder muscles that were within reach.

"Damn bucket seats," Robin cursed as she tried to reach over to Jess's far shoulder.

Jess chuckled and said, "So you've got some experience with bench seats? Or do you usually just head right for the back seat?"

Robin blushed and replied defensively, "No, I've never had bench seats."

"And...?"

"And what?"

"You didn't answer the second part of the question."

"Okay, so I might have had a couple of occasions to test out the back seat of a car, but that was many years ago."

Jess turned on her side to face Robin, smiling at the young woman's embarrassment. She reached over and gently touched her cheek. "You know, you're really cute when you blush."

"It's too dark for you to tell whether I'm blushing," Robin replied indignantly.

"Yeah, but I can tell anyway," Jess said self-assuredly, causing Robin's cheeks to flush even more.

Robin reached up and held Jess's hand to her cheek, closing her eyes at the feelings that were quickly rising to the surface. *I can't believe what a simple touch can do to me.*

"Robin, I..."

The cell phone rang loudly, startling both women. Robin's eyes flew open. *Oh shit, I'm going to kill you for this, Capi...*

Robin dug her phone out of her jacket pocket and returned her seat upright. Jess did the same as Robin quickly finished her call, telling Capi that she could be there to pick her up in another twenty minutes.

Robin looked over at Jess, wondering what might have happened if they hadn't been interrupted. "Sorry about that," she said apologetically.

"Hey, it's no problem. I should be getting back anyway, to check on my team."

They drove to the hotel in silence, Robin thinking about how much she wished she were going to stay with Jess that night, and Jess thinking about how much she wished Robin wasn't going out to a women's bar. By the time they arrived at the hotel, Jess's earlier depression had returned.

Robin pulled up in front of the lobby and turned to Jess, noticing the sad expression on the coach's face once again. "Is your headache back again?" she asked as she reached across and put her hand on Jess's shoulder.

Jess flinched noticeably, and Robin removed her hand. "Yeah, I guess it is. I'd better go take some aspirin." She couldn't bring herself to look at Robin, and just wanted to get out of the car before things got any more uncomfortable. She opened the door, and with a brief glance back at Robin, said, "Thanks for the ride, and I hope you have a good time tonight." She smiled weakly and got out of the car before Robin could reply.

Robin just sat there, dumfounded at the change that had come over Jess during the ten minute car ride to the hotel. *What just happened? Everything was fine—great, even.* Half of her wanted to run after Jess and find out what was wrong, and the other half was telling her to give the coach some space. Since

Capi and Carmen were waiting back at the arena, she decided she'd have to figure out what went wrong some other time. *If she'll even talk to me about it.*

Chapter 31

Robin, Capi, and Carmen sat at a table near the dance floor, which was crowded with women out on a Friday night in Seattle. The fact that a major women's basketball tournament was going on at the same time didn't hurt the bar's attendance. They recognized a number of women that they had seen earlier at the Arena, and many were still sporting clothes in various shades of purple and gold.

"How about another round? I'll buy," Carmen offered, getting out of her chair.

"Sure, but the server will probably be around in a few minutes if you want to wait," Capi replied.

"I don't mind getting them. Besides," Carmen gave a little sly smile, "I think the bartender likes me, so maybe I'll get a free round."

"I'd like you, too, if you tipped me five dollars for a six dollar order," Robin quipped, having been at the bar earlier with the SID.

"Hey, just maintaining good relations with people that count," Carmen replied with a big grin. "It's something you learn in business school."

Capi just shook her head as she watched Carmen walk to the bar. *It's not exactly a swagger, but she's not lacking in confidence, that's for sure.* She looked over to Robin, who was smiling back sympathetically at her. "I think this might be more than I can handle," Capi said ruefully.

"Oh, come on. It's good for you. Get you out of your comfort zone for a little while," Robin teased.

"Well, at least I'm going to get a free dinner out of it. You'll be buying tomorrow night."

Robin just raised her eyebrows with an admiring look on her face. "I think you're going to like having someone pay attention to you for a change. See if you can just enjoy it, okay?"

"I'll try," Capi replied as Carmen returned to the table. She set three pints of beer down, and then held her hand out to Capi, asking her if she'd like to dance. A slow song had started and the dance floor was quickly filling with couples. Capi blushed slightly, but took the offered hand and got up to join Carmen. Robin just watched with a smile as they made their way onto the dance floor.

Carmen took Capi's hand and held it to her shoulder while putting her arm around the taller woman's waist. They maintained a very small distance between them, talking and smiling as they moved easily in time with the music. Robin was just thinking they looked good together when her attention was drawn to someone that was standing beside her chair.

"Hi there, I'm Melinda. Are you here by yourself?"

Robin looked up to see attractive blue eyes smiling back at her.

"Uh...no...actually, my friends are just dancing. They'll...uh...they'll be back in a minute," she stammered.

"Would you like to join them? On the dance floor, I mean?"

Robin wanted to say no in the worst way, but couldn't think of a reason to turn down the invitation. Melinda was a nice-looking woman, probably in her late twenties, and had an open, sincere, look on her face. Robin smiled and said, "Sure, that would be nice."

They found a small opening on the crowded dance floor, and Melinda took one of Robin's hands and laid her other hand lightly on the small woman's shoulder. Robin returned the gesture and relaxed a little, not sensing any predatory motives on Melinda's part.

"You didn't tell me your name," Melinda said, smiling down at the shorter professor.

"It's Robin." *Why is everyone in the world taller than me?* "Do you live here in Seattle?"

"Yeah, I'm an engineer at Microsoft. I've lived here for

about five years now. How about you?"

"I'm from Oregon—Comstock. I teach at Northern Oregon University."

"Really?" Melinda asked, impressed. "You don't look old enough to be a professor."

Robin laughed. "I hear that all the time, but really, I'm older than I look."

"So what are you doing in Seattle? Just come up to enjoy our night life?"

"No, we're here watching the Thanksgiving tournament at the UW."

Melinda looked questioningly at Robin, obviously not knowing about the tournament.

"Basketball?" Robin prompted. "You must not be a fan, huh?"

"Actually, I hate sports. I'm more into the theater and the arts."

Robin felt an irrational sense of relief at that revelation. *Well, this would have been a short courtship, if it were a courtship at all.*

"I'm afraid I know next to nothing about the theater and arts," Robin replied. Melinda looked surprised, but didn't pursue the subject further. The song ended, and Robin quickly said, "Well, I'd better get back to my friends. Thanks for the dance." Melinda smiled and nodded, and didn't look overly disappointed that Robin wasn't inviting her back to the table. As she neared the table, she saw Capi and Carmen watching her with big grins on their faces.

"Whaaat?" Robin asked, trying to look innocent.

"Oh, nothing," Capi replied. "We just leave you alone for two minutes and the next thing we know, somebody's picked you up and has you in their arms on the dance floor. You were never that easy for me."

"You never asked me to dance, as I recall," Robin retorted.

"Oh, well, in that case, would you like to dance?" Capi said, one eyebrow raised in challenge.

"I'd love to," Robin replied seductively, holding her hand out to Capi.

They both laughed, and Capi got up to join Robin on the dance floor. Carmen looked a little confused at the banter between the two best friends, but quickly started a conversation with a group of women at the next table and soon had them all charmed into buying her another drink.

"So, how was she?" Capi asked Robin once they had found a space on the dance floor.

"She was very nice, thank you. Her name is Melinda, she's nice-looking, very smart, has a good job, and hates sports."

Capi laughed. "That must have ground the conversation to a halt."

"Yeah, that was pretty much the end of it. So how is it going with you and Carmen?"

"She's sweet, she's charming, she's funny, and she scares the hell out of me."

Now it was Robin's turn to laugh. "How long has it been since someone has really made you feel special?" She looked more seriously at her good friend. "You deserve that, you know? You make people feel special all the time."

Capi smiled back gratefully, and said, "Thanks. I have to admit it does feel good."

"Then just go with it, okay? There's nothing to be afraid of."

The three women stayed late at the bar, talking, laughing, and dancing. Robin was approached a number of times while Carmen and Capi were off together, but she politely refused any more offers to dance. As the night wore on, she started thinking more about Jess, worried about how the coach was feeling. *Maybe I shouldn't have left her alone like that. What if she's really sick? Yeah, but what if she really just wanted to be alone? Maybe I'm pushing her too much.* Robin looked around at the multitude of women in the bar, wondering why she wasn't the least bit interested in any of them. *There's only one woman I'm interested in, and she's not here. But how long can I keep hoping for something that might never happen? How many opportunities do I turn down in the meantime?* Robin sighed deeply, knowing she wasn't going to be interested in anyone but Jess for a very long time.

"Hey, Robin, you're looking a little tired over there," Carmen noted, bringing Robin out of her thoughts. "It's pretty late, maybe we should be getting back."

"Yeah," Capi agreed, noticing the tired look on Robin's face. "I can see that I'm going to have a hard time getting you out of bed in the morning."

The three women finished their drinks and made their way out of the bar, groaning as they encountered the ever-present winter rain. It was only a short ride to the hotel, and in no time Robin was asleep in her room. Capi was in the next bed over, having a more difficult time finding sleep, thinking about the evening's events and how she was feeling about one small, attractive, dark-haired woman she'd left down the hall. Carmen had thanked her for a wonderful evening, and had reached up to give her a small, sweet kiss before going into her room. Capi could still feel the soft lips on hers and the unmistakable tingling that reached to her fingers and toes.

Jess awoke the next morning feeling restless and unsettled. She searched her half-awake brain for the source of her discomfort, upset once again when she found it. She looked at the clock and saw that it was six a.m., and decided she needed to get out of her hotel room. She donned her running clothes and shoes, and headed for the elevator. Once out on the dark streets, she pushed herself until she was breathing heavily, finding some perverse solace in the punishment.

I wonder how late they stayed out last night? Of course, that's assuming they even came back...Oh, stop that. Of course they came back. Give Robin a little credit, will you? She's not exactly the type to go home with some stranger from a bar. No, but she's certainly the type to make new friends easily, and the "going home" part might be just a few weeks away. Jess increased her speed up a hill, mad at herself for not being able to control her negative thoughts.

This could all be avoided if you'd just figure out how to make a place for her in your life, you know. Robin's made it pretty obvious that she wants you, not somebody else. Jess relaxed a little at that thought, and slowed her pace to something she could maintain for an hour. By the time she got back to the hotel, she was feeling exhausted, but better and more relaxed. As Jess was walking through the hotel lobby, she saw Carmen sitting off to one side, drinking coffee and reading the morning paper. She detoured over toward the SID, who looked up from her paper as she approached.

"Hey, Coach—how was your run?"

"It was good. In fact, I'll bet I feel much better than you look this morning."

Carmen looked a little guilty as she replied, "Yeah, I think we stayed out a little too late last night, and probably drank a little more than we should have. I'll be surprised if we see Capi and Robin before noon."

Jess paled a little and asked, "Did they have a good time last night?"

"Oh yeah. I suppose that after living in Comstock for a while you go a little crazy when you finally get out to a real bar."

"Yeah, I suppose so," Jess replied half-heartedly. "Well, I'll leave you to your recovery. I trust you'll be in top form by game time."

"You can count on it," Carmen replied, giving the coach a confident smile.

Jess walked off toward the elevators, the good mood that she'd found by the end of her run long gone. She spied the door to the stairs next to the elevators and took them two at a time for the eight flights to her floor. She could barely breathe by the time she got there, the punishment once again seeming fitting for her complete failure in her personal life.

Robin awoke with a headache and a foul taste in her mouth from too many beers and too much smoke in the bar the previous evening. She groaned as she turned over and opened her eyes.

"Hey, Sunshine," Capi teased. "I thought maybe you were going to sleep all day."

"What time is it?" Robin asked grumpily.

"Eleven fifteen."

"Why are you so chipper? Did you already get coffee?"

Capi's smile broadened. "As a matter of fact, a secret admirer of mine sent coffee and rolls to our room this morning, along with a paper." She pointed over to the table where a carafe of coffee was sitting with a plate of cinnamon rolls.

"And a rose?" Robin said incredulously, pointing to a single stem in a glass vase sitting on the table. "Did something happen last night that you didn't tell me about?"

"Hey, what makes you think something had to happen?

Maybe some people are just more romantic than you."

Robin groaned and sank back on her pillow again. "Man, you have it bad, don't you?"

Capi laughed and said, "You're just jealous. Come on, get up and have some coffee—you'll feel better."

Jess was running her team through the defensive scheme she wanted to use for the Washington post players for the fifth time. Their shoot-around had started at eleven; it was now twelve-thirty and they hadn't covered nearly as much as Jess had hoped they would. Her headache had returned, and she felt like nothing she said was getting through to her players. *I guess we're just going to have to rely on what got us this far. If I work them any longer, they're going to be too tired for the game tonight.* Even though the team was running through the drills at half-speed, Jess could sense their fatigue, both mental and physical. She blew her whistle and called them over.

"Okay, let's call it quits. Everyone make twenty-five free throws and meet back on the bus in twenty minutes. We'll go back to the hotel, check out and go to dinner at two-thirty. Then we'll come back here and watch the first game until it's time to get taped. Any questions?"

No one had any, so they dispersed to the baskets to shoot their free throws. Jess went over to get a drink and asked the trainer for some aspirin. She sat down to watch her players shoot free throws, and found herself thinking about Robin. *I wonder what she's doing this afternoon. Will I get a chance to see her before the game? Probably not. And probably not after the game, either, because we're going to have to get going right away.* She took a deep breath and blew it out. *How can I miss her when I just saw her last night? And why am I always thinking about her when I should be concentrating on my job?*

Jess looked around the arena at the banners of the Pac-10 schools. *How many of them have women coaches? All of them.* She was somewhat surprised at the realization, not having thought about it before. *And how many of those women are gay? I have no idea. I don't even know for sure if some of them are married. So why am I so sure that everyone would know if I was gay?*

She was staring into space when LaTeisha came over and
snapped her fingers in front of Jess's face. "Hey Coach, everybody's on the bus waiting for you."

Jess jumped to her feet with an embarrassed look on her
face. "Sorry. I guess I just spaced out there for a minute."

"Yeah, I guess so," LaTeisha replied with a concerned look.
"Are you worried about the game tonight?"

"No...I mean, yes...Yeah, I'm worried about how we're
going to defend those damn post players," she said, quickly
thinking of something to say, since she couldn't tell her assistant
that she had actually been lost in thought over a young economics professor.

Capi and Robin arrived at the arena just in time for the start
of the five o'clock game. They took their seats behind the visitors' bench, although they could have sat just about anywhere
they wanted. Most Husky fans wouldn't start arriving until about
halftime. Robin looked around and saw the NOU team lounging
in the bleachers at one end of the court. Some were reading
homework that they'd brought along, but most were just talking
and watching the other teams warm up. The assistant coaches sat
nearby, but Jess was nowhere to be seen. Robin felt a wave of
disappointment roll over her, since she was hoping to get a
chance to talk to Jess before the game. She was still worried
about how the coach was feeling after her abrupt departure the
night before.

"Hey there, is this seat taken?" The low, sensual voice sent
a shiver through Robin's body, and she looked up to see deep
blue eyes looking down at her. She couldn't help the full smile of
relief that broke out on her face.

"Actually I was saving it for someone special," Robin
replied, motioning for Jess to sit down.

The tall coach sat down partially facing the younger woman
and put her arm around the back of Robin's seat. "Did you guys
find something fun to do all day, or did you spend the time
recovering from last night?"

Robin blushed slightly, thinking about how she had barely
gotten dressed by early afternoon. "Well, we wanted to make
sure we got our money's worth out of the hotel, so we stayed

there until we had to check out."

Jess smiled knowingly at Robin and shook her head.

"Are you feeling better today?" Robin asked with a look of concern. "I was worried about you last night."

Too worried to have a good time at the bar? Jess thought hopefully. "I'm feeling okay. It's just been a stressful weekend." *You have no idea how stressful.*

"Yeah, I'll bet it has been," Robin replied sympathetically. "But just think how good it's going to feel when it's over, and you've won your first tournament."

Jess smiled at Robin's optimism. "We can't afford to get ahead of ourselves," the coach warned. "I'm worried that we might be a little too comfortable after last night."

"Well, I'm sure if anyone can get them mentally prepared, you can," Robin said confidently.

Why does she believe in me like that? Jess searched Robin's eyes for a reason, and saw admiration and affection looking back at her. *I don't know what I did to deserve it, but now I feel like I can't live without it.*

"Hey, Coach," Carmen interrupted them from the aisle, "they're ready for the pre-game interviews."

Jess let her gaze linger on Robin for just another moment, a silent understanding passing between them.

"Good luck," Robin said softly. "You'll do great."

"Thanks," Jess replied, and let her hand fall down to Robin's shoulder for a brief moment before getting up and following Carmen out to the press room.

"...and coaching for Northern Oregon University, in her first season, Jessica Peters," the Washington announcer intoned in the somewhat nasal monotone reserved for references to the opposing players and coaches.

Robin looked down at the imposing figure of the coach, towering over her team as they sat in front of her listening to last minute instructions. Jess was wearing a black shirt with very subtle white vertical lines running through it, and a pair of black pleated pants that seemed to go on forever down her long legs. *Oh my, how am I going to keep my eyes on the game,* Robin thought to herself. She took her program and fanned her face a couple of times, drawing a smirk from Capi.

"Oh, like you're any better," Robin challenged. "I was about to hand you a napkin a minute ago when you were staring over at the press table."

Capi laughed and said, "Some pair we are, huh?"

The game progressed through the first half with NOU staying just a couple of points ahead of the Huskies. They were clearly playing at their best, hustling after loose balls, helping on their match-up zone defense, and hitting over fifty percent from the field. Jess was worried that they could be playing so well and not winning by more. At halftime, she praised her team for their solid play, and told them to just keep playing the way they were. The zone defense was controlling the Huskies' inside game, and as yet, they hadn't been hurt too badly by outside shots.

The teams were equally well matched in the second half. The Huskies tied the game a couple of times, but each time NOU would make a small run and get back up by four or five. With two minutes left, the Bobcats had their biggest lead of the game at eight points. Washington called time out, and Jess's team came sprinting over to the bench.

"Okay, we're going to stay in our match-up zone, but you need to pay more attention to their three-point shooters now. If the ball goes into the post, everyone can't collapse to help, okay? And we need the weak side defenders to rotate around and cover the open players."

Unfortunately, in the other huddle the Washington coach was a step ahead. "I want the ball to go in to the post from the left wing. They're going to collapse on you like they have all game, so I want you to kick it back out to the point, okay. Now their weak side player is going to be rotated over to the point, so you need to move it quickly to the weak side wing, who will be open for the three-pointer, okay?" Heads nodded vigorously and the players sprinted back out onto the court.

The next two times down the court, the Huskies ran the play to perfection, cutting the lead to two with forty-five seconds left. Jess called time out to regroup. She huddled up with her assistants on the court to discuss strategy.

"I think we need to go back to player-to-player," Pam insisted. "We can't keep giving them those open looks."

"And their posts really haven't been hurting us that badly,"

LaTeisha agreed.

"Yeah, but that's because the zone has been double-teaming them the whole game," Jess countered. "We just need to move our feet faster on defense, and anticipate where the pass is going."

The assistants knew their role, and knew when to stop arguing and start supporting the head coach. They nodded in agreement, and Jess went over to talk to her team for the thirty seconds that were left in the time-out.

"We're getting burned on the weak side, so we need to keep our weak side defender home. If the ball goes in to the post, I want the person defending the passer to make a move toward the post as if you're going to double-team, but then I want you to pop back out to cover your player, okay? Hopefully, they'll pass it back out when they see the double-team coming, and if not, you posts are just going to have to play solid one-on-one defense."

The teams returned to the floor and Jess's team brought the ball up court. After a few passes around the perimeter, the ball went into the high post at the free throw line. She looked for the high-low pass to the low post, but hesitated a second too long before throwing it. The defender knocked the pass away and the Huskies had it back with twenty seconds left. They worked ten seconds off the clock, and then threw the pass in to the post from the wing. The wing defender faked the double-team, but before she could get back to her player, the post had passed it back and the three-pointer was on its way.

"IT'S GOOD! IT'S GOOD!" the partisan announcer yelled as the final horn sounded.

Jess's team was in shock on the floor, having blown an eight point lead in two minutes, while the coach strode down the sidelines to shake the Husky coaches' hands. Her eyes were blue chips of ice as she returned to her bench, grabbed her clipboard and strode off the floor. A reporter intercepted her halfway, and in an amazing display of self-control, Jess tersely answered a few questions. The reporter could tell that he was walking on thin ice, and quickly let the coach go.

Jess got to the locker room and threw her clipboard against the wall. *God damn it. I have never been so out-coached in my life. What an idiot.* "Stay in the zone, let them take the three-pointers," she mocked herself. *Why the hell didn't you listen to your assistants? You don't pay them not to think, do you?*

A few of the players straggled into the locker room, and Jess composed herself enough to offer some condolences. The post-game scene was quiet and depressing, and everyone hurried to get on the bus and get out of Seattle.

The ride home was dark and quiet. They didn't get away from Seattle until ten p.m., and they had to stop and pick up dinner to-go at the nearest Subway. Many of the players fell asleep quickly, while others stared dejectedly out the windows, listening to music on their headphones. Jess was in the front of the bus, reliving the end of the game over and over again in her head, and wishing the bus could go faster.

Behind her, Pam worked on some statistics from the game when Carmen approached and slid into the seat next to the assistant coach.

"Hey, Carmen."

"Hi, how do they look," she asked, nodding toward the stat sheet Pam was working on.

"They actually look pretty good. It's one of the best games we played all year if you go by the statistics."

"Too bad they don't give the trophy to the team with the best statistics, huh?"

Pam chuckled. "I guess that would take away a little of the excitement, wouldn't it?"

"Yeah, I suppose so." Carmen tried unsuccessfully to stifle a yawn.

"What's the matter, didn't get enough sleep last night?" Pam asked teasingly. "I heard the bar was hopping."

"Who'd you hear that from?" Carmen asked, surprised.

"The Washington trainer is an old friend of mine from my college days, and she was out last night, too. She said you guys were having quite the good time."

"Well, I don't know about anyone else, but I've never seen so many good-looking women in one place before. Not that I was looking at more than one of them, of course," Carmen added quickly with a smile.

"Yeah, right. I heard that Robin was quite the babe-magnet. Had women asking her to dance all night, huh?"

"Well, she did a pretty good job of fending them off, although I did see her getting up-close and personal with one nice-looking woman on the dance floor."

In the seat in front of the two women, Jess felt her stomach clench and she thought she might be sick. *Jesus, this weekend just gets better and better.* She jumped out of her seat and stormed to the back of the bus where she found an empty seat among her sleeping players.

The bus pulled into the NOU arena parking lot at one-thirty, and the players quickly unloaded their gear and took off for their dorms and apartments. Jess went to her office to drop off her briefcase, and then headed down to the locker room to make sure everything was closed up. Her headache had returned, and she was becoming increasingly depressed that she was going home to an empty house instead of getting to see Robin. So it was with great surprise that she opened the door to find the young professor sitting on a bench, leaning against the lockers.

"How did you get in here?" she asked, startled.

"It's nice to see you, too," Robin replied with a little smile. "I was waiting in the parking lot and Carmen told me you'd be making a final stop here before you left. I thought maybe you'd like some company."

Jess looked at the young, attractive woman sitting in front of her, who always seemed to be there when she needed her. She couldn't help herself. Despite the tournament loss, despite her worries about Robin at the bar, despite the headache that kept hounding her all weekend, all she wanted was to wrap the small woman in her arms and never let her go.

Jess walked slowly toward Robin, the look in her eye a smoldering testament to her feelings. Robin stood up to meet the taller woman, her eyes darkening as she looked up into the face of desire. Despite the signals she was getting from Jess, and despite the fact that every fiber of her being strained to be with the coach, Robin waited for Jess's touch. She couldn't afford to be wrong again—to push Jess into something she wasn't ready for.

She didn't have to wait long.

Jess reached her hand behind Robin's head and drew her

face closer. Her other hand found the small of Robin's back, and their bodies were pressed together. Slowly, Jess lowered her head to Robin's slightly parted lips, her eyes never leaving Robin's until they fluttered closed at the first soft contact.

Robin groaned and her lips parted further, eagerly accepting Jess's passionate kiss. Her hands caressed Jess's back and reached up to tangle in long, thick hair. She felt her knees growing weak and Jess guided her backward, pinning her against the lockers, the coach's strong thigh pressing between her legs.

Jess's lips never left Robin's, while her hands frantically worked to unbutton the younger woman's shirt. She felt the silk fabric of Robin's bra, and her breathing picked up. Pushing the shirt off her shoulders, Jess slowly kissed her way down Robin's neck, her hips and thigh keeping a steady rhythm between the shorter woman's legs.

Robin threw her head back as she felt Jess nip at her neck and shoulders. Her chest heaved, and she wanted nothing more than to feel Jess's lips on her breasts. In answer to her prayer, Jess unclasped her bra and tore the offending garment away, replacing the warmth of the silk with the warmth of her mouth. As Jess slid down Robin's body, she unzipped the loose-fitting jeans, sliding her hands inside the cotton Jockeys and around the slim hips, drawing the small woman even closer.

Robin gasped for air, and tried to maintain consciousness under the assault on her senses. "Jess," she whispered. "Are you sure this is what you want?"

Jess didn't even pause. "This is exactly what I want," she said between kisses. "This is exactly what I need, and I've just been too stupid to admit it." She rose up to look Robin in the eye again. "I'm so sorry I turned you away before. Please let me make up for it now," she said, her eyes darkening even further.

Robin wrapped her arms around Jess's neck and pulled her close again. "Just don't make me regret this later," she said, her mouth millimeters away from the coach's.

"Never again," Jess whispered, and her lips seared the truth of that statement into Robin's soul. Jess pressed Robin even harder against the lockers, one hand slipping between them, down to the unzipped jeans and into the warm wetness that waited.

Robin gasped and her body arched in response. In what seemed like seconds, but surely must have been minutes, her hips jerked and she cried out Jess's name, wrapping her legs around the tall woman, pinned between the strong body and the lockers.

Jess's face was buried in the small woman's neck as she felt Robin respond. She held on to the trembling woman, maintaining contact for as long as she could, before her own legs gave out and they sank to the carpeted floor together. Jess held Robin in her arms, rocking her gently, saying, "Never again, never again."

Chapter
32

Robin lifted her head from where it was buried in Jess's neck and looked the tall coach in the eye. "Where did that come from?" she asked breathlessly.

Jess smiled. "Weeks of frustration, and the fact that you are absolutely irresistible," she replied as she bent her head and softly kissed the smaller woman's forehead.

Robin returned her attention to the tender neck and nibbled softly at the smooth skin. Jess leaned her head back, closing her eyes and moaning softly. As Robin's hand started to unbutton Jess's shirt, the coach halted her by gently grasping her wrist.

"Could we continue this at my place? I don't even want to think about what we just did in my team's locker room."

Robin laughed and said, "Don't want to push your luck, huh? What time do the janitors come in, anyway?"

"I have no idea," Jess replied honestly, "and I don't want to find out firsthand now."

Robin extricated herself from the coach's strong body, and stood up to find the clothes that had been tossed off in the heat of the moment. Jess just watched admiringly as the young woman pulled her shirt back over her shoulders, and then was pleasantly surprised and aroused as Robin took her silk bra and slowly pushed it down the cleavage of Jess's shirt.

"Hold that for me until we get home?" she said seductively.

"I think I can manage that," Jess said, her eyes smoldering

once again. She reached for Robin's hand and led her out of the locker room, not releasing it until they left the outer doors of the arena. They walked to Robin's car, and Jess stood outside talking to the young woman through the open window.

"Why don't I follow you to your house; you can drop off your stuff and get a change of clothes, and then I'll give you a ride to my place."

"Okay," Robin replied, looking a little confused, "but I could just bring my own car over there and then you won't have to worry about giving me a ride back tomorrow."

"I don't mind, really," Jess said quickly. "I'll see you at your place," she said, already halfway to her own vehicle.

Robin rolled up her window and started her car. *I wonder what that's all about. It would seem a lot easier if I just had my own car there.* A look of realization came over Robin's face. *That's it, isn't it? You don't want my car there; you're afraid someone might see it. Oh Jess, you're just not going to make this easy, are you?*

In the other car, the coach was trying to rein in her emotions, which had been on somewhat of a roller coaster over the last twenty-four hours. She was ecstatic over what had just happened in the locker room, but still more than a little nervous about everything. *I can't believe we just did that in the locker room. What came over me? I don't even remember thinking about it. I guess that's good, because if I had been thinking, I never would have done it, and I'm* definitely *glad I did it.*

But what is this going to mean for the future? For my job? Jess's mind put a halt to that line of thinking. *You already tried to put your job first, and look where that got you. You are* not *going to pull back from this again. So you'd better just find a way to make it work with your job.*

They arrived at Robin's and the young woman ran into her apartment to grab some clothes for the next day while Jess waited in the car. They then made the short trip to Jess's apartment and unpacked what they needed from the weekend.

It was three a.m. before they slid between the sheets of the queen-sized bed, and Robin snuggled in close to the taller woman, laying her head on her shoulder. Despite their earlier intention to continue things when they got home, Jess's gentle stroking of Robin's back quickly put the young woman to sleep. Jess followed soon after, the stresses from the weekend flowing out of her body to be replaced by the contentment of having Robin by her side.

Jess awoke earlier than she'd hoped, given the late hour they'd gone to bed. It was light outside, though, and she could see the peaceful look on Robin's face as the small woman continued her slumber unabated, curled up close to Jess's side. The coach gently moved some stray locks of blond hair off of Robin's forehead and stroked her fingers lightly over the tousled head. She examined her own feelings and thoughts about the previous night, and found that she only felt happiness and relief, rather than the fear and panic that had accompanied their first time together. She knew that she needed this woman in her life like she'd never needed anything before, and although that thought held its own element of fear, it also brought a sense of peace that Jess could feel deep within herself.

Green eyes blinked slowly open, and seeing the look of open adoration on Jess's face, quickly darkened with desire. Robin stretched her naked body and slowly draped herself over Jess, the feel of skin on skin igniting her senses. "Good morning," she whispered hoarsely, bringing her lips up to meet Jess's.

"Mmmm, I never knew mornings could be so good," Jess replied, capturing Robin's lower lip between hers.

"Well, I'd say you have a lot to learn then," Robin said, straddling the tall woman's hips while kissing her way toward Jess's ear. The coach ran her hands over Robin's strong back, gripping her hips and pulling her closer. "I seem to recall we left some unfinished business last night," Robin breathed into the hypersensitive ear, causing Jess to moan softly.

Jess tangled her fingers in Robin's hair and brought the young woman's mouth back to meet her own. Lips parted and tongues met in a slow, sensual exploration. Jess's hands ran up and down Robin's bare skin, softly brushing the sides of the young woman's breasts that were pressed up against her own. Jess broke the kiss and gently pushed back on Robin's shoulders, her hands trailing down to caress the soft breasts that were now exposed. Her heavily lidded eyes were locked on Robin's face, as the young woman slowly closed her eyes and tilted her head back, arching into Jess's hands.

Robin's hips started moving of their own accord, pressing her wetness against the taller woman's abdomen. *How can I be so aroused so fast? Wasn't I just asleep a minute ago? How does she do this to me?* Taking a deep breath to regain some control, Robin gently grasped Jess's wrists and pinned them beside the tall woman's head, lowering her mouth once again to nibble on an earlobe.

"I want to make you feel the way you made me feel last night," Robin said huskily. "I want to make you lose control, forget where you are, think of nothing but my touch and how it makes you feel," she whispered between kisses to the soft neck just below the ear. "I want to make you think of nothing but the two of us."

Jess writhed beneath Robin's weight, desperate for more contact between them. Robin was more than happy to oblige, and soon the tall woman was gripping the sheets, head thrown back, and calling out the young woman's name again and again.

Slowly, Jess returned to earth, her chest heaving and her breathing ragged. She desperately reached for Robin, needing to hold her close, and the young woman quickly covered the long body with her own, burying her face in Jess's neck. They stayed that way for a long time, Jess stroking her hands over Robin's back while the young woman murmured sweet words of reassurance in her ear.

It was noon before the two women finally lay exhausted in the bed, sheets tangled between their legs. Jess was on her back and Robin was on her side, tracing long patterns down Jess's arm with her fingers.

"Jess?"

"Hmmm?"

"Are you sure you're okay with this?" Robin asked, nodding her head toward their naked bodies in a gesture meant to capture the events of the past twelve hours.

Jess turned to face Robin, her expression serious. "I'm more than okay with this, Robin. This is what I've wanted all along, I just wasn't willing to admit it. Or maybe I wasn't able to admit it," she said with chagrin.

"But are you still worried that it's going to affect your job?"

Robin asked with a worried expression on her face.

Jess sighed. "I don't know how this will affect my job, and I'd be lying if I said I wasn't worried about it. But *not* being with you was affecting my job, too. I don't know where my head was at the end of the last game, but it certainly wasn't where it needed to be." Jess reached up and stroked Robin's hair softly. "All weekend I was thinking about you...how much I wanted to be with you—*needed* to be with you...how much I hated the thought of you being with someone else because I turned you away..."

Robin looked startled. "What do you mean, me being with someone else?" she asked incredulously. "Jess, there's no one else. What made you..."

"I know, I know," Jess cut in. "But when you went out Friday night, I couldn't help but think about how you would eventually look for someone else if I couldn't give you what you wanted. The thought of you in someone else's arms, even just on the dance floor, almost killed me."

"Oh Jess," Robin said sympathetically, reaching over to wrap her arms around the tall woman. "You know, I only danced with one woman Friday night—other than Capi, and she doesn't count—and all it did was reinforce what I already knew. I don't want to be in anyone's arms but yours."

Jess hugged Robin tightly, hardly able to believe that this woman would really want her—only her—after what she'd put her through earlier that year. *I promise I won't mess up this second chance. There just has to be a way to make this all work out.*

Jess pulled back from Robin a little. "You know, I...I need to be discreet about this...about us," she said somewhat apologetically.

"I can understand that," Robin assured her. "It's not like I'm in the habit of broadcasting the details of my personal relationships to the world," she quipped.

"I know that, but you've probably been more open about your relationships than I can afford to be."

Robin looked a little concerned. "Well, I don't need to offer the information to anyone, but if someone asks me directly, I don't think I can lie. But Jess, I don't expect anyone to be asking me questions like that anyway. Are you concerned that someone will ask you?"

"Not really, I guess," she said unconvincingly. "At least, not if we don't give them any reason to."

"Well, maybe we're just worrying about something that isn't even a problem yet," Robin replied with a reassuring smile. A small voice in the back of her head sent warning signals that there was danger ahead, but she didn't want to spoil the happiness of the morning with unnecessary worry.

"Hey, do you have any idea how hungry I am right now?" Robin asked, changing the subject.

"I'm sure I have no frame of reference for the bounds of your appetite," Jess said with mock seriousness. "Would you like me to make some French toast? You've got evidence that I can do that without poisoning you."

"Let's go," Robin replied enthusiastically as she climbed off the bed and held her hand out to Jess. As she saw the coach's magnificent—and naked—body rise up from the sheets, she couldn't resist taking her in her arms once again and kissing her until she had forgotten all about breakfast.

Jess and Robin saw each other every day over the next week, but not nearly as often as the economics professor would have liked. The coach was busy getting ready for a road trip to California over the upcoming weekend, and there was only one night that Robin was invited to stay over at Jess's apartment. Robin's rational mind told her that Jess was worried about being discreet and she should let the coach set the pace for a while until she got more comfortable with their relationship. Her emotions, however, were screaming at her to find a way to spend more time with the busy Coach.

On Thursday, the two women met for morning coffee at the Java Connection. Jess's team was scheduled to leave that afternoon for their flight to southern California.

"So do you think your team is ready for the weekend?" Robin asked.

"Well, we've had a really good week of practice. It took them a couple of days to quit talking about the loss last weekend, but I think that's ended up motivating them to work even harder."

"How do you think you'll match up with the two teams you're playing against?"

"We play Long Beach State on Friday night, and that will be a tough game for us. They're looking pretty strong this year. But Sunday's game should be easier for us. I'll be disappointed if we don't win that one by ten or more."

Robin looked down at her hands that were nervously playing with the stir stick from her coffee. "You know, flights to L.A. are pretty cheap right now. It wouldn't be a very expensive trip for me to come and watch," she said, looking up with trepidation to see Jess's reaction.

The coach quickly looked away from the table and cleared her throat. "You know...I don't think that would be such a good idea," she said softly, returning her eyes to look pleadingly at Robin. "What are people going to think if you fly all the way to southern California to watch us play?"

"Who's going to think anything?" Robin said defensively. "The players? The trainer? The manager? We already know the SID wouldn't have a problem with it."

"Some of my kids are from southern California, and their parents are likely to be at the games," Jess argued.

Robin looked at her in complete disbelief. "How in the world would their parents even know who I was, let alone who I was sleeping with?" she asked incredulously. "Jess, don't you think you're being just a little bit paranoid here?"

"Look, Robin, you agreed that we could be discreet about this, and I just don't think that having you follow me to southern California is very discreet."

Robin took a deep breath and willed herself not to lose her temper. *She's about to leave for four days and you don't want her to leave while you're mad at each other,* she admonished herself. "Okay, I see your point," she conceded quietly, although she couldn't quite look the coach in the eye when she said it.

An awkward silence ensued for a couple of minutes before Jess finally spoke up. "I'm sorry this can't be the way you'd like," she said softly. "But I'm doing the best I can right now."

Robin looked at her with genuine empathy in her eyes. "I know you are. And I'm sorry that I was pushing you too hard. Let's just forget that I even mentioned it, okay?"

"Okay," Jess replied, but both women knew that it wasn't really okay, and each would spend much of the weekend thinking about whether there was any way to make it better.

Chapter
33

"What's the score?" Capi asked, slightly out of breath from rushing into Robin's apartment after picking up a pizza.

"It just started and it's 6-4 Long Beach," Robin replied, turning up the radio.

Robin moved the papers she was grading off to the side of the table and got out plates and napkins for the pizza.

"You want a beer, or something else?"

"That depends...Are you going to make me help grade those papers?" Capi asked, nodding toward the stack of homework.

"Of course. You're the one who calls yourself an economist trainee," she joked.

"Then I'd better have the beer."

Robin got out a couple of microbrews and poured them into chilled glasses from the freezer. They dove into the pizza while listening to the radio announcer give the play-by-play. The game was staying close through the first half, although a few of Jess's players were getting into foul trouble.

"Oh my! I can't believe that call!" the partisan announcer yelled. "That's three fouls on Schmidt and that's really going to hurt us. Let me tell you folks, that was one of the worst calls I've ever seen in my twenty years of broadcasting. Schmidt had perfect position and the offensive player just ran her over. I don't know what...Oh no. Coach Peters has just gotten a technical foul. She is absolutely livid out there. Her assistants are trying to restrain her, but she's halfway out on the court yelling at the official who made that call. She'd better be careful or she's going to get thrown out of this game."

Robin put her head in her hands and groaned. "Oh jeez, she's going to hate herself for this later."

The foul shots and the additional free throws from the technical put Long Beach up by eight with only a few seconds left in the half. They then inbounded the ball down low, where NOU was now missing the tall presence of Schmidt, and scored again at the buzzer. In a matter of seconds, they had gone from being within four points to being down by ten.

After a break for commercials, the play-by-play man came back on. "Well, that was a real killer at the end of the half. Coach Peters was still yelling at the ref as she was leaving the court. We'll have to see how the team responds to this when they come out for the second half. Let's look at the first half stats now, which have just been handed to me by Sports Information Director Carmen Ricardo, who we are very pleased to have helping us out with our broadcast tonight."

Robin smiled over at Capi, who was immediately blushing. "So how are things going with one very charming SID? You're looking a little guilty over there...Is there something I should know about?" Robin asked teasingly.

"Things are going very well, thank you, and I think you know everything you need to know," she said smugly.

"Okay, now I know you're not telling me everything. Let's hear it."

Capi proceeded to tell Robin about a week that included fresh flowers, a candlelit dinner, and sweet notes and e-mails arriving at unexpected times. "She's one of the funniest people I've ever met. I can't believe how she can make me laugh. When I hear from her, I just forget all about the bad things that have happened that day and I'm instantly smiling. I think my staff is wondering if I'm on drugs or something, but they're not going to complain about a good thing."

Robin laughed and reached over to give her friend a hug. "That's great, Capi. She sounds really special, and the best part is, she obviously thinks you're really special...which you are."

"Okay, that's enough about me," Capi said self-consciously. "Let's hear about you and the short-tempered basketball coach."

Robin sighed and proceeded to tell Capi about the events over the last week, ending with their unfortunate conversation at the Java Connection. "The worst part was having her leave for four days without really getting a chance to make up for that," Robin said with chagrin. "I sure hope she's forgotten all about it by now."

Jess had sent the team and other coaches into the locker room for halftime, and was standing outside the door trying to regain her composure.

What in the hell was I thinking? I guess that's a stupid question, isn't it? I hardly ever lose control like that. And of course, what I'm really mad about is that I made the mistake of leaving Natalia in there with two fouls and only a minute left in the half. So I go and take it out on somebody else because I'm mad at myself, right? Just another case of losing focus, which I seem to be doing a lot of lately. And do I even want to think about why I'm having trouble focusing? No, let's not go there right now. I'm just glad she wasn't here to see this.

Jess cleared her mind of the events at the end of the first half and strode purposefully into the locker room. To her surprise, she saw looks of pride and admiration on her players' faces instead of the disappointment that she expected.

Well, maybe it pays to stick up for them once in a while. Show them how much I care about what's happening out on the court. Of course if I could do it without giving away four points, that would be even better.

"Okay, listen up everybody. We're only down ten points and most of those we gave to them. So we know we can play with this team in the second half. We're going to have to adjust to the officiating—we can't have two or three people fouling out and expect to win. And we can't be giving them free throws on technical fouls, either," she said with a little self-deprecating grin to let them know she was including herself among the people that had to adjust to the officiating. She went on to make a few defensive adjustments to give more help to Natalia and hopefully avoid further fouls, and then made sure that they were pumped up for the start of the second half.

Jess's team came out strong and narrowed the gap to three points by the ten minute mark of the second half. Natalia had picked up her fourth foul, and two other players had three.

Unfortunately, this made them play more tentatively, and Long Beach immediately pressed the action, driving to the basket in an attempt to draw fouls. The strategy worked, and with four minutes left, both Natalia and Bennie had fouled out. With their two best players on the bench, NOU was overmatched and ended up losing by nine. Overall, Jess wasn't too disappointed, given the hole they had dug for themselves before the half, and she congratulated her players on a good effort as they came off the floor.

Jess was feeling better about her own second half performance, maintaining her focus and doing what she could to keep her team in the game. She sat in the locker room, going over the stats and reflecting on the game. *It was all so much easier when I didn't have other things on my mind, like a personal life. But I know one thing for certain, I'm not leaving for a trip again while we're mad at each other. All I've wanted to do since we left is call her and straighten things out somehow. Maybe I was wrong not to want her here with me. I mean, I do want her here with me, but I just can't believe that others wouldn't think it was strange and start wondering about our relationship.*

"Coach?...Coach?" Heather stood next to Jess trying to get her attention from whatever thoughts she was engrossed in.

"Huh?...Wha...Oh, sorry Heather, I didn't see you there," Jess replied, a slight blush creeping up her cheeks. "What can I do for you?"

"My parents wanted to know if they could join the team for dinner tonight."

"Oh, sure. Do they know where we're going and how to get there?"

"I'm just on my way out there to tell them," she said, nodding her head at the locker room door.

"Okay, no problem. I'd like to meet them and get a chance to talk to them." Jess smiled. Since she hadn't recruited most of her current team, she hadn't met many of the parents yet.

"Cool," Heather replied, skipping out the door. After giving her parents directions, Heather and Chris sat together waiting for the others to make it back to the bus.

"You should have seen Coach in the locker room," Heather said. "She was like in some other world, and I had to practically yell at her to get her attention."

"Really? Maybe she was daydreaming about strangling that official. Did she have a sinister grin on her face?"

Heather laughed. "Wasn't that incredible to see her lose her cool like that? She's always so totally in control—I wonder what happened?"

"I don't know, but she's seemed preoccupied since we left Comstock." She leaned over and whispered conspiratorially, "Do you think she's missing somebody back home?"

Heather grinned and replied, "Do you really think they're like, together? I don't even want to think about Coach doing the nasty with my econ professor."

"It sure beats a mental image of her with that assistant football coach that was hanging around earlier in the year, don't you think?"

"Yuck. Did you have to say that?" Heather replied with a sick look on her face. "Actually, I think it's kind of cute to think of Coach and Dr. Grant together, I just don't want to think about it in too much detail, okay?"

"Okay...Hey, shut up 'cause here she comes."

Robin and Capi sat at the table, grading the last of the economics homework.

"I guess they held their own in the second half anyway," Robin noted. "Too bad they got so far behind at the end of the first half."

"Well, those officials sounded terrible. They must have gotten them off a list of Long Beach State alumni," Capi said dryly.

"Yeah, but they've got to expect that kind of thing on the road and be able to adjust," Robin reasoned.

"I suppose. Hey, what should I give someone who labeled the axes on the graph wrong and drew the marginal cost curve upside down?"

"Well, did they at least label it as a marginal cost curve? You can give them a point for that."

Capi rolled her eyes at Robin. "You asked them to draw a marginal cost curve, Robbie, so of course they labeled it that way. Do you want me to give them a point for this mark over here where they accidentally dropped their pencil, too?" she asked sarcastically. "Maybe you should tell them that all marks on the paper will count for something, and we'll at least get some interesting art work to grade."

"Hey, just because I like to give students the benefit of the doubt doesn't mean that I'm giving away points," Robin said defensively.

"Whatever you say," Capi agreed unconvincingly.

"Can I ask you a question?" Robin said seriously.

"Since when do you have to ask that?" Capi replied.

"Would you feel okay if Carmen said she didn't want anyone to know that you were seeing each other? I mean, would you think she was ashamed of you, or of your relationship?"

"I don't think we're going to be able to have this conversation if we use Carmen for the example, because I can't imagine her trying to hide her feelings about anything. So let's just talk about you and Jess, okay? How does it make *you* feel? Do you think she's ashamed of you, or of what you have?"

"Well, I guess at some level she must be ashamed of it, because she's willing to accept the standard of others that says there's something wrong with it."

"I'm not sure that means she's ashamed of it," Capi replied. "We probably all accept certain standards and regulations, even if we don't agree with them, because we don't think we have a choice. I think Jess is wrong, though, about how much people actually care about her personal life. But I'm not in her business, so I can't honestly say that I know what it's like for her."

Robin took a sip of her beer and looked depressed. "I just don't know how long I could live in some kind of secret relationship, always worrying about whether someone would find out about us. That's just not me."

Capi looked sympathetically at Robin. "Nobody should have to live like that, Robbie. But hey, it's way too early to be giving up. Give Jess a chance to get used to the whole thing. Maybe she'll come around and find a middle ground somewhere."

"Yeah, maybe. You know, I think this stuff has me down right now because we left each other after a little fight on Thursday. All I can think about now is how stupid that was. I keep wondering if she's still mad at me, and if she's going to want to see me when she gets back."

Robin could feel the tears stinging the back of her eyes when the phone rang.

"Hello?"

"Hey, how are you?"

"Jess?"

"Were you expecting someone else?"

"Yes...I mean no. I...I just wasn't expecting you to call. I mean...I thought you'd be busy with your team," Robin added hastily as she wiped the tears away with the back of her hand. Capi smiled knowingly at Robin and made a motion to indicate that she'd go wait in the other room.

"Well, I've only got a few minutes because we're at a restaurant, but I was afraid if I didn't call now that I wouldn't catch you before you went to bed."

"Hey, you can call me anytime, you know. It doesn't matter if you wake me up."

There was an awkward silence as both women wondered how to bring up what was really on their minds.

"Too bad about the game tonight," Robin said sympathetically. "But you did better in the second half anyway."

"Please tell me you didn't listen on the radio," Jess said hopefully, cringing at the thought of Robin knowing about her tirade against the referees.

"Every minute of it. Even the part where the visiting Coach's body was taken over by aliens, and she went ballistic at the refs," Robin said teasingly.

Jess groaned. "How embarrassing. You must think I'm an idiot. That might have cost us the game."

"You may be a lot of things, Jess, but an idiot is not one of them."

"Well, sometimes I do some really stupid things...Like leaving on Thursday without calling to say I was sorry for getting mad at you," she said softly.

Robin felt the tears spring back into her eyes. "Hey, I'm the one who should apologize. I'm sorry that I'm always pushing so hard, Jess."

"No, you shouldn't have to apologize for just being honest about what you want," Jess said emphatically. "Especially since it's the same thing I want. I just haven't figured out how to fit it all into my life yet. Do you think you can be patient with me, even when I'm completely impossible to live with?"

Robin sniffed and took a deep breath to steady her voice. "I'll do my best to be patient, if you'll forgive me when I fail." Her voice caught on the last word.

"Hey...you're not crying are you?" Jess asked softly, concern lacing her words.

Robin couldn't find her voice to respond.

"Please don't cry, Robbie. I promise we'll work this out when I get back, okay?"

"I'm sorry, Jess," Robin choked out. "I just wish you were here."

"Me too...More than you know."

Another silence extended for a few seconds, and finally Jess cleared her throat. "I'm really sorry, but I'm going to have to get back to the table. Are you going to be all right?"

"Yeah, I'll be fine," Robin reassured her. "You've got enough things to worry about without worrying about me this weekend, okay? I'm here for you Jess, and I'll be here when you get back, I promise."

"Thanks," the coach replied sincerely. "You don't know how much I needed to hear that."

"Always."

"I'll see you soon, okay?"

"Okay...I can't wait."

Chapter
34

Saturday was a day for the players to take it easy and visit some of the attractions of southern California. Jess arranged for Pam and LaTeisha to take a group to Universal Studios for the day, but the head coach couldn't afford not to do a little recruiting while she was in the area. There was a high school tournament nearby with some great Division I prospects, so Jess headed there for the afternoon. It wasn't hard to spot the other college coaches in the gym when she arrived, armed with their notebooks and decked out in apparel announcing their respective universities. Jess purposely took a seat well away from the rest of them, not interested in any socialization with other coaches. After watching for about a half hour, she looked up from her notebook to see a young woman approaching with Cal-State Monterey emblazoned on her warm-up jacket. Jess didn't recognize her, so was surprised when she sat down next to her in the bleachers.

"Hi, aren't you Jess Peters from Northern Oregon?" the woman asked with a friendly smile.

"Yes, I am," Jess replied, somewhat warily.

The other woman extended her hand and said, "I'm Sara Graebel. I was an assistant coach there for a couple of years under Coach Thompson." Coach Thompson was Jess's predecessor at NOU, but Jess didn't recognize Sara's name from his previous staff.

"You must have left before last year, then," Jess replied, and

Sara nodded in acknowledgement. "And I take it you're at Cal-State Monterey now," she said pointing at the school logo Sara was wearing.

Sara smiled broadly and said, "Yeah, I've moved up to the head coaching ranks, and now I know how easy I had it when I was an assistant."

Jess laughed and started to relax in Sara's easy-going presence.

"I made a lot of good friends while I was at NOU. Do you like it there?" Sara asked.

"So far, I like it a lot. I think Comstock is just about the right size town for me. And being in L.A. this weekend has confirmed that even more," she said wryly.

"Yeah, southern California does take some getting used to, but I'm from here originally, so it doesn't bother me too much. You know, I was talking to an old friend of mine from NOU the other day, and she said your program was doing great. I think she might be a friend of yours—Robin Grant?"

Jess was clearly startled but tried hard not to show it. She desperately quashed the paranoia that was trying to rise to the surface and finally replied, "Yeah, she is a good friend of mine. How did you get to know Robin?" *Please, please don't let her be an old girlfriend of Robin's.*

"Well, I started out being friends with Robin's roommate, Ellen, but we kept having so many problems that I would find myself talking to Robin all the time, so we ended up being closer than Ellen and I were. I probably don't have to tell you how easy it is to talk to Robin—she just knows how to make you feel better all the time," Sara said with a wistful smile on her face.

Jess couldn't help but smile in return, knowing exactly what Sara was talking about.

The game they were watching came to an end, and the next one wasn't scheduled for another hour. Sara asked Jess if she wanted to go with her to get a latte at Starbucks, and Jess surprised herself by saying yes. She wasn't sure if it was Sara's friendly demeanor or the fact that she wanted to know more about Sara and Robin's relationship that was driving her, but she got up and followed the Monterey coach out the door.

Sara and Jess spent the next hour comparing notes on the high school players they'd seen, and discussing the differences in recruiting between Division I and II. Jess found Sara to be

intelligent, witty, and extremely easy to talk to, and she started
wondering why she had always avoided socializing with other
coaches in the past. *I was probably afraid that some of them were
gay and I'd be associated with them,* Jess thought, and then
immediately realized how stupid and narrow-minded that was.
She took a discreet look at Sara as they were driving back to the
gym and decided that there was absolutely no way for her to
know whether or not Sara was gay, and that it wouldn't have
made one bit of difference in the conversation they were able to
enjoy.

That afternoon, Jess and Sara watched another game while
they compared their experiences of living in Comstock and
working in the NOU Athletic Department. Jess was starting to
feel like she'd known Sara for a long time, and was sorry to see
that it was getting late and she needed to get back to the hotel.

"Be sure and say hi to Robin for me, okay?" Sara asked.

"Sure. Do you guys get a chance to talk to each other very
much?"

"Not really. You know how it is once you move away—it's
just hard to find the time. But I wish I could find time, because
Robin is really a special woman," Sara said sincerely.

"Yeah, she is," Jess agreed with a distant look in her eyes.

Just then another woman approached them and Sara's face
broke into a big smile. "Hey, Char, you're here early. Did you
get all your work done this afternoon?"

The other woman smiled back at Sara, but the smile faded
just a little when she noticed the tall, attractive coach that Sara
was talking to. "I got enough done so that I won't have to go
back in tomorrow, and that's what counts," she replied to Sara.
She waited expectantly for Sara to introduce her to the potential
competition.

"Oh, sorry. Charmaine, this is Jess Peters, the new coach at
Northern Oregon University. Jess, this is Charmaine Jackson—
she's an attorney in Monterey."

*Take a lesson, Jess. She introduced her as "an attorney,"
not "my friend" or "my roommate" or "my partner." You're so
worried about what people will think Robin is to you, but she
doesn't have to be anybody but Robin, the economics professor.*

The two women politely shook hands, although Jess felt like
she was being scrutinized for any wrong move she might make
toward Sara.

"You ready to go?" Charmaine asked Sara. "We've got dinner reservations at seven, you know."

"I remember, and I'm ready whenever you are." She turned back to Jess. "I can't tell you how glad I am that we got to meet and talk for a while. I really miss parts of Comstock and NOU, but I'm glad to see that the basketball program is in such capable hands," she said as she held her hand out for Jess.

Jess said, "Thanks," and clasped her hand warmly.

"And I'm especially glad that Robin has found someone like you for a friend. Be good to her, okay?" Sara asked, raising an eyebrow and looking knowingly at Jess.

Jess could feel herself blush a little as she replied, "Okay, I will."

"See you at the convention?" Sara asked, referring to the annual coaches' convention held in conjunction with the NCAA finals.

"Yeah, sounds good," Jess replied, giving a wave to Sara and Charmaine as they walked away.

I'm not sure what just happened there. It was like she knew that Robin and I were together. I didn't tell her that, did I? Did I give it away by something else I said? Surprisingly, Jess didn't feel the least bit panicked by the thought that Sara might know about her and Robin. In fact, she felt an overwhelming desire to talk to Sara more about it. She realized then, that she didn't have anyone in her life that she could talk to about these things. Robin was her best friend, but whom could she talk to about Robin? *I've never wanted to talk to anyone about my personal life before. But deep down, I* want *some people to know about Robin and me. I...I guess I'm proud of it.* That thought shocked Jess to her core, yet made her inexplicably happy to admit it. She smiled to herself as she gathered her things and left the gym.

Sunday's game was scheduled for two p.m. so that Jess's team could get a flight back that night. As expected, the game was much easier than Friday night's had been, and NOU won easily. The coach maintained her focus and composure for the entire game, but when it was over, she couldn't wait to get back to Comstock.

After showers, the team was bussed to the airport where

they had an hour and a half wait before their flight. They used the time to get some dinner and then sat around the boarding area reading or talking. Jess tried to call Robin a couple of times, but didn't get any answer at the professor's apartment. As she walked back from the phones the second time, she noticed Chris and Heather watching her with interested looks on their faces. *Now what are they up to? I swear those two are joined at the hip, the way they're so inseparable.* The proverbial light went on over Jess's head and she did a double take at her two players. *Do you think they're...No, don't even think about that. They're children, for God's sake.* Of course, Jess knew that wasn't true, but sometimes she couldn't help but think of them as her own offspring, and you just didn't think about your own kids having sex together. Jess shook her head and put the thought out of her mind.

She returned to her seat and tried to spend some time going over the stats from the weekend, but finally had to give up because she just couldn't keep her mind on anything except the small, blond professor that was waiting for her back home. *What is the matter with me? I feel like I've been away for a month. I can't remember ever missing anyone so much in my life. Is it going to be like this for every trip I make this season? God, I hope not, because I'm not sure I can stand it.*

*I wonder what she's doing right now...*Jess closed her eyes and leaned her head back on her seat. *Maybe she's at work, or maybe she's out with Capi, or maybe she's just taking a walk by herself and thinking about me...*

Robin was just finishing up her hike in the school forest near Comstock. It was only five o'clock and already starting to get dark. *I can't wait until solstice so that the days start getting longer instead of shorter. This is definitely the hardest time of the year to live in Oregon*, she thought as the rain dripped off her hood. Despite the dreary weather, though, Robin couldn't deny the sense of excitement that had been coursing through her body all day. Her inability to sit still had led her to the forest two hours ago to try to dissipate some of the excess energy. She brought her Walkman and listened to the second half of Jess's game. The post-game interview with the coach had nearly done her in—hearing Jess's voice and yet knowing that she wouldn't get to see her until late tonight, and maybe not until tomorrow if their plane got in too late. She was hoping that Jess would come by no matter what time she got home, but was trying to mentally prepare herself for a different outcome.

Robin grabbed some dinner on her way home, and spent the evening watching Sunday night football. At ten, she finally gave up and went to bed, the earlier anticipation having turned to disappointment. She tossed and turned in her bed for at least an hour, sleep eluding her.

Maybe their flight got delayed. Or maybe she just had too many things to do when they got back. There must be lots of things that need to get taken care of at the end of a road trip, right? Or maybe she was just too tired, and wanted to get a good night's sleep. Lord knows she wouldn't have gotten that over here, Robin thought wryly. *Or maybe she just wanted to be by herself tonight. Just because you want to spend every waking minute with her doesn't mean she feels the same way...*

The knock on the door sent Robin flying out of her bedroom. She didn't even think about the danger of opening her door in the middle of the night without checking to see who was there. She wasn't disappointed, though, as she flung the door open and saw a travel-weary, but happy coach smiling back at her.

Robin couldn't help it—she threw herself at Jess and wrapped her arms around her neck, burying her face in the dark hair.

Jess dropped her bags where she stood and returned the hug, holding the small woman as tightly as she could, and thinking that nothing had ever felt so right before in her life.

Chapter
35

"Robbie," Jess said softly, giving the sleeping woman's shoulder a little nudge, but getting no response. "Robin." Louder this time, with a stronger shake, and sleepy green eyes blinked halfway open. Jess was leaning over the bed, having already dressed.

"Hmmm? What time is it? It's still dark out."

"Shhhh, you can go back to sleep, but I need to get home so I can get in to the office early today. I just wanted to say good-bye." Jess leaned over and gave Robin a tender kiss on her fore-head.

Robin sat halfway up and blinked her eyes in at attempt to awaken her senses. She looked over at the clock and her eyes widened. "Jess, it's only four a.m."

"I know," Jess said, "but I woke up and couldn't get back to sleep, so I might as well get a head start on the day."

"But..." Robin sat up even further. "Can I at least make you some coffee before you go?"

"Nooo," Jess said soothingly, pushing Robin gently back down onto the bed and climbing up to lay beside her. She gently pushed the hair back from Robin's face, while kissing her softly on the cheek. "Just go back to sleep. I'll call you later in the morning, and we can have lunch together, okay?"

"Mmmmm." Robin closed her eyes again and relaxed into the gentle touch of Jess's fingers in her hair. In less than a minute, she was back asleep.

Jess quietly got off the bed and left the room, gathering her bags from the living room where she'd left them the night before. She silently let herself out of the apartment and headed for her car. She looked around at the parking lot and the other apartments, glad to see that everything was dark and quiet. *At least chances are pretty good that no one would have seen my car here between late last night and this morning.*

When Jess got back to her own apartment and unpacked her bags, the lack of sleep suddenly hit her. She and Robin had made love late into the night, but her nervousness about staying overnight at Robin's had kept her from sleeping well and led to her early departure. She decided that she would just lie down for a few minutes to rest her eyes, but before long she was sleeping soundly. She didn't wake again until nine a.m.

Oh damn, Jess cried to herself as she looked at the clock. *How did this happen? I was just going to rest for a few minutes...*

She quickly headed for the shower and managed to get herself ready for work in twenty minutes. When she arrived in her office, she already had a voice-mail message from Robin, and she called her back right away.

"Robin Grant," the professor answered her phone.

"Hi, it's me. Sorry I wasn't here when you called."

"Hey, that's okay. Did you have a meeting or something?"

"Uh...no...actually, I fell asleep when I got back home this morning and I just got in," Jess said sheepishly.

"Oh...well, I hope whatever you needed to get there early for was able to wait for you," Robin said, somewhat disappointed that Jess could sleep at home but not at her apartment.

"Yeah, that's not a problem. Say, are you still interested in lunch?" Jess said in an attempt to deflect the conversation from her morning's hasty retreat from Robin's.

"Sure, but can we go at one so I can play basketball at noon?"

"Okay, how about if I come by the rec center and pick you up?"

"Okay, see you at one...And Jess?"

"Yeah?"

"I missed you this morning when I woke up," Robin said softly.

Jess could feel herself blush, even though she was alone in her office. "Yeah, me too," she replied self-consciously.

There was a long silence, and Robin finally said, "I guess I'll see you later."

"Okay, bye."

How can everything be so easy when we're alone together, and so hard as soon as I'm back in the real world? Jess thought to herself. *Even now, when I'm sitting alone in my office, I feel like the eyes and ears of the whole Athletic Department are on me. And I feel guilty—like I'm doing something wrong. Am I? I guess that's the big question, isn't it?*

A few days later, the NOU team was gearing up for another non-conference game. Jess's team had two more games at home before they would take a short break over Christmas. Classes were over for fall term, and players could spend more time in the gym without distractions. The team was just finishing up a short practice in the late morning before their game, when Robin showed up at the arena. Sensitive to Jess's desire to be "discreet" she hadn't been coming to practices lately, and this time she stayed well up in the bleachers until the practice was over and the team had left the floor. She then headed off to Jess's office to find her.

"Hey there," Robin said cheerfully, standing in the doorway to Jess's office.

Jess looked up, startled to see Robin there, but quickly broke into a smile. "Hi, what are you doing way over here? Come on in," she said, waving Robin into one of the chairs in front of her desk.

"Your team looks like they're ready for the game tonight," Robin said.

"Did you watch practice?" Jess asked, surprised. "I didn't see you there."

"That was the idea," Robin said sarcastically. "If you didn't see me that means nobody else would have either." She knew her sarcasm was harsh, and she instantly regretted it when she saw the hurt look on the coach's face. "I'm sorry, Jess. I didn't mean that the way it sounded."

"Sure you did," Jess replied despondently. "I know you don't understand why I'm having such a hard time with this, and I don't seem to be able to explain it to you very well."

"No, that's not true, I do understand." Robin looked down guiltily at her hands. "I guess I'm just not used to it, and it's frustrating to have to hide something that means so much to me," she said sincerely, looking up to meet the coach's eyes.

Jess looked over Robin's shoulder at the open door, wondering whether their conversation could be heard outside of the office. She lowered her voice and said, "It's hard for me, too, you know."

"I know. Look, Jess, I didn't come over here to make you feel bad, and I'm really sorry I brought it up. Can we change the subject?" she asked with a pleading smile.

"Sure," the coach said easily, returning the smile.

"I...uh...I was wondering if you had plans for the Christmas break."

Jess had a moment of panic. *She's not going to ask me to go home with her and meet her family, is she?*

"Uh...no, I guess I don't. Christmas usually isn't a very big deal for me. We never have much time off between games and practices at this time of year, so I was planning on just hanging around here and catching up on a few things."

"Well...um...do you think you might like to get away for a little while...with me?" Robin asked hesitantly.

Jess couldn't help but smile reassuringly at Robin. "I could maybe get away for a couple of days. But I thought you'd go home for Christmas. Won't your family miss you?"

Robin looked chagrined. "My mom is always trying to guilt me into coming home for Christmas, but the last couple of years I've just told her that I don't want to fly to the Midwest during the winter, and especially not over Christmas. She seems to accept that, but then she expects me to come home twice during the summer."

Jess laughed. "Well, their loss is my gain. Where were you thinking of going?"

"Well, I rented a house in Sunriver and thought maybe we could go skiing. Mt. Bachelor isn't very crowded until after Christmas, so I thought we could cross-country ski on Christmas Eve and downhill ski on Christmas Day."

"Can you promise I won't break my leg and be on crutches for the rest of the season?" Jess teased.

"No, but I can promise to wait on you hand and foot if that happens." Robin smiled.

"Hmmmm, that might be worth it. I think I'll try out some of the black diamond runs."

A knock on the doorjamb interrupted them. Jess looked up to see LaTeisha standing there and tried to put a more serious expression on her face.

"Sorry to interrupt, Coach...Oh, hi Robin. How are you doing?"

"Good, thanks. How are things going with you?" Robin said with a friendly smile in return.

"Well, Coach here is keeping me so busy I can't even get into any trouble," she said with mock regret.

Robin laughed easily, but Jess cut in and asked LaTeisha what she needed.

"Eastern's here for their shoot-around a little early. I was wondering if you knew when the men were going to be in the gym today."

"Hey, I'll get out of your way and let you get some work done," Robin said apologetically, rising out of the chair and heading for the door. "I'll talk to you later, okay?" she called back to Jess.

Jess had a look between frustration and disappointment on her face, but she called out an "okay" in return, and Robin was gone.

"She's really nice—I like her," LaTeisha said approvingly, looking at Jess.

Jess found she couldn't hold the gaze without blushing and looked out her window while mumbling, "Yeah, I think so, too."

The assistant coach lowered her voice and said, "You could do a *lot* worse, you know."

Jess's jaw dropped and she stared at LaTeisha, unable to respond.

"What? You think I'm blind or something?"

"I think you're out of line," Jess said seriously.

"Well, maybe I am, but I'm going to tell you what I think anyway. I've seen the ups and downs you've gone through this fall, and I think you could use somebody to talk to every once in a while. Maybe that's not me, because I work for you, but I'm offering just the same."

Jess looked coldly at her assistant coach for a long while before responding. "Tell Eastern they can have the gym until two o'clock," she said, returning her eyes to her desk and picking up some paperwork, clearly dismissing the assistant coach.

LaTeisha let out a sigh and slowly turned and walked out of the office. *That went well,* she thought ruefully.

Jess stared at the papers in her hand, looking right through them. She was angry at her assistant coach for bringing up her personal life at work, for implying that she *needed* someone to talk to, and for making her think again about how difficult this all was for her. But finally she had to admit that she was really angry with herself for her reaction to LaTeisha's comments and the way she treated her assistant coach. *Like you've got so many friends that you can afford to lose any. Just last week you were wishing you had someone you could talk to, and now someone offers and you freak out. What's the matter with you?*

Jess was unable to concentrate on her work, and decided to go home for a run before coming back in for pre-game preparations. She gathered up her things and walked out of the office without talking to any of her assistants, not yet ready to confront LaTeisha again.

Chapter
36

Robin and Capi were seated about four rows behind the home team bench for the game with Eastern. Since the students were off-campus for the holiday break, the crowd was relatively small on a week-night. The seats behind the home team bench were packed, however, mostly with family and friends of players and coaches.

Robin noticed that Jess came out of the locker room with an "all-business" look on her face, and maintained a little scowl throughout the pre-game warm-ups. She kept to herself, standing off to the side and not interacting with her assistants. *I hope nothing went wrong since I saw her this afternoon.* Robin looked around at the players. *It doesn't look like anyone's injured or anything. I wonder what she's upset about?*

The warm-ups finished, the players were introduced, and the game got underway. NOU quickly jumped out to a ten point lead over the undersized Eastern team. Robin was cheering enthusiastically from her seat, and at the first time out, the woman seated next to her gave her a little smile as she sat back down.

"You seem like a loyal fan," she said warmly. "Do you come to most of the games?"

"I try to come to all of them," Robin replied. "I'd go to all the away games, too, if I could. I love basketball."

"You sure seem to know a lot about the game. Are you related to one of the players?"

"Oh, no. Why do you ask?"

"I just thought that most of these seats were reserved for the players' families and friends," the woman replied.

"Well, actually, the coach is a good friend of mine, so she gave us the tickets."

"Really? Which coach?"

"The head coach, Coach Peters," Robin said with a little proud smile.

The woman looked a little surprised, but recovered quickly. "Well, we're Heather Martin's parents—number twenty-two out there. I'm Patti and this is my husband Jim," she said, nudging her husband to get his attention.

"Glad to meet you," Robin replied, shaking both of their hands. "I'm Robin Grant, and Heather is actually in one of my classes—economics. And she's doing very well."

"You must be quite a good teacher then," Patti replied, "because math was never one of Heather's strong suits."

Robin laughed and said, "Well, there's actually more logic than math at this level of economics."

Capi leaned over at this point and interjected, "But she *is* a very good teacher—she's just too modest to admit it."

Robin blushed and introduced Capi to the Martins. The time-out ended and everyone's focus returned to the game. The Bobcats picked up the pace even further, and by halftime they had a fifteen point lead. As they left the court, despite the good play and big lead, Jess was still scowling.

In the locker room at half time, Jess let the players sit and rest for a few minutes. She sat away from the team, looking over the stat sheets from the first half. The assistants stood on the other side of the room, waiting for Jess to come over and discuss the second half strategy.

"What do you think she's so upset about?" Pam whispered to LaTeisha. "The game couldn't be going any better."

LaTeisha looked a little guilty. "I'm afraid she's mad at me, and the rest of you are suffering through association."

Pam looked at her with surprise. "What did you do?"

"I asked her something a little too personal this afternoon, and she took offense...told me I was out of line and hasn't spoken to me since."

"Ouch," Pam said sympathetically. "What did you ask her?"

LaTeisha rolled her eyes. "You think I'm going to tell you

that when I'm already in trouble? Shhhh. Here she comes," she whispered as Jess got up and walked toward them.

The head coach looked at Pam and Jeff and asked, "Anything you think we need to do differently in the second half?"

"No, things look great, coach," Jeff replied, and Pam nodded. LaTeisha just kept her mouth shut and waited. Finally Jess turned toward her and raised an eyebrow in question. The assistant coach just shook her head no, and looked down at the floor.

"Okay then, we'll keep things the way they are. I may want to try some different defenses later in the game if we stay ahead by a comfortable margin. Help me make sure everybody gets some playing time tonight, okay?"

The coaches nodded again, and Jess turned to address the team.

Back in the bleachers, Robin had returned from the concession stand with a hot dog, popcorn, soda, and M&M's. Capi just smiled at the young woman's appetite and got up to let Robin into her seat. In between bites, Robin continued her conversation with Patti and Jim Martin. By the end of halftime, Robin knew where they lived, where they grew up, how many kids they had, where they both worked, and whether or not they would be at the next game.

As the teams came out of the locker room, Robin met Jess's eye as she walked back onto the court. The head coach quickly looked away, the serious expression still on her face that had been there since the beginning of the game. Robin was starting to get worried that something bad had happened, and that somehow it involved her or her relationship with Jess. *Just when it seems like we're making a little progress, something happens to set us back again. I wonder what it is this time...*

The game progressed as expected, and the Bobcats won easily. Everyone got plenty of playing time, and Jess was able to experiment with different defensive schemes in a game situation. All in all, the game was a huge success, but the head coach couldn't have looked less pleased as she shook the opposing coaches' hands and stalked off the court.

Jess talked very briefly to her team in the locker room, answered a few reporters' questions, and escaped to her office as soon as possible. Once there, she sank wearily into her chair and closed her eyes. She asked herself what it was about the encounter with LaTeisha that afternoon that made her so upset.

I know that I'm not used to sharing my personal life with my colleagues, but it has to be more than that. I guess what upsets me the most is that if LaTeisha knew about Robin and me, maybe everyone knows. Jess shook her head. *No, not everyone sees me every day like my assistant coaches do, so that's probably an irrational fear. And it's not like she thought there was anything wrong with it—my God, she was practically congratulating me. Come on, admit it. You just over-reacted like you always do.*

Jess heard the outer office door open, and the assistants came in. She could hear them dropping off their things and closing down their offices for the night, and then she heard the outer door open and close as they left. She sighed deeply and pushed herself out of her chair, turned out the light and left her office. As she walked by LaTeisha's office, she was surprised to see the light on and the assistant coach sitting at her desk, staring out the window. *I need to clear this up right now,* Jess thought.

She knocked on the open door and LaTeisha swiveled around in her chair.

"Can I come in?"

"Oh...yeah...sure." LaTeisha motioned to the empty chair in front of her desk. They sat in silence for a moment before LaTeisha cleared her throat and said, "Look, Coach, I'm really sorry..."

"No," Jess interrupted. "Don't apologize...please. I...just let me say this, okay?" Jess paused and took a deep breath. "I appreciate what you were trying to say to me this afternoon, and I shouldn't have gotten so mad about it. But I...I'm not in the habit of talking about my personal life, and I don't think I want to change that now."

LaTeisha looked down at her hands and remained quiet.

"I guess what I'm saying is that I think we have a really good working relationship, and I'd like to keep it that way. Do you think that's possible?"

The assistant coach raised her head and looked Jess in the eye. She saw the steel curtain that the head coach had drawn across her emotions, and knew that she was not going to be the one to get past it. She nodded her head once and replied, "Yes, I think it's possible, and I'd like it very much if we could just take

up where we left off before I opened my big mouth this afternoon."

Jess smiled just a little, and said, "I think that would be
great." She rose out of her chair and extended her hand to
LaTeisha, who gripped it firmly. Jess held on for a long moment,
her eyes relaying her gratitude for the assistant coach's understanding. "I'll see you tomorrow, okay?"

"Okay," LaTeisha managed to smile in return, relieved that
things might possibly be better the next day.

Robin had waited for Jess to return to the court after the
game, but after the players emerged and another twenty minutes
had gone by, she decided to leave. She went looking for Capi,
and found her at the press table talking to Carmen.

"Hey, didn't you find Jess?" Capi asked, noticing the glum
look on Robin's face.

"No, I think she must want to be by herself tonight. She
seems to have disappeared."

Capi looked concerned, but said, "Well, maybe she just got
tied up with something. Why don't you come out with us for a
beer, and then you can call her later?"

"Oh, I don't know...I think I'd just as soon head home. But
thanks for the invitation."

"Are you sure? Come on—it'll cheer you up," Capi said,
giving Robin a reassuring pat on the back.

"No, really. You go ahead. I just don't feel like staying up
that late. Have a good time, okay?"

"All right, if you're sure..."

"Yeah, g'wan. I'll talk to you tomorrow."

Robin waved goodbye to Carmen and walked dejectedly out
of the arena.

Jess left the office feeling much better than she had all
night, and headed back to the court to see if she could find
Robin. By the time she got there, only the clean-up crew was
left, and Jess's mood deteriorated once again. *I can only imagine
what she's thinking—I stomp around all night like a moody bitch,*

*and then I disappear without even talking to her. God, why does
she always have to bear the brunt of my problems? And how long
will she be willing to do that before she just gives up on me? I*
have *to figure out some way to reconcile my personal and professional lives before I mess everything up and end up with nothing.*

Jess got in her car and decided to drive past Robin's to see
if she might be home and still up. Unfortunately, there were no
lights on in the apartment when she got there, so she continued
to her own apartment. She tossed her briefcase on the couch and
was heading for the kitchen when the phone rang.

"Hello?"

"Hey, you're home."

"Yeah, I just walked in. Where are you?"

"I'm at home...where did you think I was?"

"Well, I just drove by there and there weren't any lights on
so I didn't stop."

"Really? You were just here? You should have knocked. I
just crawled into bed about ten minutes ago."

"Well, I didn't want to wake you up..."

"Jess, how many times do I need to tell you that you can call
or come by any time you want? In case you haven't figured it out
yet, I *like* to talk to you." Robin lowered her voice and added,
"And I like seeing you on my doorstep even more."

Jess smiled and felt a warmth spread throughout her body.
"You have no idea how good that makes me feel right now."

"Hey, did something happen today? You sure didn't look
very happy at the game."

Jess sighed. "I was just my typical insensitive self and over-
reacted to something LaTeisha said this afternoon."

Robin waited for a moment, but when it appeared that the
coach wasn't going to elaborate, she prodded, "What did she
say?"

"She said she liked you—thought you were nice."

Robin was confused. "And that made you mad? Thanks a
lot."

Jess laughed, relieving a little of her tension. "And then she
told me I could do a lot worse."

"Oh...Why...How would she know about us?" The pieces
were starting to fit together for Robin, and she knew the coach
would probably not react well to someone assuming she was gay.

"That's what I'd like to know. Here I thought we were being

discreet and someone I'm not even that close to personally knows about us."

"But Jess, you work with her every day. I'm sure she sees things you're not even aware of."

"Yeah, but that's exactly my point. Maybe it's just not possible to keep these things discreet." Jess took a breath to calm down. "I just don't know yet what this is going to mean for my job."

"So what did you say to LaTeisha?" Robin was almost afraid to ask.

"Oh, in my very mature way I told her that she was out of line, and I didn't speak to her for the rest of the day."

"Oh, Jess."

"But I finally came to my senses and talked to her after the game, and I think we got things straightened out. I told her that I'd like to keep my personal life personal, but that I was sorry for the way I acted. I think we're okay now."

Robin could understand why Jess had reacted the way she did, but certainly didn't agree with it. Nevertheless, she felt bad for the head coach, and wished there was something she could do to make things easier for her. Unfortunately, she couldn't think of a single thing—it seemed that Jess was going to have to figure this out for herself...if that was possible.

"Robbie?"

"Hmmm?" Robin was drawn out of her musings.

"How would you feel about seeing me on your doorstep right now?"

"Mmmm, that would be a *very* nice surprise," Robin drawled in a low voice.

"That's what I was hoping you'd say," Jess said, smiling once again. "I'll be right there."

"I can't wait."

They hung up and Jess didn't even bother to change out of her work clothes. In five minutes she was knocking on Robin's door, and smiling as a bare arm snaked out to grab her and pull her into the apartment. Robin was wearing a form-fitting tank top and boxer shorts, and she led the tall woman into the bedroom by the hand. Once there, Robin turned and put her arms around Jess's neck, pulling her down for a soft kiss.

All of Jess's fears and frustrations drained out of her at the touch of Robin's lips. This was the feeling she couldn't deny, no matter how much thoughts of her job tried to interfere. She belonged in this woman's arms, and she would find a way to keep Robin in her life, because she could no longer live without her. Jess wrapped her arms around Robin and pushed her back toward the bed, never breaking the kiss.

The back of Robin's knees hit the edge of the bed, and as the young woman lowered herself onto the bed, her lips trailed down Jess's neck. She reached for the buttons of the coach's shirt, and was soon pushing the garment off of Jess's shoulders, unhooking her bra, and kissing the soft swell of her breast.

Jess tangled her fingers in Robin's hair, pulling her tighter to her arching body.

Robin fumbled with the zipper to Jess's pants, but soon had them off as well. She pulled the tall, and now very naked, woman down on top of her as she reclined back on the bed. Jess's breasts were poised just above Robin's face, and the young woman proceeded to lose herself in sensations she could no longer control. Hours went by as the two women repeatedly explored each other's most intimate places, desperate to feel the total release and acceptance that only they could give to each other. Finally exhausted, they fell asleep with legs and arms still tangled together.

Jess sat in her office the next day, trying to keep her eyes open when all she really wanted to do was take a nap. She'd gotten up early that morning and returned home to shower and change, after maybe four hours of sleep.

She was trying to concentrate on some scouting reports for her upcoming game, but her mind kept wandering to thoughts of Robin. After the previous night, the coach was more determined than ever to figure out a way to reconcile her job with her personal life. Jess's computer chimed with the notice of a new mail message. She clicked on the icon and saw an address she didn't recognize.

Jess—
How are things in Comstock? I read about your most recent win in the paper. It sounds like your non-conference season is going well.

I wanted to let you know about a high school player I saw the other night. Her name is Michelle Starling and she's from Carson City. She is definitely Division I material, but she's at a small school so no one is giving her much attention. I tried to recruit her to Monterey, but she has her heart set on Division I, so I told her I'd make a few contacts for her. If Division I doesn't work out for her, hopefully she'll think of me first when she starts looking at Division II schools.

It was sure nice talking to you last week. Say hi to Robin for me, OK?
Sara Graebel

Jess called Pam into her office and asked her to look into Michelle Starling. After the assistant coach left her office, Jess sat back in her chair and thought about how much she had enjoyed her earlier conversation with Sara. *I sure wish I had someone like her around to talk to more often.* Jess's eyes widened as she realized there was no reason she couldn't talk to Sara more often. While she didn't feel comfortable talking to someone like LaTeisha about her personal life, maybe someone hundreds of miles away that understood what she was going through would be the perfect solution. In a moment of extreme courage, Jess did something completely out of character—hit "reply" on her screen and started typing.

Sara—
Thanks for the tip! I'll check Michelle out. It's hard to hear about all the good kids in small schools, so I really appreciate your willingness to share that information.

Hey, I feel a little weird about asking this, but I was wondering if I could ask your advice about something kind of personal. (You can say no and delete this right now.) I've never really had to think about how my personal life and my professional life go together—I guess because I've never really had much of a personal life! Anyway, what I'm wondering is how you handle your job without giving up your personal life, and how you handle your personal life without losing your job. If you don't feel comfortable discussing this with me, I understand. Believe me, I don't feel comfortable discussing it with other people either! But I found it really easy to talk to you when I was in California, and you're a long ways away so you can't see just how uncomfortable I am!

Thanks again for recruiting tip! I look forward to hearing from you.

Jess

The coach hit "send", sat back in her chair and tried to slow her racing heartbeat. Her palms were sweaty and she was already wishing she could take back the message. Her phone rang and she almost jumped out of her chair in surprise. Dealing with the routine demands of her job turned out to be a good diversion for her, though, and ten minutes later she was surprised to see the notice of a return message from Sara on her computer screen.

Jess—

I'd be happy to talk to you about the challenges of blending a coaching job with a personal life. And I'm going to assume that we're talking about a personal life that involves two women, OK? (If not, you can delete this right now. <g>) Of course, I can't speak for everyone, but this just hasn't been an issue during my career. I certainly don't go out of my way to tell people about me and Charmaine, but I don't hide it either, and I think most people figure it out on their own. I suppose there are athletic directors who would have a problem with this, but it's hard to believe that there's an athletic director in a major program today that hasn't had some gay coaches on his or her staff.

The other issue is recruiting, and we've all heard the horror stories of opposing coaches supposedly using the "gay" label against an unmarried woman coach. But I think there's more rumor than truth to that, and I think it's becoming more of a non-issue every day. I suppose there are still some homophobic parents out there, but I don't think most athletes even think about things like that when choosing a school and a coach. Maybe I'm incredibly naïve, but that's been my experience.

Have you had some specific problems there at NOU? I always thought the athletic staff there was pretty progressive.

Well, I hope I've been at least a little bit helpful. Do you mind if I ask whether your personal life involves Robin? If so, you're one lucky woman!

Sara

Jess let out the breath she'd been holding while reading

Sara's letter. She smiled at the reference to Robin, knowing that she felt very lucky indeed.

Is it really possible that this is all just a non-issue? That I've been killing myself over something that no one else even cares about? I find that really hard to believe. I suppose the truth lies somewhere in the middle.

Jess sat deep in thought for a long time, before finally deciding that she needed to take a walk and clear her head.

Over the next couple of days, she and Sara wrote back and forth, discussing the specifics that were on Jess's mind. Although she wasn't completely convinced that she didn't need to be paranoid about her relationship with Robin, Jess was at least starting to feel better about things, and was especially happy to have someone to talk to about her personal life. Of course, it didn't hurt that Sara was many miles away, and Jess was not likely to run into her any time soon.

Chapter
37

"Wow, look at that view. It's like a winter wonderland," Robin exclaimed. The trees were laden with snow from last night's storm, and they sparkled in the sun like a million diamonds. She and Jess had been cross-country skiing up the side of a ridge all morning, and now they were overlooking a tree-covered basin flanked by Broken Top, a jagged peak in the Cascades.

Jess caught up to Robin, breathing heavily from the climb. She was not as experienced on cross-country skis, but she could almost make up for it with her natural athletic ability and her long strides. Nevertheless, the thin air at 6,000 feet was taking its toll.

"That's incredible," Jess managed between breaths. They couldn't have asked for a better day. The temperature was around 35F, and they had been peeling layers of clothing off all morning. Robin was now clad in only a thin polypropylene undershirt and thermal tights, and Jess couldn't help but admire the part of the view that included the young woman.

"You like what you see?" Robin asked, raising an eyebrow.

"I like the view from here just fine," Jess replied with a seductive smile. She moved up behind Robin, straddling the shorter woman's skis, and wrapped her arms around her waist. She leaned over and softly kissed an exposed earlobe before resting her chin on Robin's shoulder. "It's beautiful," she whispered, "and so are you."

Robin turned her head to meet the taller woman's lips, and she lost herself in a soft, but passionate kiss. Her knees were threatening to buckle when she finally broke it off, breathing as heavily as she had been while climbing the ridge.

"I can't believe what you can do to me with just a kiss," she breathed.

"That was not just a kiss," Jess replied, equally breathless. "I didn't know it could be so warm standing in the snow in the middle of winter."

Robin leaned her head back on Jess's shoulder, thinking that life couldn't possibly get any better. However, her stomach chose that moment to growl loudly, and Jess chuckled as she felt the vibrations under her hands. "I guess that means it's time to stop for lunch, huh?"

"Sorry, I didn't mean to disrupt the mood. I guess I don't have any control over my appetite."

"As if we didn't already know that," Jess teased.

They found a fallen log to use as a seat, and unpacked the lunch of cheese, crackers, fruit, and chocolate. Robin made a little sandwich of cheese and apple between two crackers and offered it to Jess. The coach took it between her lips, capturing a few fingers along the way.

"Hey, don't be starting anything you can't finish," Robin warned.

"Who says I can't finish it," Jess replied with a raised eyebrow.

Robin smiled. "You think you could keep me warm enough not to get hypothermia from bare skin on snow?"

"Oooh, a little challenge," Jess said, leaning over to capture Robin's lips. Without breaking the kiss, she put her arms around the smaller woman and pulled them both backwards until they slipped off the log into the soft snow behind them.

"Yikes! You got snow down my back!" Robin shrieked.

Jess laughed and pulled the young woman on top of her, brushing the snow off her back. They were nose to nose as they smiled at each other, glad beyond words that they could have this time together away from the pressures and problems of their everyday lives.

Robin snuggled her head into Jess's neck and hugged the tall woman tightly. She could feel the heat radiating between their bodies, but the rest of her was starting to get chilled. She shivered once, and Jess rubbed her back briskly, trying to warm her up.

"I guess we'd better think about getting started again before you get too cold, huh?" Jess asked.

"Mmmm, I suppose so, but it's hard to leave this spot," Robin mumbled from where her lips were softly kissing Jess's neck.

Jess chuckled and replied, "Well, I'll bet we could remember where we left off once we get home and are sitting in front of a nice warm fire."

"Oh, that does sound good," Robin said, shivering again and lifting herself off the taller woman.

They quickly ate the remaining lunch, gathered up their things, and got back on the trail. Robin set a brisk pace in an effort to get her circulation moving again, and soon they were making their way back down the ridge. It only took them about half the time to get back to the car as it had taken them to climb the ridge, and they easily made it back home in time to prepare a nice dinner. Afterward, they settled in front of a roaring fire, sipping a glass of wine and appreciating the feel of tired muscles after a long day of skiing.

Robin leaned her head on Jess's shoulder, staring into the fire. Her hand was tracing an idle pattern on the coach's thigh.

"Jess?"

"Hmmm?"

"You wouldn't be mad at me if I got you a Christmas present, would you?"

Jess turned and smiled at Robin. "Well, that might depend on what you got me, I suppose."

Robin smiled back. "Well, then I guess I'll have to give it to you in order to find out, huh? Wait here." She got up and walked to the bedroom, returning with two packages, one small and square, and one long and round. She handed her the small, square one and said, "Open this one first."

Jess smiled and took the package, then pulled Robin down to sit next to her again. She leaned over and gave the young woman a soft kiss on the lips and whispered, "Thank you."

"But you haven't even opened it yet," Robin protested.

"It doesn't matter what it is...The fact that it's from you, and you're here giving it to me, is all the Christmas present I could want."

Robin blushed and took the coach's face into her hands, kissing her soundly. "I'm afraid the present isn't nearly as romantic as you are."

Jess chuckled and pulled away to open her present. Inside the box she found a pair of black flannel boxers with "NOU Bobcats" written on the waistband, and a white T-shirt with the fighting Bobcat logo.

"Pajamas," Robin explained.

Jess grinned and replied, "Does this mean you want me to wear more clothes to bed?"

"Well, I do enjoy taking them off," Robin retorted, "but I really got them for when you're traveling. I didn't think you should still be wearing those Idaho State clothes."

"I'm sure my team would appreciate your efforts. Unfortunately, they never see me in my pajamas."

"Hey, you never know when there's going to be a fire in the hotel and you're going to have to go running out in your PJ's."

Jess laughed and hugged the small woman, thanking her once again.

"Here, now open this one," Robin said while handing over the long, round package.

Jess unwrapped it to reveal a beautiful graphite fly rod. Her eyes widened in surprise, and she looked up at Robin.

"I built it for you," Robin said somewhat shyly.

Jess looked back at the rod and said, "You're kidding. How did you do that?"

"Well, if you buy the blanks at the fly shop, they let you use their equipment to add all the hardware."

"So you put on the guides, and the handle, and the reel attachment?" Jess looked more closely at the careful application of thread covered with epoxy to hold the guides in place.

"I was going to use orange and black thread, but I thought it would be too tacky." Robin looked down self-consciously. "So I decided to try to match the blue of your eyes instead."

"It's beautiful," Jess exclaimed, looking up again at Robin. "I don't know what to say...Thank you." She set the rod down and gathered the young woman into her arms, hugging her tightly. She pulled away slightly and reached into her pocket for an envelope. She handed it to Robin and said, "Merry Christmas."

Robin took the envelope and opened it, finding a card with

Santa spinning a basketball on his finger. Inside, Jess had written:

Robbie—
The end of my season won't be complete if you're not there with me. When (not if!) we make it to the first round of the NCAA's, will you come along? All expenses paid, of course. Please say yes!
Love, Jess

Robin looked disbelievingly into the coach's eyes. It was only a few weeks ago that they had argued over whether it was okay for Robin to go to an away game, and now Jess was inviting her to the post-season tournament. *What could have caused you to change your mind so quickly? Not that I'm complaining.*

"Well?" Jess asked with a raised eyebrow.

"Oh..." Robin realized there was a question she had neglected to answer. "Yes. Absolutely yes." And she threw her arms around the coach's neck, pulling her in for a kiss to emphasize the point.

Chapter
38

Robin lay snuggled in Jess's arms in front of the fireplace, both women watching the fire, thinking about how wonderful this Christmas was turning out to be.

"Jess?"

"Hmmm?"

"Have you thought much about what you want for the future...I mean, not for the forever future, but just the near future?" Robin asked with hesitation.

"Are you talking about my career future or my personal life future?"

"Well, both, I guess."

Jess thought for a moment. "Well, for my career future, I'd like to win enough games this year to make it into the NCAA's, and then have a great recruiting year." Jess paused, thinking beyond this first year. "I guess every coach's ultimate goal is to win a national championship, but you just don't get there overnight. I just hope I'm still at NOU working at it five years from now."

"Do you think you'll move onto a bigger program if you're successful at NOU?"

Jess held Robin tighter and kissed the top of her head, sensing some insecurity in the young woman. "I don't have any particular aspirations to coach at a powerhouse like UCONN, or Tennessee, but I certainly would listen to any offers that might come my way in the future." She tilted her head to look into

Robin's eyes. "Does that worry you?"

"No...well, I guess it does a little...Okay, a lot. But I know it comes with the job, and I would be so happy for you if you got a chance to do what you've dreamed about all your life."

Jess smiled at that. "What about you?" she asked. "What do you want for your career future?"

Robin laughed lightly and replied, "Tenure—what every assistant professor wants. But seriously, I love Oregon, and I'm here as much for the things I can do outside of work as for the things I do at NOU. I'd be happy to get tenure here and stay for a long time."

"Is there anywhere else you've ever thought about living?"

"Hmmm." Robin thought. "There's nowhere I'm dying to move to, but I guess there are some other places I would consider living, like Montana, or Colorado, or New Mexico, or Northern Arizona..."

"Nothing in the east?"

"I'd be really surprised if I ever found myself east of the Mississippi River again. I suppose I could live in Wisconsin or Minnesota, but that might be too close to my mother for my sanity."

Jess chuckled. "I don't really see myself going east either. I think the west just kind of gets into your blood."

Robin fidgeted a little bit and cleared her throat. "And what about the future of your personal life?"

Jess kissed Robin again and replied, "Mmmm, I'm very happy with my personal life at the moment." She pulled away a little and looked into Robin's eyes again. "I think things have been a lot better for me lately...I...I'm feeling more comfortable about who I am, and what it means for my job. And...and I've realized that I want you to be a part of my life, and I can't keep that part completely separate from the rest of my life. I don't *want* to keep it separate."

Robin felt the tears spring to her eyes. She buried her face in the tall woman's neck, trying not to turn into a blubbering idiot. Jess held her tightly and soothed her with soft words of reassurance.

Finally, Robin looked at Jess with red eyes. "I was afraid there was never going to be a place for me in your life, Jess. What made you change your mind?"

"Oh Robin, I had to find a place for you. Couldn't you see

how much I needed you?" She looked sincerely into the young woman's green eyes. "I just had to step back and open my mind a little bit. When I did, I realized that everyone wasn't out to get me. They weren't all looking for some weakness or flaw that they could exploit. In fact, most people I come in contact with are actually on my side. I don't know why I always had this feeling that I was alone in everything."

"You're not alone, Jess," Robin said, smiling up at the coach. "There are a lot of people at NOU that want very much for you to succeed."

Jess smiled back with a little twinkle in her eye and replied, "I've even found a supporter in California—from another coach, of all people."

Robin looked questioningly at the coach. "Really? Who would that be?"

"An old friend of yours, as a matter of fact," Jess replied with a sly grin on her face. "I ran into Sara Graebel when I was recruiting at a high school tournament on our last trip there."

Robin looked startled, thinking about her own conversation with Sara and hoping that it hadn't come up when Jess and Sara were talking. She didn't want the coach to think that she had betrayed her confidence.

"How did you meet her?"

"She came up and introduced herself to me. We had a really nice talk—just about basketball...recruiting...working at NOU. We even went out for coffee afterward. She's really nice. I can see why you two were friends when she was here."

Robin smiled at the memory of time spent with Sara at NOU. "Yeah, she was a lot of fun to be around."

Jess watched the fire dying down to glowing embers. "When we got back from that road trip and I had that run-in with LaTeisha, I decided I really needed somebody to talk to about what I was going through. It had been so easy to talk to Sara that I just decided to bite the bullet and ask her if I could talk to her about some personal things."

Robin looked really startled at that. Jess was simply not the type of person to reach out to someone else for help with personal problems. Yet she was incredibly proud of the coach for being willing to do it. *I guess that's a sign of how much our relationship means to her,* she realized with an undeniable amount of pleasure.

"So you just called her?"

Jess chuckled. "No, I wasn't that brave...I e-mailed her." Jess proceeded to tell Robin about the series of e-mails between Sara and her, and how it eased a lot of her fears about her job. "I'm not saying I don't still feel the need to be discreet, but I'm hoping I can put the paranoia to rest," she said with a self-deprecating grin.

Robin hugged the tall woman tightly and said, "You don't know how good it makes me feel that you are willing to try so hard to make this work with your job, Jess. You could have just given up, you know."

Jess pulled back and looked intently into green eyes. "No I couldn't, Robin. I tried, remember? I can't give up on you...on us."

Robin searched the blue eyes for any sign of doubt, but found only sincerity and promise. She couldn't stop the smile that spread across her face. "This is the best Christmas ever," she said, leaning in to lightly brush her lips against Jess's. The coach pulled her tighter and returned the kiss with a passion that promised that the holiday was only going to get better.

Chapter
39

January brought the start of the conference season for Jess, and the start of classes for Robin. Conference games were generally played on Thursday and Saturday nights, unless the television schedule dictated a Sunday afternoon game. Since the women alternated their home and away games with the men's team, Jess was out of town from Wednesday to Sunday just about every other weekend. Robin was teaching every day of the week, which precluded her from taking any long weekends in order to watch an away series. Robin was frustrated at the lack of time she got to spend with Jess, just when she thought their relationship had the chance of settling down. Midway through the season, it was all she could do to suppress her frustration on the few occasions she did get to spend some quality time with the head coach. Jess could sense that something was wrong, but she was helpless to do anything about it. At the halfway point, they were scheduled to play their bitter rivals, the Southern Washington Hawks, at home on Friday night, which would at least give her a rare two-day weekend free.

Jess's team had continued its preseason success, and had won all its home games and at least gained a split on the road. They stood in third place in the conference, just a game back of Stanford and Southern Washington. However, Jess was not completely happy with the team's performance in recent weeks, and she was particularly disappointed in the play of one temperamental point guard. Bennie had been showing up just a little late for a few practices and had been clearly taking the path of least resistance in most drills and scrimmages. Jess had warned her about being late, and tried to push her harder in practice. In games, Bennie had been able to rise to the occasion, but Jess didn't know how much longer that would last.

Two days before the Southern Washington game, Jess called her assistants in to her office to see if any of them knew what Bennie's problem was.

"I don't know, Coach, but I've noticed it, too," LaTeisha offered.

"Maybe she's having problems with school," Pam speculated. "Have we gotten any progress reports back yet?"

"Yes, and while they're not glowing, she's not really doing that badly," Jess replied.

"Well, maybe it's personal then," Jeff said.

"Or maybe this is just her usual style," LaTeisha countered. "Maybe she was just on her best behavior at the beginning of the season to impress the new coaches."

"Hmmm." Jess's brow furrowed. "I hadn't really considered that. Maybe I'll give a call to one of the previous coaches and see what their experience was."

Jess dismissed the assistants from her office and decided to call Sara, who would have been involved in recruiting Bennie, even though she didn't coach her at NOU. In reality, she was glad to have the excuse to call Sara and talk to her new confidante.

"Hi Sara, this is Jess Peters."

"Jess. How are you doing?"

"Good—how about you?"

"Great—we're really doing well in our conference play so far. Is everything okay with you and...well...I mean, is everything going okay for you there?" Sara wasn't sure how comfortable Jess was in talking openly about her and Robin, since they had only discussed relationships in general in their previous e-mail correspondence.

"The job is going okay, and I guess the personal life is going as well as it can for a basketball coach in season that is on the road for half her life," Jess chuckled.

"Don't I know that," Sara sympathized. "Char is threatening to find a surrogate partner during the season."

Jess laughed, although she couldn't help but cringe at the

thought of Robin finding a substitute for her under any circumstances.

"Hey, I'm actually calling with a basketball question, not a personal question."

"Sure, what is it?"

"You recruited Bennie Gonzales out of high school, right?"

"Ahhh, Bennie...I sure did. Now there's a player with unlimited potential."

"No argument about that, but we're having a little trouble getting her to reach that potential, mostly because she insists on doing the minimum necessary to get by. Does she have a history of that?"

"Oh yeah, that was definitely her rap in high school. I talked to Coach Thompson last year, and he had the same problem with her as a freshman. He said that at the beginning of the year she worked hard, probably because she wasn't sure if she was going to get a starting position or not. But once she had that sewed up, she definitely slacked off."

"Hmmm...well, I kind of thought that might be the case, but I wanted to make sure before I talked to her about it."

"Well, good luck. Trying to motivate players like that is one of the hardest parts of our job."

"That's for sure," Jess agreed. "Hey, I'm afraid I need to go, but it was nice talking to you again."

"Sure, no problem. Good luck with the rest of your season."

"Thanks, you too."

Jess hung up the phone and thought about how she was going to approach Bennie. She knew one thing—showing up late to practices was not going to be tolerated.

That afternoon's practice followed the same pattern as previous ones, with Bennie showing up about ten minutes into the warm-up and stretching time. Jess stood on the side of the court, giving the point guard a look that would have dropped her in her tracks, if she'd had the guts to look back at the coach. Instead, she took a place as far away from the coach as she could get and joined the stretching routine. Jess deliberately walked around to where Bennie was hiding out, and simply stood there watching. Throughout the practice, Jess made a point to be standing near

Bennie, clearly making the point guard nervous, but also giving her little opportunity to slack off. At the end of practice, Jess called the team together.

"You all know that this is a very big game for us this Friday. If we win, we have the chance to be tied for the conference lead going into the second half of the season." She saw a few excited smiles appear around the group, but they quickly faded as Jess got serious and her eyes turned to blue chips of ice.

"Unfortunately, not everyone is taking this as seriously as they should. And if there's one thing I will NOT tolerate, it is someone letting her teammates down. This basketball team may not be the most important thing in your life, but when you are in this gym, it is the ONLY thing in your life." Jess's glare was directed straight at Bennie, who was looking intently at her shoelaces.

Jess took a deep breath to calm herself. "It appears that we need a little review of some team rules. I expect people to show up on time for practice and games. If I thought the beginning of practice wasn't important, I wouldn't make you be here. However..." she walked slowly around the group to stand next to Bennie, "...since Bennie doesn't seem to think that the beginning of practice is important for her, she will sit out the first half of Friday's game. Tara, you'll be starting at point guard." The look on the players' faces was one of shock and dismay. They all knew how important Bennie was to the success of their team, and now they were all going to suffer because of her actions.

"Is there anyone else who needs to be reminded of the rules?" Jess looked seriously around the group, most of who quickly looked down when their eyes met. This was not the way that Jess wanted to leave her team after a practice, but they would have another practice before Friday's game, and she thought that it might do the players good to go home and think about how serious she could be about her team.

"The rest of you can go; Bennie, I'll see you in my office in ten minutes." With that, Jess strode off the court, leaving the team talking in hushed tones as they made their way to the locker room.

Ten minutes and thirty seconds later, Bennie was reluctantly knocking on Jess's door. Jess looked at her watch and sighed. *You'd think she might have been a minute early under the circumstances.*

"Come on in, Bennie. Have a seat," Jess said, motioning to the chair in front of the desk. Bennie shuffled over and slumped in the seat, not looking up.

Jess sat and looked at the young woman for a few moments, trying to decide on the best approach to take. While she knew that the half-game suspension was necessary for her team rules to have any integrity, she didn't think that an adversarial approach was going to work with the recalcitrant player.

"Bennie, is there some reason you've been showing up late for practice?"

Bennie just shrugged and shook her head no.

"Do you think you work as hard as you can when you are at practice?"

This time, Bennie just shrugged, unwilling to admit that she might be able to try harder.

"What do you think would happen if you tried as hard as you could in every drill? In every scrimmage? Are you afraid you'd get tired? That you wouldn't have enough left to get through the rest of the practice?"

Bennie's eyes rose briefly to meet the coach's, and then quickly returned to her lap. She mumbled a very quiet "No."

"Are you afraid that if you put it all on the line that you'll be opening yourself up to possibly fail?" Jess paused to let that sink in. "A lot of players feel that way, Bennie—that if they just hold something back, then they can say they weren't trying their hardest if something goes wrong. Is that how you feel?"

Bennie shrugged again, but was obviously taking in something that she hadn't thought about before.

"Well, I want you to think about that a little, okay? I want you to think about how you can go through your whole life just trying to get by, and then you'll get to the end of it and what will you say? 'Whew, I made it?' Just 'making it' isn't good enough, Bennie. It's not good enough for you, and it's not good enough for my team. The only way you can really make sure you don't fail is to go out there every day and do your absolute best. Do you understand what I'm saying?"

Bennie finally looked up and quietly said, "I guess so."

Jess smiled just slightly at her, and replied, "Well, you think about it over the next few days, especially while you're playing the back-up point guard. You're going to see how much your team needs you, and how much more you can do for your team if you give them everything you've got."

Bennie started to get out of the chair, obviously wanting desperately to escape from the coach's office.

"Sit down, Bennie. There's one other thing. You need to apologize to your team for coming to practice late. I'd like you to do it tomorrow at the beginning of practice. Do you think you can do that?"

Bennie looked like Jess was asking her to stick needles under her fingernails, but she finally said a reluctant "okay" when she realized the coach really wasn't giving her a choice.

"Great." Jess smiled more broadly this time. She got up and walked around her desk, leaning on it just in front of where the player was sitting. "Bennie, you're a very important part of this team, but I care about you as more than just a player—I hope you know that. If there's something that's bothering you or you need to talk to someone about anything, I'm willing to listen, okay?"

Bennie nodded again, although it was clear that she thought the coach was the last person in the world she would go to if she had a problem.

"See you tomorrow, Bennie."

The point guard rushed out of the office, leaving Jess shaking her head and wondering if she'd really made any progress at all. *I guess the next week or so should tell. I just hope this doesn't cost us the game on Friday. Not that I'd change my decision if I knew it would...*

It was halftime of the Southern Washington game, and Robin sat in her seat feeling frustrated like the rest of the fans. Well, at least half of the fans, since the Hawks fans had showed up in force and were easily out-cheering the hometown fans, who had a lot less to cheer about. NOU was down fifteen at halftime, the result of turnovers and an ineffective offense without their starting point guard. Tara had been playing her best, but it just wasn't good enough against Southern Washington's experienced backcourt.

Robin slumped in her seat and scowled. "I HATE the Hawks," she muttered to Capi. "And I hate the damn Hawk fans, and that damn Hawk mascot."

Capi laughed at her friend's frustration. "You've only lived here three years—how can you hate the Hawks so much?"

"It's easy. They think they're so much better than us, and then they go out and prove it every year in almost every sport. Who wouldn't hate them?"

Capi laughed even harder. "Oh come on. We have a better gymnastics team than they do."

Robin rolled her eyes. "You know they don't HAVE a gymnastics team, smart-ass."

"Okay, okay, but what about softball and volleyball? We beat them sometimes in those sports. And we've even beaten them in football every once in a while."

"Yeah, but there's only one sport I *really* care about, and that's women's basketball, and I haven't seen us beat them in the three years I've been here. And it's not looking good tonight."

"No, it's not," Capi agreed. "But things might be different if Bennie was playing. Do you think she'll play in the second half?"

"I sure hope so. Jess said it was just a half-game suspension, but I'm worried that it might be too late to dig ourselves out of this fifteen point hole."

Robin's premonition turned out to be right, as the Bobcats fought back gallantly in the second half, only to end up losing by four. The green and yellow clad fans whooped it up around the arena as the opposing coaches shook hands at the end of the game.

"Ugh. I think I'm gonna throw up," Robin said, looking around at the celebration. "And Coach Runyan has that smug look on her face. How can Jess even shake her hand?"

"Well, Jess is obviously a lot more gracious than you are," Capi noted, as the tall, dark coach made a point of shaking the opposing players' hands as well before striding off the court to the locker room.

"I don't know how she does it," Robin replied. "She has more self-control than anyone I've ever met. Maybe too much, sometimes."

Capi looked at Robin inquisitively. "What is that supposed to mean? You guys aren't having problems again, are you?"

Robin sighed. "No, I'm just frustrated because I hardly ever get to see her. And then when we do get to spend time together, I end up picking a fight or pouting over something stupid, just because I'm so frustrated. It's like a Catch-22. Pretty soon she's just not going to want to spend time with me, and I won't blame her."

"Hey, it sounds like you're feeling way too sorry for your-self," Capi admonished. "Where's that self-assured, fun-loving woman that I've had a crush on for three years?"

Robin smiled gratefully at Capi. "If I'm at all self-assured it's because you've done such a good job of building me up, and we both know that crush ended with your first glimpse of a cer-tain sports information director."

"Oh no, you'll always be my first love," Capi teased. "Everyone else will just have to settle for being second best."

"Well, here comes second best now, so maybe you'd better watch what you say," Robin said in a hushed tone.

Capi blushed as she turned to see Carmen walking their way. The SID smiled broadly at Capi, making her blush even more.

"Yeah, you sure look like you're settling for second best," Robin said in her best sarcastic tone.

Carmen greeted them both and sat down in the empty seat next to Capi, laying her hand on the tall woman's thigh in a casual sign of affection.

"Do you two have plans for the night, or could I take you out for a drink?" Carmen asked, leaning forward to look at both women.

"I don't know, Capi, do you think we'll get a better offer?" Robin said with mock seriousness.

"Well, there were those two women in the hawk hats that were giving us the eye earlier..."

Robin couldn't keep a straight face any longer and burst out laughing. "Oh God, Carmen, please—anything but a Hawk fan."

"I'm not quite sure how to take that comment," Carmen said, feigning a look of hurt.

"It's okay, honey, she was only kidding," Capi said, patting Carmen on the leg solicitously. "Come on, let's get out of here and find a bar that isn't decorated in green or yellow."

The women got up to leave, and Robin saw Jess coming back out from the locker room. "Hang on you guys, let me just go tell Jess what we're doing. I'll be right back."

Robin walked up to the coach, who had been intercepted by the Senior Women's Athletics Administrator. She stood off to the side, waiting patiently until they finished their conversation. As the administrator walked away, Jess turned to Robin with a look of welcome relief. She took a step closer to the smaller woman and wished she could just pull her in for a much-needed hug. *That's what my straight colleagues can do with their partners; it's just not fair, is it?*

"God, that was a hard loss to swallow," Jess said.

"Yeah, but you did pretty well considering you didn't have your starting point guard for the whole first half. That should make you feel pretty good about the rematch at the end of the season," Robin said optimistically.

"I suppose so, but it's hard to think about that right now. I guess mostly I want to forget about this game and start looking forward to the second half of the season...and hope that no else finds a need to test the team rules." She looked at Robin hopefully and said, "If you're not busy you could come over and help me forget..."

Robin's smile faded a little as she replied, "Well, I told Capi and Carmen I'd go out for a beer with them, but I can tell them to go ahead without me..."

"No, no, you should go," Jess said quickly. "I didn't know you had plans."

"But Jess, we hardly ever get to see each other, and I can see Capi anytime," Robin protested.

Jess smiled reassuringly at the smaller woman. "Why don't you go out for one beer with them, and then come over. It will take me that long to finish things up here and get home anyway, okay?"

Robin didn't look like she was quite convinced, but she acquiesced anyway. "Do you want me to bring anything with me when I come?"

"Just me," Jess said very softly, a half-grin spreading across her face.

Robin blushed furiously and slapped the tall coach on the arm. "And now you expect me to just go out with my friends for a while?"

Jess just turned to go and shot another grin over her shoulder while waving good-bye.

Robin stayed for the minimum time necessary at the bar

with her two friends before heading over to Jess's. Her repeated glances at the clock resulted in endless teasing about her single-mindedness, but Capi finally urged her to go.

"It's not like you're really here with us anyway. And Carmen's just been dying for a chance to get me alone, so you'd be doing her a favor," Capi said with a wry grin toward the SID.

Carmen rolled her eyes. "It's true, she's been resisting all of my charms, but I think she's just about to give in, and another hour alone with her is all I'll need."

Robin laughed and smiled gratefully at her friends. "Well, I hope you have as much fun as I'm going to have tonight," she said with a wink.

"Whooo-boy, let's not go there," Capi said, fanning herself with a menu.

Robin just grinned and gave Capi a hug before she headed out of the bar.

When she arrived at Jess's, the coach had changed into a pair of sleek black running pants and a black NOU T-shirt, complementing the dark hair and blue eyes. Robin raked her eyes over the tall coach, and walked slowly up to her. Jess's eyes locked on Robin's, and a smile played across her lips.

"Have you been waiting long?" Robin asked softly.

"Just my whole life," Jess replied, taking the small woman in her arms and bending down to kiss her soft lips.

Robin drew back and whispered, "I'm so glad you're home this weekend. I miss you so much when you're away."

Jess leaned her forehead on Robin's. "I miss you, too, but it just makes these times we have together all the more special."

"Do you really have the day off tomorrow?"

"Yeah, I thought the team could use the break, and God knows I could...especially if I can spend it with you."

"Hmmm, we'll have to see if you earn it or not," Robin said in a sultry voice next to Jess's ear while she pushed the coach backward toward the couch. Just as the back of her knees hit the couch, Jess spun Robin around and lowered her gently, following quickly to straddle her with arms and knees.

"That sounds a little like a challenge," Jess purred. "I think I just may be up to it." Jess took hold of Robin's wrists and held them above the small woman's head. Her torso pinned Robin to the couch, and she started a sweet torture with her lips and tongue. Robin writhed beneath her and Jess took both of Robin's wrists in one hand, her other hand roaming the young woman's body, caressing and inflaming her senses.

"Jess, please..." Robin panted.

"Please what?" Jess asked without pausing in her ministrations.

"I need to feel you...feel your skin...take these clothes off..."

"So impatient," Jess teased, even as she unbuttoned Robin's shirt with her free hand. "Don't move," she warned as she released the smaller woman's wrists. Jess quickly stripped off her own clothes, and then returned to the task of removing Robin's. As she stripped the pants over her feet, Jess knelt back down on the far end of the couch and kissed her way up Robin's bare legs. The young woman reached to tangle her hands in Jess's hair.

"Uh-uh," Jess said, grabbing her wrists and putting them back over her head before returning to her pleasurable task. Robin groaned and closed her eyes, gripping the material of the couch in her fingers. Jess proceeded to cover every inch of the young woman's body with soft lips and caressing hands, finally concentrating on the place she wanted it most, and sending Robin over the edge to a place she'd never been before.

"Oh God," Robin breathed as she slowly regained her senses. "What did you just do to me?"

Jess grinned and said, "I hope I just earned the right to spend tomorrow with you."

"Tomorrow, the next day, next week...I think I'm in debt for a long time."

"Hmmmm, mission accomplished," Jess said as she held the small woman tightly.

Robin managed to repay a little of her debt later that night, and the two women went to sleep exhausted, not rising until late the next morning.

Chapter
40

The second half of the season started well for Jess's team. Bennie was showing up on time, and while she may have still held back a little in practice, she was definitely working harder than she had before. It even seemed to rub off on the rest of the team, and Jess couldn't have been more pleased with their effort. The result was a four-game winning streak, sweeping the Washington schools on the road, and the Arizona schools at home. In mid-February, the team was traveling to the Bay area for the all-important match-up with Stanford. First, though, they had to defeat Cal on Thursday night, and Jess was worried that the team might overlook the Bears in their anticipation of the Stanford game.

As the team waited at the airport for the short flight to San Francisco, Jess noticed that Heather stood over by the window, staring out at the planes taking off for the last twenty minutes. She looked around to find Chris and saw the young woman talking on the phone, smiling and laughing. She didn't think too much more about it, and didn't notice that the two women didn't sit together on the plane for the first time all season.

On Thursday, the team had a good shoot-around at the Cal arena, which turned out to be a precursor to how the game would go. NOU came out aggressively on defense, and harassed the Cal guards into numerous turnovers. Natalia dominated inside on offense, and Bennie kept feeding her the ball for easy baskets. The only downside of the half was that Heather had thrown the ball away repeatedly on fast breaks, and was 0 for 6 from the field. At halftime, Jess patted her on the head and told her not to press—just let the game come to her. Heather bit her lip and nodded, not looking up from the locker room floor.

The Bobcats went on to win by fifteen, a margin that would have been even bigger if Jess hadn't played the subs for the last seven minutes. All in all, she thought the game was a great tune-up for the Saturday game with Stanford. She just hoped that Heather would come out of her slump by then, especially since the young woman was so upset by her play that she cried in the locker room afterward.

On Saturday afternoon, Jess was reviewing some scouting reports for that night's game when there was a knock on her hotel room door. She went to open it and was surprised to see Heather standing there.

"Hi Heather, what can I do for you?"

"Um...I was wondering...could I come in?"

"Oh, sure," Jess said, stepping aside and waving the young woman inside. Jess walked over to the table where she had been working and pulled a chair up to face hers. The player sat down and looked at her hands that were fidgeting nervously in her lap.

Jess waited for a few moments, and when it appeared that Heather was too nervous to start the conversation, Jess said, "Do you want to talk about the game on Thursday? I know you didn't play as well as you'd like, but I don't think you should be too worried about it, Heather. Everybody goes through slumps."

At that, Heather started crying, and Jess thought she had somehow said the wrong thing. "Hey, it's nothing to get so upset about," Jess said reassuringly.

"No, you don't understand," Heather sobbed, leaning her forearms on her legs. "It's not about the game...I mean, it is, but it isn't."

Now Jess was really confused, but she decided that she should wait and let the young woman explain before she said anything else wrong. She reached over and rubbed Heather's back in a soothing motion, waiting for the player to compose herself.

"My life is all screwed up right now, and...and I don't know who else to talk to...but...well, I thought you might understand because you're...well, because of you and Dr. Grant."

Jess's hand flew off Heather's back like she'd been burned,

and she sat back in her chair, looking disbelievingly at the young woman. Heather looked up through tear-filled eyes that were pleading for compassion and sympathy. Jess swallowed hard and fought her every instinct that was telling her to run—to deny what Heather had said and end the conversation right there. *No, you can't do that again. You stay right here and give this woman the support she needs.*

Jess cleared her throat to buy a little more time to think. "Heather, let's just back up a little bit. Why don't you tell me why you think your life is all screwed up." *Okay, that's it—don't deny it but you don't have to confirm it either.*

Heather's tears flowed harder as she said, "It's Chris...she...she says there's someone else, and she doesn't want to be together anymore."

"I see..." Jess thought hard. *What in the hell is the right thing to say?* "When did she tell you this?"

"Last Monday. I...I didn't even know anything was wrong," Heather wailed.

"Hey, hey..." Jess soothed. Her mind was at war with her body, the latter wanting to reach over and comfort the young woman, and the former warning her not to touch the player. The coach tentatively put her hand on Heather's arm, and the young woman immediately leaned over and started sobbing on Jess's shoulder. She clumsily patted Heather on the back, and after a few moments the player sat back up and wiped at her eyes.

"I'm sorry...I..."

"No, that's okay, you don't have anything to be sorry for," Jess said emphatically. She got up and retrieved some Kleenex from the bathroom, offering it to the young woman whose sobs were lessening.

"I don't really know what to say, Heather," Jess offered lamely as she sat back down. "These things are painful, and there's really nothing I can say that will make you feel better about it. It's just going to take time."

"But everything was fine between us," Heather protested.

"Hey, you're so young, Heather. Things can change so fast when you're twenty years old. Chris probably had no intention of finding someone else. Sometimes these things just happen, and there's no good reason for them."

"But...do you think she might change her mind...might come back to me?"

"I don't know, Heather. It's possible. Have you talked to her about it?"

Heather looked down sadly. "Yeah...she...she said that it's already over between us...she doesn't feel the same way anymore. I...I just can't believe that she won't change her mind if I could just figure out the right thing to say to her."

"Sometimes it's not in your control, Heather. At some point you just need to say to yourself that you did everything you could, and it's just not your fault if it doesn't work out. But right now, I think you need to take care of yourself, and do the things you need to do for your own sake."

"Like what?" Heather asked with some skepticism.

"Well, for one thing, you can try to find some success in other aspects of your life, like basketball, for example. Instead of letting this control your thoughts and ruin your game, why don't you concentrate on the game and let it take your mind off your troubles? I know it's not that easy, but if you really work at it, I'm sure you have the mental discipline to focus on the game for a couple of hours."

Heather raised her head, looking for the sincerity in Jess's eyes to match her words, and managed a small smile when she found it there. "Yeah, I guess I could try," she offered softly.

"Why don't you start tonight, okay? Just give it a try. I believe you can do it, Heather—I really do."

Heather looked hopeful as she got up to leave.

"Thanks, Coach...and thanks for talking with me."

"Anytime, Heather—I mean that."

Jess closed the door behind Heather and leaned back into it, sighing heavily. *God, I hope I said the right things.*

The bus arrived at the hotel to pick the team up for the game, and Jess noticed that Heather looked much better. She sat by herself a few rows behind the coach wearing her headphones, and appeared to be successfully avoiding Chris.

Jess thought about how she might change the substitution pattern to minimize the amount of time that Heather and Chris would be playing together. She didn't want to change Heather's starting role because she wanted to show the player that she still had confidence in her. She was a little worried, however, about how long she could leave Heather in such an important game if the young woman wasn't playing up to her usual potential.

Jess watched the pre-game warm-ups carefully, and Heather seemed very focused. She kept a serious expression on her face, and although she wasn't interacting with her teammates as much as usual, that was probably understandable. As the starting line-up was introduced, Heather sprinted onto the floor, but kept her eyes forward as she ran through her teammates who were slapping her hands. If the situation was affecting Chris at all, it wasn't obvious to the head coach.

The opening tip went to Bennie, and almost before she could look up, Heather was sprinting toward her basket ahead of the Stanford defense. Bennie fired the pass to her for the easy lay-up, and NOU took the first lead. As the Cardinal came down for their first offensive possession, Heather was matched up against their high scoring "2" guard. She picked her up at half-court and proceeded to deny her the ball, despite having to fight through three or four picks that were being set in an attempt to free her up. The Cardinal eventually had to settle for an off-balance shot by one of their post players that missed badly, and Natalia grabbed the rebound and quickly fired the outlet pass to Bennie. Heather was again streaking down the sideline, but there was one Stanford player back defending. Heather did a jab-step into the lane and popped back out to the three-point line where Bennie threw her the pass. She didn't even hesitate as she took the three-pointer, and was already heading back down court as it swished through the net.

A little smile played across the head coach's lips, even though she had been saying "No!" as Heather was taking the quick shot with no rebounders. *Good for you. I knew you could do it.*

About fifteen minutes into the game, the score was even and Jess could see that Heather needed a rest. She told Chris to go in for her, and as Heather came off the court she deliberately avoided the hand that Chris offered her, her eyes focused on the bench. She went down to sit at the end, and Jess followed her there, kneeling down in front of her with a hand on the player's knee. Jess turned her head so only Heather could hear her and said, "You're doing great—I'm really proud of you." The mask that Heather had been wearing the whole game slipped a little as she smiled slightly at the coach. Jess smiled back and returned to her seat, focusing once again on the game.

By halftime, NOU was up by four and the team was excited as they entered the locker room. Jess could hear players saying, "We can do this!" and the optimism was almost contagious. However, Jess had been around long enough to know that Stanford was not going to come out in the second half without making some adjustments, and beating them on their home court would be a rare feat for any team. The head coach tried to temper the optimism without losing the enthusiasm, and after making a few adjustments of her own, sent them back onto the court for the second half.

As expected, Stanford started the second half with a new look, switching defenses repeatedly, and pushing the tempo of the game. They were paying more attention to Heather, who was finding it difficult to get free for a shot. To her credit, she concentrated on defense, passing, and rebounding instead, and other players were able to benefit from the double-teams she was drawing.

With a minute left in the game, NOU was up by one and Stanford had possession. As they reversed the ball around the key, Heather anticipated the pass to the weak-side player and neatly intercepted it, heading down court for a lay-up. She was fouled hard going to the basket, and landed heavily on the floor. She slowly got up, and limped toward the free-throw line, barely putting weight on her right ankle. The referee asked her if she was all right, and she waved her off, saying she would be fine. With the crowd behind the basket waving balloons and jumping up and down to distract her, Heather made both free throws, putting NOU up three with thirty seconds left.

Stanford called time-out and Jess pulled Heather aside. "Are you okay?"

"I'm fine," Heather replied, not meeting the coach's eyes.

Jess looked skeptically at the young woman. "Jump on your right leg for me."

Heather's face contorted with pain and frustration as she shifted her weight to her right leg, which immediately gave out.

Jess put her hands on Heather's shoulders and bent her head to look into the player's eyes, which were filling with tears. "Heather, we wouldn't even be in this game if it wasn't for you. But you're in no shape to play. Go get some ice on that ankle so it doesn't swell up on you."

Heather limped off toward the end of the bench, met half-way by the trainer who put her arm around the player's waist and acted as a crutch for her. Jess watched her for a moment, and then quickly strode over to where the team was huddled with the assistant coaches.

"Chris, report in for Heather." She waited until Chris got back from the scorer's table and then knelt in front of her team. She could barely be heard over the noise of the Stanford band and the cheering crowd. "We can't let them shoot the three!" she shouted as the players bent their heads closer to try and hear her. "We're going to go with the straight player defense, but you need to watch for the inside-out. Don't be sucked into the key if they throw the ball into the post. Natalia, you're not going to get any help inside." The tall post player nodded with a look of determination on her face. "If we play good defense for thirty more seconds, we can win this game." Jess looked around at the faces and was pleased to see that no one seemed hesitant or scared. She stood up and put her hand out, the others quickly reaching in to join hands, and said, "Defense," which the team repeated in unison before heading back onto the court.

As the team waited for Stanford to break their huddle, Jess called Chris and Bennie over and told them to switch their defensive assignments, giving Bennie responsibility for Stanford's star player. The Cardinal in-bounded the ball at the end line, and worked some time off the clock. With about ten seconds left, Chris's player had the ball and faked one way before driving hard down the right side of the lane, leaving Chris trailing help-lessly behind. Bennie immediately left her player to help out, leaving Stanford's star wide open for a three-point shot when the driving player passed her the ball. The shot dropped through at the buzzer and the place erupted.

"Overtime! We're going to overtime!" the announcer screamed.

Jess did her best to remain composed as she called her team back over for the brief intermission before the overtime began. The players were stunned, though, and Jess knew that the momentum was squarely in Stanford's favor. On top of that, NOU was going to have to play the overtime without Heather, who had clearly been the spark for most of the game.

Jess did her best to pump up the team, and they left the huddle with determined looks on their faces, but it didn't take long for Stanford to reel off six quick points without answer. NOU ended up losing by four, and Jess watched as a line of very disappointed players filed past her on their way to the locker room.

The coach couldn't have felt more frustrated herself. They had missed an opportunity to beat one of the premier teams in the country on their home court, had missed an opportunity to take sole possession of first place in the conference, and had lost a starter to injury. *It's going to be a long trip home,* Jess thought dejectedly as she made her way off the court.

Jess walked wearily down the hall to her hotel room after telling the players to meet for breakfast at six the next morning. "What a day," she sighed to herself, thinking back to the difficult conversation with Heather earlier that afternoon. Heather had been in tears again after the game, and Jess could only imagine how devastating the combination of injuring her ankle, losing the game, and dealing with a broken heart would be. As her coach, Jess couldn't help but feel responsible and wished there were something she could do to help the young woman out. Feeling tired, depressed, and above all, lonely, she pushed open the hotel room door, thinking that she would give anything to be back home with Robin.

The scent of flowers hit her immediately, and Jess looked up to see a dozen roses arranged in a vase on the table in her room. She stared incredulously at the bouquet, and slowly walked over to the table. She slid the card out of a small envelope that just said "Jess" on the outside, and a smile slowly spread across her face.

Jess—
Happy Valentine's Day! I'm thinking of you always...
I love you—
Robin

Jess couldn't believe it. *She...she loves me? Can that be true?* She read the card again and decided that maybe the day wasn't so bad after all.

Chapter
41

Robin was laying on her couch late Saturday night after listening to the basketball game on the radio. She had the latest Indigo Girls CD playing in the background, and she was staring at the ceiling.

One of these times, Jess is going to win a close game. She works so hard and I just feel so bad when things don't go right for her. Especially when she's on the road and has to go back to her hotel room by herself. She sighed heavily. *What I wouldn't give to be there right now...*

The phone interrupted Robin's thoughts and she flew off the couch to answer it.

"Hello?"

"Hey, are you still awake?" Jess said softly.

"Mmmm, I was hoping it would be you," Robin replied, settling back down on the couch. "How are you doing?"

"I'm doing much better now than I was a few minutes ago."

Robin smiled. "Really?"

"You're incredible, you know that? How did you know I'd be coming back to my hotel room in a state of near depression and would need something to cheer me up?"

"Believe me, I was hoping those roses would be for a celebration, not condolences. But I'm really glad if I could make you feel a little better."

"You always make me feel better...Just talking to you can make me almost forget about losing that game...in overtime...after being ahead by three with thirty seconds to go...Okay, I admit I haven't forgotten about it at all."

Robin laughed and Jess couldn't help but join in. "One of these times the luck will go your way, Jess."

"Well, I hope so, because I'm really getting sick of telling the team how much we can learn from these losses."

"Just wait, there'll be a close game that really counts down the road, and you're going to come out on top. In the end, things are going to go your way because you've earned it."

Jess was quiet for a moment before responding. "You know, it really means a lot that you believe in me like that. I've never had that before—I always thought I had to do it on my own."

"Hey, I'm here for you anytime you need me," Robin said with conviction.

Both women were silent for a few moments, the power of their words sinking in.

"I miss you," Jess said softly.

"I miss you, too. Will I get to see you tomorrow?"

"I sure hope so. We get in around eleven. Can I stop over on my way home?"

"I'll be here waiting."

"Great. You know, I think I might even be able to sleep tonight now," Jess said, realizing how much better she felt.

"I hope so...I'll be thinking of you."

"Mmmm, me too."

"I'll talk to you tomorrow, Jess. Sweet dreams."

"You, too." The coach paused for a minute, sucking in a breath. "And Robin?"

"Yeah?"

"I love you, too."

The end of the conference season was shaping up as a race for second place between NOU and Southern Washington, with Stanford remaining a game ahead and likely to win the conference title. NOU's conference didn't have an end-of-season conference tournament, so the final standings were especially important for determining who would be selected to the NCAA tournament. Although the NCAA selection committee often went at least three deep in their conference, Jess didn't feel confident that third place would be good enough. Since the Bobcats hadn't made post-season play in a number of years, and also had a fairly weak non-conference schedule, the only way they could guarantee making the playoffs was to place second in the conference. Southern Washington would be their last regular game of the season, and the outcome was likely to decide their fate.

The week before the Southern Washington game, NOU hosted the southern California schools and was able to maintain their tie for second place by beating both teams. Since Saturday night was the last home game of the season, there was a reception following the game for family and friends of the team. Robin was delighted when Jess invited her, and even more delighted when she said that Capi could come, too.

The reception was held in the Alumni Room of the arena, and a nice spread of appetizers, pizza, and soft drinks was laid out when Robin and Capi arrived. There were around twenty-five others there, although the team and coaches had not yet returned from the locker room. The two women filled their plates, grabbed something to drink, and found a place at one of the tables. After a few moments, they were approached by Patti and Jim Martin, Heather's parents.

"Mind if we join you?"

"Mmmph!" Robin tried to respond with a mouth full of pizza while gesturing to the empty seats at the table.

"Good to see you again," Capi quickly filled in. "What did you think of the game?"

"I thought it was great," Patti replied, sitting down next to Robin. "I was really glad it wasn't so close, because I've had enough of those nerve-wracking games this year."

"Well, I think winning a close one might have been a better tune-up for next week, " Jim replied while taking the chair next to Capi. "They're going to have to play better than they did tonight if they expect to beat the Hawks on their home court."

"Oh, you're always such a spoil sport," Patti admonished. "Can't we just be happy they won and enjoy it?"

Robin couldn't help but smile at the banter, but decided that a little intervention wouldn't hurt. "Well, I'm happy they won, but I do agree that next week's game is going to be tougher. Are you going to be there?"

"Are you kidding?" Patti responded. "We wouldn't miss it. How about you?"

"Oh yeah. As much as I hate going up there to that old dungeon they play in, and having to put up with those Hawk fans, I wouldn't miss it either."

Capi and Jim had started their own conversation, and Robin and Patti concentrated on their food for a few moments. Robin's attention was caught by the arrival of the coaches and players, who were quickly monopolized in conversations with parents and friends. Patti looked over at Robin and saw the look of open admiration on the young woman's face.

"Coach Peters has really done a wonderful job, hasn't she?" Patti said with an indulgent smile towards Robin.

Robin blushed when she realized she'd been caught staring. "Oh...yeah, the team is doing great."

"Well, it's basically the same team they had last year, and they're doing much better, so I think the coach can take the credit for that, don't you?"

"*I* think so, but you'll probably never hear Jess say that," Robin said, thinking of how much emphasis the coach put on the "team" concept.

"Well, Heather can't say enough good things about her," Patti replied, looking over at the tall woman who was working the room like a politician. She turned back to Robin with a serious look on her face. "Did you know that when Chris left Heather a few weeks ago, Coach Peters was the one who helped Heather get through that? She'd probably still be moping around today if the coach hadn't been so compassionate."

Robin nearly spit her soda out her nose. She managed to swallow and then started coughing violently. Capi slapped her on the back a couple of times, asking if she was all right. The young woman managed to nod, although her face was getting darker from lack of oxygen. Finally she managed to take a deep breath, and her color started to return to normal.

"Sorry," she croaked, "that just went down the wrong way I guess." She took a few more deep breaths and then returned her attention to Patti. "So Heather is doing better now?" She managed to not look completely dumbfounded by the news Patti had just sprung on her. *What did Jess think when Heather approached her about that? And why didn't she tell me about it?*

"Oh, yes. Much better. You know how kids that age are. They think they've found the love of their life, until the next love of their life comes along. Heather is already looking back and wondering what she saw in Chris."

Robin managed to smile and nod, but for once in her life, was having trouble maintaining a conversation. She was saved when Heather came bounding over to their table, hair still wet from the shower.

"Hey, mom. Did you like the game?" Heather then noticed who her mother was sitting with and somewhat shyly added, "Oh, hi Dr. Grant. How are you?"

"Fine, Heather. You did great tonight. Your ankle seems to be fully recovered and your scoring average has really picked up in the past couple of weeks."

"Thanks. Coach Peters has been helping me with some stuff, and I think I've got a lot more confidence in my shot now."

"Well, it seems to be working. Keep it up for next week, okay?"

"I'll try," Heather replied, and then sat down to talk to her mother.

Since Capi was still talking to Jim, Robin took the opportunity to watch Jess make her way around the room. The tall, attractive woman towered over most of the parents she was talking to, and Robin could see the respect and admiration in their faces. As Jess finished one conversation and turned toward another couple, her eyes met Robin's across the room. For just a moment, the professional façade softened and a little smile quirked her lips. Robin smiled back, feeling a warmth spread throughout her body that was out of proportion with the small gesture from the coach. *God, I love her.* The thought startled Robin, and for a moment she worried that she'd said it out loud, but since the other conversations were still going on around her, she relaxed and thought more about her feelings.

I've never felt anything like this. I was sure I was in love with other people before, but it never felt like this. She's all I think about anymore. And I want to be with her all the time—to fall asleep every night and wake up every morning with her. But I'm afraid she's never going to want to live together. She'd be too worried about how it would look. Robin sighed sadly. *Is there any possibility of a future with a basketball coach?*

"Hey, what was that deep sigh about," Capi said quietly, leaning over toward Robin.

"Oh, nothing. Just doing a little pre-worrying about the future."

"Hmmm, well maybe we should just stick to worrying about the present, what do you think?" Capi asked with a reassuring smile.

"Yeah, you're right. And the present looks pretty damn good, so I think I'll just quit worrying altogether."

"That's my girl." Capi smiled.

On the other side of the room, Jess was talking to a group of parents when she noticed that Bennie was sitting off by herself, eating her pizza. Jess excused herself and went over to talk to the young woman. She sat down next to her and gently placed her hand on the player's shoulder.

"Hey, Bennie, you did a great job tonight."

"Thanks," the player mumbled, giving the coach a quick glance.

"You know what I was most proud of?" Jess asked with a little twinkle in her eye.

"Mm-mm," Bennie replied with a little shake of her head.

"That you worked so hard that you actually had to ask to come out of the game."

Jess saw a very small smile work its way onto Bennie's lips. "I'll never penalize you for that, Bennie. I'll just let you catch your breath and get you back in there as soon as you're ready, okay?"

Bennie nodded, and Jess realized that she wasn't going to get any real conversation out of the point guard. *If there's one thing this job makes you good at, it's one-sided conversations,* Jess thought ruefully. "Try to have a little fun tonight, okay? You earned it." With that, Jess got up and gave Bennie's shoulder a little squeeze before she walked away.

Before anyone else could corral her, Jess quickly strode over to Robin's table. The young woman gave her a warm smile as she approached and the coach looked down self-consciously. Jess greeted them all, and then leaned down to say a few things in Heather's ear. The player nodded while looking across the room, and then got up. Jess said "Thanks," and then took the seat that Heather had vacated.

"Congratulations on the win tonight, Coach," Jim boomed in his best fatherly voice. "Do you think you're ready for next week?"

"We'll have to play a lot better than we did tonight if we expect to beat the Hawks," Jess replied, while Heather's father beamed at the confirmation of his earlier observation.

"Well, I'm sure if anyone can get them ready, you can," Patti said with complete confidence.

"Thanks, but it's ultimately up to the team to decide how much they want it."

Robin mentally rolled her eyes as the conversation went exactly according to script. She checked out for a few minutes and looked around the room again. She saw Heather approaching Bennie with two drinks in her hand, offering one to the point guard. Bennie looked surprised at the gesture, but graciously accepted the drink. Robin saw Heather motion to the chair, and Bennie nod before the blond woman sat down. Robin watched for a while longer, while Bennie lifted her head more and more, looking up and smiling at Heather, and eventually they seemed to be settling down into a relaxed conversation. Robin realized that there was a lull in the conversation, and she brought her attention back to the table. When she looked at Jess she saw that the coach was also looking over at Bennie and Heather with a rather satisfied smirk on her face.

Later that evening, Robin and Jess were lying together on the couch in Jess's living room, watching the late edition of Sports Center. Robin was fading fast, and rested her head on Jess's shoulder and closed her eyes. The tall woman hugged her tightly and clicked the TV off with the remote.

"Am I keeping you up?" Jess asked.

"Am I still up?" Robin quipped. "Feels like bed to me." She nuzzled her face in Jess's neck and kissed her softly.

Jess chuckled and kissed Robin's forehead in return.

"Hey, I forgot to tell you what Patti Martin said to me tonight," Robin said, pulling away and looking somewhat accusingly at Jess.

"What?" Jess replied innocently.

"Right in the middle of a gulp of soda, she says 'Jess really helped Heather get through her break-up with Chris.' I nearly spewed my soda across the table. How could you not have told me about that?"

Jess got a worried look on her face. "So her mother knows, too. I didn't know she had talked to her mother about it." Jess looked away, her mind racing with a million thoughts at once. *What did she tell her mother about me? Does her father know, too? Did they talk to any other parents? Do all the players think Robin and I are together?*

Robin gently touched Jess's cheek and brought the coach's gaze back to meet her questioning eyes. "What's wrong?"

Jess looked down uncomfortably. "It's just something Heather said when she first came into my room. She said that she thought I would understand because of you and me."

Robin's eyes opened wide as she looked in disbelief at the coach. "You're kidding."

"No."

"How would she know about you and me?"

"That's what I'd like to know. How did LaTeisha know?" Jess looked at Robin with frustration written on her face. "How can it be so obvious when I try so hard to be discreet?"

"Hey, they're just making assumptions, Jess. They can't really know," Robin tried to reassure her.

"Yeah, and maybe it wouldn't be a problem if the assumptions weren't true, but in this case, they are. I couldn't exactly deny it if someone came out and accused me."

Robin pulled away from Jess with a hurt look on her face. "What do you mean, 'accused you?' Do you think you're committing a crime or something? I thought you weren't ashamed of what we have."

A look of distress came over Jess's face. "You know that's not what I meant...Robin, you just don't seem to understand the implications for my job if everyone knew that I was...that you and I were..."

"You can't even admit it to yourself," Robin said with more disgust than she had intended. "Everything was fine when you thought no one knew about us, but it's obvious you still think that this relationship is wrong somehow."

"*I* don't think it's wrong," Jess protested. "But other people do, and some of those people could influence whether I keep my job or not."

"I thought we had gone beyond this choice between me or your job," Robin accused.

"We have. But I didn't think it was going to mean that everyone would suddenly know about us." Jess looked to the ceiling and pushed her hair back off her forehead with a sigh. "I just need some time to think about what all this means, I guess."

Robin stood up abruptly. "Fine. Take all the time you need." And she headed for the door.

"Robin! Wait. Where are you going?"

"To spend some time with friends who aren't ashamed of me."

"But..." The door slammed behind the young woman, leaving Jess to collapse on the couch in frustration.

Chapter
42

After a fitful night of little sleep, Jess finally got up at six a.m. Sunday morning and put her running clothes on. She went out for a grueling five mile run, finding as many hills as possible to punish herself.

Why does this have to be so hard? God, I feel like we've been through all this before. In fact, I know we have. I thought we agreed that we didn't want people to know, and now it seems like everybody knows. Why would she be surprised that I got upset about that? And what does she want me to do now? I can't just pretend I don't feel this way...

Jess finished her run feeling drained and depressed. She walked back into the apartment and immediately felt stung as she remembered Robin walking out the night before. She quickly walked through the living room to the bedroom, not even looking at the couch.

Thirty minutes later, Jess was in her kitchen, finishing her first cup of coffee and fidgeting by the phone. *Well, I might not know what to say to her, but I've got to try to say something. I'm not going to get anything else done today until we work this out. If we work this out.* That thought made Jess's stomach clench in despair, and she vowed to not even consider that outcome. She took a deep breath and reached for the phone.

No answer.

Jess looked at the clock and saw it was only seven-thirty in the morning. *She never gets up early on a Sunday—how could she be gone already? Unless she didn't go home last night...*

Jess paced around the kitchen for fifteen minutes before she finally gave in and grabbed her car keys. She made the short drive to Robin's apartment and confirmed that the young woman's car was not there.

Oh come on—quit being paranoid. She probably just couldn't sleep and got up early to get some coffee or something. Jess rummaged through her glove box to find a piece of paper and a pen. She scribbled a quick note and wedged it into the doorknocker on Robin's apartment. With a heavy sigh, she turned around, got back into her car, and headed for her office.

"So I finally get you in my bed, and all you want to do is talk about another woman," Capi said with a teasing smile.

Robin rolled over and gave her good friend a hug, burying her face in the taller woman's shoulder. "I'm sorry," she said, and started to sob again.

"Hey, I was just kidding," Capi reassured her, rubbing her back soothingly.

"I know, I just can't stop crying. What is the matter with me?"

"You're in love—it's a common ailment that turns women into blubbering idiots."

"Oh, that's helpful," Robin replied.

The two women had been up all night talking, and even though Robin was completely exhausted, she couldn't stop thinking about Jess. And thinking about Jess made her upset all over again, which would lead to more talking. The sun had finally come up, and Capi was wondering if she was going to get any sleep at all.

"Robin, why don't you just give yourself a little time to think about things. You don't have to figure everything out right now. Just relax and try to get some sleep, and then we can talk again later, okay?"

"Okay. I'm sorry I'm keeping you up, Capi. I should have just gone home last night..."

"No, I'm glad you came over here," Capi said reassuringly. "I've told you before, I'll always be here for you, and I meant it."

Capi worked her fingers into Robin's hair and started to gave the young woman a gentle massage. Before long, the exhaustion took over and Robin's eyes finally closed. Capi sighed with relief and quickly followed Robin into sleep.

Capi awoke four hours later and got up to make a pot of coffee. She was just pouring two cups when Robin appeared in the kitchen, hair wildly out of place and eyes barely open. Capi couldn't help but grin at the sight. "So this is what I've been missing every morning, huh?" she teased.

"Hey, you're not looking so hot yourself," Robin retorted, shuffling over to get her cup of coffee.

Capi laughed and steered Robin over to the kitchen table where the toaster, bread, and peanut butter were waiting. "Maybe some peanut butter toast will cheer you up," Capi offered.

"I don't think so, but thanks," the young woman replied, sipping her coffee but ignoring the food.

"How about half a piece? You have to eat, you know."

"Oh, all right," she gave in. "I'll try, but no guarantees."

Robin nibbled on her toast, her thoughts clearly somewhere else. "What am I going to say to her when I see her again?" she blurted out.

Capi looked up, startled by the change in topic. She took a deep breath and tried to focus her thoughts back on Robin's personal problems. "Well, what do you want to say to her?"

"Other than how crazy she makes me?" Robin sighed. "I really don't know. I guess I want to let her know how I feel, and make it clear that I can't be in a relationship that she thinks is somehow wrong."

"That seems perfectly reasonable to me. It's one thing to recognize that other people might have a problem with your relationship, and another to just give in to that sentiment as if you agree with it."

"I just don't see why she thinks she has to deny it. If other people want to make assumptions, just let them," Robin said with frustration.

Capi reached over and rubbed Robin's arm reassuringly. "You know, maybe the two of you should just take time out for a while—until the season is over. The pressure on Jess right now is probably pretty intense, and maybe she'll be able to see things more clearly in a few weeks."

Robin looked at Capi with a mixture of hope and despair.

"You're probably right, but I don't know if I can get through a few weeks feeling like this."

"You don't have to look at it like things are over between the two of you. You'll just be taking a little break while things are really stressful for her."

Robin sighed. "I guess you're right. At least I can have hope that things will work out."

"Of course they will," Capi said confidently.

Jess was in her office, trying to concentrate on some scouting reports for the upcoming Southern Washington game, but her thoughts kept straying and finally she just threw her pencil across the room.

"God damn it. Why can't I keep my mind on my work?" She sighed heavily, leaned back and closed her eyes. She nearly jumped out of her chair when the phone rang, and she grabbed for it as fast as she could.

"Hello?"

"Aren't you supposed to say 'NOU Basketball, Jess Peters'?"

Jess exhaled audibly with relief. "Hey, thanks for calling me," she said softly. She was dying to ask Robin where she'd been all morning, but she bit her lip. "Are you okay?"

"I've been better, but I'm okay."

"Look, Robbie, I'm really sorry about last night...I didn't mean to upset you. I...I guess I'm still struggling with some things that I thought I'd gotten past."

"I know, Jess. I guess I was expecting too much to think that you could just instantly change the way you've thought about these things for years and years. So...I thought...maybe we should just cool things off until after your season is over."

Jess felt her heart start to break. *Cool things off. What is that supposed to mean? Is this just a nice way to let me down? Is she just going to wait until the season is over to tell me?*

"Are you still there?" Robin asked after a few moments of silence had gone by.

"Yeah," Jess choked out, finding her throat suddenly constricted. "What...What do you mean by cool things off?"

"Well, I just thought...Since you've got a lot of pressure on you right now, with your job and the end of the season and everything...Maybe it would be better if we just backed off for a while, you know? You won't have to worry about people seeing my car at your apartment, or seeing you leave my place in the morning—that kind of stuff."

"Oh...well...yeah, I guess that might be a good idea," Jess said without conviction.

"Okay then...good...I guess that's what we'll do," Robin said awkwardly.

Jess didn't respond.

"You know, it's not like we can't see each other, or talk to each other, Jess."

"Yeah, I know. It'll be fine, I'm sure. You're right that things are pretty intense for me at work right now, so a few less distractions would be good for me," Jess replied, not wanting to let on how upset she was.

"Okay then...Well, I don't want to keep you from your work, so I'll talk to you soon, okay?"

"Sure. See you later."

They hung up, neither one knowing how upset the other really was.

The week went by with neither woman calling the other. The thought of trying to have a conversation that would somehow appear casual, and that wouldn't slip into a discussion about their relationship, was enough to deter them both.

Finally on Friday morning, Robin couldn't stand it anymore. Jess was going to leave for Erving early that afternoon for their most important game of the year, and there was just no way that Robin wanted her to leave without at least wishing her luck. After stalling and fidgeting in her office for a good twenty minutes, she finally reached for the phone and dialed.

"NOU Basketball, Jess Peters."

"Now that's how I expect you to answer the phone," Robin said with a smile in her voice.

After a slight pause, while Jess was obviously composing herself, she replied, "Hey, it's good to hear from you."

"I just wanted to call and wish you luck tonight."

"Thanks, a little luck never hurts, but I'm hoping we're so

prepared that we don't even need luck on our side."

"I'm sure you are," Robin said. "I'm going up there with complete confidence that we can finally stand up to all those Hawk fans and tell them who's really number one in this region."

Jess couldn't help but laugh at Robin's sense of rivalry. "If my players are half as motivated as you are, it shouldn't be a problem."

There was an awkward pause as both women tried to decide whether to leave the conversation casual or try to talk about what was really on both their minds.

You're the one who wanted to cool things off for a while, so don't go bringing up other subjects now, Robin admonished herself. "Well, I'd better let you go—I'm sure you've got lots of last minute details to attend to. I'll see you at the game, okay?"

"Okay. Thanks for calling."

They hung up and each felt just a little bit better than they had all week.

Chapter 43

Robin and Capi were seated in the section behind the visitors' bench, and recognized a number of other people from last week's reception. The arena was packed almost entirely with green and yellow-clad fans, although there were two or three small pockets of orange and black visible. The teams had returned to the court after the National Anthem and were now waiting for player introductions. Robin nervously rolled her program in her hands, looking at the two benches and trying to assess the relative intensity of the teams. Her attention was drawn to the coaches, who were standing off to the side while the players were introduced.

Jess was dressed in black pants and black silk shirt, with only a few gold accents in her earrings and bracelet. Robin thought she looked almost dangerous, and suspected that was probably the intended message. The opposing coach, on the other hand, was wearing a mini skirt that barely covered her rear, and a tight-fitting jacket with nothing apparent underneath. Dark stockings over impossibly long legs and three-inch spike heels completed the outfit, and Robin thought the whole thing screamed "hooker!" *Well, we know who the straight men in the crowd will be rooting for.*

After player introductions, which included an extended tribute for those seniors graduating from the Southern Washington squad, the game finally got underway.

Natalia won the tap and Bennie brought the ball up against

tight player-to-player pressure. She looked inside, but the Southern Washington post players were big and denying the easy entry pass, so she passed the ball to the wing. The weak side post player popped up to the free throw line for the pass, and executed a perfect "high-low" pass to Natalia for the easy bucket. The Southern Washington coach was screaming at her post defender to "watch that high-low!" as they ran back up the court on offense, stomping her foot for good measure.

Robin leaned over to Capi and said, "I hope she doesn't break one of those heels. I don't think those shoes were meant for that kind of stomping."

Capi laughed and slapped Robin on the arm. "Hey, we're here to watch the game, not the coach."

Both teams continued to push the ball inside to their post players, each having success. At the first officials' time-out, NOU was up by three as the players sat on the bench in front of Jess.

"Listen up!" she shouted over the noise of the band that had been conveniently located in the end zone facing their bench. "We're going to switch to our match-up zone, okay? I want to see a lot of help on the post players. And let's anticipate those passes. We've seen everything they're running, and we should be able to get into the passing lanes and get some steals." Jess finished the time-out by setting up an in-bounds play under their basket. The team ran it to perfection, setting a double screen for Bennie who nailed the three pointer from the top of the key.

On Southern Washington's next possession, the match-up zone surprised them, and by the time they recognized it and adjusted, there were only seven seconds left on the shot clock. They ended up taking a desperation shot that rebounded long off the iron, setting up a fast break for NOU. Bennie dribbled to the top of the key, hesitated as if passing to Heather on the wing, and then blew by the defender for the reverse lay-up. The lead had grown from three to eight in under a minute, and the Southern Washington coach called a thirty second time-out.

"Man, I'm glad I'm not in that Southern Washington huddle right now," Robin said, looking at the team getting chewed out by the coach that towered over all of them. In contrast, Jess was smiling and congratulating her players on their execution, encouraging them to continue to work hard for the rest of the first half. The players responded and NOU left the court at halftime up by ten.

Robin relaxed in her seat for the first time since the game started. "I don't know if I can take another half of this," she said to Capi, fanning herself with her program.

"Maybe you should walk outside and cool off for a while," Capi replied. "It does get hot in here, not to mention loud."

"I'm afraid to walk alone in hostile territory," Robin joked. "Especially since we're up by ten."

Capi looked at her black jeans and orange NOU sweatshirt. "What makes you think they'd know you were rooting for the Bobcats?" she quipped.

Just then, Carmen walked up to their seats and Capi's smile got bigger. "First half stats for you," the SID said, handing each of them a sheet of paper.

"How do we rate this V.I.P. treatment?" Robin asked.

Carmen leaned in close, putting her hand on Capi's thigh as she did so. "I can't resist two such beautiful women, and I thought maybe it would improve my chances of getting a date with you after the game."

"Ahh, flattery will get you everywhere," Robin replied, while Capi just rolled her eyes. Carmen smiled seductively at them both and bounded off to return to the press table.

"Jeez, you shouldn't encourage her," Capi said, feigning exasperation.

Robin's attention was diverted to the court where NOU was running back out for the second-half warm-up. The coaches walked out after the players, with Jess the last one onto the court. Robin found herself drawn to the sight of the tall coach, her heart aching from the lack of contact over the past week. *She does seem to be pretty focused on the game. Maybe this little separation has been a good thing for her.* That thought made Robin distinctly uncomfortable, wondering if they would ever be able to get back what they had before. *Is this just proving that she does better when she doesn't have to worry about her personal life? That maybe our relationship is incompatible with her job?*

"Hey, are you okay?" Capi interrupted her thoughts, looking at her pale face with concern.

"Oh...Sorry. Yeah, I'm fine. Just thinking about some things, I guess."

"I thought you were going to give that a rest for a couple of weeks and not think about it," Capi admonished.

"It's just not that easy," Robin protested. "We don't talk about it with each other, but that doesn't stop me from thinking about it just about every minute of the day."

Capi patted her on the back. "Well, it's only another week until the tournament starts, so maybe the problem will be over soon."

Robin's expression turned even more depressed. "What am I supposed to do now about her invitation for me to come to the first round of the tournament?"

"What do you mean?"

"Well, she invited me when everything was fine, but now that she's worried again about what people think, she probably doesn't really want me to go."

"Hmmm, well, let's not worry about it until we have to, okay? Something tells me I might want to be going to that tournament, too," Capi said, looking suggestively over at the press table. "So we can just go together and you won't have to interact with Jess if she doesn't want you to."

Robin nodded, but her shoulders slumped in defeat.

It wasn't long, however, before Robin was back into the game, all thoughts of her personal crisis behind her. NOU came out in their match-up zone at the start of the second half, but Southern Washington's guards were finding their range from the outside and were making NOU pay for their double-teams of the post players. With only five minutes left in the second half, the lead was reduced to two and Jess took a time-out.

"We're going to go back to the player defense, okay? But we still need to get that weak side help when the posts are fronting their players. I also want you guards to start picking up their ball handlers full court. Have you got enough left in you for that?" She looked specifically at Bennie to see if the player would be willing to put out the effort necessary for a full-court, player-to-player press. The point guard just nodded confidently, and Jess gave her a very slight smile in return.

The change in defense disrupted the Southern Washington offense for the next couple of times down the court, and the lead increased to four. The teams then traded baskets until there was a minute and a half left to play. On Southern Washington's next possession, Bennie got screened by one of the big posts when her player cut down the lane, and Natalia was too late in coming to help. Bennie scowled at her teammate, obviously mad that the pick hadn't been called out. She took the inbounds pass and ran the ball up the court, stopping at the top of the key and launching a quick three-pointer. It missed badly and Southern Washington converted the long rebound into a fast break basket. With forty seconds left and a tie game, Jess called time-out. She pulled Bennie aside while the assistant coaches talked to the rest of the team.

"Bennie, you don't have to do everything yourself out there. If you give the ball up and work to get open, you're going to get a better shot than that last one you took. And if you all work together, it won't matter who gets the shot, because it's going to be an easy one. Do you understand what I'm saying? You've got to trust your teammates, okay?"

The point guard nodded, her eyes never leaving her shoes. Jess led her back to the huddle and quickly diagrammed the play she wanted them to run on the next possession.

NOU worked twenty seconds off the thirty-second shot clock before advancing the ball toward the basket. Bennie dribbled to the wing position, waving Heather through the key to the other side of the court. Natalia was posted up at the free throw line on the ball side, and the other post player cut up toward the free throw line on the weak side, drawing her defender away from the basket. Bennie tossed the ball into Natalia at the high post and took a step toward the top of the key. As her defender turned her head to watch the pass, Bennie took off on the back door cut to the basket. Natalia threaded a perfect bounce pass around her defender and Bennie went in for the open shot.

And missed it.

Southern Washington grabbed the rebound and with eight seconds left on the clock called their last thirty-second time-out. Jess went out onto the court to meet Bennie and put her arm around her while walking back to the huddle.

"That's okay, Bennie. You ran the play just like we drew it up and you got the shot we wanted. They don't always go in." She stopped and turned around to look at the dejected point guard. "Look at me, Bennie." The player reluctantly brought her eyes up to meet Jess's. "You're never going to think about missing that shot again, you hear me? The next time, you're going to do nothing but focus on that rim, and the shot's going in, okay?" Bennie brightened up a little and nodded with determination.

The two joined the rest of the team in the huddle and Jess set up their defense for the in-bounds play. As NOU broke their huddle, Heather grabbed Bennie's arm and pulled her close to whisper something in her ear. Bennie looked up and gave her a little smile, and Heather slapped her on the butt as she returned to the court.

As Southern Washington lined up to throw the ball in from under the NOU basket, the Bobcats matched up with them. Natalia was guarding the player throwing the ball in, her height and long arms making it difficult for the player to see the court. The Southern Washington guards were side by side at the free throw line and Bennie's player took advantage of a good screen to get open for the pass. Bennie worked her way around the screen and quickly got in the face of the ball handler. As the Southern Washington player made a crossover dribble to change directions, Bennie got her hand on the ball and sent it about five feet away from the two players. Without a moment's hesitation, Bennie dove for the ball and got there just before the Southern Washington player. She looked up to see Natalia still near the end line and managed to flip the ball over her head to the tall post player, who laid it in as time ran out.

The stunned Southern Washington crowd went silent, while the few Bobcat fans erupted in cheers. Robin was jumping up and down, and hugging everyone around her. The players had run out onto the court and Bennie had collapsed under a pile of celebrating teammates. Jess had also shot off the bench when Natalia's shot went in, but she quickly regained her professional demeanor and went down the sideline to shake the Southern Washington coaches' hands. Afterward, though, she nearly sprinted onto the court to join her team in the celebration. She finally made her way to Bennie, and the two of them looked eye-to-eye and saw the mutual respect there. After a brief pause, Jess grabbed the small guard and hugged her close.

"You made the extra effort, and you trusted your teammate. I'm really proud of you, Bennie," she whispered in her ear.

"Thanks," was all the player could choke out, overcome by the emotion of everything that had happened.

Robin watched the celebration from the stands, happy for Jess and the players, but feeling a sense of loss at not being able to really share the moment with the person that meant the most to her in the whole world. She thought about all the tournament games she'd seen on TV, where the coaches happily kiss their spouse after the big win, and couldn't help but be a little angry at the unfairness of it all. But the worst part was, even after they were out of the limelight tonight, things would still be difficult for them.

Whose idea was it to cool things off for a while, anyway? she thought dejectedly. *But I can't deny that the results were pretty good for Jess's team, can I? I wonder if she's going to think that our separation had anything to do with tonight's win. Or if maybe...just maybe, she's wishing she could celebrate with me as much as I wish I could celebrate with her.*

As Robin watched the team slowly make their way off the court, Jess turned and looked up at the stands behind the visitors' bench, searching for someone. When her eyes met Robin's, there was an unmistakable connection, but Jess's elation over winning the game was clearly dampened by her recognition that things weren't the same between the two of them. Robin did her best to give Jess an encouraging smile, not wanting her disappointment in their personal life to mar this special occasion for Jess.

"Hey, you about ready to go?" Capi called out to her.

"Huh? Oh, sure, just let me get my coat," Robin replied, bending over to gather her things. She straightened up and looked around the arena with satisfaction. "Well, for once we get to walk out of here without getting heckled by a bunch of Hawk fans gloating over their win."

"Yeah, in fact I've never seen a place this big empty out so fast," Capi chuckled.

The two women wandered over toward the press table to make arrangements with Carmen, and then headed for the exit. Robin looked back at the court one more time and sighed wistfully before turning to leave.

Saturday morning Jess was relaxing in her kitchen, drinking a cup of coffee and reading the newspaper account of last night's game. She hadn't slept well, whether because of the excitement over the game, or the distressing situation with Robin, or both.

Why do things have to be this way? I just can't believe there's not a middle ground somewhere. She thought more about her feelings, and realized that she was the one reluctant to meet in the middle. *It only takes one person—the wrong person—to know about us, and my job, my whole career, could be history. All these things I've worked so hard for.* She sighed audibly. *But on the other hand, I know I'm not going to be happy without Robin in my life. Could it possibly be like Sara describes it—that even if people think they know, they won't care? Could I really just tell someone who asked that my personal life is not their concern, without panicking and giving everything away? Maybe I do need a couple of weeks to sort this all out.*

Sunday afternoon was when the NCAA Tournament Selection Committee would announce the pairings and locations for the first rounds. Jess and her team were going to meet at the Alumni Room in the arena to watch the selections on ESPN, and friends, family, and fans were invited. Jess knew they weren't going to be hosting the first-round games, since those were allocated to the first and second seeds, but she was hoping that they wouldn't be sent all the way across the country to the east. And she was really hoping to avoid the games hosted by Tennessee and UCONN, knowing that those teams would be virtually impossible to beat on their home courts.

When she arrived at the Alumni Room, her players were scattered about, talking with friends and family while waiting for the show to begin. Jess looked around, hoping just a little that Robin might show up. But she knew that this was exactly the kind of event that made her nervous about being seen with Robin, and she was sure the young woman knew that, too. *And, after all, that's the point of all this, right? To not have me worry about these 'awkward' situations while we're trying to make it through the playoffs. But which is worse—to worry about how it would look if she were here, or to worry about why she's not here?*

A few minutes before the selection show was to begin, Jess called her team up to the two tables at the front of the room to watch together. The players huddled together nervously, many of them holding hands while they listened to each pairing as it was announced. Finally, they heard their own name:

"The second game at Louisiana State will be between the

eleventh seed, Florida, and the sixth seed, Northern Oregon University."

A cheer erupted from the crowd, and the players talked excitedly among themselves. Jess was pleased with their seeding, but not thrilled with the prospect of traveling to Louisiana, two time zones away from their usual routine. However, she set aside those worries for a few minutes and just sat back to reflect on the fact that they were one of sixty-four teams to make it into the NCAA tournament, and she'd done it in her first year at NOU. There was only one thing that could make her life better right now.

Chapter
44

The next few days were hectic for Jess, overseeing travel arrangements and preparing her team for a game that was only five days away, one of which would be taken up almost entirely by travel. Due to the quarter system of NOU, the players would be taking final exams for winter quarter that week, which made scheduling practices difficult. There were also hours of film to watch in an effort to scout a team that played at the opposite end of the country.

In the midst of all this, Jess was progressively more preoccupied with thoughts of Robin. She missed the unwavering support that Robin had offered her, the relaxing times that they could spend talking or just lying around with each other, and she especially missed the intimacy that she'd waited thirty-four years to find, only to risk losing it so quickly. She found herself more depressed with each passing day, realizing how much the young professor's presence meant to her. On Tuesday night, she was up late reviewing scouting reports at her kitchen table when she found her thoughts on Robin once again. *Is she having as hard of a time with this as I am? What if she's discovering she doesn't really need me...or even want me around? She obviously has friends like Capi that accept her for what she is and don't make her live some kind of double life. Maybe she's discovering that she could never really be happy living with a basketball coach.* Jess's head dropped into her hands, and she couldn't stop the tears that started. Soon her shoulders were heaving with

sobs, and she finally just let the emotion overtake her, crying
until the tears would no longer come.

After a fitful night of little sleep, Jess was back in her office
early on Wednesday. She logged onto her computer and her
heartbeat picked up when she saw that she had a new message
from Robin.

Jess—
*How are you doing? I hope all your preparations for the
playoffs are going well. Things must be really hectic for you.*
*I wanted to see if it was still OK with you if I went to Loui-
siana for the game. If it's going to make you worried about what
people will think, or distract you in any way, I'd be willing to
stay home. Things seem to be going pretty well for you right now,
and I don't want to do anything to change that.*
*I'd be making the trip with Capi, so hopefully no one would
think I'm there to be with you. I'm sure you'll be so busy you'll
hardly even see me.*
*It's really OK for you to ask me to stay home, so please be
honest about what is best for you.*
Hope to hear from you soon.
Robin

Jess felt a mixture of relief and despair. She was thrilled to
hear from Robin, and glad that she still wanted to go to the
game, but she was distressed by the overall tone of the letter.
*How could we have become so distant from one another in such a
short time?* She realized that Robin was just following their
agreed upon course of "cooling things off" for a while, but reading her words that were so reserved and formal had a depressing
effect on the coach. Nevertheless, after a few moments of
thought she composed a message in reply.

Robin—
*I would love for you to come to Louisiana and watch our
games. I'm sorry if I gave you the impression you wouldn't be
welcome. Nothing could be further from the truth. In fact, if you
remember, this trip is supposed to be on me. I have two tickets*

*for you—I'll put them in campus mail. And if you tell me which
flight you want to take, I'd like to get that for you, too.*

*You're right that things are going well for us right now, and
I'm busier than I've ever been. As much as I'm looking forward
to these playoff games, the end of the season will bring some
welcome relief. Hopefully it just won't come too soon!*

Good to hear from you—

Jess

She sank back in her chair and stared at the computer
screen. *Why didn't I tell her that I miss her? Why didn't I tell her
how miserable my life is without her? Am I just being stubborn,
or am I afraid that she doesn't want to hear it anymore? Could
her feelings for me have changed that quickly?* Jess didn't want
to think too much about that last thought, and was relieved when
the computer notified her of another new message.

Jess—

*Thanks for the offer on the plane ticket, but I think it would
be easier if I just got it myself. It was nice of you to get the playoff tickets, though—thanks! I know Capi will really appreciate
that, too.*

*Best of luck in your first game (not that you'll need it)! See
you in Louisiana—*

Robin

Jess sighed, wishing Robin's letter didn't sound so much
like a "friend," but knowing that it was all she could expect
under the circumstances. *It will probably be easier this way for
the trip—for both of us.*

Chapter
45

Robin and Capi flew into Baton Rouge on Friday, arriving with just enough time to check into their hotel room before heading off for the game. They would have liked to fly in the day before, but grades needed to be turned in before Robin left, and that meant grading sixty-five final exams in less than twenty-four hours. The young professor was exhausted by the time they landed, but she got her second wind when they entered the arena and felt the excitement surrounding playoff basketball.

Although the arena wasn't very crowded yet, the NOU cheerleaders had made the trip and were making up for any lack of noise from the crowd. It was still early and the home team, LSU, wouldn't be playing until eight o'clock, so many fans would arrive midway through the first game.

Jess's team was going through warm-ups and looked more than a little pumped up for the game. Everybody seemed to be running a little bit faster, jumping a little bit higher, and encouraging their teammates a little bit more than during the regular season. Robin thought they displayed a good combination of excitement and confidence, and decided that Jess had done a masterful job of preparing them for the game.

Her eyes drifted over to the coach, who stood on the sideline watching her team go through their pre-game routine. Jess looked just as intense as the players, her mind clearly focused on the upcoming game. So Robin was surprised when Jess turned and looked into the stands, their eyes meeting for what seemed like minutes, but was clearly only a few seconds. Robin could see a gamut of emotions run through the blue depths, changing from the intense game look, to a genuine happiness at seeing her there, and finally to a pained look of profound regret before she quickly looked away. Robin's heart ached with the desire to just hold Jess in her arms and bring back the look of happiness that she had seen there only weeks ago.

Jess led her team off the court for a final pep talk, returning with about ten minutes left in the warm-up. The excitement was building in the arena—spectators, players and coaches all knew that the season would end for one team that night. Finally, the teams were introduced, the players took the floor, and the referee tossed the ball up in the center circle. After a few times up and down the court where both teams either missed shots or committed turnovers, the nerves seemed to settle down and play improved.

NOU had a decided advantage inside, and Jess's game plan obviously called for the offense to focus on post play. The guards pounded the ball inside, and when Florida finally started double-teaming the posts, they would kick the ball back outside for open shots. By halftime, the Bobcats led by twelve and the Gators had not yet found an answer to NOU's inside game.

Jess didn't change her strategy for the second half, but Florida got more physical on defense, pushing the post players out beyond their comfort zone before they could get a pass. Despite her strident protests to the referees, no fouls were called and it was obvious that tempers were flaring on the court, as well as on the bench. The crowd was back in the game, cheering loudly as the Gators inched their way back into contention. The lead was down to five when Jess finally called time-out. As her team ran over, she strode out on the court to plead her case to the referees.

"My post players are getting beat up out there. How can you not see that?"

"That's enough, coach. I don't want to hear any more," one of the male referees said patronizingly.

Jess's nostrils flared and her eyes narrowed. "I don't care whether you want to hear any more or not. I'm going to tell you when I think my players are getting cheated by the officiating."

The whistle for the technical was quick in coming, and LaTeisha grabbed Jess and turned her back toward the bench before she could get her second technical, which would result in ejection. Jess took a few deep breaths to regain some semblance of control and moved over to where her players were huddled. Once again, she noticed a hint of pride in the players' expressions, and even though her temper had cost them two points and possession of the ball, the added determination by the players more than made up for it. When they returned to the court, they matched Florida's physical play and proceeded to go on an eight to zero run that gave them a commanding lead they never relinquished. As the final buzzer sounded, the bench swarmed the court while Jess and her assistants walked down the sidelines to shake hands with the opposing coaches.

"Nice game," the Florida coach said sincerely while clasping Jess's hand in both of hers. "That was a very strategic technical you staged there," she added with a smile.

Jess smiled back a little sheepishly. "I wish I could say it was planned, but I'm afraid I just lost my temper."

"Well, whatever it was, it worked. Congratulations, and good luck in your next game."

Back in the stands, Robin and Capi were celebrating with the Martins, who had also made the trip. "They really picked up the intensity after that technical, didn't they?" Jim Martin commented. "I didn't know Coach Peters had such a short fuse, but the team really responded in a positive way."

"Well it was hard to watch our players get beat up like that," Robin retorted. "If it had been me, I would have gotten the technical about ten minutes earlier."

"You're probably lucky you didn't get one from the stands," Capi replied, referring to Robin's spirited advice to the referees throughout the game.

"Hey, she was just sticking up for her partner," Patti defended. "I can certainly understand—I was about to go out on the court myself and defend Heather from that big goon that was pushing her around."

Robin smiled, even as she paled a little from Patti's reference to Jess as her partner. *I should correct her—this is just what Jess doesn't want to have happen.* She was distracted from her thoughts, however, when Jim suggested they go down and wait for the team to come out of the locker room.

"Come on, you two, we'll be back in plenty of time for the next game," he said, motioning to Robin and Capi to join them.

The four of them went into the hallway near the locker room

entrance and only had to wait about five minutes before the players started coming back out. Patti and Jim went off to talk to
Heather, leaving the other two women to wait for Jess. Robin
was nervous about seeing the coach, but she kept telling herself
that a true friend would be there to congratulate her, and she
hoped she'd always at least be a true friend.

"Are you going to be okay with this?" Capi leaned over and
whispered to her.

"Yeah, I think so. I just hope she's okay with it."

"Of course she will be," Capi reassured her.

Robin smiled gratefully back at her friend, and then her
attention was drawn to the door where Jess and her assistants
were emerging. They stopped to say a few things to the other
fans that were milling around, and then Jess saw Robin and Capi
and quickly walked over.

The coach gave Robin a dazzling smile, obviously happy
with her team's performance, and equally happy to see the young
woman there.

"Congratulations, Jess. Your team played great," Robin
said, offering her hand somewhat awkwardly. Jess took Robin's
hand and held it, along with the young woman's gaze, a little
longer than was probably expected.

"Thanks. I'm really glad you guys could make it," she said
sincerely, looking over to include Capi in the conversation.

"Hey, we wouldn't have wanted to miss that awesome display of referee baiting," Capi teased, easing the tension that
seemed to surround them.

"Oh jeez, is that all anybody is going to remember about the
game? I've already had three reporters ask me about it," Jess
replied.

"Well, you have to admit it seems a little out of character
for you," Robin said with a smile.

"And it did seem to make a difference in the game," Capi
added. "Are you sure it wasn't just a little bit premeditated?"

"Believe me, I would never have said that if I'd actually
stopped to think first," Jess assured them.

Just then Carmen walked over and the three women turned
to greet her. She gave Capi a big hug and an extra squeeze of the
hand before releasing her. "Are you guys staying for the next
game?" Carmen asked.

"Of course. We have to check out the competition for

tomorrow," Robin replied. "Aren't you staying?" she asked, turning to direct the question at Jess.

"We're staying too," the coach answered. "I have to scout, and I think it's important for the team to see who they'll be playing and try to pick up on some of their strengths and weaknesses. Besides, I want them to have the whole tournament experience while they're here—you never know when you're going to get back again."

"Oh, you'll be back next year," Carmen said confidently. "I'm counting on the Final Four by then."

Jess laughed. "Let's not get ahead of ourselves, okay?" She turned to Robin with an apologetic look on her face, and lowered her voice. "I'd better get out there before the game starts. Thanks for being here—it really means a lot to me."

"I wouldn't have missed it," Robin replied with a bitter-sweet smile on her face.

Jess turned and headed back out to the court, while Robin waited for Capi to make plans with Carmen for later in the evening. Robin watched the coach's back as she walked away, fighting an irrational urge to run after her and somehow make the past few weeks just go away.

After the second game of the evening, which LSU won handily, Robin, Capi, Carmen, and the Martins were having a drink in their hotel bar when the coaches arrived. Jim waved them over to their table and rounded up a few more chairs. Capi quickly moved her chair over and made a space between her and Robin.

"Hey Jess, come on over here and tell us what you think we're going to have to do to beat LSU on Sunday," Capi called out to the coach.

Robin blushed a little at Capi's obvious manipulation of the seating arrangements, but was happy to see Jess smile and relax into her chair.

Conversation resumed around them, the Martins quizzing the assistant coaches about their scouting report of the next opponent. Capi and Jess were discussing how to handle LSU's transition game, and Robin took the opportunity to just sit back and think about why this level of companionship seemed fine if she and Jess weren't lovers, but somehow unacceptable if they were. *I just don't understand it. It's not like I'd be draping myself all over her, or saying inappropriate things. But if we were lovers right now, she probably wouldn't have even wanted to sit with us.*

"...don't you think, Robin?" The young woman was startled out of her thoughts and realized that Capi had asked her a question.

"Huh? Uh, sorry Capi, I spaced out there for a minute, what did you say?"

Capi laughed. "Are we keeping you up past your bedtime?" she teased. "I said, I think Bennie should have an advantage against their point guard, what do you think?"

"Oh, yeah, Bennie is a lot quicker than she is," Robin agreed.

"Well, as long as I can keep Bennie playing within the system, I think she'll do fine," Jess added. "But if she takes it as some kind of one-on-one challenge, it's going to be a problem."

"It seems like she's really settled down in the last couple of games though," Robin noted.

Jess gave a little smirk as she replied, "I think Heather has had a little bit to do with that. I talked to her about her role as a captain on the team, and she seems to have taken a personal interest in getting Bennie to be a little more of a team player. Sometimes teammates can be much more effective than coaches," she noted wryly.

Robin nodded her head, amazed once again at how Jess was able to bring together this group of players in her first year as head coach, and lead them all the way to the NCAA playoffs. *Even if I didn't love her, I'd think she walked on water*, Robin thought to herself. She raised her eyes to find Jess looking back at her, and she blushed, thinking Jess had somehow read her thoughts. Capi had turned to talk to Carmen once again, and the two women were left to their own conversation.

"Have I told you that I think you're a great coach?" Robin asked quietly.

Jess smiled shyly. "Maybe once before, but I think you might be biased."

"Well I'm not the only one who thinks so, but you're right, I might be a little bit biased."

Jess shifted uncomfortably in her seat, wishing they weren't in the middle of a bar with seven other people. She wanted to touch Robin in the worst way—to hold her hand, touch her face, wrap her arms around her—and she clasped her hands together to keep them from wandering without her permission.

"I'm really glad you made the trip," Jess said again. She glanced around to see that no one was paying any attention to them, and lowered her voice even further. "If you weren't here, I'd just be thinking about you all the time, and then I wouldn't be focusing on my team."

"But I thought having me around was a distraction to you," Robin said, somewhat surprised at Jess's words.

"No," Jess protested. "You've never been a distraction, Robbie. I admit I worry about what other people think, but I've always been more distracted when you're not around."

"If only I could figure out a way to be invisible," Robin joked, but regretted it when she saw the hurt in Jess's eyes.

"I'm sorry you can't just be yourself around me," the coach said, looking down at her hands.

"Hey, I was just kidding," Robin tried to explain. "I know that what other people think is important for your job."

Further conversation was interrupted when Jim Martin called out to Jess from across the table. "Hey Jess! How are you going to keep your team from being affected by the hometown crowd? You could hardly hear yourself think in there during that second game tonight."

"I'm counting on you to be louder than them, Jim," Jess replied with a smile. "And Robin's got to count for at least a hundred of them, don't you think?"

Everyone around the table laughed at that, and the conversation returned to a group discussion of Sunday's game. After a little while, LaTeisha looked at her watch and said that they were way past curfew. The curfew didn't apply to the coaches, of course, but they decided that they should head back to their rooms and make sure that the team had settled in for the night. Everyone said their goodbyes, and Robin watched Jess walk away, wishing they had more time to talk privately.

As Robin looked wistfully after the departing coaches, Patti moved over into the seat next to her. "So, you want to talk about it?" Patti asked, gently putting her hand on Robin's forearm.

Robin looked at her, startled. "Talk about what?"

Patti smiled understandingly and said, "It doesn't seem like

things are going so well between you and Jess. I know it's none
of my business, but I just thought you might want someone to
talk to."

"Uh, look Patti...I think maybe you've got the wrong idea
about Jess and me...I mean, I can't really talk about it..." Robin
found herself flustered and unsure of what to say.

Patti's eyebrows furrowed as she tried to understand what
Robin meant. "But Heather told me you two were...You mean
you're not?"

Robin blew out a breath in frustration. She couldn't just lie
to someone she had come to know as a friend, but she didn't
want to say something that would implicate Jess at the same
time.

"The truth is that I would like nothing more than to be with
Jess, but she doesn't think that's possible with her job. She says
that other coaches would make an issue of it in recruiting, and
parents wouldn't want their kids to play for her."

Patti looked outraged. "You've got to be kidding. What parents wouldn't want their daughter to play for a coach like Jess?
She's taught Heather more about basketball, and life for that
matter, than any other coach she's had."

"I know, and I keep telling her that, but I'm sure there's
some truth to what she's saying. There are plenty of homophobic
people out there," Robin said with resignation. "So, the truth is,
Jess and I aren't partners, we're just friends right now." Robin
decided that really was the truth, and she didn't have to say anything about whether she and Jess had ever been more than that.
She thought it was the best she could do under the circumstances.

Patti had a look on her face that told Robin she was trying
to think of ways to "fix" this problem, and Robin worried about
where that effort might go. "Please, Patti, don't say anything
about this to anybody else, okay? Jess is already sensitive
enough about it."

Patti's eyes came back to Robin's and she looked sympathetically at the young woman. "This must be really hard for
you, isn't it?"

Robin felt the tears sting the back of her eyes and she
quickly looked down at her lap. "Harder than anything I've ever
been through," she replied quietly.

Patti put her hand over Robin's and said, "You just hang in

there, okay? Things will work out—you'll see."

With that, she got up, retrieved her husband and said good-bye to the three women still at the table. Capi noticed that Robin was feeling a little down, and suggested that they all head back to their rooms. After saying goodbye to Carmen, Capi put her arm around Robin's shoulders and they headed off to bed.

The next morning, Jess was up at six, sitting at a corner table in the hotel coffee shop and reading the paper when Patti Martin approached her. "Hi, Coach, mind if I join you?"

Jess looked up, surprised that anyone else was up that early, but quickly motioned for her to have a seat.

"You're up early," Patti observed. "Have trouble sleeping?"

"I always get up this early," Jess replied. "But...the truth is, I did have trouble sleeping last night. Must have been all that excitement from the game."

"Yeah, I suppose so." Patti looked away as if in thought. "I've never really thought about how hard it would be to be a coach. You know, late nights, working on weekends, pressure from fans...It must be really hard to have a personal life, isn't it?"

Jess narrowed her eyes, wondering where Patti was going with this line of conversation. "Yeah, it can be hard, but we all know what we're signing up for when we become coaches," she replied.

"Still, it seems like it's easier for the men coaches, don't you think? They have wives that can follow them around to games, and if they have kids, the wives seem to take care of the family."

"Well, there are a few women coaches who have husbands that do that," Jess said somewhat defensively.

"Yeah, but what if you don't have a husband? What if you don't want a husband? Then how are you supposed to have any kind of personal life?"

Jess looked the older woman squarely in the eye, raising one eyebrow. "Patti, what exactly are you getting at? Just say it, okay?"

Patti smiled back in return. "Okay, you got me. I never was any good at beating around the bush. Look, I just want to tell you that we, Jim and I, and lots of other parents, think you are the best thing that could have happened to this team. We're going to support you for what you do on the court—for how you treat our daughters, and how you give them a role model they can strive for. And because we care about you, we want you to be happy in the rest of your life, too. And we're going to be there to support you, no matter what." She paused and looked sheepishly at Jess. "I guess that's what I really wanted to say."

Jess just looked at Patti for a long time, a mixture of emotions running through her. Finally, she just said, "Thanks, Patti. That means a lot to me. I wish all parents could be like you."

"Hey, there are more like me than you think," Patti replied. "Trust me, I talk to them."

Why do I find that frightening? Jess thought, but she managed a weak smile. Patti got up to leave, giving Jess a pat on the shoulder as she walked by. The coach sat there for a long while, staring ahead and thinking, *What in the hell just happened here?*

Chapter
46

Robin and Capi were returning to their hotel room after dinner on Saturday night when they ran into Carmen in the hall. She invited them both out for drinks at a nearby pub, but Robin declined, saying she was tired from the night before and just wanted to spend the night reading and relaxing. She encouraged Capi to go, however, knowing that she had been monopolizing her friend's time. It was obvious that the other two women were desperate to spend some time alone together, and Robin was happy that they would finally get the opportunity.

She went back to her room, changed into a T-shirt and boxer shorts, and had settled onto her bed with a good book when there was a knock on her door. She got up and was surprised to see Jess standing on the other side. She quickly opened the door and stood aside for her to come in.

"Hi...are you busy? I probably should have called first..."

"No, no...come on in. I was just reading a book."

Robin walked back over to the bed she had been lying on and sat on the edge. "Have a seat," she said, motioning to the other bed across from her. Jess sat down and looked around the room.

"Where's Capi?"

"She went out with Carmen. They were going to check out that pub down the street. They just left, so I don't expect her back anytime soon. In fact, I'm not sure I expect her back at all," Robin said with a wry smile.

Jess smiled back. "Carmen seems pretty stuck on her—she

hardly even flirts with other women anymore."

Robin laughed. "I think the feeling's mutual, although Capi is a little scared about playing with fire. She's definitely going to be cautious about giving her heart away too soon."

"Well, she probably still has a little bit of her heart set on you, too."

Robin blushed a little. "Oh, I think she's been over me for a while now."

"You're not that easy to get over. I should know—I tried once." Jess lifted her eyes to meet Robin's. "I...I guess that's what I wanted to talk to you about. I know you said you wanted to wait until after the season was over, but I was hoping maybe we could talk about it now." Jess looked over at Robin hopefully.

"Are you sure, Jess? You've got the biggest game of the year coming up tomorrow..."

"That's exactly why I'm sure I want to do this now," Jess said emphatically. "Robin, all I do is think about you...about us...about how I want things to be different. And...and I know that I worry too much about what other people are going to think about our relationship."

Robin looked at Jess skeptically. "So how are things going to be any different for us in the future?"

Jess looked down at her hands. "I think I'm slowly beginning to understand that having my career doesn't mean that I can't have a personal life. I know I've said this before, but I obviously didn't feel it in my heart, or I wouldn't have been so paranoid."

"And what makes you think you can really mean it this time?" Robin asked, trying not to sound harsh or accusing.

Jess looked Robin squarely in the eye, trying to show the sincerity in her words. "Well, for one thing, I think I finally recognize the support that I have from a lot of different people associated with my program. And I don't think those people would just stop supporting me if they knew I was having a relationship with a woman."

Jess got up and moved over to sit next to Robin. She put her fingers under the young woman's chin and brought Robin's eyes up to meet hers. "But more importantly, I've learned that I care more about you than I do about my career. I desperately want to have both, but I know now that my career wouldn't mean a thing if you weren't there to share it with me."

Robin blinked away the tears that were forming in her eyes, wanting so much to believe that Jess meant it this time...that the coach would be able to accept their relationship, and not be ashamed of what they had. *Oh God, how do I know whether to believe it or not? How many times can I give her my heart, only to have her break it again?*

Robin looked away and wiped her eyes with the back of her hand. "I don't know Jess...I don't know what to believe any more."

"Believe in me, Robbie." Jess reached over and gently turned the young woman's face back toward hers. As she lowered her lips toward Robin's, she looked at her through half-closed lids and whispered, "Please believe in me."

Robin closed her eyes and felt the incredible softness of Jess's lips. Then the coach's hand moved to the back of her head, pulling her more forcefully into the kiss. Robin hesitated for a moment, then wrapped her arms around Jess's neck and returned the kiss with a passion born of weeks of frustration.

The kiss seemed to last for an eternity, and when they finally parted slightly to catch their breath, Robin searched Jess's eyes for any sign of doubt, but found only sincerity. She closed her eyes and leaned her forehead on Jess's, sighing deeply. "I love you," she whispered. "I love you so much it hurts, and I won't be able to stand it if we have to go through this again."

"We'll never have to go through this again. I promise," Jess whispered back, moving her lips across Robin's temple and then over her sensitive ear. "I love you, too, and I'll never be ashamed of what we have."

Jess's low voice in her ear inflamed Robin's senses and she threw her head back, exposing her neck for Jess's eager kisses. She leaned back on the bed, pulling Jess down with her, and their legs and arms became entwined as their bodies searched for more contact between them. Jess lifted up long enough to pull Robin's T-shirt off, a soft moan escaping her throat when she saw there was nothing underneath it. She slowly bent her head to kiss the soft swells of Robin's breasts, and the young woman arched into the caress. Jess increased the intensity of her kisses, and Robin tangled her hands in Jess's thick hair, gently pushing her further down her body. Jess put her fingers under the waistband of Robin's shorts and slowly pulled them off her legs, her lips following the path with a trail of kisses. She then worked her way back up the insides of Robin's legs, which parted willingly in response.

"Now, Jess, please," Robin pleaded while gripping the sheets of the bed and writhing in anticipation. When she finally felt the warmth of Jess's lips and the pressure of her tongue, she moaned loudly. "Oh God, yes!" she cried, and Jess's own passion took hold, driving her insistently until she heard Robin scream her name and felt her convulse one last time. Jess held on tightly while Robin slowly relaxed, the aftershocks continuing for minutes. Finally, Jess pulled away and kissed her way back up Robin's stomach. The young woman couldn't wait, and she reached down and pulled Jess up, claiming her lips in a searing kiss. When Jess broke away for a breath, she saw the tears in Robin's eyes and moved her lips to kiss them away.

"Are you okay?" she asked softly.

Robin nodded her head, not trusting herself to speak.

"I love you," Jess whispered. "And I love making love with you." She continued to place soft kisses on Robin's face, and the young woman's emotions finally settled down.

Robin kissed Jess back and then held her out at arm's length. "What are you doing in all those clothes?" she asked with an accusing look.

Jess looked down at herself sheepishly, realizing that she hadn't even taken her shoes off. "I guess I just got too carried away to notice."

"Well, I think I might have to do something about that," Robin said as she pushed Jess over onto her back and unbuttoned the coach's shirt, making sure to follow the path of her hands with her lips. The pile of clothes next to the bed grew steadily larger as the moans became louder. Before long, Jess was also calling out to a God that she didn't know she believed in.

Afterward, Robin buried her head in the warmth of Jess's neck and hugged her tightly. The tall woman rubbed her hands across Robin's back soothingly, and before long, exhaustion overtook them and they fell asleep in each other's arms.

Capi quietly slid the key card into the hotel room door, trying not to wake Robin. She and Carmen had stayed out until around eleven, and then had gone back to Carmen's room for another few hours. But Capi didn't want to leave Robin alone for the night, knowing that the young woman was struggling with her feelings toward Jess, and in need of a good friend.

She tiptoed into the room and nearly fell over a pile of clothes at the end of Robin's bed. *What the hell,* she cursed to herself, barely catching her balance. The light from the moonlight was just enough for her to see a lump in Robin's bed that was clearly too big for the small woman alone. *Oh shit! Who in the heck would she have brought back to her room? It's gotta be Jess, doesn't it? And if it is, what's she going to do if she wakes up and sees me here? I've gotta get the hell out of here.*

Capi turned around and snuck back out of the room, stopping to get her toothbrush on the way. She quietly closed the door behind her and sank against it with a sigh. *Man, she's gonna owe me big time for this one.*

The click of the door closing caused Robin's eyes to blink open. She wasn't aware of what had awakened her, but she was acutely aware of the warm body that was entwined with her own.

Oh my God—we fell asleep. She looked over at the nightstand and saw that it was two a.m. *How could we have done that? Jess is going to have a fit.*

"Jess...Jess, honey," Robin said while gently nudging the sleeping woman.

"Hmmm...what...what's wrong?" Jess blinked her eyes a few times, trying to figure out where she was and what was happening.

"I'm really sorry. I guess we fell asleep...I should have woken up sooner..."

"Robin..."

"I don't know what I was thinking. I shouldn't have let you fall asleep..."

"Robin..."

"I hope no one has been looking for you. I'm sure you can get back to your room without running into anyone..."

"Robin!"

The young woman finally stopped babbling and looked at Jess. "What?"

Jess gave the young woman a reassuring smile. "It's okay. I'm not worried about it." She leaned over and gave Robin a gentle kiss, which immediately eased the young woman's fears. "It's not like I'm out cheating on my spouse or anything."

Robin couldn't believe that Jess was so calm. *Maybe she really meant it when she said things would be different now. So why do I feel like we did something wrong?* She shook her head at the irony of it all. "I guess I'm the paranoid one now, aren't I?" she laughed.

"Well, I probably should have told one of my assistants where I'd be, but I'm sure no one has sent out a search party looking for me. I should probably get back to my room, though, just in case I have any messages waiting for me."

"Okay," Robin replied, extricating herself from Jess and sorting through the clothes on the floor.

Jess made herself presentable enough for the unlikely situation of being seen in the hallway at two in the morning, and gave Robin one last kiss before slipping out the door.

Capi returned to their room about ten on Sunday morning, wondering if she should knock or just use her key. *She has to be gone by now, doesn't she?* She decided it was probably safe to just go in, and she looked up to see Robin sitting by the window, reading the morning newspaper and looking like nothing was out of the ordinary.

Robin smirked at her and said, "Just getting home? Must have been a good pub you two found."

"Hey, I don't want to hear another word about what *I* did until you tell me who was in that bed with you when I came home last night."

Robin looked horrified and her hand covered her mouth. "You didn't come home last night..."

"Of course I came home last night. Surely you didn't expect me to spend the night with someone else when I had you waiting here. I certainly wouldn't expect you to desert me for somebody else," she said with mock indignation. She couldn't keep the smile from reaching her lips, though, and soon they both broke into laughter.

"I can't believe I didn't wake up when you came in."

"Oh, you must have been exhausted from...well, from *talking* all night, right?"

"Right. How did you know?"

"Come on, spill it. I want to hear every detail," Capi commanded, and the two of them spent the next hour trading stories of the previous evening.

Chapter
47

Robin and Capi arrived at the arena about an hour before
game time. They didn't want to miss one minute of the excitement and suspense of the evening's match-up, and this gave them
an opportunity to compare the two teams during warm-ups. The
arena was already more crowded than it had been for NOU's first
game, and the LSU band was there in force. Although the seats
immediately surrounding the two women were full of Bobcat
fans, they were a very small minority in a sea of purple and gold.

Jess's team was shooting around at their basket, the organized warm-up not starting for twenty more minutes. Robin
noticed that Bennie and Heather were working together, one
rebounding for the other and making sharp passes for spot-up
shooting practice. When they switched roles, they would give
each other a high-five and a few words of encouragement. After
ten minutes of this, they started working out one-on-one, and it
was obvious to Robin that the physical nature of the play was
half the fun for them. She thought it was a good sign that the
players could be laughing and having fun while obviously working hard and being competitive. She had been worried that the
team would come out too serious and end up being tight for the
game. She was just thinking about what a master Jess was at preparing her team for games, when the tall coach walked up the
aisle and sat down in the empty seat next to her.

"Hi," Jess said, giving Robin one of her drop-dead gorgeous
smiles as she sat down. "Sorry I didn't get a chance to call you

this morning. Things got pretty hectic with all the game preparations."

"That's okay," Robin reassured her. "Capi and I have been
pretty busy ourselves, seeing as it was the last day to shop for
souvenirs, right Capi?" Robin said while giving her friend a
nudge.

"Oh...yeah, right," Capi replied, her attention being brought
back from the court. "Hey Jess, how are you doing? I hope you
weren't as tired as Robin was this afternoon," she said with a
smirk.

Robin elbowed Capi hard in the ribs, but Jess just gave Capi
one of her half-grins accompanied by a raised eyebrow.

"I felt great this afternoon, but then I made it back to my
room for at least part of the night."

Robin blushed furiously and couldn't believe that this conversation was going on around her. "Hey, is your team excited
for the game?" Robin asked in an obvious attempt to change the
subject. Jess and Capi both just sat back in their seats and smiled
smugly, allowing Robin to breathe a sigh of relief.

"Well, I'd better get back down to the bench," Jess said,
returning her attention to Robin. She lowered her voice and said,
"I just wanted to say that I'm really glad you're here, and I'm
really glad about last night."

Robin smiled shyly and replied, "Me too. Good luck in the
game."

The coach made her way back down to the sidelines and
watched the remainder of the warm-ups. By the time player
introductions were made, the arena was nearly at capacity and
Robin could hardly hear herself think. She could see the level of
nervousness increase in the NOU players, but after Jess huddled
with them for the final time, they came out looking confident
and relaxed.

NOU pushed the pace at the beginning of the game, Bennie
passing the ball ahead to Heather at every fast-break opportunity. Even when they couldn't get a breakaway lay-up, they often
ended up with a player advantage and at least got an open jump
shot. After eight minutes, NOU was up by seven and the LSU
coach called time-out to adjust her transition defense. The Lady
Tigers responded and Bennie had to start setting up their half-
court offense. NOU had a size advantage in the middle, but the
LSU players were quick and able to knock down many of the

entry passes. LSU ended up getting some fast breaks of their own off of steals, and soon the game was tied again. The teams traded baskets until halftime, and when Jess's team left the court at the break, they were up by only one.

She looked at the faces surrounding her in the locker room and saw the openness and trust that she had worked so hard to earn during the year. She knew that she could give these players the motivation and strategy they needed to face an opponent like LSU, but she wasn't sure they had the horses to pull off the upset. Their advantage was their underdog status, though, and Jess knew they had to go out there with a "nothing-to-lose" attitude. She rallied her team with a reminder that there was no tomorrow—no reason to save anything for another day. She urged them to leave everything they had on the court that night, and the team charged back out for the second half, hungry for the chance at an upset.

Of course, the LSU coach had years of experience on Jess, and she was not about to let her team come out unsuspecting of NOU's desire. The Lady Tigers were even tougher in the second half, determined not to see their season end on their own home court.

The game stayed close for the first fifteen minutes of the second half, NOU able to capitalize on some power moves by Natalia, and LSU able to take advantage of their quickness to get some open shots. Unfortunately, Natalia was prone to reach over the back of the smaller LSU post players rather than move her feet to get position, and she ended up getting her fourth foul with five minutes left to play. Jess took her out for a short rest, but knew that she was going to have to go back in quickly if NOU was to have a chance. By the time Natalia returned at the three-minute mark, NOU was down by four.

The next time down the court, Bennie spread the offense out and made a move on her defender at the top of the key. As she drove down the right side of the lane, Natalia's defender came over to help, and Bennie wrapped a pass around the LSU post to Natalia who was now left with an open lane to the basket. As she went up for the lay-up, she was fouled hard, but kept her concentration and put the shot in. She added the free throw and they were within one.

As LSU in-bounded the ball, Bennie put full court pressure on their point guard. She overplayed her to the right, forcing her to dribble toward the sideline. Heather recognized the opportunity for the double-team, and as Bennie cut off her player at the sideline, the LSU guard reversed her dribble right into Heather who neatly stole the ball away. Bennie was already heading down court, and Heather lobbed her the ball for the easy lay-up.

As Bennie set up for the full-court pressure again, the LSU guard smartly passed the ball ahead to one of her forwards and the Lady Tigers set up their half-court offense. The ball went to the wing and the low post player moved to the free throw line to get the pass. The rest of the LSU players cleared out of the lane, leaving Natalia to try to stop the post player one-on-one. While this would have been an easy task if the player had stayed in the low post, out at the free throw line, Natalia was vulnerable. The smaller LSU post faked the outside shot, and when she got the big center off her feet, she quickly drove around her to the left. Natalia did what every player does in that situation—whether they have four fouls or not—she reached out and fouled her before she could reach the basket.

The referee signaled to Jess that Natalia had fouled out of the game, and the coach took the full thirty seconds to decide on a substitute, hoping to ice the free throw shooter a little. When the teams lined up for the one-and-one, the handful of NOU fans were doing their best to disrupt the shooter, but the stands behind the basket were full of quiet LSU fans and she calmly sank them both.

Jess could see a little of the wind go out of the sails of her players after Natalia fouled out, and she called time-out to try to keep the momentum from swinging too far the other way. But when they went back onto the court without their dominant center, the offense floundered and they ended up with a thirty second shot clock violation. With only a minute left in the game, LSU had the ball and a one-point lead. They used up twenty-eight seconds off the shot clock before heaving up a desperation three-point attempt...that went in. The fans went crazy which seemed to rattle the NOU players, and the result was an off-balance shot from the baseline that missed badly. LSU rebounded and Bennie immediately fouled the player. But with a four-point lead and only ten seconds to go, the pressure was off and the player sank both free throws. LSU allowed Bennie to dribble the length of the court for a meaningless basket and the game was over.

Jess stood and stared out at the court for a moment, watching the pandemonium surrounding the LSU players. *Next year that's going to be us,* she vowed, and she turned with purpose and went to shake the LSU coaches' hands.

Robin watched Jess congratulate the LSU coaches, then shake the hands of the LSU players, and then finally gather her own players around her for some final words before letting them go off to talk to friends and family. Despite the loss, Robin could see the pride in the head coach's actions, and she knew that the players had nothing to be ashamed of. Jess would find a way to turn this loss into a learning experience, and they would be stronger next year when playoffs came around.

After the brief team huddle, Robin and Capi walked down to the court. Jess was talking to some reporters, and Capi went off to find Carmen. When the coach finished with her interview, she saw Robin standing by the bench and their eyes met across the court. Jess slowly started to walk over, getting intercepted repeatedly by parents and fans, but her gaze always returned to meet Robin's. Finally, she made it over to where the young woman waited and saw the questioning look in her eyes. Knowing what Robin was asking, and not thinking twice about who might be watching, Jess enfolded the smaller woman in her arms and hugged her tightly. From different places across the court, a player's mother and a Director of Student Affairs were watching with identical smiles of satisfaction.

Epilogue

"This is beautiful, Jess," Robin exclaimed, looking out over the valley from the end of the road where they had parked. The two women got out of the car and walked to the edge of the road. "How did you ever find this?"

"My real estate agent brought me up here last week. I couldn't believe the view when I saw it—I felt like I was in an airplane."

The patchwork of the valley was laid out before them, sunlight through the clouds adding patterns of light and dark. On the horizon, Mount Hood and Mount St. Helens loomed above the foothills.

"Can you imagine living someplace like this and waking up to this view every morning," Robin said wistfully.

"I couldn't have imagined it before, but I can now," Jess said, taking Robin's hand and turning to face her.

Robin looked at her quizzically, and waited for Jess to explain.

"I had a meeting with Butch today. He offered me a contract extension and a substantial raise."

"That's great, Jess. He must be worried that you're going to get snapped up by some bigger school." Robin's smile faded a little as it hit her that maybe Jess did have offers from other schools. "You...Did you accept it?"

Jess smiled back at the young woman's uncertainty. "Of course I accepted it. I don't have any interest in looking at other schools right now. In fact," Jess tilted her head to look directly into Robin's eyes, "I'd like to settle down here a little more."

She shifted her feet nervously. "The truth is, I brought you out here because...well, I thought maybe...I wondered if you might consider building a house with me."

Robin looked at her with a mixture of shock and disbelief. "Are you serious?"

Jess smiled and pulled Robin in for a hug. "Completely serious," she whispered in the ear next to her lips. "I want us to live together, and I want it to be in a home that we both feel is our own."

Robin pulled back a little and looked up at the coach. "But Jess, I could never afford to live in a place like this," she said, looking around at the large view lots.

"Neither could I, by myself, but if we live together, we can. I already talked to my agent about it, and she said it shouldn't be a problem." Jess started to get a little nervous as she realized that Robin hadn't accepted her proposition yet. "But if you think it's too early to move in together, or you want to live by yourself, I'll understand, really..."

Robin halted Jess's words by pulling her head down for a reassuring kiss. Their lips parted just slightly and Robin murmured, "Nothing could make me happier."

Available soon from
Yellow Rose Books

Lost Paradise
By Francine Quesnel

Kristina Von Deering is a young, wealthy Austrian stunt-woman working on an Austrian/Canadian film project in Montreal. On location, she meets and eventually falls in love with a young gopher and aspiring camerawoman named Nicole McGrail. Their friendship and love is threatened by Nicole's father who sees their relationship as deviant and unnatural. He does everything in his power to put an end to it.

Meridio's Daughter
By LJ Maas

Tessa (Nikki) Nikolaidis is cold and ruthless, the perfect person to be Karê, the right-hand, to Greek magnate Andreas Meridio. Cassandra (Casey) Meridio has come home after a six-year absence to find that her father's new Karê is a very desirable, but highly dangerous woman.

Set in modern day Greece on the beautiful island of Mýkonos, this novel weaves a tale of emotional intrigue as two women from different worlds struggle with forbidden desires. As the two come closer to the point of no return, Casey begins to wonder if she can really trust the beautiful Karê. Does Nikki's dark past, hide secrets that will eventually bring down the brutal Meridio Empire, or are her actions simply those of a vindictive woman? Will she stop at nothing for vengeance...even seduction?

Turning the Page
By Georgia Beers

Melanie Larson is an attractive, extremely successful business executive who shocks herself by resigning from her job when her company merges with another and relocating. While trying to decide what to do with her life next and at the urging of her uncle, Melanie heads to Rochester, New York, to stay temporarily with her cousin Samantha. She hopes to use her business savvy to help Sam sort out the financial woes of her small bookstore. During her stay, Melanie meets and becomes close to the family that owns the property on which Samantha lives, the charming Benjamin Rhodes, a distinguished, successful businessman, as well as his beautiful and intriguing daughter Taylor. Surprised by what and how she feels for each of them, Melanie is soon forced to face the facts and re-examine what's really important to her in life, career and love.

Prairie Fire
By LJ Maas

A dying Shaman whispers a cryptic message, "The buffalo must run free..." In this sequel to *Tumbleweed Fever*, we continue the story of Devlin Brown, an ex-outlaw, and Sarah Tolliver, the woman of her heart.

The Shaman's words are translated by a Choctaw Medicine Man and now Sarah and Dev must convince the ranchers around them to destroy the wire fences that contain their cattle in order to avoid certain calamity.

Amidst the beautiful and, sometimes unforgiving, land of the Oklahoma Territory, the two women begin a new life together. Adventure and Mysticism abound as they revisit the Choctaw camp where Devlin grew up. Sarah must decide whether she will undergo the Clan rituals that will allow her to join with the former outlaw in a ceremony that will bind their hearts together forever.

Other titles to look for in the
coming months from
Yellow Rose Books

Daredevil Hearts
By Francine Quesnel

Heartbroken Love
By Georgio Sicily

Many Roads To Travel
By Karen King and Nann Dunne

Ricochet In Time
By Lori L. Lake

Love's Journey
By Carrie Carr

R.L. Johnson is a university professor who always wanted to be a basketball coach. She lives in the Pacific Northwest where she enjoys flyfishing, skiing, and playing basketball, volleyball, and softball.